Critical Acclaim for Neal Asher

"If you like SF and you want some good, old-fashioned, seat-of-the-pants story telling then Asher is the hot ticket." —*The Third Alternative*

"Playing like a turbo-charged mi_____ *Ientity, The Departure* moves at Asher_____ *K*

"I had an absolute blast with th_____ : better and better." —*Falcata Times blog*

"Asher…projects the terror-haunted sensibility of our time into a future of limitless brutality…Asher displays great virtuosity." —*The New York Times Book Review*

"Gritty. Now there's a word you don't often hear in connection with science fiction—and more's the pity…This unique style is all Asher's…deeply satisfying…. And, he leaves you eager for more…" —*SF Site*

"Asher's galaxy is full of color and sleaze, and his story rattles along at high speed. There are surprises, double-crosses, elaborate lies to be seen through, astonishing escapes from certain death, and last-minute reversals. Fast-moving, edge-of-the-seat entertainment." —David Langford

"Asher…writes with a low-key, mordant sense of humor, never really going for over-the-top, laugh-out-loud moments. He creates a sort of dissonance with his remarkable imagination and clear prose. He'll describe something so patently weird and oversized, something so incredible, so complex, so insanely bloody or vicious with an utter clarity and aplomb that is seemingly at odds with what we're seeing. He charges into the absurd with a gusto that is courageous and outrageous." —Rick Kleffel, *The Agony Column*

"If anyone still imagines that likening an SF author's work to actionthriller-horror genres means that it can't really be SF, or that it can't be good SF, then t_____ *Interzone*

THE OWNER VOL. 3

JUPITER WAR

Other Books by Neal Asher

Cowl
The Owner Trilogy
  The Departure
  Zero Point
  Jupiter War
Agent Cormac
  Shadow of the Scorpion
  Gridlinked
  The Line of Polity
  Brass Man
  Polity Agent
  Line War
Spatterjay
  The Skinner
  The Voyage of the Sable Keech
  Orbus
Novels of the Polity
  Prador Moon
  Hilldiggers
  The Technician

Short story collections

Runcible Tales
The Engineer
The Gabble

Novellas

The Parasite
Mindgames: Fool's Mate

THE OWNER VOL. 3
JUPITER WAR

NEAL ASHER

NIGHT SHADE BOOKS
NEW YORK, NEW YORK

Night Shade books may be purchased in bulk at special discounts for sales
promotion, corporate gifts, fund-raising, or educational purposes. Special
editions can also be created to specifications. For details, contact the Special
Sales Department, Night Shade Books, 307 West 36th Street, 11th Floor,
New York, NY 10018 or info@skyhorsepublishing.com.

Night Shade Books® is a registered trademark of Skyhorse Publishing, Inc.®, a
Delaware corporation.

Visit our website at www.nightshadebooks.com.

10 9 8 7 6 5 4 3 2 1

Library of Congress Cataloging-in-Publication Data is available on file.

ISBN: 978-1-59780-493-6

Cover illustration by Jon Sullivan
Cover design by Claudia Noble
Interior layout and design by Amy Popovich

Printed in the United States of America

To those private companies that are making the plans and actually developing the technology to mine asteroids, build orbital hotels and build bases on the Moon and Mars.

Ignore your detractors and keep looking at the stars.

1

THE GOOD WILL OF THE PEOPLE

It can been seen that, despite her brutal treatment of anyone who ever stood in her way, Serene Galahad's reign was still contingent on the good will of the people of Earth. However, the knowledge of the "common man" was limited; he thought that Alan Saul had attacked Earth and released the Scour—the pandemic that annihilated nearly half of Earth's population of eighteen billion—almost certainly killing someone the common man knew. Under Serene Galahad that same common man seemed to have acquired more personal freedom and more material wealth, while his ruler apparently strove to avenge his losses. Of course, he did not know that the greater freedom he enjoyed was due to Saul wiping out Committee infrastructure and frying a large proportion of those who had formerly wielded the whip. Nor did he understand that his greater material wealth was precisely because the Scour had killed billions of his fellows. Nor did he realize that Serene Galahad was entirely responsible for the Scour. The gratitude he felt for his current ruler was unwarranted, and the sense of motivation that had him turning up at the factory gates early was based on a lie. This sort of ignorance, unfortunately, has been the lot of the common man since the dawn of time.

EARTH

The sun was shining on what had been Chairman Messina's small patch of Tuscan countryside. There were lemons on some of the trees and green oranges on others, while below them carefully tended succulents had opened red, orange, white and yellow flowers to the morning sun. Light glinted brightly off an all-chrome shepherd as it strode on patrol near the fence, and razorbirds roosting on a watchtower could almost be mistaken for seagulls. But all this brightness seemed just a veneer over blackness to Serene Galahad.

As her limousine drew up beside the building, Serene felt that its dressing of stone and red pantiles, concealing its recent lineage, was merely a facade of a similar nature, but one that covered failure. She stepped out of her vehicle before Sack, her dehumanized lizard-skin bodyguard, could open the door for her, and she pushed her sunglasses up onto her hair. Already the troops from the two armoured cars were piling out and heading for the two entrances—and going in fast, their instructions clear.

"It should just take a few minutes," Sack informed her, looming at her side.

She shrugged, not really concerned, and continued to survey her surroundings without interest. Coming from inside the building she could hear shouting, a scream, the sound of glass breaking. Of course it wasn't necessary for her to be here for this, but maybe it could bring her back into focus; maybe this was the remedy she required. Eventually, just as the shepherd disappeared from sight behind some olive trees, Sack told her, "They're ready."

She began walking towards the main entrance, Sack still at her shoulder and two armoured guards moving ahead. One of the guards held the door open for her while the other one moved on into the corridor beyond. Meanwhile, Sack drew his antiquated automatic and proceeded with it pointing down at his side. There was no need, because no one here—except her troops—was armed. The staff here had all been thoroughly vetted, and none of them would even consider violence against her . . . until it was too late. She moved on past a room full of computers and wall-spanning information screens, another room containing tiers of shelves crammed with old paper files, but with search-and-sort robots, looking like the offspring of document scanners and spiders, crawling along the shelves. And finally she came to a door outside which four of her troops had already gathered.

Serene paused as they moved aside; she glanced at a smear of blood on the floor and wondered if some of those working here might have guessed in advance, or had just been a bit too tardy in following orders. She looked up at the sign on the door, which announced "Tactical" the smaller text below this reading "Data Acquisition, Collation and Assessment—Positive Response Planning." She snorted, then reached down and extracted her new Black Oval palmtop from its pouch at her belt.

"Ma'am?" Sack enquired, gesturing towards the door.

She nodded and he opened it for her; she strode on through.

The entire staff of this main tactical unit was present in the room. Some were seated at consoles, but most were herded back against the far wall. Near the door, some desks had been shoved over to one side, leaving just one, the chair behind it facing the room. Troops stood watchfully to either side of it.

Serene moved into the room, pulled out the chair and sat, placing her palmtop carefully before her, tapping it once and watching in satisfaction as it hinged open, expanded its film screen and projected a keyboard onto the desk surface. She reached out but, anticipating her, it had already called up the list of the thirty-four personnel here which she had been looking at earlier.

"Merrick Myers," she stated, looking up.

The woman was clearly reluctant to come forward, but others moved aside quickly and someone behind her gave her a shove.

"Ma'am," said Myers, achieving a ridiculous mix of bow and curtsey.

"You are the officer in charge here," Serene declared, "but the blame cannot be wholly attributed to you. Your final assessments for submission to me are made up from a collation of data and assessments gathered from other tactical units. It is the case that what you present to me can only be as good as the data you receive."

Myers looked quite relieved to hear this and seemed about to say something, but Serene held up a hand to cut her off and continued, "Nevertheless, the fact remains that, despite having the best data and tactical programs available, along with the application of the minds of a total of four thousand two hundred and three tactical analysts, 'Tactical,' still got it wrong."

"Ma'am, if I could—"

"You will be silent!" Galahad spat. Then, after a pause to calm herself. "Time and time again your 'tactical assessments' underestimated Alan Saul. The failure of Tactical is no small matter. You have allowed the greatest mass-murderer in human history to escape our grasp. And because of that you have also jeopardized the future of Earth. We still do not have the Gene Bank samples and data that would enable us to regenerate Earth's ecosystem."

Serene found herself growing irate again as she mentally reviewed what she had just said, and as doubt nibbled at her certainty. Was the blame really all theirs? Yes, of course it was, damn it! She had done everything she could and, as had been the case throughout human history, had been let down by her advisers. She could only work with what she *knew*. It was their *fault*.

Serene flicked to another list and then fed that into a particular program. This was a random selection of ten per cent of other tactical personnel in places like this, both on Earth and in orbit—a number that rounded up to three hundred and eighty-six.

"This cannot go unpunished," Serene continued. "However, I am not so stupid as to allow such a punishment to destroy or cripple an important resource. I have therefore chosen a method suitable to our location here in Italy: I am using the old punishment called decimation." She set the program running, watched a loading bar appear, rise to its maximum and then disappear.

"For those of you unacquainted with the word, decimation was how Roman commanders punished troops guilty of cowardice or rebellion. One in ten was selected and killed." She now went back to her previous list of those here and fed that into the same program as well, but paused it with the parameters set. "Right now, three hundred and eighty-six of your fellow tactical analysts both on Earth and in orbit are learning what their strangulation collars are for."

At this announcement many in the crowd before her reached up to finger the hoops of bright metal fastened around their necks. As was usual in this sort of situation, they were seeing or hearing others being punished and assumed this was an object lesson for them; that this time they had escaped.

"Here, gathered before me," said Serene, "I have the cream of Tactical—the best analysts and programmers available—and I cannot blithely kill off one in ten of you."

Ah, the relief in their expressions . . .

"Your failure is almost of an order of magnitude worse than that of your fellows, therefore you are all going to die."

It took them a moment to realize what she had just said, a moment for them to begin to protest and mill like sheep being circled by wolves, and just a moment for Serene to set the program running again. Some of them began screaming and protesting, those seated leaped out of their chairs, and all of them groped ineffectually at their now closing collars. A couple ran towards her, the man ridiculously wielding a litter bin. Sack's automatic cracked twice, both head shots, one lifting the top of the man's scalp and the other hitting the woman's nose before exiting in a spray of brains and bone behind her. They both went down, and behind them computers crashed to the floor, as desks and chairs were overturned in a writhing and choking mass of dying humanity.

Serene turned to Sack. "That wasn't really necessary, now, was it?"

"My apologies, ma'am," he replied woodenly.

Serene took in the look of horror on the faces of some of the troops, though most remained hard faced and unreadable. It occurred to her that Sack might have killed those two so as to end their suffering swiftly, but then she immediately dismissed the idea. A man like him didn't get to the position he held without becoming callously inured to this sort of incident.

Just as on other occasions like this, she noticed the sudden smell of shit, though this time the only collar failure was one that closed too quickly and all the way, severing a head and sending a spray of blood that even reached her desk. She closed up her palmtop, stood, picked it up and returned it to its pouch.

By now the choking sounds had ceased, though chests were still heaving and legs kicking. Serene abruptly stepped back, bored with this now, and realizing that though she had felt her malaise lift for a moment, it was back in force.

"Take me home," she said to Sack, before heading for the door.

MARS

Var slowly hauled herself to her feet, feeling weak, shaky and nauseous, and only just beginning to accept that she wasn't on the brink of dying. It was a strange mental state to emerge from; she had given up her responsibilities, had nothing to do, and how uncomfortable and filthy she felt had been irrelevant. But her anger at Rhone, for first trying to kill her out here on the surface of Mars, then leaving her to die when her oxygen ran out, helped her feel alive again. For this had not faded and now became the anchor that stabilized her. And her brother, who had miraculously crossed the solar system to bring her oxygen, seemed to inject some steel into her backbone with the steady regard of his weird pink eyes. She straightened up, gazed at him for a second, then transferred her attention to the vehicle he had arrived on.

The dust having rolled away, the machine was now clearly visible. On seeing its similarity to an early rocket-propelled precursor of vertical take-off jets she had christened it a "flying bedstead"—and now felt no need to question that label. On the dusty rust-coloured ground rested a cube-shaped framework from which projected steering thrusters, one pointing towards Var and two pointing left and right, with presumably a fourth projecting from the other side. Within it, a single acceleration chair faced up towards the sky, with hardware from the cockpit of a space plane installed in front of it. Behind the chair, two cylindrical fuel tanks had been mounted horizontally, and beneath them the main engine pointed towards the ground.

"I would have said 'impossible to fly' had I not seen you flying it," she rasped.

"The word 'impossible' has always been given a severe battering throughout human history, and recently has been dealt a near fatal blow," he reminded her.

She felt slightly demeaned by his dismissive attitude, and wished she hadn't used the word "impossible" but instead enquired about the technicalities of flying such a machine. His remark had referred to this Rhine drive he had used to bring Argus Station here. Arrogant of him, she felt, but supposed it did seem pointless discussing the difficulties of flying the contraption that stood before her when he'd recently totally shafted conventional physics. She studied him and he seemed blank to her; not quite as human as the brother she had once known, but was she misremembering? Perhaps it was the effect of those . . . eyes, and the knowledge of everything he had managed to achieve?

"What happened to you, Alan?" she asked, trying hard to connect.

"I may retain that name, but little else of the brother you knew." He glanced up the valley, seemingly impatient with her. "We'll talk while we walk."

Swallowing a snappy reaction, she waved a hand towards his vehicle. "Can't this thing get us back to Argus?"

"No." He turned and headed back towards it with the long gliding steps necessary here. "An Earth-format space plane would have fallen like a brick in Martian atmosphere. I had to strip one down to achieve the correct weight-to-thrust ratio, and physically it could not include any more fuel than this used to get me down here." He reached up beside the seat and detached a backpack, pulled it down and slung it over one shoulder, and turned back to her.

"So we have to go to Antares Base?" she said.

He nodded. "We have to get your Mars-format space plane flying again."

"We don't have any fuel for that either."

"Not a problem as, right now, my robots are constructing a drop canister to get some down to us." He paused reflectively. "It should come down, twenty hours hence, within just a few kilometres of the base."

"But we do have the additional problem that I am no longer in charge," she replied. "Rhone is probably now in control of Antares Base, and its weapons."

He waved a dismissive hand. "Something to be dealt with in due course."

He'd stolen a space station and all but destroyed the Committee, so perhaps had some reason for self-confidence, but she found his arrogance nevertheless distasteful. No matter what he had done, a single bullet could still kill him. He turned jerkily and began heading away, kicking up small clouds of dust. Var hesitated, not much in love with the idea of tagging along behind, of being in second place, then reluctantly acknowledged to herself that she was alive only because of him and she hurried to catch up, her legs leaden and a pain nagging in her chest from what was probably a cracked rib.

"Where are you heading?" she asked.

"There's a cave system leading from Coprates Chasma to that cave you were moving your base to. That will get us close without being seen."

She had considered going that route herself, but just hadn't possessed a sufficient air supply. Noting the weight of the pack he carried, she felt sure he must have brought extra oxygen bottles along. Yes, of course he'd brought extra; of course he would never make a stupid mistake like forgetting to bring enough air.

"So, tell me, Alan," she said, moving up alongside him, "how come you're here now?" It was merely a conversational gambit, and he accepted it as such.

"You could say," he began, "that my birth into this incarnation was from a plastic crate on the conveyor of the Calais trash incinerator . . ."

Throughout the Martian afternoon they trudged on up Coprates Chasma, with rouge dust hanging in the air over their trail while Saul, in terse and perfectly correct sentences, told her what had happened to him and what he had been doing over the last few years. Var was appalled. Her brother had always appeared pragmatic and mostly emotionless, yet there had never been any indication that he could also be so murderous. But, then, this person beside her was not quite the brother she had known and, in truth, she had previously never had any idea that she herself could become such a ruthless killer. Perhaps they shared the same genetic trait.

Their walk brought them to a triangular cave piercing a steep cliff and, as they scrambled over fallen rubble to reach it, Var realized that Alan seemed just as exhausted as she felt. But he finished his monologue.

"In a state comparable to unconsciousness, I had calculated that what we now call the Rhine drive was our only hope." He shrugged. "I was arrogant and I was wrong because Galahad's warship, the *Scourge,* still managed to intercept us."

Var felt slightly surprised at this admission of error.

He halted and turned to look at her. "Her troops boarded Argus and a lot of people died. We came close to losing and it was only by my boarding the *Scourge* and penetrating its computer system that we managed to prevail."

"So what did you do?" Var asked.

"I penetrated their ID implants and activated the biochips—killing them all with the Scour virus lying latent within them." He faced forwards and moved on. "We got the drive running again after that and hit the *Scourge,* which had retreated, with our drive bubble. That ship is back on course for Earth, and now doubtless full of corpses." He paused contemplatively as they walked, then added, "In reality the only person the Rhine drive actually saved was you."

Var felt a surge of resentment at that, then shook it off as she contemplated all he had told her. So that was it: end of that chapter and turn over the page. He had summarized some of the most catastrophic events the human race had ever faced, also events that had opened out vast horizons; all had, as their root cause, himself. She found that somehow . . . unfair.

"So what now?" she asked, as they reached the cave mouth. "You always wanted to build spaceships, Var—that is one memory I retain," he replied. "Give me your opinion of Argus Station, in that respect."

She shivered and, despite her weariness, felt a sudden excitement. "It was a stupid design." Yes, it was, but she couldn't help feeling as if she was about to deliver a proposal to some Committee technology-assessment group.

"How so?" he enquired, flicking on his suit light to punch a beam into the dusty dark ahead.

"The initial aim was to build a ring station that could be spun up for centrifugal gravity. They first put in the structural supports and then began building the ring, and only realized halfway through that they had positioned it over the Traveller engine, so wouldn't be able to complete it if they intended to use that engine again—which they did. Then, instead of moving the engine so that it pointed either up or down in relation to the ring's axis, they decided to turn the ring supports into the spindles for cylinder worlds, then went on to build the arcoplexes. It was a government hash from the start."

"Very true," Saul agreed.

"We'll have to move it," Var opined.

"The engine or the station rim?" he asked.

"The Traveller engine, effectively, since we really need to get that asteroid out of there, cut it up and turn it into something useful."

"So you propose a ring-shaped spacecraft with the engine jutting below?"

"I propose no such thing."

He wasn't walking into the cave, just leaning a hand against the wall of stone as he waited to hear what she had to say. In just a short exchange, this conversation had moved on from apparently idle speculation. But she felt sudden misgivings. After all he had done, why would he need her expertise? Was he just offering a sop to her pride? No, she couldn't allow that thought to take hold: she could be just as good as him, just as successful. She closed her eyes for a second to try and remember the schematics of the Argus Station, and then consider what could be done with it.

"The Alcubierre warp," she said, her eyes snapping open, "what is its size and shape?"

"It *presently* generates at a diameter of seven kilometres—a kilometre from the station rim all round. It is oblate, with an axial thickness of four kilometres, though with half-kilometre indents at the poles."

"I notice your emphasis on 'presently,'" remarked Var.

Saul nodded. "Without the Argus asteroid at the centre of the station, the warp would be spherical."

"So that changes the kind of ship you could build," said Var. "If you intend to retain the drive you already have."

"True," Saul agreed. "What design of ship do you propose?" "They were a little two-dimensional in their thinking when they built the station. If the ship itself was spherical, you could build in greater structural integrity, maybe even position new arcoplexes inside it and move the Traveller engine round and then out along one axis—that is, if you feel you need to retain that engine."

"With the Rhine drive, we essentially fly blind," he observed non-committal.

She couldn't help but feel he had been coaxing her to her next words. "You've managed to create a warp drive—something long considered impossible in conventional physics circles—so what about Mach-effect propulsion?"

"I have been considering it," he acknowledged. "As with the Rhine drive, it may be that we already have a large portion of the necessary hardware in place simply with the EM field equipment."

"I see."

"So, what would you do first?"

"You'll need a lot of construction robots, and a lot more materials than you can obtain from the Argus asteroid. Robots first, then start building the skeleton of the sphere—"

He abruptly stepped away and gazed up at the sky.

"Brigitta and Angela," he said, "I have sent instructions to the system which concern you. When you've finished clearing that mess in there, I want Robotics operating at full production. I've also instructed Le Roque to give you everything you need." He paused for a second, listening to a response, before continuing. "Yes, he's having the smelting plants extended." He then turned to Var. "It begins," he explained. "Shall we?" He gestured into the cave ahead then led the way in.

Of course, once they got deep inside the cave he would be out of contact with the computer systems of Argus Station. He'd set things in motion just then, which seemed fast for someone used to the bureaucratic delays and screw-ups usual in her previous employers. It was also exhilarating, but for the feeling that she was somehow being shifted into place like some game-piece.

ARGUS

Hannah gazed at the swirling debris spreading out from the ring side bearing installation of Arcoplex Two, noting the flare of welders throughout the station amid constant robot and human activity.

"Madness," she exclaimed in exasperation. "He's risking our lives to save a sister he doesn't even remember."

Even as she finished this outburst she felt mean and selfish and began to question her motivation. He wasn't risking their lives because they could survive without him. With the Rhine drive, they could now avoid anything Earth threw at them, and they probably also possessed enough expertise to repair the station and return it to self-sufficiency. Materials and energy wouldn't be a problem: the former could be gathered within the Asteroid Belt, or elsewhere in the solar system; while for the latter they could fly close to the sun, use their mirrors and solar arrays, and be away again before Galahad could send anything after them.

So why am I angry? Hannah wondered.

It was because she loved Saul and didn't want him to die. It was because, without him now, she would feel alone. No. That didn't really work. If she was truthful she had to admit she did not love him. She had once had an infatuation for the man he had previously been, when both man and infatuation had been human things. But loving the Alan Saul who rescued her from Inspectorate HQ London had seemed more akin to loving some especially efficient weapons system. And now he existed in an area far outside cosy one-on-one human relationships, having risen to the position of godhead or *Owner,* which was the title he had assumed out of contempt for all other titles, or perhaps arrogance. So what was bothering her?

Possessiveness.

Somehow he belonged to her, and she realized that this concern of his for his sister—his risking *his* life for this Var Delex, by flying that contraption of his to the surface of Mars, alone—was the source of her pique. She was jealous, and knowing that only annoyed her further. And, by Le Roque's silence over radio, she guessed her reaction had made him uncomfortable. He was embarrassed for her.

Hannah swung round to watch an ant-like construction robot emerging from one of the empty rooms inside the installation. It was clutching a human corpse in its big two-fingered forelimb. The corpse wore a grey vacuum combat suit painted with the symbol of the rising sun on the chest and back. This was not one of the *Scourge* assault troops Saul had killed with the Scour, for the head was missing and misty vapour trickled from numerous bullet holes. The corpse was off on its journey to be placed first in the hopper of a big robot normally used to carry construction materials, then conveyed, once that robot had a full load, to the overflowing rim mortuary. It struck Hannah that this task must be now becoming quite familiar to the robots here.

"Did he have to kill them all?" she asked abruptly, then winced. Where had that come from?

"I'm guessing he didn't have time to be selective, Hannah." Le Roque's tone sounded somewhat patronizing over the com link. "And if he hadn't been so drastic, we might all either be dead or imprisoned by now."

Yes, those were the plain facts, but she didn't want to apologize for her outburst. Why the hell should she? She'd been shot at, she'd killed people, become an unwilling participant in slaughter, damn it! Still, she pulled back on any further outbursts. Le Roque had suffered similar woes, and he had also lost friends. She realized she was behaving like a brat, and it was time to stop.

"So, what do we do while he's gone?" she enquired as she began heading for the arcoplex elevator at this end. "Has he relayed any instructions?"

Le Roque emitted a dry laugh. "Oh, he's given us some chores to be getting on with while he's out of contact in a cave system down there. The detail on them came close to crashing the system, until he slowed things down a little."

"What?"

"We all have our instructions, and reconstruction is ramping up to the maximum possible given the limited power available, and we've restarted mining operations on the asteroid. I'm trying to get a handle on it, but it's not all obvious. He has some robots building a fuel drop tank for the Mars space plane down there, and Brigitta and Angela are running Robotics at full capacity."

"More robots?" Hannah queried.

"More robots," Le Roque confirmed, "though we have to await some new schematics that he'll send once he's back in contact. We also have provisional—but yet to be approved—designs for thousands of different station components, including what look like new arcoplex spindles."

Arcoplex spindles? Hannah wondered as she stepped into the elevator. "Okay," she said, "I'm heading back to my cabin now." She cut the link.

Suddenly feeling very weary, Hannah leaned back against one wall of the elevator, almost glad that the damage to Arcoplex Two had made it necessary to cut its spin again. She was pleased not to have to trudge through an artificial one gravity to her quarters near her laboratory. As the doors opened to admit her to the arcoplex, she opened her suit visor and was immediately hit by the smell of burned plastic and cooked human flesh, and sharply reminded of what had happened here. To distract herself she thought about the meaning of the instructions Saul had issued.

He seemed to be mapping out the immediate future and keeping everyone busy, but what about afterwards? Obviously he was aiming to rebuild Argus Station, almost certainly turning it into the spaceship he had once named it. Doubtless he intended to ensure it was self-sufficient, manoeuvrable, powerful . . . and then? Did he intend to move against Earth or move away? Did she, in all honesty, have any chance of understanding his future aims and divining his present plans?

MARS

Saul had understood, from the moment Var breathed easily again, that it was time to start acting and stop reacting. Images from Earth he had viewed during his descent to Mars showed that, while the *Scourge* had been out here hunting them, Serene Galahad had not been idle. He counted at least ten mass drivers operating, the framework of three huge ships taking shape amidst the ever-expanding Mars Traveller construction station, also a structure down on Earth that already looked like a test bed for something similar to the Rhine drive. If he continued just *reacting* they would die, so he needed to work harder and faster than the sum industrial and technical might of Earth.

"We'll need more power than what's available out here," said Var.

Saul focused his human facet on her, aware already that he was dealing with someone angry and prideful and little in love with being merely a subordinate. Whether his sister had always been like that he did not have sufficient memory of her to know. He also wondered if her recent experiences here might have changed her.

"Fusion should supply enough power to begin the work, but, yes, I agree: we need more power." He turned and stepped into the cave. "I'll take Argus close to the sun when we are done here."

"And what do you intend to get *done* here?"

"As I said, I want to get the Mars-format space plane up and running," he said. "The people here will be relocated to Argus while I strip Antares Base of anything useful, like the fusion reactor."

"You'll give them no choices?" she asked, apparently pleased by the idea.

"They can stay on Mars and die, if they so choose," he said bluntly.

The floor of the cave was uneven, and in places they had to scramble over boulders, after which Saul found himself panting, despite weighing just over a third of what he weighed on Earth. Deeper in, he began to note calcite formations—the nubs of stalactites and stalagmites that had never had a chance to get as big as anything similar on Earth. They had to be billions of years old.

"But, still, there is the problem of Rhone," Var observed.

Saul grimaced, annoyed with himself now because he had not thought to bring a weapon. Just getting here and rescuing his sister had been an unchar-acteristically overriding concern, while anything after that, down here, had seemed of little importance compared to everything else he had needed to do.

Now, because he hadn't been paying attention, the problems down here could become critical. Once out in the open again, he could take over their systems, but there were no readerguns he could use to remove Rhone. He and Var could sneak in and maybe seize some weapons—he had confidence enough in his own abilities in that respect—but all that seemed untidy, and there was still a chance that one or both of them might get killed.

"What do you suggest?" he asked, turning to study her.

"I want to kill Rhone," she said tightly, leaning against the cave wall and seemingly grateful for the pause. "But that's personal. Maybe, if you can link me through, I can talk to the whole base—let Rhone and the rest know the situation and get their response."

It was vague, imprecise.

"You could demand that Rhone step down," he suggested.

"I don't want to be *their* leader."

"You've fallen out of love with the idea?" Saul commented, moving on.

"Give me something to build and teams to command, and I'm fine. Making life-and-death decisions about people's future I'm not so fine with."

Of course, her pride had taken a heavy blow, and now Saul had offered her a way out. She wanted to deal with the nuts and bolts of a major space engineering project, as if that would be so much easier.

"I collected what data we have on you," he said. "On top of all your other qualifications you're a synthesist, which makes you much more qualified to lead people than many others who would like the job, including this Rhone. Sometimes the job chooses you and there are no other options."

He considered Hannah up on Argus as he said this: how sometimes it was necessary to accept responsibility because really there was no one else who could.

They trudged on through the darkness with long slow steps, their suit lights stabbing ahead of them. In his mind, Saul tracked their position on an old seismic map of this cave, pausing occasionally to study his surroundings. Some hours of silence passed as they laboured on, at one point crossing the bed of an ancient underground stream scattered with rounded pebbles. As he paused to aim his light in each direction along the pipe cut through the rock on either side of them, Saul understood that Var's decision to take Antares Base underground had been the best one in the circumstances, but that would have come to nothing once the might of Earth reached out here. It really did not matter how capable were the individuals or minor groups scattered about the solar system, because they simply could not bring to bear the kind of resources Serene Galahad had available. He started to move on, but Var suddenly swore and sprawled on the ground.

"You okay?" he asked.

She got back up onto all fours, then probed her side with one hand. "I need to rest."

"Are you hurt?"

"Cracked rib, but that's not my main problem." She stood up. "Thinking I was going to die, I didn't waste much of the little time I had left on sleeping."

"We'll take a break here," Saul said. "Do you have food?"

"Some."

"Then eat and rest." Saul stepped over beside the wall of the stream bed and sat down, feeling grateful for a break himself. Var sat opposite him, sucking from her suit spigot for a while, but did not seem inclined to talk further. He watched her eyelids sag then finally close, detected the change in her breathing, and envied her—she'd fallen straight into a deep sleep. Checking his own physical condition, he felt no need for sleep, for he had slept long enough, but did feel the need for his body to recharge. He sucked from his own suit spigot—a protein paste packed with sugars, vitamins and minerals—until it was dry. He then switched over to fluids and gulped down a litre of some unidentifiable citrus liquid. Then he consciously ramped up the activity of his organs, cleaning out poisons and recharging all round, doing the best to bring his body to optimum efficiency in the shortest time. But even all this, involving considerable detail, occupied only a small portion of his intellect, so he considered other matters meanwhile.

Saul summoned up in his mind a schematic of the standard construction robot, along with ideas he had played with before about how it could be vastly improved. At present it was a singular machine and, though it looked like an ant, the idea of social insects had not been taken to its logical conclusion, and beyond. The robots must be designed as parts of a logical whole—all their components rendered interchangeable down to even their minds. Robots that consisted of three body parts and three sets of limbs should be made capable of both separating and conjoining. He visualized robots with just one body section and one pair of limbs mating up with similar fellows to create robots with any number of body sections and pairs of limbs, even up to centipede monsters. Outlining this general idea, he next concentrated on the specific: the alloys and meta-materials to be used, the dimensions of all the components, a new design of processor to run a whole new kind of software. Seven hours later, by the time Var reopened her eyes, he had perfected every detail.

"I'm sorry about that," she apologized.

"No problem at all," he replied, standing up. He really didn't resent the delay at all because he felt stronger after those hours of respite, and knew he had designed something truly inspired, even for him.

When they moved on again, Var wanted to talk. Hours passed as she picked at him for details of recent events. In turn, he tried to fill in some of the blanks in his recollection of her history, and occasionally ventured to fill the blanks in his own. He thus learned more about their parents, about their sheltered upbringing, about the tutors he drained of knowledge and discarded, and his steady progress to adulthood. It was all distantly interesting, but Saul could find no emotional connection there. Really, Var was telling him stories about someone else. Then, coming with a kind of inevitability, her next question focused on something he had been skirting around within his own mind.

"So, you'll turn Argus Station into something bigger and better—a spaceship the like of which has never been seen before," she said. "Then what?"

There was the question. Until they first started up the Rhine drive, every effort made had been towards survival. Now the *Scourge* was no longer a problem and, with luck, it would be some time yet before Earth could send anything else against them.

"Then I leave," he replied.

"Leave?"

"The solar system."

"There will be some aboard Argus who won't like that."

"I'd like to offer them an alternative, but that's not feasible. I could take Argus to Earth right now, but there are Earth's defences to consider and also the fact—which I have made plain to them—that their next destination once they set foot on Earth would be an adjustment cell."

Glittering dust still hung in the air in front of them, even though it had been several days since the mining ahead had ceased. Many more hours had passed since their rest and, glancing at Var, Saul could see that she was again as weary as he himself felt. It would be better, he reckoned, if they did not approach the base in this state. Recollecting what he had seen on the way down, he said, "There are some pressurized cabins at the head of the shaft this Martinez began opening out?"

"Yes—and I don't think Rhone would have had time to close them down." She paused thoughtfully. "In fact, I wonder what he is doing, and what he now thinks is best for the base. He must know by now that the *Scourge* isn't coming here, and that puts him in a bad position. The base either has to be moved underground entirely or everything that has already been moved underground has to be brought back to the surface. Will your people up above have spoken to him?"

"I left instructions for them to ignore any communications sent from anyone but me."

"He'll be shitting himself," said Var. "He gambled on Serene Galahad and lost, so he might now be desperate enough to do something stupid."

Metal glinted under their suit lights and in the next moment they stepped out onto an area of compacted rubble. Looking up, Saul could see, silhouetted against the night sky of Mars, the scaffold leading up to the surface and the derrick above with the lifting platform firmly in place underneath it. No connection here with Argus which, by his calculation, sat just above the horizon and would fall behind it in just another half-hour. He would have liked to have put it geostationary above Antares Base but, with two moons whipping about out there, it was easier to put it into a stable orbit.

The cave directly ahead had been greatly enlarged and at their limit their suit beams vaguely picked out regular shapes: stacks of regolith blocks brought down from the old base, an ATV plus trailer, piles of equipment in plastic packing cases and other stacks of steel frames rescued from a geodesic dome. There were robots here, too, just a couple of them looming in the dark like steel herons. Saul reached out to them and found them on standby, but resisted the temptation to power them up and seize control of them. There seemed no point.

"We'll have to climb," Var pointed out.

"Is that a problem for you?" Saul asked.

"Not at all."

The low gravity made climbing so much easier. However, the low air pressure threatened to rack terminal velocity up high should either of them slip and fall. But, of course, as Saul reminded himself, his sister was quite well aware of that. He reached out and closed a hand on one of the nearest scaffold poles and found his grip firm. Without further ado, he began hauling himself upwards. It was easy enough, and he only had to pause once to rest, wedging himself between the pole and the rock wall of the shaft. Checking Var, he saw that, despite her cracked rib, she had not needed to rest. When he reached the top of the scaffold she was there to help him out onto the surface. He still wasn't up to full fitness and wouldn't be for some time yet.

"Thanks," he said, because that was what you were supposed to say.

As he moved away from the shadow of the derrick he could sense the Antares Base computer network, far over to his left, like a three-dimensional flow diagram for a heating system. He could link into it from here, but there seemed no point at the moment. Instead he gazed at Argus over on the horizon. Now that its smelting plants were extended and gleaming like eyes in dimly reflected sunlight, it reminded him of how it had looked from the surface of Earth.

A second later he was fully connected with the station's computer system, whereupon he immediately inserted his new robot schematics, also instantly generating an order for the necessary materials from the smelting plants. Next he tracked down Brigitta Saberhagen to her cabin, checking recent history to discover that she had only gone to bed after being awake for nearly forty hours. He left her alone and instead found the connections to ten particular minds and riffled through them to find the one he wanted.

Judd was one of those minds. The proctor was an amalgam of human and machine, either an android or a cyborg, the product of research carried out in Humanoid Unit Development aboard this station. On discovering the proctors here and understanding the horror involved in that research, Saul had considered destroying them, but he had activated them, and now found them indispensable. In a way, they were more like him than any human aboard.

Judd was repairing and rerouting damaged optics leading from the Rhine drive to Tech Central, assisted by a human team of four people, one of them in an EVA unit. He sent Judd the schematics of the new robots, meanwhile idly checking what the other proctors were doing. Paul was in the Arboretum, pruning shattered trees and replanting those that had been uprooted. Two more proctors were out on the Arboretum skin, working with human teams and construction robots to remove vacuum penetration locks and to make repairs, while the rest were scattered around the station in similar pairs, doing similar work. They never slept, these proctors, though they did take time out for themselves, sitting like natives around technological camp fires, communing in some manner Saul did not want to intrude on because he felt that seeing through their eyes was more than enough.

"Interesting," said Judd.

"When you're done there, I want you to assist the Saberhagens," said Saul. "Let them take the lead, and only intervene if they start to go wrong."

"I will be done in two hours."

"Good."

A further search now revealed Angela Saberhagen standing on a newly replaced glass floor above the robot factory, smoking a hand-rolled cigarette. Saul initiated a connection through her fone.

"Don't you know those are bad for you?" he remarked. "The least of my worries," she said, taking another drag.

"How close are you to getting the factory up and running?" he asked.

"You already know," she replied bluntly.

"Very well. I have a schematic for new robots for you to build, and the materials requisitions have gone to the smelting plants," he said. "I want you to retool as quickly as you can. Whenever you need to sleep, I want the work to continue, so I've sent Judd to assist."

She gazed up at the nearest cam. "New robots . . . How long before you start replacing us outdated humans, Alan?"

"That will never happen," he replied, and cut the connection. It was, he considered, a relevant question. He could allow the people up there to update themselves in the same way he himself had been updated, but he knew what the inevitable result would be. They would then be in competition with him, his power would be diminished and some would try to take it away from him. He might lose control. This was the same fear that turned democracies into totalitarian regimes and he wasn't immune to it. In fact, he did not care to be immune to it. The people aboard Argus would remain under his heel until he found some viable way to be free of them, though for the moment, he wanted that way not to necessitate exterminating them.

Even as he considered this quandary he accessed some of the brain-implant designs Hannah had stored in her system. He needed something to raise the people there above simple humanity—which, as his new robots came online, would be all but obsolete—but not something likely to raise them beyond his control. Where, though, in the plans developing both inside and outside his skull, to insert human beings? He saw them as control nexuses: either mentally controlling subgroups of robots or else controlling complex telefactored machines. Transforming them to his purpose would seem as dictatorial as the Committee, but what use were they to him if they were not . . . useful?

"So how *are* things there?" asked Var.

He pointed to the station. "The smelting plants are extended. One of them is already at work, while the other will be ready within a few hours. The robot factory will start producing our workers within that time too."

"We just need to get back there, then," she said, turning away and striding over to one of the cabins.

Saul hurried after her, crammed himself into the small airlock with her, and soon the both of them were inside the cabin itself. Var immediately undid her helmet and took it off.

"At last," she said, then turned and stepped through a door into the small washroom and toilet.

Saul removed his helmet and sniffed the stale air before surveying his surroundings. Along one wall of the cabin stood a single workbench loaded with equipment: dismantled electric motors, some hydraulic rams, a vice and a wide selection of hand tools that were run from pressure lines coiling down from a pipe along the ceiling. The rest of the room was occupied by a scattering of chairs around a low table improvised from food and drink boxes, with similar boxes stacked by the near wall, some foam mattresses and rolled-up sleeping bags, and a single desk with an old-style computer sitting on it, optics leading up from this machine into the ceiling.

He sat down at the desk to turn on the computer, and what had been a hazy and distant network suddenly etched itself into his brain as the computer connected to Antares Base and he linked to it via its modem. He slowly began to open up the bandwidth and explore, sampling here and there until he found the protection securing the computer in Mars Science, which he broke with a thought. He then speed-viewed the recorded exchanges between Rhone and Serene Galahad, understood the man's fears, lack of imagination and naivety, and moved on to locate the cam network and see what the base staff were doing.

The medical bay contained four bullet-riddled corpses on gurneys, while a doctor Saul soon identified as Da Vinci sat on the floor with his back against the wall, drinking some concoction out of an Erlenmeyer flask—probably surgical alcohol cut with fruit juice. Sixty of the personnel were confined to their rooms, each room locked down from Mars Science, while the rest occupied a community room. Those who were armed were gathered about Rhone himself on one side of the room, most of the rest sat in nervous silence while a few of them were arguing with Rhone and those accompanying him.

They wanted assurances but he now no longer had any to give them. He spoke eloquently of the tragic deaths of Var Delex and Lopomac, and expressed his displeasure at how some had sought to blame these deaths on him. The "some" were, Saul suspected, those four corpses in Da Vinci's surgery. No one believed him, even those around him with the guns, but those busy arguing obviously weren't prepared to state that outright. He talked about how they must now work together to survive and how the damage done during that lunatic move under-ground must be swiftly reversed. When they asked about Argus, he told them it was irrelevant, since there was no way anyone on the station could get to them. It seemed everything Saul was hearing had already been said and that Rhone was now reaching the end of his patience. The people were dismissed to their rooms with the instruction to await their work orders, and a warning that disobedience would not be tolerated. Saul with drew—he now knew all he needed to know.

2

SCRAPPAGE

With the ID implant, with cams covering just about every populated area, with "adjustment" to correct people's behaviour and with the shepherds, razorbirds and spiderguns for enforcement, the death rate due to "technical errors" was high under the original Committee. After Alan Saul destroyed much of this apparatus, Serene Galahad discovered that the consequent reduction in control led to greater productivity. However, her Committee instincts had not changed and, also viewing human beings as a plague upon her beloved Earth, it seemed a logical step for her to tighten her grip in a much more direct way. The strangulation collar was her solution. During her time as absolute dictator of Earth, nearly a billion of these devices were manufactured and placed around the necks of those holding essential positions and, as with any such hurriedly mass-produced technology, there were errors. These would not have mattered too much, were it not for security measures within the collars that read any error in the device as an attempt to remove it, and so prompted it to kill the unfortunate wearer. How many people died as a result can only be estimated, since those who died were always conveniently claimed to have been guilty of some crime. A conservative estimate puts the figure at two million, but it could in reality be as high as ten times that.

ARGUS

The shooting continued all around them, streaks of tracer bullets cutting through smoke and debris. The air quality, Alex noted, was getting quite bad, and he had to keep snorting dirt and splinters out of his nose. This was the problem with fighting in zero gravity: the detritus thrown up by bullets and explosions didn't just settle back to the ground.

Alex blinked, reached up to his face and touched the moisture below his eyes. In this state of meditative recall, replaying memories in order to analyse tactics and learn from mistakes, it all seemed so immediate. But he knew his tears weren't due to the sharp memory of dust in his eyes.

"It was confusing at first," Messina continued. *"There I was, with no memory of my past—doing what I was told while trying to understand the hatred directed at me. I was assaulted frequently, and nearly got killed on the last occasion. But now my confusion is gone."*

"It's gone?" said Alex, noncommittally.

"They tried to keep it from me, of course, but the image of the face I possessed before is not something that can be concealed for long."

Alex looked round to see Messina up on his knees now and gazing back, resting his shoulder against the penetration lock.

"I know who I was," he said—a little sadly, Alex thought.

"You were Chairman Alessandro Messina, ruler of Earth," Alex stated firmly. *Then his gaze strayed to what he assumed was a chunk of debris sailing through the air towards them. It took him half a second further to realize his mistake.*

Alex shuddered, his body trying to respond to something that had happened just a couple of standard days ago now. He opened his eyes and surveyed his surroundings as he prepared himself for the worst memories. His small cabin was located in a workers' dormitory fixed between lattice walls. The door was locked and, for now, this place had become a prison. But Alex felt fine with that. The cabin was comfortable enough, and the medic had already seen to his various wounds. He had some bottles of drink and even some food, a hammock and a combined zero-gravity toilet and shower unit, the latter of which he had used and as a result felt the cleanest he had felt in a long while. This was substantially more than had been available to him for the many months during which he had scrabbled to stay alive, trapped in a zero-gravity hydroponics unit. He was okay with the solitude, too, because he needed to straighten out his thinking. He closed his eyes again and returned to the not too distant past.

"Grenade!" he shouted, heaving himself to his feet and reaching for Messina.

The erstwhile ruler of Earth stood up, ready to throw himself clear, then took a couple of steps, forced forwards by the impact of the bullets hitting his back and blowing chunks of flesh and rib out of his chest. Alex rolled aside, firing at a half-seen figure, coming back up onto his knees as the same figure staggered, then he sighted properly and emptied the new clip into it. He saw bits of his target flying away, before the grenade detonated and picked him up in a hot fist.

Screaming somewhere . . .

This was where it got difficult. The blast had thrown him into foliage, where he finally slammed to a halt against a solid branch. With his ears ringing, he had dragged himself back to the penetration lock. There he had found the Chairman's remains slowly revolving in the air above him, like some grotesque expanded sculpture constructed of offal. He had gone into the trees and found the assailant dead, cut in half, but that hadn't been enough.

He didn't care about his own life any more. Chairman Messina was dead and there had to be payment. Firing ahead . . . Not even trying to take cover, Alex propelled himself through the trees to where the floating debris mostly consisted of chunks of hardening breach foam. A penetration lock protruded from the ground, three of the assault force from the Scourge gathered around it. As one of them turned towards him, Alex braced himself against a trunk and fired his rifle from the hip—half a clip, picking them up and sending them tumbling, blood misting around them.

The next attacker he found opened fire on him from concealment in thick bushes, branches shattering all around him. Alex threw himself towards those bushes, emptied the rest of the clip, inserted another and kept his finger on the trigger. A figure, just glimpsed, tried to escape, shattered assault rifle tumbling away. Alex kept firing until there was no more voluntary movement there, snatched ammunition clips from a belt half-concealed by a bulging mass of viscera, moved on . . .

Tactical analysis: you weren't conserving ammunition.

He killed again, then again. He responded to direct fire against him by just confronting it and moving in, firing continuously.

Tactical analysis: how the hell did you survive that?

Through the killing haze he started to realize something was wrong with the attackers. They seemed to be responding to him too slowly. When a grenade flung him tumbling, he located its source and fired on a soldier who seemed to be trying get back out of the Arboretum through a penetration lock. Bullets tore flinders from the lock, but only briefly before they ran out. Alex reached down for another clip as he flung himself forwards, but found none. Hardly thinking about it, he discarded his rifle and drew his commando knife as he came down on the man fumbling to open the lock. The man seemed hardly able to defend himself as Alex dragged him round, scanned the armouring of his VC suit, then drove the carbide blade towards a weak point under the arm. He shoved it in to the hilt, then tilted it down, slicing to the heart, blood jetting out.

Next he was strangling someone, with no recollection of the intervening time. After that it seemed he could only find the dead or dying. He caught one soldier slowly towing himself along the base of the Arboretum dividing wall, pulled him up and gazed in puzzlement at the bloodshot eyes and foam around his mouth, before snapping his neck.

Tactical analysis: they were dying of the Scour virus.

Finally he realized the shooting was over. Then, almost as if operating on some homing instinct, he made his way back to where Chairman Messina had died. He went down on his knees, covered in blood—most of which was not his own.

It was over.

Alex drew the sidearm he had taken earlier from the other corpse here and which, during his killing spree, he had completely forgotten. He put the barrel in his mouth and there he paused for a brief eternity, until he realized he had no reason to pull the trigger . . .

Alex was a clone of Chairman Alessandro Messina, but also a soldier who was surgically and chemically programmed to be totally loyal to that one man. He had been loyal. He had remained loyal to the best of his abilities, even when Messina had been mind-wiped and turned into someone else—even until the end. But he didn't pull the trigger because the initial programming was not so strong any more, and he was now older and wiser than a clone new from the vat. He realized in that moment, as so many people do, that having a new purpose might be better than blowing out the back of his skull.

"I know what you're capable of," the commander of the station police, Langstrom, had said, shortly after finding him in the Arboretum. "I can offer you a place with my men. You'd be one of the first to be issued with weapons if we're attacked again which, considering our recent history, seems highly likely."

Alex had not even needed to think about his answer.

"No," he'd replied, "I need a totally new purpose, preferably with less guns and blood involved."

Langstrom had then not known what to do with him, hence Alex ending up in here.

Floating above his hammock, Alex opened his eyes, reached up to wipe his face with a shaking hand. He was covered in sweat but now felt he had severed some link to his past. It was as if he'd finally shaken off a fever. He reached down and grabbed the edge of the hammock, using it to drag himself to the wall. A swift kick against it sent him drifting across the room to a pack, gecko-stuck to a wall-shelf. He took out one of the bottles inside, uncapped it and squeezed its contents into his mouth. After a moment he lowered the bottle and stared at it, realizing he'd been given beer—something he'd only ever sampled once or twice in his life before. He took another swallow, and another—then heard the door lock clunking, before a knock on the door itself. He waited, expecting someone to come in, then registered that the person outside was being polite.

"Come in," he said, feeling foolish.

The door swung open and in stepped a giant shaven-headed brute of a man. Alex instinctively pushed his gecko soles down against the floor and took a step back, gripping the plastic bottle more tightly, while briefly scanning the room for a more effective weapon.

"Hello, Alex," the man said mildly, as he folded his arms.

Alex peered at him, with memories slowly surfacing. Of course, here was a man it had been necessary for him to know when he'd been in Messina's fast-response protection team.

"Ghort," he said.

Ghort nodded and smiled cautiously.

"I'm surprised you're alive," Alex added. "Or should I say I'm surprised you still have a mind."

"Only the murderers were mind-wiped," Ghort explained. "Even though I was one of the Chairman's bodyguards for ten years, I never actually murdered anyone. I told him I'd only kill to defend him or myself." He paused reflectively. "I could, of course, say the same about you. It's arguable that you're responsible for a considerable number of deaths aboard this station, and therefore I'm surprised Saul didn't kill you when he captured you, or have it done afterwards."

"Perhaps it's because of my lack of free will," Alex suggested.

Ghort's expression hardened. "Something we are all lacking now."

Alex just stared at him for a long moment, then asked, "What do you want?"

"Commander Langstrom told me," said Ghort, "that you want an occupation that doesn't involve guns and blood. Well, I've had you assigned to my team in Construction and Maintenance, and we have work to do, a lot of it, right now."

Alex hadn't really thought about what he wanted, just about what he didn't want.

"Okay," he shrugged.

Ghort led him out into a station that seemed to have become, in just a few hours, even more chaotic than it had been during the height of the recent battle.

MARS

While Var slept, Saul dropped his body into a similar state of somnolence, but one without the loss of awareness and volition.

In his mind, like a librarian after a recent rush, he began cataloguing and filing, returning books to their correct shelves, clearing up the rubbish and polishing the floors. He felt a slight irritation at not being able to access the whole of his mind, which included his organic backups in Hannah's clean-room and the whole Argus computer network, but spread across these and everything currently in his skull there was a great deal of redundancy. Much of what he was now doing inside his head would act as a template to lay over some other work in progress elsewhere, when he could again access it. However, the situation wasn't ideal and would become less tenable in the years, decades and perhaps centuries to come . . .

Yes, centuries . . .

Acceptance had slowly crept up on him. He now perfectly understood the changes he had made to his own body even before Smith had erased the earlier Alan Saul, and was now recognizing what other changes he could make. He knew that this, combined with his mental backups, meant that corporeal immortality lay within his reach.

He again considered other possibilities that had occurred to him during the trip out to the Asteroid Belt, and which had been affirmed by recent events. The Alexes were tank-grown clones of Chairman Messina. They were grown to adulthood so fast that the tanks they grew in required powerful cooling systems, so energetic was the cell growth, and each produced an adult Alex in just a few years: a blank slate on which Messina wrote the mind of his choosing. However, the methods of indoctrination used had been crude—surgery even being required. Now, with everything Hannah was coming up with, it should be possible simply to copy across from another mind. Saul could now substantially reduce the danger of physical death to his body in the same way as it had been reduced for his mind. He could make copies of himself. He could, in fact, use copies of himself for risky ventures such as this present one.

Cowardice?

Saul allowed himself a smile. What exactly was cowardice? He'd been in turn frightened, angry and exhilarated while hacking a bloody path from the Calais incinerator out here, but had never backed away from danger. Then, again, as he had seen it at the time, he could never have been safe while the Committee had the power to take away his life. Now that he was, to stretch a term, "safe" from the Committee, other considerations were coming into play. And the main one of these was how much did he value his own life; a life that now might just go on and on? No, he defined cowardice as sacrificing his integrity in order to stay safe, and not as the eliminating of unnecessary risks to his life.

Saul further pondered on the future and, for the first time in a while, felt a surge of unaccustomed excitement. A whole universe lay out there to explore. The Drake equation remained to be solved, while its resultant paradox, described by Fermi, needed to be investigated. Knowledge within and without stood ready to be gathered . . .

Now, venturing into astrogation data residing inside the hardware in his skull, Saul began mentally exploring the mapped planetary systems that lay beyond Earth, wondering where to go beyond the solar system. Perhaps first some of those least likely to contain life, while he gathered resources and explored the worlds within; perhaps a pause in the light of some binary star system while growing clones of himself and imprinting upon them some honed-down and thoroughly human copy of his mind? Maybe he could bathe in the light of a red hypergiant while extending and cementing his knowledge. So many possibilities.

But one not to be ignored.

He grimaced. Yes, the one possibility he must not ignore was that though he was powerful and now possessed a drive that could take him out into the abyss, Earth did not lie so far behind him. He had managed to extend his mind, but already Serene Galahad had created her comlifers—humans with hardware in their skulls much like his own and similarly linked into computer systems—who were only a step behind him. And, though he had taken Hannah Neumann away from Earth, the slow accretion of knowledge could lead, within just a few years, to bio-interfaces equivalent to the one in his skull. Rhine had managed to design a working warp drive and, with Earth's resources, Galahad appeared likely to come up with something just like it, and soon. But Galahad was just the latest example of the kind that came to dominate the human race;

the near stars, he realized, would never be a safe enough distance away. He would need to lose himself out there, find a place and make himself a fortress.

Then of course there were other things to speculate on. The Drake equation posited that there should be intelligent life out there, but the Fermi paradox posed the question of why it had not been seen. Perhaps the answer to that was related to the likes of Serene Galahad and himself? Too much power in the hands of too few, genocidal rulers, and dark inwardly turned realms where free beings had become just cogs in a machine, perhaps races intolerant of competition dropping warp-drive weapons on inhabited worlds, perhaps whole races sliding into the mental self-destruction he himself had faced when he uploaded Janus? For all he knew, he could be heading out into something more potentially hostile than a solar system controlled by Galahad and her ilk.

The hours slid by as Saul created models in his head of nightmare alien cultures, of dystopias, utopias, of intelligent life based on something other than carbon, and on the myriad possibilities based on carbon alone. At some point his mind slid into the utterly esoteric, and also into a state closer to human sleep. He immediately grasped for himself the utility of this lucid dreaming state and allowed it to continue, and only rose out of it as watery Martian morning wafted its reluctant light through the windows of the cabin. He stood, headed over to the bathroom, attended to the needs of an unfortunately weak human body, gazed at his face in a mirror on the wall, noted how he needed a shave and a haircut but how these faults humanized him, washed his face then returned to the main room and turned on the lights.

"It's time?" said Var, immediately sitting upright in her sleeping bag.

"We move," Saul agreed, stepping over to the chair he'd draped his VC suit on.

Var scrambled out of her sleeping bag, frowned at him, then headed for the bathroom. He pulled on his suit, swapped out the oxygen bottle, checked over Var's EA suit and replaced the air bottle for that too, finishing just as she returned, and handing it over.

Riding on the Martian dawn came his full self, and he felt a visceral pull as they stepped outside, and for a hundred metres after that, as they trudged across the dusty ground. Then he was in and connected to Argus Station, expanding and updating.

Even at that moment, his robots were preparing to launch the fuel drop tank from Docking Pillar Two. Initial thrust came from a dismounted space-plane steering jet, which would be ejected in Martian atmosphere. The thing would take re-entry heat on a ceramic shield, open out parachutes to slow it further, then inflate air bags for a bouncing landing. Now it was nearly complete, he saw, in an instant, some adjustments he could make: how with the addition of an extra parachute and a reduction of the fuel load he could insert some extra weight behind the heat shield; and he issued his instructions. Really, he should have thought of this earlier.

"So what's the plan?" Var asked.

Saul gazed ahead towards Shankil's Butte. In just two hours his package would arrive here on Mars. "You know the plan," he said.

"I mean: how do we deal with Rhone?" she asked, irritated.

Antares Base sat as clear in his mind as Argus Station, but the latter was of more interest to him at the moment. In the few seconds it would take before Var became impatient he further checked the situation up there.

Already two of his new conjoining robots were rolling off the production line. Both smelting plants were running, and producing components for both Robotics and the massive reconstruction of the station into a spherical space-ship. The robot mining machines on the asteroid had nearly filled both of the big ore carriers to keep that process going. However, power supplies were at full stretch, while all the building and manufacturing were nowhere near their proposed maximum, so Saul needed to limit their stay here. It was time to get things done.

"Perhaps, when we are a lot closer, you should speak to him," he suggested to Var. "Your suit radio is in range of the base even now. You can tell him that I've come to rescue them, to relocate them to Argus; that his earlier actions are understandable and are forgiven."

"You fucking what?"

"What else did you intend to say?"

"Something, but I wasn't going to talk about forgiveness."

"Try, anyway—and I'll ensure that everyone there also hears your exchange. Perhaps if he's not agreeable you can slant your persuasion at everyone else there . . ."

She glared at him suspiciously.

What she said didn't matter all that much, anyway. Rhone would respond precisely as Saul expected him to. Gazing into the base, he could see a man struggling to find some solution to the insoluble, but certain that his grip on power was the right one. Such men always had a maximum response even for small outside threats. It made them feel worthy, useful, that they were *doing* something.

"He'll send his people out to take a shot at us," said Var.

"Of course he will," Saul replied. "So we need to get to the cover of Shankil's Butte before you speak to him." He picked up his pace.

"I still don't see how this advances our cause any," Var protested. "I can probably get us inside without him knowing . . ."

Looking through the base cams, Saul counted eight armed staff. Checking the records there, he saw that most of these were from Mars Science, though some were from Maintenance and Construction. The head of the latter, Martinez, was one of the corpses still lying on a gurney in the medical area, so obviously the eight here were the only ones Rhone trusted with weapons. Saul calculated that Rhone would send a minimum of four of them outside.

"In fact you could not get us in without him knowing, since he's paranoid enough to be running a recognition system through the exterior cams," said Saul. "I, however, can get us in, but what then?" He glanced at her. "Eight of his people are armed."

"You're as irritating as ever," she replied. "You're not going to tell me what you're planning, are you?"

Saul analysed that and realized that some human element of him was being wary of letting her know how ruthless he intended to be. He considered the idea of detailing his plans to her but then, deciding he did not yet want to explain the cold reasoning behind them, rejected it.

"You'll have to trust me," he said. Var growled in irritation.

It took them an hour to reach Shankil's Butte, a partially collapsed monolith of wind-carved sandstone cut through with layers of conglomerate. On the collapsed side, a path wound up through fallen rubble to the top and, without hesitation, Saul began to tramp up this for no other reason than to gaze at the view, which included the base itself lying a couple of kilometres beyond. As he wended his way up, the fuel drop tank launched from Argus Station, which was now well above the horizon but not visible in the daylight sky. Soon they reached the canted summit of the butte and gazed out at the base. The remaining hexes and linking wings were clearly visible, with stacks of regolith blocks and other building materials marking out where much of it had been disassembled.

"Here," said Var.

Saul turned to see her prodding at something on the ground with her toe and then gazing back the way they had come. He walked over and peered down at an assault rifle clip lying by her feet.

"It was from here that one of Ricard's men shot my friend," she explained.

"You killed Ricard and his men," Saul noted.

"Will it ever end?" she asked.

"Everything ends," he opined, turning away and finding a rock to sit down on, and again studying the base.

Over to the right he could see the Mars-format space plane, parked by a low building to one side of a couple of fuel silos, at one end of a rough airstrip where rocks had been dozed to either side and holes filled in and packed down. Checking trajectories in his mind, he focused on the far end of the strip. Half an hour to go now.

"Time for you to talk to Rhone," he said.

"You're sure?"

"Have you ever known me not to be?" he asked, not sure *what* she had known about him.

Var made some adjustments on her wrist console, while Saul reached out to the base and established multiple links between the radio receivers there and the internal public address system. "This is Var Delex calling Antares Base," she said, her words echoing in his mind as he heard them at both ends. "I need to speak to you, Rhone. There're some things you need to know." Saul watched the sudden panic stirred up at the other end.

Rhone, who had been working at a console in Mars Science, now banished the supplies lists from his screen and called up control schematics for the communication system, immediately trying to shut down public address. Saul allowed him a few tries, then put up the words "Talk to Var" on his screen, before freezing out his keyboard.

"Can he hear me?" Var asked on a private channel.

"Yes, he can hear you," Saul told her, "and so can everyone else in the base."

"Listen to me, Rhone," she continued on an open channel, "the *Scourge* isn't coming. In fact, Earth now has nothing capable of getting out here, and won't have anything for years yet."

Saul didn't disabuse her of that notion, as she would learn about the huge orbital activity around Earth soon enough.

"You can, if you wish, rebuild the base where it is or move it underground as we planned, but your chances of survival won't be much different from before. However, I have an alternative offer."

Rhone had now moved to another console and had summoned a few of his armed staff. He there used the dishes on the roof of the base to triangulate Var's position. Saul let him do that, as he wanted Rhone to know precisely where they were.

"Alan Saul is here on Mars, Rhone, and he is about to deliver fuel for our space plane. I'm leaving Mars with him to join him on Argus Station. All the staff of Antares Base are welcome to join him too . . . all the staff, Rhone. I understand why you did what you did and, though I'm not prepared to forgive it, Alan Saul is."

"Shouldn't you talk to her?" asked one of those with Rhone.

Rhone rounded on him. "If we submit, Galahad will end up killing us. Var is either lying or doesn't know what's happening around Earth . . . and do you think for one moment that someone who has stolen a space station and launched an attack against Earth that killed millions gives a fuck about us?"

"Still . . ." replied the man, uncertain.

"You saw that thing that came down?" Rhone asked. "It had just one pilot, and I'm surprised it reached the ground in one piece. We have the advantage now, especially if Saul is outside. Just think how grateful Galahad would be if we could capture him alive or even have his corpse to show her. You two, take Piers and Thorsten out there." Rhone checked his screen. "They're on Shankil's Butte. Capture them if you can, or bring back their corpses."

So far so predictable: he was sending his most trusted lieutenants to do this job. Replaying cached base recordings, Saul confirmed that all four of them were either directly responsible for or closely involved in the recent killings there.

Rhone now keyed into the frequency Var was using. "Var, what a surprise to hear from you." He grimaced as his own voice was repeated over the PA system. "I was sure that fall killed you."

Of course Rhone had told everyone in the base that Var had suffered an unfortunate accident. Would she now let him get away with that?

"Well, I'm alive . . . and I'm waiting for your answer to Alan's proposal," was all she said.

Rhone shut off com and turned to others who had joined him. "They're desperate to get to our space plane. We *do* have the advantage here." Those others, unarmed staff of Mars Science, spectators, nodded dubious agreement. He ignored them as he opened up com again. "I'll be needing guarantees. Perhaps we should continue this discussion inside . . . Also, I need to confirm that Alan Saul is indeed with you. I don't see why he would risk his life coming down to the surface."

Var turned to him and Saul nodded and spoke. "This is Alan Saul. I came down to the surface of Mars to rescue my sister, whose married name is Delex but whose maiden name was Saul. Everything Var has told you is true. You must also be aware that aboard Argus Station we now have a working version of the Alcubierre drive, which effectively takes us out of the reach of Serene Galahad. We are also completely self-sufficient, have a great deal in the way of resources and can survive out here. Think very carefully about your next decisions, Rhone."

Rhone sat back, his expression blank as he glanced at a screen showing his four recruits coming one after the other out of a base airlock. Meanwhile, the fuel drop tank had begun its descent and opened its first parachute.

"Galahad is building ships, fast, and I'm told it's likely they will have similar drive systems," said Rhone.

"That's true," said Saul, glancing at Var and seeing her frown. "But there are other truths you seem to be avoiding. A moment ago you wondered if someone like me, who has killed millions, would give a fuck about you all, yet you seem to be forgetting how Serene Galahad released the Scour on Earth and killed *billions*. Do you think she cares about rescuing you for anything other than punishing you on ETV prime-time?"

"So you say," replied Rhone.

Saul saw no point in arguing further. This man knew for certain that the Scour had originated from ID implants. "I'll want your decision soon."

Rhone turned to stare up at one of the base cams, now aware that Saul had indeed penetrated the place. Maybe that would be enough to sway Rhone, but Saul doubted it. He swung his attention out towards the horizon, beyond the airstrip. The drop tank had now opened out its second and larger parachute and was inflating its gas bags. Saul estimated that it would be visible within the next twenty minutes. He looked back towards the base. All four of Rhone's most loyal people were now outside, three of them moving away from the base in Saul's direction while another was driving an ATV round from the other side.

The timing was almost perfect but—even down to his walking pace in getting here to this butte—Saul had ensured that.

ARGUS

Ghort's first instruction, upon handing over a powered socket driver—the only tool Alex could first be trusted with—was: "It's pointless trying to race the robots, but I'm fucked if I want them more than ten joints ahead of us by end of shift."

The task was simple enough. Structural members were to be anchored to the top and bottom faces of the fifteen-kilometre circumference of the station ring. This first involved cutting away marked-out areas of cladding material to expose one of the stress beams—a beam nearly a metre square, precisely following the curve of the station and made of a complex lamination of bubblemetal and graphyne. With the section of beam exposed, they attached a jig, which Ghort positioned precisely with an integral laser survey device, before heaving the U-plate in to slot over the beam and then clamping it down. Akenon and Gladys then towed over their multi-weld unit and, using nickel-carbon and high-temperature epoxy wire, welded the plate in position. Then the three of them unloaded the beam-end joint from their dray and it was Alex's turn, using his socket driver to tighten, to the correct tension, the eight bolts the others quickly started in their threaded holes in the U-plate.

The first time Alex had tried to tighten a bolt, he ended up spinning round in vacuum on the end of the socket driver, while the other three laughed. That was the limit of his hazing, however, for there was work to be done and one of the construction robots working along the adjacent beam had already finished its joint and was moving on to the next. Thereafter the work became just mechanical, repetitive and somehow comforting. Alex had assumed that while performing this task, he'd have too much time to reflect on his past, but it didn't work out that way. All he thought about was the next thing to do, how he could position himself so as not to get in the way of the others, how quickly he could lean in to tighten the bolts and how best to position himself while doing so. However, as they progressed and the nearby construction robot ran out of joint ends and had to wait for one of its kin to bring another load, there was finally time for banter.

"We're fast becoming fucking obsolete," said Gladys, pointing back along their course around the rim, where a hemispherical robot on gecko treads was now pausing regularly beside each of their previously affixed joint ends.

"What's it doing?" Alex asked.

"Inspecting our work," she replied. "Used to be it was us inspecting *their* work."

"Don't exaggerate, Gladys," said Akenon. "Last thing you inspected was the crabs on your snatch."

"Go fuck yourself, Ake."

"Sure, I got less chance of catching anything nasty that way."

"Right," interjected Ghort, as Alex leaned forward and began tightening down the latest set of bolts, "we'll take a break after this one." He pointed across to the outer edge of the station ring, where there clung a mobile over-seer's station, overlooking the webwork of beams of partially constructed floors extending from the outer rim.

Alex wound in the last of the bolts and stood upright. They'd now been working solidly for six hours, and muscles he was unaware of during the most severe forms of combat training were now aching. This was the perfect reminder of something one of his instructors had once told him: "Never underestimate the strength of manual workers. You might exercise and train for three or four hours a day, but that length of time involved in hard physical activity only gets them as far as their first tea break." He stretched his back, then opened the gecko pad on the side of his socket driver, before stooping to secure the tool down by his feet. He quickly followed the other three as they headed towards the overseer's station.

"All this has got to go." Ghort gestured to the partially completed new floors. "He wants a clean rim, so all those extensions you guys had started on now have to be dismantled."

"I guess he knows what he's doing," said Gladys, her voice subdued.

"More so than any Committee bureaucrat," remarked Akenon contem-platively.

Since he had first met them Alex had noticed how Akenon and Gladys always talked in hushed tones when the conversation turned to Alan Saul—the *Owner*. However, Ghort's attitude was rather more difficult to pin down. The man seemed to continue working dutifully, as instructed, but his expression closed up when the Owner was mentioned, and he became hard faced and acerbic whenever the conversation turned to politics, any hazy concepts such as freedom or any speculation on what their future might hold.

They passed through the airlock two at a time and, once inside, Ghort delivered the welcome news that the place was fully pressurized, which apparently meant no food paste or metallic-tasting fruit juice from their suit spigots today. After they removed the helmets of their heavy work suits, Akenon popped open the case he had lugged in. Taking out Thermos flasks of hot coffee and individual boxes of pasteurized and sealed sandwiches, he handed them round. Sipping coffee through a straw, Alex headed over to the windows and gazed across the face of the rim. Gladys shortly came up to stand beside him.

The rim face extended for hundreds of metres inward, at which point the station enclosure rose up in a slope for just over two kilometres to the jutting prominence of Tech Central. Over to the right of that, the rest of the station, along with a truncated view of an extended smelting plant, lay silhouetted against the rusty brown face of Mars.

"Never seen it like this," she said, gesturing to the scene before them.

"Well," said Alex, "I suppose it looks a bit different to Earth." He nodded towards Mars.

"I don't mean that," she said, and stabbed a finger, "I mean the robots."

It seemed that the enclosure was another item that "had to go," because large areas of plates had already been stripped away, while yet more were being rucked up, like fish scales, and carried off. Both there and around the rim, the robots swarmed like steel ants, and the station seemed to be dissolving in some areas and re-crystallizing in others even as they watched.

"What's that about robots?" Ghort asked, moving up beside them. This interruption reminded Alex that Ghort, though trained in construction before a delegate had spotted his talent for thumping people, was not an old hand like the other two. Alex would have expected seniority issues to arise from the order delivered from on high that Ghort should become foreman of this small team, but the other two seemed perfectly happy with having him in charge. Alex also sensed that this wasn't down to sheer luck, but to a certain individual's ability to slot personalities together with the ease of Lego bricks.

"They were never this integrated before," said Gladys, still watching the robots. "We'd get work orders, a specific job to do, and that would get slotted into the system of a team of robots, and they'd set to work. We had to iron out any errors, sometimes stop them working and ask for reprogramming to include stuff they weren't programmed to do."

"The robots are more efficient now," suggested Alex.

"Nah, the robots were always fine if they were programmed right. The problem was everything behind them."

"Crap in crap out," said Akenon, round a mouthful of sandwich.

"Never seen them running this fast," continued Gladys. "They just ain't stopping. The bloody things are even *anticipating* now, and covering stuff that shouldn't be in their programming. I saw one stop halfway through a job to repair some weapons damage to a beam junction. If one of them ran into anything like that before, it just shut down to wait for its new instructions."

"It's him," Alex suggested, noting a brief and quickly suppressed flash of anger in Ghort's expression.

"Yup," Gladys agreed, "it certainly is."

As he later walked out to start the next six hours of their shift, feeling buoyant after solid food and hot coffee, Alex considered how he was now part of something awesome and thus understood the attitude of his co-workers to the Owner. As he began work once more, he was thinking again about nothing beyond the next bolt to wind down, and then how best to apply the diamond cutting wheel Ghort had begun instructing him on how to use, and how best to make sure he didn't slice a hole in his suit. The time seemed to flash by till, when Ghort called a halt, Alex stuck his tools to the deck with a feeling of weary satisfaction.

"It's only eight beam ends ahead," said Akenon. "That'll do."

Another small victory in the human—robot race, with the necessary handicap applied.

Back inside the station, Gladys commented, "The new boy didn't slow us down."

"The new boy done good," said Ghort drily, slapping Alex on the shoulder.

Alex was amazed at how happy he felt to be complimented on performing such simple tasks so ably, and puzzled too because he felt the urge to cry.

Everybody seemed to be working at a frenetic pace, so it should have come as no surprise to Hannah to find tasks queued up in the station's system for herself, too. In her personal queue she found the names of everyone aboard the station listed in order of importance under "neural tissue samples," though with a vague proviso in there of "scheduled when available." On top of that it turned out that a long production floor, provided with power and plumbing points but no equipment, beyond the sealed door adjacent to her clean-room, was to be opened to her. It seemed that this was where she would be growing those tissue samples in aerogel matrices and setting up production of the cerebral hardware and bioware required to link those people the samples were taken from to their backups.

Hannah sighed. She had always preferred focusing on research and did not enjoy the work involved in mass manufacturing the product of such research. However, she couldn't really fault Saul in his aim to give the people here a chance at a form of immortality.

Investigating further, she found that this was not the last of it. He wanted her setting up artificial wombs and other related devices and, by the look of the list, this meant human cloning. She was uncomfortable with that, but saw how it related to the growing of neural tissue samples: backups for both body and mind. Neither was she comfortable with the plug-ins: exterior hardware that made a link between the internal bioware in their skulls and their backups, and which also enabled limited access to the station's computer systems and its robots. That gave her pause as she realized that Saul wanted the people here to take some steps up the same ladder he himself had climbed, but did not want them to climb too far. She could see that, with this set-up he would always remain in control: able to shut down that exterior hardware and boot people out of the system at will. Was that moral? Was it right? She didn't know, but recognized that it was certainly a precaution she would also take, were she in his position.

There came a knock at her door as it opened, and in stepped Le Roque. Hannah gazed at him in puzzlement. "I don't often see you down here."

He frowned at her. "Well, that being the case, you shouldn't have scheduled me to come here. I was about to get something to eat and then catch some sleep. Apparently you want to take neural tissue samples from everyone aboard the station, so you can repair brain damage like you did with Saul."

It was to be a gradual dissemination of the knowledge: let it spread throughout the station rather than announce it. Don't actually conceal it but don't make an effort to let everyone know. This was the kind of news that could cause extreme reactions, both positive and negative. Being able to live forever was a dream of humanity, but never being able to die could be the most extreme of nightmares, especially when your entire experience of life until now had been under the Committee. This could result in people clamouring at her door either to demand immortality or to lynch her. Tell them before you take the sample, had been Saul's message, therefore give them the choice. "True," she said, "but I didn't expect anyone here just yet—the scheduling is automated."

"You're not ready? I can always come back another time." There was no point in opening up her surgery for this task, since it was a quick clean anaerobic operation—inducer to numb the nerves then a narrow-gauge drill needle straight through the skull to take a small biopsy. In her experience, people hardly felt it, though it was always best to go in through the back of the head so they saw neither the drill needle nor the operation itself.

"No, we may as well get it done now." Hannah waved her hand towards her laboratory's surgical chair. "But you need to understand the implications of this, and I have to give you the option to refuse."

Le Roque stared at her. "I know all I need to know: this increases my chances of staying alive should I get a head injury."

"It's more than that," Hannah explained, "and the possibilities are more extensive. I grew samples from Saul's brain in an aerogel matrix which he connected to via the bioware in his skull. This gave him a backup to his entire mind." Hannah did not continue, because she could see that Le Roque now understood.

"Immortality," he said, wide-eyed, excited. "You'll be setting up artificial wombs and a cloning facility . . ."

"I'll divide the samples," said Hannah. "Some will be used for tissue repair if required. If the damage is too extensive then I see no barrier to the possibility of download into a cloned body."

"So when do I get this bioware?"

"When your backup is ready," Hannah replied.

"Is this only for a select elite?" he asked, now starting to see the drawbacks.

"For everyone, but in order of their importance to Saul." Hannah paused. "Do you want this, then?"

"Of course I do—I'd be a madman not to want it." Le Roque went over to the chair and sat down decisively. Hannah eyed him for a moment, then stepped over to get her equipment out of a nearby cupboard. She also retrieved a powered sample case with nutrient feeds to fifty temperature-controlled glass sample tubes. She would check the system again, but reckoned she had a busy time ahead of her.

She was not wrong.

After Le Roque, Rhine paid her a visit, then came the Saberhagens. The next person to arrive after them she waved straight to the chair, which worried the man because he had merely come to unseal the door leading through to the adjacent production floor. Between sampling operations, Hannah also began to track down the equipment she would need, some of it held in stores and some of it in closed-off laboratories or other facilities scattered throughout the station, and put through the necessary orders for it to be relocated. Not everything was available, however. The boxes of aerogel with their micro-tubule feeds and other support mechanisms required a special order to various sections of high-tech manufacturing aboard the station and would have to be assembled here.

I need more staff, she thought, and immediately felt a tightness at the back of her throat and tears welling behind her eyes. Her assistant James had been, in the short time she had known him, one of the best. Now he was lying out in the rim morgue. No backups for him; no second chances for him. She allowed the unfairness of this, of life, circumstances, all of it, to wash over her, then she let it go. In this moment she was at the start of something that could stack the deck on the side of humanity, or at least those aboard this particular station. So she got back to work.

3

WHERE ARE THEY?

Enrico Fermi posed the question "Where are they?" and, being a man of his time, felt sure that the aliens had wiped themselves out with nuclear weapons. And now, long past those innocent nuclear years, in an age of cynicism and self-knowledge, we can think of a thousand answers to his question. They screwed their planet and died, or their planet changed and screwed them. They killed themselves with a whole range of weapons: nuclear, biological, robotic, nanotech or something we've yet to think of—but will. They found the perfect EMR frequency to fry their brains or disrupt their genome. A solar flare, meteorite, close nova or some other astronomical event took them out. The exigencies of evolution turned out to be that brains don't breed, which would surprise no one. Their society was taken over by some self-destructive meme: they started to fear their sun, so built orbital shields and froze to death; they feared the next ice age, so built orbital mirrors and cooked; or they feared overpopulation, so used mass sterilization and died out. But, of course, all of these are a few numbers in Frank Drake's equation to calculate the number of alien civilizations out in the universe, and it is probable we won't know those numbers until we can go out there and start counting—we'll never know the answers until we've survived them.

EARTH

The darkness had lasted for days. Serene Galahad did nothing, ignored all enquiries, ignored all demands on her time, and just stewed in depression. But that was passing now and at last she had begun taking an interest again—glad to discover that everything she had put in motion had not stuttered to a halt without her. There was, she decided, something to be said for delegation.

50

Though, annoyingly, the new tactical team located just across the estate from her seemed to be delivering very guarded assessments with unacceptable error bars.

Now, at last, she had begun to widen her focus—no longer contemplating how nice it would be to activate the Scour in every ID implant on Earth, sweep all the pieces off the board and let it return to a state last seen just after the last major extinction event.

As she strolled out onto an upper sun deck extending from her Tuscan home, Serene was now thinking clearly enough to be puzzled by some of the retrospective data delivered from Tactical. The crew of the *Scourge* had put their ship on a course back to Earth, and Tactical had no clear explanation for that. Serene agreed with that, even though she had more data than the tactical analysts themselves. The timings were all wrong, for the *Scourge* had separated from Argus Station before the Scour had begun killing the assaulting troops and the crew. Perhaps Alan Saul had warned them that they were about to die? Even that didn't really make sense, because surely they would have assumed he was lying. Like the analysts, they didn't know that the virus came directly from their ID implants . . .

She untied her robe and dropped it over the arm of the comfortable recliner provided for her up here, stretched out her arms to enjoy the Italian sun on her naked body, then gazed out across the neat groves of olive, orange and lemon trees towards the nearby fence. A shepherd was picking its way through the trees, this monstrous spidery machine of polished chrome and white plastic permanently on patrol there, while in the branches of some of the trees roosted birds like hawks but fashioned out of razors.

Some clear danger must have driven Captain Scotonis to undock his ship from the station while the assault force continued its attack. Perhaps he had decided to put some distance between himself and it, so as to deploy his main weapons again. That was really all that made sense, according to Tactical. Afterwards, as he realized that he and his crew were dying, some homing instinct must have kicked in for him to put the ship on course back to Earth. It would have been good to find out for sure, but the *Scourge* was no longer responding. Of course the crew were beyond making any response, but something must have happened aboard to damage computer systems—perhaps an explosion—and now the ship was completely silent.

In reality, Serene was glad no one on board remained alive to stand as a reminder of her failure out there. Sometime hence, when the ship came back within reach, it could quietly be taken to dock, the bodies cleared out and a new crew put aboard, then it could return to service. However, there were so many people who knew of her failure, and it took all of her self-control not to erase them, just as the crew of the *Scourge* had been erased. She wanted them gone. She wanted a fresh start: a new approach. Unfortunately, those same people were too useful and too deeply involved in her present major off-Earth projects. Serene shook her head in pique, sat down in her recliner, raised the back, then took off her sunglasses and closed her eyes.

Professor Calder was one of them. He was out there now at the old Mars Traveller orbital factory complex, building her an Alcubierre drive which, in just a few weeks, would be ready for testing. Unlike the wider population of Earth, he and thousands working for him knew all—except for the Scour-related details—of what had happened out at the Asteroid Belt, but she couldn't kill them, or him.

Serene shrugged: *whatever*. Getting rid of Calder would be stupid, and she had to admit that news of his further progress out there had gone some way towards lifting her malaise. Anyway, even people on Earth knew the truth. Previous ETV stories about the *Scourge*'s successful destruction of the Argus Station were undermined by their distrust of any proclamation from government, along with the present irritating resurrection of the Subnet and its images, somehow obtained directly from the Hubble, of Argus Station sitting in orbit over Mars. And there were limits on how many people she could kill before inefficiencies started kicking in.

The story now being spread among those who knew for sure that Argus still existed was that Saul had used computer penetration to defeat the troops, and had then killed Scotonis and his crew by clipping the *Scourge* with Argus's Alcubierre warp. It was a story close enough to the truth to be maintained.

"Your coffee, ma'am," said Sack.

Serene glanced round as her crocodile-skin bodyguard stepped out with a silver coffee pot, cream jug and sugar bowl on a silver tray. He strode over to her and dipped to place the tray on the pedestal table beside her. While he poured, and then stepped back, as previously instructed, she watched him. She now knew that he had no one, no relationship, and she studied his face for some sign of a reaction to her nakedness. She was just considering ordering him to take up the pot of sun cream on the floor beside the pedestal table, wondering what keroskin hands might feel like on her body, when her PA leader Elkin and two aides stepped out and stood there with attentive patience.

"I was told to inform you that your new aero is ready, ma'am," Sack added.

The machine was a behemoth: twenty-four fans run on separate hydrogen Wankel engines, laminated impact armour, auto-defences, a helium bubblemetal structure also incorporating helium closed-cell gas bags so that, even if every engine was destroyed, it would still float to the ground rather than drop like a brick.

Serene added cream and sugar to her cup and stirred. "Then perhaps, after this morning's meeting, it's time for me to take it for a spin." She paused with the spoon held up as she considered. "I think we'll go to Madagascar to see how things are turning out there."

ETV had broadcast news of a terrible outbreak of the Scour on that huge island—one that had completely depopulated it. Now the only humans to be found there were in the clear-up teams steadily stripping away the island's layer of concrete, carbocrete and steel—the environmental scum humans always generated. It had been, Serene felt, a rather impulsive decision of hers to activate the Scour in every ID implant there, but the results were pleasing. A chameleon and four plant species, all thought to be extinct, had been rediscovered.

"Yes, ma'am." Sack moved back and Elkin moved forward.

A lusciously sexual woman, wearing a primly loose-cut suit to try and hide her curves, she carried a single notescreen keyed to Serene's voice and functioning on predictive search so Elkin could provide facts and figures in an instant. The two aides were both pretty, blond men who possessed cerebral hardware just a few iterations below that of the seven comlifers guarding the computer systems of Earth. They were twins and the product of a genetic tweak for intelligence that Serene knew had proved successful in the past, two further examples of which were also aboard Argus Station. Through them Serene's orders would be acted upon instantly. They were a perfect choice, though Serene wondered how much their pretty appearance had affected Elkin's decision to employ them.

"I take it the teleconference room will be ready"—Serene checked her watch—"in twenty minutes, as I specified, and that all those I summoned to be here in person have now arrived?"

"All but Delegates DeLambert and Chayter, who have simultaneously been delayed by scramjet faults," replied Elkin, with no need to check her screen.

Serene nodded, aware that the two delegates mentioned had allowed political manoeuvring to get in the way of the efficient running of their regions, and had thus dropped low in production stats.

"Have them killed, at once," she instructed. "And tell their queued replacements to link in via teleconference."

Elkin nodded to the aide on her right, who merely blinked. The order had instantly been relayed and, even at that moment, two strangulation collars would be closing. Delegation certainly had its usefulness, since Serene had not even needed to put down her coffee cup. She took a sip, contemplating further tasks she intended to delegate.

"Now give me a precis of the expert assessment requested on Project Push," she instructed.

"With the resources in place, Calder can meet all the offworld targets," Elkin began. "As you have already divined, the problem is in getting those resources in place. Societal Asset's living standards will drop, while the general working week will have to be increased to one hundred hours. Those with critical placements will need to work longer still and will need support. However, robot manufacturing and our mining operations have sufficient redundancy already. Calder has already pushed high-tech manufacturing up to spec too." Elkin paused, looking uncomfortable.

"Go on," Serene prompted.

"It can therefore be achieved, unless we have another out-break of the Scour in some critical area."

"I see, well, let's just hope that doesn't happen." Serene waved the thought away. "What suggestions have been made?"

"We could increase production of military-grade stimulants and make them available to the working population, and also offer further achievement bonuses."

"The stimulants are a good idea, but we already offer bonuses."

"A suggestion has been that we offer things difficult for many SAs to buy via increased community credit," said Elkin, thus ensuring that Serene knew the suggestion did not come from her. "It has been suggested that bonuses could include removal of strangulation collars, actual cash for black-market purchases and higher placements in queues for advanced medicine."

Serene nodded, finished her coffee, then poured herself another cup. "So, does anyone offer any guarantees that, with such bonuses, my targets will be met any sooner?"

"No, ma'am, these are just suggestions based on mass psychological assessments of the SA population."

"So, even without such bonuses, we will still have the core stations expanded and fully weaponized within two months, and three working space battleships ready in six months?"

"That is the expert assessment."

"Very well," said Serene, "we'll offer the extra bonuses. We need to be ready as quickly as possible. Set things in motion—I want my delegates and other administrators able to respond immediately after I've made my announcement to them."

Elkin now glanced at the aide on her right, who also blinked as he issued the orders that would effectively put the entire planet on a war footing. It was, after all, completely necessary to get those ships and Earth's defences ready, and *yesterday* if that were possible. With this new drive of his, and what it could do to any object it came into contact with, Alan Saul had now become an even greater danger than before. Moreover, she still needed Earth's Gene Bank back, and she still needed him visibly punished for his sins. Alan Saul had to die; therefore she needed the means to kill him.

Serene paused reflectively. For such a large change in the very structure of how Earth operated, she felt the need to announce all this to her delegates, and over ETV to the world population at large. She wanted the orders to be less impersonal, wanted the world to know the importance of this, but it also occurred to her that her taking such drastic measures in response to Saul might be perceived as a sign of fear.

"Sack, Serene beckoned him over "get that new aero ready. We're going to Madagascar after I've got this nonsense out of the way. I could do with a bit of a break and then, afterwards, we'll take a tour on the way back to ensure our delegates are working diligently." And maybe, during that trip, those hands . . .

News of her visit to the big island would spread—and so would her apparently nonchalant attitude to the immediate follow-up to her recent orders. Also the future threat of her maybe turning up unexpectedly right on a delegate's doorstep would prove motivational. Anyway, she felt that it might be a good idea to get a complete assessment of the Madagascar situation before she tried something a bit more ambitious, like, for example, Scouring the human scum from somewhere else equally containable—Indonesia, perhaps. Of course that would all have to wait until after all the human scum still out there had served her purposes.

MARS

"He's given them orders to capture us," said Saul, "and if they can't do that, then to kill us. Since they're armed and we are not, I think the former would be more likely."

Yes, he was keeping something from her, but this was no game. For a moment, earlier, she had sensed a cold distance in him. He had some sort of surprise in the offing, something that was going to turn things their way, but it seemed likely to be something nasty and he wasn't sure how she would respond. Now he was coldly factual again, and Var felt she knew what the surprise was going to be. He was going to kill them.

"They'll be here within twenty minutes," she said.

"Certainly," he agreed.

She was damned if she was going to ask him again how he intended to respond. She'd been thinking about this all the way from the underground base, and now realized there could be only one answer. When the *Scourge* had engaged Argus Station, it had been fired upon. The Argus Station was now somewhere above them and probably had workable weapons aboard that he controlled. He must intend to hit the approaching four from orbit, thus reducing the odds against the two of them, but then? Var turned from him to watch the ATV pull to a halt beside those proceeding on foot, and the three of them climbing inside. All of them wore vacuum combat suits obviously salvaged from Ricard's men, and all were armed with assault rifles. She grimaced, not liking the idea of seeing the ATV destroyed, even though it would be of little use where she hoped to end up. Then she too found herself a rock, and sat down.

"There," he said, pointing towards the base airstrip.

Three dots resolved in the sky, grew larger, soon becoming identifiable as an object like a football coming down with two in-series parachutes attached to a line behind. Just a few metres from the ground, right at the far end of the airstrip, it shed its two chutes then hit and bounced. As it bounced for a second time, its outer layer of airbags was already deflating and thus absorbed even more of the shock of its ensuing impacts. Soon it was rolling, soggily, a great cloudy trail of dust behind it, finally coming to halt right up against one of the two fuel silos as its air bags continued deflating.

"Good shot," said Var, the skin on her back crawling. Was it pure luck that the fuel drop tank had come down precisely where required? Or had Saul been able to make such a precise atmosphere insertion and adjustments, on its way down, to put it there? If it was the latter explanation, then he had just done something no one else had managed throughout the history of orbital drops on Mars. She shivered, then shrugged—no, just a lucky shot.

The gas bags finished deflating, and were sucked away into their compartments to deposit a cylindrical tank on the ground. A hemispherical heat shield on the end of it detached and fell away, exposing gleaming equipment underneath—by the looks of the tangle this probably comprised all the pumping gear and hoses. Var transferred her gaze back to the ATV. It was about ten minutes away now—about halfway between the base and the butte.

"Isn't it about time you took your shot?" she asked casually. "What will you use, a railgun missile or a laser? Or did that maser work out?"

He glanced at her. "None of them. They were all wrecked during the *Scourge*'s attack and are now either being rebuilt or salvaged for undamaged components—the rest going into the smelters."

"What?" Var stood up; then, distracted by a silvery flickering, she glanced over towards the airstrip, where she could see a faint dust trail leading away from the drop tank. Something must have overheated and blown up, scattering debris—probably one of the canisters that inflated the gas bags, but nothing large enough to damage a drop tank.

"I have been pondering something," he said. "Will those who supported Rhone be a help or a hindrance to me? Should I let them live even though they killed your friend Lopomac and have murdered people in your base? Should I capture them all, find out who the killers are, and have Hannah mind-wipe them?"

"What?" said Var, immediately feeling stupid for repeating herself, and hating it.

Saul stood up. "Let's go down to meet them."

"Are you crazy?" She paused. "You *are* crazy."

"Trust me," he said, and gave a perfunctory smile. It wasn't a very good smile, but then he'd never really been able to muster a sincere one ever since he'd realized, at a young age, how most people were idiots to him. What he thought of other people now had to be a matter for much concern.

He headed for the path leading down off the butte, and Var hesitated before following. She had no choice but to trust him now because, with the open ground all around them, there was nowhere to run. It seemed he had walked them both into a trap.

The ATV had drawn to a halt at the base of the butte and its four occupants were now outside it. Saul paused beside a boulder just before he—and she—stepped out into sight.

"So, should I let them live?" he asked again.

"Only if they're no danger to us," Var replied sharply, angry because she still had no idea what he had planned.

"Very well." He turned away from her. "This is Alan Saul," he began, addressing the four gathered around the ATV as he stepped out from behind the boulder. "I suggest you put your weapons on the ground and step back from them."

"And I suggest you walk over here," replied someone whose voice was vaguely familiar, but whom she couldn't put a name to as she too stepped out. "I also suggest you put your hands on your heads and walk very slowly. Whether we have bodies or living prisoners for Galahad is a matter of indifference to me."

"No," said Saul patiently, "you'll put your weapons on the ground now and step back from them. This is the only chance you will get."

"And why the fuck should we do that?" asked the same voice as the four stepped away from their vehicle and began to approach.

"Because this one warning is the extent of my generosity to murderers."

What the hell was he doing? Var suddenly felt very vulnerable as one of the four began raising his assault rifle to his shoulder. She felt a moment almost of betrayal. Because of everything he had done, her brother must have some insanely over-inflated opinion of his abilities. Did he really think these four would give up so easily? Did he really think the presence of Argus above and the lack of any support from Earth here would be enough to make them rethink?

"Please keep your finger off the trigger," he said mildly. "Last chance for you all."

"One in her leg," said one of them. "She might survive if we get a patch on."

A series of short thrums carried on the thin air. Dust exploded around the four, and they danced and spun in explosions and jets of vapour. Bits of EA suits and bits of human being sprayed out, rifles tumbled away, and the four went down.

"I needed them away from the vehicle," Saul stated.

"It came down with the drop tank," she said, suddenly understanding, "behind the heat shield."

"Certainly," he said as, with delicate sinister steps, a spider gun rose from behind another nearby boulder and stalked closer, two of its weaponized limbs not wavering from the four corpses. "Now let's take their ATV and go and pay Rhone a visit. I want to be back aboard Argus before the next Martian sunrise."

EARTH

The giant aero was half a kilometre long, with a hammer head to the fore containing flight and weapons control, and also Serene's personal cabin with its viewing lounge. The long and fat main body contained quarters for the crew and her extensive staff, engines sitting over six fans, fuel tanks, weapon turrets that could be extended above and below, but with the largest area taken up by space-hogging helium-filled closed-cell foam. A further six Wankel engines, driving six fans for both lift and steering, sat in movable extended nacelles.

Serene's motorcade arrived even as the fuel hoses were being detached and the crew filing aboard. She gazed from her limousine at the behemoth and allowed herself a wry smile. Here was a quite practical demonstration of her power down here on Earth, but her thoughts were occupied by her tenuous hold on power beyond Earth's atmosphere. She had seen how an Alcubierre warp bubble could tear apart anything it touched, and the danger remained that Saul might, at any moment, decide to obliterate her installations up in orbit, and she needed something to counter him, hence the delay of a week before starting this trip.

She had given Calder full control of all orbital resources and the power to demand resources from Earth's industries. She had also instituted changes down here that should more than double supply from Earth. However, it had been necessary to alter Calder's main aim of building three workable Alcubierre drive battleships: Earth's defences needed to be upgraded first. To begin with, she had not known how, but a study conducted by a specialist tactical team had come up with the answer.

While under warp, the Argus Station had struck an asteroid and the tidal forces at the edge of the warp had torn the asteroid apart. However, the impact had also shut down the warp itself, and it had taken quite some time before Argus had managed to generate another one. This, then, was its weakness as a weapon. "They are correct," Calder had said, after reading the tactical team's report and talking to the new tactical adviser, Peshawar. "The Newton impact required to shut down the warp is measur-able. It is also evident that once the vessel generating this warp has set its course, it cannot deviate."

"We need a larger railgun system up there," Peshawar had noted, "to give us the required coverage. It's not the case that we can target the warp vessel at long range, since we cannot predict when it will stop and change course, thus avoiding long-range fusillades. However, the closer the vessel gets to Earth, the fewer course-change options it will have."

Which was, Serene had reckoned, just a fancy way of saying Saul could dodge the shots on the way in, but had less chance where the firing became gradually more concentrated. Now many of the components, including thousands upon thousands of the missiles those weapons fired, were being made down on Earth and sent into orbit by mass driver. Up there they were being assembled in the core and construction station, to be sited both there and in other positions up in orbit. Within just a week they would have four or five ready to fire, which would make the installations above just a little bit safer. Peshawar opined that at least fifty needed to be built to stop Argus Station in mid-flight, but he added that one attack initiated by the station would leave it vulnerable, since its warp bubble would then be down long enough for just a few railguns to disable it permanently.

Serene opened the door of her limousine and stepped out, Sack immediately at her side, Elkin and her two aides moving in, other PAs, executives and support staff swarming all around them like pilot fish about a shark. Beyond the razor-mesh fences, readergun towers and stalking spiderguns, she could see shepherds striding over compacted rubble, while beyond them dust clouds arose around the yellow and orange safety-painted steel of automated demolition machinery whose blades, wrecking balls and giant air chisels were tearing into the surrounding sprawl. This abandoned section of sprawl now being cleared for her private aeroport was one of the few places such machines were still at work. Elsewhere across Earth, sprawl clearance, but for a few special exceptions, had mostly been put on hold so that every resource could be concentrated on the work underway in orbit. It was annoying, but necessary.

"Update me." Serene crooked a finger at Elkin, then turned and swept towards the ramp that had been hinged down from the body of the aero.

"Production in all sectors dipped by eight per cent, due to retooling, but is now up by twenty per cent," Elkin replied as she fell in at Serene's shoulder. "However, the impact of this has yet to be felt in orbit, due to various bottlenecks."

"Like what?"

"Transport is the main problem: conveying materials to the mass-driver facilities and spaceports. Simultaneously there are some delays in getting space planes commissioned."

"But no more than expected?"

"Precisely as expected, ma'am," said Elkin, "but with the good news that the two mass drivers previously thought to require a complete rebuild were not as badly maintained as reported, and will be online within ten days."

Serene paused at the foot of the ramp. "So why is that?"

"The manager of the Antarctic driver was found to be massaging the figures and, shortly after the head of the inspection team threw him out of the overseer's station on the top of the driver, the manager of the Sri Lanka Sigiria driver discovered some errors in her figures and was able to manage a test power-up the very next day."

"I take it the leader of that inspection team was promoted?" Serene began to climb the ramp.

"The South Zealand and Antarctic delegate did promote him to head of regional inspection, also allowed his collar to be removed and his wife to have access to treatment for bone cancer." Elkin paused for a second. "I have a focus group investigating the possibility that perhaps his wife's condition was the reason for the inspector's diligence, and that therefore those with similar motivation might be moved into critical positions."

"Very good."

The stick had certainly been shown to work, and now the carrot seemed to be working too. As she entered the aero, Serene reflected on her basic aversion to the idea of using reward as a means of motivation, and realized that this was because, fundamentally, she just didn't much like human beings. Glancing at Sack, taking a seat beside her, his suit tight against bulky muscle overlaid with alien keroskin, she considered how this instinct probably influenced how she had started to feel about him, too.

MARS

Saul strode on past the corpses and opened the outer airlock of the ATV, then paused and turned. Var had halted by the dead and was gazing down at them. Doubtless he had lost her now just as, to a certain extent, he had lost Hannah.

"The cold reality is that each of them was either a murderer or had assisted in committing murder," he said by way of explanation—or perhaps justification.

She turned to him abruptly. "And that bothers you?"

"Not much," he continued, "but they were in my way, so I removed them."

"You could have brought the spidergun into view while we were still hidden," she stated, "and they would probably have surrendered instantly."

He walked back over to stand beside her as she stooped beside one of the corpses to undo a belt holding a holstered sidearm, then stood up to buckle it around her waist.

"I'm sure those two," she gestured to a couple of the corpses, "were the ones who shot Lopomac, and also took a shot at me."

"They also killed other personnel, after Rhone's return." Saul pointed to a third corpse. "This one too."

"Then fuck them." She stooped again to pick up an assault rifle and some spare clips.

"Yes, quite," said Saul, realizing he had half expected the kind of moralizing he received from Hannah. "Their lives turned on this moment, yet one of them decided to reach for a trigger."

"No need to go on," said Var grimly, turning away and trudging towards the ATV.

Saul overtook her and stepped inside the vehicle first.

She followed him inside as he plumped himself down in the driver's seat. As she closed the outer airlock door he started up the vehicle, took hold of the control column and turned it round, sending the ATV speeding back towards the base. A moment later, he summoned the spidergun, and it was soon flowing along beside them.

"The circle closes," said Var.

"In what respect?" Saul asked.

"I was just thinking about the last time I drove back to the base this way," said Var. "I had one of Ricard's shepherds chasing me and ready to grab me once I stepped out."

"And you gave it Gisender's corpse," he stated.

"I did, yes."

At that moment, back in the base, Rhone was getting the bad news.

"Alan Saul is with her," said someone in Mars Science. "They're gone."

"What do you mean 'gone'?" Rhone asked, looking up. The man shrugged. "He's got a spidergun with him."

Rhone had simply no reply for that. He gazed at his screen, watching the approaching ATV and spidergun emerging clear out of the dust, then tapped at his fone with his forefinger before turning to gaze up at the nearest cam.

"Who do you trust in there?" Saul asked Var.

"Only Martinez, the head of Construction and Maintenance, and Carol Eisen, both of whom were with me from the start," Var replied.

Saul winced and calculated that Rhone's chances of leaving Mars alive had now nosedived from a point barely above zero. "They are among those who were killed. They're both lying on a gurney in your medical area."

Var dipped her head and squeezed her eyes shut. After a moment she raised her head and stared forward blankly for a moment, before turning to him. He realized then that she had already suspected this but had not wanted to ask. "How did they die?"

"Carol received a single shot through the head, which looks like a routine execution. They must have nailed Martinez outside, however—multiple gunshots and his body dehydrated."

"Bastard," Var spat.

"Is there anyone else there you trust?"

"Dr Da Vinci has always seemed honest enough, but I can't say that I completely trust him," she replied. "He turned against me once he suspected I was murdering personnel."

Saul recollected his earlier view of the doctor sitting on the floor of his surgery and getting drunk. The man had obviously not liked the manner in which Rhone had assumed power. Gazing at him now through a cam covering the surgery, Saul watched him struggling alone to insert one of the corpses into a body bag. He was evidently hungover and looked thoroughly miserable.

Switching back to Rhone, Saul addressed him, and the entire base, through the PA system: "You've been updated on the situation now, Rhone, and must be aware that you've run out of options. I have a spidergun with me and I am now coming to take control of Antares Base."

Rhone sat rigid in his chair, staring blankly at his screen. Others in Mars Science were watching him warily. Sitting in a chair by the door with an assault rifle cradled in his lap, one man closed his eyes and shook his head, then raised his rifle and ejected the clip. Sensible of him, Saul thought.

"The two armed individuals currently in the community room and Hex One will proceed to the base medical bay and hand over their weapons to Dr Da Vinci," Saul continued. "After which they will release all those who have been confined to their cabins. I then want you all to gather in the community room."

"And what about me?" asked Rhone, sitting back and crossing his arms.

Saul ignored his question, instead addressing the man sitting by the door, whose name he'd just unearthed from the base's records. "Thomas Grieve, I have individual instructions for you." The man looked up. "I want you to take Rhone to his cabin and lock him inside. Afterwards you take your weapon to Da Vinci and leave it with him, then head over to the community room."

Grieve sat indecisively for a moment, his gaze straying to one of the screens in Mars Science that showed Saul's approaching ATV, with the spidergun pacing alongside. Grieve abruptly reinserted his rifle clip and stood up, walked over to Rhone and just stared down at him. After a moment Rhone rose, looking tired and stooped, then trudged out of Mars Science with Grieve following behind him. Shortly after they departed, the other staff there began heading off towards the community room.

"Good," said Saul.

"So that's it, we're done?" Var asked him disbelievingly.

"Would you have preferred further bloodshed?" Saul enquired. The first two armed men had now reached Da Vinci and were handing over their weapons, as instructed. The doctor handled these with distaste, quickly depositing them on a gurney and tossing a sheet over them. Meanwhile, Rhone trudged into his own cabin and sat down on the bed. Grieve secured the door, then hurried off to find Da Vinci, who received his gun with similar distaste. On his way out after Grieve, the doctor locked the door behind him. There was nothing quite like a spidergun at your back to smooth things over, Saul felt. Some while later, as he finally drew the ATV to a halt beside the base, he began focusing his mind on the next objectives, already selecting staff, according to their records, for the various tasks he wanted performed.

The spidergun entered the airlock leading into the base first, Saul and Var following. Saul noted that his sister had left the assault rifle behind but brought her sidearm with her, and he wondered if this was as a precaution or if she had in mind a particular use for it. He meanwhile built up a work roster within the base's system. Crews would have to head out to where Var had previously been relocating the base and there collect a list of items he had just collated, which was just about everything bar the regolith blocks. Another crew would prepare the space plane, whose system he had already penetrated, running diagnostic checks and listing the maintenance needing to be carried out. It would also need to be fuelled. The rest would continue dismantling the base, following Var's previous plan, but with some minor adjustments. The reactor would go last, on what Saul planned to be the space plane's sixth and final run up to Argus. And now, with the spidergun proceeding through the doors ahead of him, he entered the community room.

The nervous crowd within instantly moved back, some of them tripping over chairs in their hurry to distance themselves from the spidergun. Saul reached up, unclipped his helmet and removed it. He glanced at the main screen, which now displayed assignments and itineraries, which were copied to the personal screens of every bit of computing in the room. As he surveyed those around him, he tracked Var through the base's cameras. She clearly had something else in mind and hadn't followed him inside.

"There will be no debates right now and there will be no questions," he said. "Later, when all the work down here is done, and you are all aboard Argus Station, you can debate and question all you like, but by then you will know the situation anyway."

Var had now opened Rhone's door and stepped inside. Sitting on his bed, an ancient laptop open beside him, Rhone was studying a view into the community room.

"Who killed Martinez and Carol Eisen?" she demanded bluntly.

Looking up, Rhone replied, "I'm responsible."

"I know that, but I want to know who pulled the trigger."

Rhone named three personnel, adding that two of them now lay dead in the dust beside Shankil's Butte. The third was Thomas Grieve. This was inconvenient, since Saul had included Grieve—who had worked in Construction and Maintenance under Martinez—among those assigned to taking this base apart. In his mind, just in case, Saul lined up the man's replacement as he spoke to those assembled before him.

"Your individual assignments are indicated here," he waved a hand towards the screen, "and also queued up in your personal computers. You will get to work now." He pointed to one individual: "You will lead the space-plane maintenance crew. I expect that plane to be ready for launch by this evening."

He paused and gazed around at them as, perfectly on cue, three gunshots echoed through the base. Var had made utterly certain: two shots to Rhone's chest and a final close shot through his skull. She was ruthless, his sister, and very unforgiving—a trait that Saul recognized all too well.

"Why are you all still here?" he added, moving aside and gesturing to the door.

As they quickly headed out of the Community Room, Saul contemplated what he now knew about his sister. She was undoubtedly arrogant, and he felt she detected the same trait in Saul himself. At high cost, she had chosen to be no longer subordinate to anyone and that decision had stuck. She was as ruthless as him, but still based her decisions on emotionally slanted human thought processes, just like his own emotionally slanted decision to rescue her. Putting her in charge of the reconstruction of Argus Station was the right thing to do, since it would keep her focused on the specific. However, she would, in time, become a problem.

4

TWEAKING

The technology for artificially altering the human genome has been available for a century, mainly in the form of viral recombination to negate hereditary diseases. But, as always, there are rumours of dark goings on in secret government laboratories. In these places the geneticists have tried to make the perfect soldier, have tried to classify what combination of genes leads to high intelligence or even genius. They have tried to make human beings that mature quickly, consume less and die quickly after a limited span. They have tried to make humans more disease-and injury-resistant and to even eliminate death. Anything you can think of has been tried in those dark and secret places, and all of this would have remained rumour if we on the Subnet had not reported the truth. The Committee's contempt for human life was what let the secret out. All would have remained simply rumour had they properly disposed of the failures, but they did not, as attested to the monstrous corpses pulled from the Ganges just a few kilometres down from the All Health research centre in Pabna. And we can be sure that where there were failures there were also successes, and that they live among us now.

ARGUS

Alex now stood upon one of the lattice walls beside Arcoplex Two, above the accommodation unit he had been assigned to, which lay sandwiched between the two walls below; a sensation of immanence permeated the station. And everything around him seemed slightly distorted, as if it was slightly out of synch with the surrounding universe. Yet he could not nail the reason for this, and he wondered how much was due to the vortex generator winding up to speed, or his *knowledge* that it was doing so.

He gazed across to the space-plane docks as the big manta winged Mars-format space plane, like some giant metallized fruit bat, swooped towards the limb of Dock Two for the fourth time; he felt amazed that he could now actually see both it and the dock. This was because most of the upper enclosure now rested in a small city of stacks on the upper lattice wall, just a kilometre away from him. It was proof, if any was needed, that Gladys's observation of five days ago seemed truer than ever. The robots were working much faster and more efficiently—but the humans were too. Alex could never remember anything getting done so quickly throughout his time here undercover when the Committee was in charge. Always there had been technical hold-ups, hitches in supply of materials and components, or jobs getting done in the wrong order and having to be reversed, or the work interfered with by the bureaucracy. He also remembered that the bureaucratic interference included workers disappearing because of some perceived slight towards an Inspectorate executive, and that generally everyone had worked with a complete lack of enthusiasm, doing only the bare minimum to get by.

Now the human teams were actually competing with each other and with the robots, while the robots never stopped, and the proctors, of whom everyone had been wary, had become a reassuring presence always ready to smooth out any of the few irregularities when not themselves employed on something related to the EM shield. Both smelting plants were also working, though at this distance from the sun they were not at full power, and a haze spread out behind them, marking the path of Argus around Mars. The ore transporters were on the move too, though intermittently since it was mostly salvage that was being smelted, while the smelting-plant docks continuously vibrated in sympathy with the busy roar of the rolling mills, extruders, presses and forges. Robots the size of train carriages were taking salvage to the ore carriers, then returning with components—brackets, beams, rolls of welding wire and crates of fixings—and distributing them. And the shape of the station had changed.

Not only had most of the enclosure been taken down, but incurving beams were being fitted to the rim, visible in some areas like the rib bones of titanic beasts decayed on a steel shore, slowly but surely etching out the eventual shape of this station—this ship.

"That you, Alex?" came the enquiry through his fone.

He turned to see Ghort—the man's bulk easily recognizable even in a heavy work suit—climbing up onto the lattice wall and heading over.

"It's me," Alex replied, raising a hand.

"Thought so, as most of us enjoy our free time not wearing a suit." Ghort sauntered over. "Looking good," he commented casually when he arrived at Alex's side, then his gaze strayed to the scene over beside them. "But those give me the creeps."

Even though he knew now that Ghort was perpetually probing people around him for their reactions to the situation they found themselves in, Alex had to agree. On the face of the lattice wall, near where it ended at a gap beside the curved edge of Arcoplex Two, the latest product coming out of Robotics had been arrayed in a neat square—hundreds of them—all laid out like a legion on a gamer's model battlefield. They gleamed, these things: squat cylindrical bodies supported horizontally by double-jointed limbs terminating in six-fingered hands resting flat against the deck, further cylindrical tool caches affixed to their upper surfaces, all arrayed so close together that from some angles the outlines of them looked like polished brass centipedes. Even as the two men watched, another transport trundled down from the end of the arcoplex on its gecko treads to unload yet another batch of them, forming the corner of a new square.

"We'll be obsolete soon, according to Gladys," he said.

"Maybe not just yet," Ghort replied. "The new boss has reassigned us."

That had come as a surprise. Alex had expected the Owner, upon his return, to take a firmer grip on the reconstruction, but they now had a human in charge who had been, so Alex was told, the overseer of the Traveller construction project. Even on the first day, she had started making changes, reassignments which had been annoying but after a short time seemed like a squirt of lubricating oil to the station machine. Those doing the reconstruction were now working directly under Varalia Delex, who addressed them daily over the screens, describing further the ship they were to build. She seemed to be everywhere, offering encouragement, actually asking advice, often mucking in with some of the drudge work, and just being there. This had boosted morale, as it made people realize that they truly were part of something amazing, and in the end it had been her rather than the Owner who had given the project its present shape and impetus.

"Reassigned where?" Alex asked.

"It seems these new fellas"—Ghort stabbed a finger towards the nearby legion of robots—"are taking over our job, and will be building the framework of the ship's sphere. The human teams and a lot of the older-design robots are moving above and below." Ghort gestured back towards the asteroid and to Tech Central. "We are first slicing up the asteroid—completely removing it—and then we connect all the station spokes and beam-work that used to be bolted to it to a central core, then we divide into groups. Some will be taking apart Tech Central and erecting an arcoplex spindle in its place. The one we're now in will build downwards, for two kilometres, making a tough shock-absorbing column to support a platform."

"Platform?"

"Yeah, it seems the boss isn't happy with the current position of the Traveller engine—so we're going to be moving it."

Alex stood there, dumbfounded, then ventured, "And when are we to start doing this?"

"Well, right now we've got to lock down our previous job and pack away our tools," said Ghort, "then we start on our new job once the sun is shining."

Did the tension seeming to lace the very air demonstrate that the vortex generator's effect on space-time was somehow against nature? No, Hannah decided, it was once more a demonstration of how human technology was outpacing the old naturally evolved human bodies, and further justification of everything she was doing in her laboratory and now also here in this factory area Saul had provided.

"We've been avoiding each other," said Var.

Hannah turned to study the woman stepping out from the laboratory and onto the floor of the new biofactory. In one sense Var Delex's appearance was reminiscent of one of the Saberhagens, what with her pale hair, narrow features and athletic physique. But there was something much harder ground into Var, just as the Martian rouge had been ground into her skin. The Saberhagens were youngsters—just in their twenties—this woman, being Saul's sister, had to be at least fifty years old, like Hannah herself.

"It seemed the politic thing to do for now," said Hannah. "You've had a lot to do, I understand: a lot of computer design, reorganizing—in fact all that's involved in turning a space station into a starship."

Var gazed at her very directly. "And yet I feel as if I've been given make-work, as if he left things undone just so I wouldn't feel redundant."

Hannah shrugged. "One of the penalties of serving a demigod?"

"So it would seem." Var folded her arms and leaned back against the wall. "I've tried to make the reconstruction completely mine, so as to give the human teams a human face to talk to, and I'm trying to divorce their work from that of the robots—since many of them were starting to feel outmoded."

"And it's working, so I'm told."

"It is." Var nodded in solemn agreement.

"How are things with the rest of the . . . Martians?" Hannah asked. "I understand that most of them are located here now." Along with one Thomas Grieve, who had recently been a guest in Hannah's surgery—she hoped he was the last subject she would ever have to mind-wipe.

"There were a few problems to begin with, when they found out they couldn't choose where they were assigned, and that therefore they couldn't stay together," said Var. "But growing up under the Committee results in obedience."

Hannah grimaced, decided not to pursue her thoughts about Grieve. Instead she focused on the problems about the assignment of personnel, since she had already heard and discussed them, if only briefly, with Saul.

"A good thing about humans is that they form communities," she said. "A bad thing about humans is that they form ghettos."

"Precisely what he said to me." Var frowned. "My brother seems to have become quite the philosopher. Of course, now the people from the base have to get used to their feeling of obsolescence here." She cast an eye across the various machines in Hannah's factory. "What about you?"

Hannah's hand embraced the same machines. "Not obsolete yet."

"I understand you're taking neural tissue samples from every one, apparently to be grown into grafts for the repair of head injuries," Var commented neutrally. "I also understand that you've asked for volunteers from among the staff to try out some new cerebral hardware."

Hannah flicked her gaze towards the group of four workers, all clad in paper overalls, steadily making their way up the factory as they installed automated biofactors and the base hardware of cylindrical glass growth tanks that had yet to be manufactured elsewhere. This was effectively a small job, hence the presence of only one small general-purpose robot working alongside them: a thing running on treads supporting a cylindrical upright body wrapped in a carousel of limbs sporting a variety of tool heads. She then swung her gaze to a large temperature-controlled safe.

This contained the remaining hundred and fifty cerebral interfaces. These were an older design than the one Saul currently used and were the same as those employed by the seven comlifers on Earth. They were also the kind she herself had used to wipe the minds of all the Committee delegates surviving here—biological interfaces that were the precursors to the one in Saul's head, but which in the delegates were now effectively inert, which seemed a kind of justice. Until she made more, of a better design, these interfaces would provide the link for one hundred and fifty personnel to their backups, once they were ready, and would give them limited access to the station system and the robots.

"What has he told you?" she asked.

"He talked about travelling to the stars and I talked about human mortality," said Var, "whereupon he suggested I talk to you about the work you are doing."

Hannah felt a flash of jealousy upon hearing that, for when had Saul last communicated with her about anything above the completely practical? She suppressed the reaction, then pointed to the racking fixed along one wall, which now held twenty aerogel boxes, all tubed and wired together with secondary power supplies in place and provided with optics ready to attach them to the station's computer system.

"The components are here in Arcoplex Two," Hannah explained. "Aerogel matrices in which to grow organic backups to a human mind, cerebral implants and exterior com hardware linked to those backups." She gestured to the safe. "And in another area we're installing the equipment for growing human clones."

Just as with Le Roque, Hannah needed to explain no more, for Var Delex understood at once, or maybe her suspicions had been confirmed. Her eyes grew wide nevertheless as she processed the news that the inevitability of her own death could be postponed. But then she moved beyond that.

"Cerebral bioware connecting to exterior hardware?" she queried.

Hannah shrugged, feeling somewhat uncomfortable.

"He's put in an off-switch," Var continued, "so he'll be able to sever their link to their backups." She paused reflectively. "Demigod indeed."

"I don't like it," Hannah agreed, "but—and now I'm going to sound like a Committee executive—too much freedom could be a bad thing."

"For him, you mean," said Var. "Tell me, will you yourself have this exterior hardware?"

Though one of Hannah's new assistants had taken a sample from her skull, she hadn't even considered beyond that. How did she feel about Saul being the gatekeeper between her and eternity?

"I trust him," she said. "Though he'll control my link to my backup, I will still have the chance of living forever, or at least for thousands of years, so who knows what might happen in the future? Perhaps one day he will cease to feel the need to control me."

"Or perhaps," said Var, "you will cease to trust him."

"Such cynicism," said Hannah. "Obviously you have a lot to think about and would perhaps prefer not to go this route?"

"It *seems* a road worth travelling."

"So when will you want me to take a sample from you?" Hannah persevered.

Var Delex grimaced. "Not just yet."

Hannah just watched her, still not quite understanding this woman whom Saul felt was important enough to risk his life in rescuing her from Mars.

"Later, perhaps after the current shift," Var added, "I was considering trying out this bar in the Arboretum. Perhaps you could join me and we can start to get to know each other better, since it's possible we may be in each other's company for a very long time." She gestured to the backups. "A very long time indeed."

Hannah nodded, something tightening in her torso, like that faithless friend, her panic attacks—but a much deeper and more hollow feeling, like awe. She realized that she had been so wrapped up in the detail of what she was doing that she had failed to incorporate the big picture, and yet Var's simple remark had opened her eyes.

A very long time indeed.

It was as if Saul held space hooked over his finger, drawn taut and ready to be released, but time dragged in the world he occupied, seeming a hundred years behind the intricate images he had constructed in his mind. Many weeks had passed since he had saved his sister's life and, by any human measure, his plans for Argus had advanced at an amazing rate, but Saul did not measure reality in human terms. It was all too slow; the delays between thought and action and achieving final product were interminable, frustrating. Yet Saul possessed absolute control of his own mind, so frustration, a thoroughly human malady that served no purpose, was something he could just eliminate from his skull.

Time dragged but Saul watched with the patience of Jove, while turning a human face to the world.

"From the beginning, both of you claimed you wanted to work here," he said, peering down through the glass floor at the hive of activity in the robotics factory.

"That's true," said Brigitta.

Judd was down below with a small team of humans, stripping down one of the assembly machines only because that was quicker than letting it repair itself. Such malfunctions had been a rarity since Robotics had become ever more . . . robotic, therefore the components called human and proctor were required less and less often. Thus far, three legions of the new-design robots were standing ready, gleaming out there on the lattice wall beside the arcoplex. Saul probed the neat function-ality of their minds, the perfectly in-consonance diagnostic returns from their bodies. Just a thought from him, and they would be in motion but, though *they* were ready, the station was not. Even if they had enough power, they could hardly keep operational for a day before they used everything up. Thus the smelters needed to go over fully to solar power, and begin producing components at their maximum rate. This would free up reactor power for the robots, which would supply themselves from numerous recharging points, even while solar power fed, via cells inlaid into their skins, the rectifying batteries inside their bodies. Once operating together as a large efficient machine constantly supplied with energy and components, they could *really* go to work.

Saul now transferred his human attention to the weapon he held—one of the plasma rifles Brigitta and Angela had fashioned for use in the fight against the troops from the *Scourge*.

"I want you to do something else," he said.

"Evidently," Brigitta replied.

"I want you to leave Robotics to Judd and go back to work on the station weapons," Saul continued, "including the plasma cannon I want you to design and build. I've given you some of the parameters and eventual position of all the weapons in the completed ship. I've also opened up a new area within this arcoplex for you to develop them and, if they are available, will supply the workers and robots you may require."

The twins exchanged a look, and then Angela gave a brief nod.

"Okay," said Brigitta. "Things were starting to get a bit samey here, anyway, and we always like a challenge. By the way, is there any chance of us getting our hands on some radioactives?"

Saul handed the weapon back to her. "When we go after new materials, yes, but right now it's all about energy."

"Good, because that's our big disadvantage against anything sent from Earth. Remember, they've got the nukes."

Saul nodded briefly and turned to head back the way he had come, but most of his mind was already ranging elsewhere. Much more data were available from Earth, and now he saw a further cost of having rescued his sister and salvaging the equipment and personnel from Mars. He should have attacked. Instead he should have taken Argus Station straight from the Asteroid Belt to Earth and methodically destroyed everything in orbit. Since he had not done so, Galahad had responded very quickly to the threat he represented, and he had just watched the test firing of two new heavy railguns, one from the Traveller construction station and another from Core One. Attacking now was still an option, but better for him to spend as much time in the solar system as was safe, and then just run. In the end, if he wanted to keep a lid on Earth, he would have to stay within the solar system, knocking down any attempt by the Earth-bound to reach out into orbit. Why trap himself here in such an onerous chore when a whole universe lay within his reach? At some point the Saberhagens would realize that the weapons they were building weren't intended as a defence against Earth, but against anything they might find way out beyond.

Sixth docking . . .

As Saul arrived at the elevator that would take him out of the arcoplex, his constant companion spidergun climbing in ahead of him, he mentally reached out and locked the docking clamps holding the Mars-format space plane to Docking Pillar One—the disassembled fusion reactor aboard it could wait to be offloaded—then began similarly locking down all the way across the station. The smelting plants had already finished their latest run, and the transporters running between them and the station were parked down in the bases of the smelting-plant docks. Now the smelters began pulling in the mirrors which had been supplying meagre concentrated sunlight to complement the output of the fusion reactors, while the big cable drums jerked into motion for hauling them back towards the station. Having now received the order, both human and robot work parties finished their latest jobs and began putting away their tools—the robots to then head off and cling to some nearby section of the station structure while the humans returned to their accommodation.

An enclosed walkway now led straight from the elevator exit into Tech Central. Saul took this at an unhurried pace, finally entering the cageway leading up to the main control room and propelling himself up after his spidergun. As he entered, the occupants busily working their consoles hardly spared either him or the robot a glance, having become used to seeing both now. Le Roque oversaw the team, speaking to someone through his fone, while Rhine was sitting at the navigation console. Saul headed over to stand beside him.

Rhine glanced up. "We might hit something on the way in," he warned. "Not everything is mapped."

"The chances are low," Saul opined, "something like one in a hundred for us hitting something and twice that for it to be big enough to knock out the drive bubble." He sat down at the console next to Rhine's—the one that had before been occupied by Girondel Chang, who now resided in the rim mortuary. Really, there was no need for Rhine or anyone else to be here, since Saul was in full mental control of the whole operation.

"It's going to be hot," Rhine added.

"Nothing the station cannot handle, and we need the additional energy."

To pass the time, Saul again checked the programming he had in place. The moment they arrived at their destination, he wanted action, and he intended to get that—though perhaps not from the humans aboard, since they might take a few hours to adapt.

The first smelting plant locked home in its dock, then the second. He watched as Leeran and Pike—the stalwarts in charge of those plants—and other workers there, headed towards their offices and there strapped themselves into chairs. Most of the robots were now locked in place, while just a few humans had yet to sort themselves out. Le Roque took a seat and fastened his lap strap, while those around him did the same. All of this securing and locking down was completely unnecessary if the drive functioned as before, but there was always a chance of something going wrong. This was, after all, only the third time ever this new technology had been used.

"Two minutes until shift." Saul's voice issued from intercoms all across the station. "If you've forgotten something, then it's too late now. Just leave it and get yourselves strapped in."

Beyond the windows of Tech Central, the station rim—its inwardly curving rib bones rising up all around it—seemed to lift like the lower jaw of an angler fish. Beyond that the view of Mars turned hazy. With the drive fully up to speed, Saul could now fling them away from here with just a thought, but he allowed the crew some remaining time. While that passed, he watched Hannah securing herself in the surgical chair in her laboratory, the Saberhagen twins strapping into chairs in an office adjacent to Robotics, and his sister standing, in a heavy work suit, on the rim of the station, with her feet solidly planted and a line attaching her to one of the nearby ribs. Everyone else was safely inside the station, but Saul had made no rule about how they should secure themselves, and Var was only putting herself at minimally more risk by staying where she was.

"Giving yourself a grandstand view, sister?" he asked her.

"It's a bit disconcerting out here. It feels just like I'm standing on the inner face of a tidal wave, and now the stars are changing colour and . . . damn, look at Mars."

Visible through the windows of Tech Central, Mars was noticeably changing hue, first turning as red as it was supposed to be, before intensifying to something as unnaturally bright as fluorescent paint.

"I'm surprised I'm the only one outside," she added. "I would have thought that you, at least, would also want to be this close."

"I'm even closer, since I can view through every sensor of the station," Saul replied.

"That's hardly the same."

"You're quite correct. Ordinary human senses can be so dull."

Var just snorted at that. It was time now.

"Shifting," Saul announced.

Everything beyond the station turned black, and again Saul felt as if he was folding space around himself like a thick blanket, and rolling away into another world. He visualized the warp bubble as a droplet of water skittering across a hotplate, as he counted down the seconds then minutes of their journey. It began to grow uncomfortably hot inside the station but, out on the lattice wall, the legions of robots sucked up and rectified that increase of energy into something usable, while elsewhere throughout the station Rhine's rectifying batteries rose quickly to full charge. A momentary shudder had Saul reaching down to grip the arms of his chair, but it soon passed. The warp bubble must have clipped something, or else destroyed something too small to stop their progress. Saul calculated it must have been an object massing just under half a tonne, before he sank into the esoteric maths concerning warp-bubble impacts, just to pass the remaining interminable yet fantastically short ten minutes of the journey.

Next, the universe suddenly turned the lights back on. Bright sunlight glared, as bright as Mediterranean daytime. They had just travelled across an appreciable portion of the solar system in a matter of mere minutes. Saul blinked. Would an experience as fantastic as this start to become as prosaic as a routine flight in an aeroplane? He unstrapped himself and stood up, walking over to the windows that had already taken on the tint that had disappeared when they had left Earth behind.

"How was that for you?" he asked Var.

"Like nothing else," she replied, her voice hushed, sounding slightly depressed. Saul understood her reaction. She had been excited before, but actually seeing the drive work made her feel very small, and she did not like feeling that way. Despite being busy with the reconstruction, her pride was still suffering wounds. Irritated by his sister's apparent weakness, he slid the fragment of his attention he had allotted her away and elsewhere. Light and heat suffused the station, as energy storage, which out at Mars had forever been on the point of depletion, continued to rise, and he too felt energized as a thump reverberated under his feet—Leeran and Pike obviously feeling no need to take stock, and already extending the smelting plants. The power of sunlight, it seemed, affected all of those it touched, for even now people were unstrapping themselves and checking work rosters; while others, who knew what to do, were already donning spacesuits.

The old robots first, Saul decided, feeling them unpeeling instantly from the points in the station they had been clinging to, and dispersing to obey their queued-up orders. He then felt further vibrations through his feet as the mining robots again began hacking into the asteroid below, and as the ore carts began hauling their loads towards the big transporters.

"It's like . . . like waking up," said Le Roque at his shoulder.

"We've been sad," quipped Rhine at his other shoulder. "That would be—"

"Yes, I know what seasonal affective disorder is, Rhine," Saul interrupted.

"I need to get back to it," said Rhine, unperturbed, as he turned away. "This Mach-effect stuff is fascinating."

Rhine, Saul had realized, possessed the kind of mind best kept at work so, with a little help from the proctors, he was already finessing the design for the Mach-effect drive, and deciding how best to integrate it with what they already had.

"Crazy, but brilliant," Le Roque commented, once Rhine was gone. Then, turning back to Saul: "So now we really go to work?"

"We do, and you yourself need to relocate to the secondary control centre." He glanced towards him. "They're already cutting the anchors down below."

"Quick work."

"Rhine just suggested that we're all coming out of SAD, out of suffering from a lack of sunlight, but perhaps there's more to the power of the sun than merely that." Saul considered all the possible effects of this relocation, and could not shake off the feeling that the personnel here were as linked into Argus Station, in their own way, as he himself. Certainly, new measurable power was running through everything aboard, but it seemed as if a *psychic* current had been set up, too. He did not believe in any supernatural explanation, of course, but was not prepared to discount an esoteric scientific one.

Steadily increasing activity became visible in the station outside. Saul briefly watched teams of humans and robots heading from their accommodation towards the Mars Traveller engine, which they intended to detach from the asteroid. He watched another team begin work alongside the mining robots, cutting their way towards a fault that would eventually break the steadily shrinking mass of nickel iron in two. Then, through the windows ahead, as well as in his mind, he focused on the extent of lattice wall beside Arcoplex Two.

Now.

Smooth as oil, a neat line of the new robots began flowing across the lattice wall towards the rim, the square formation they were emerging from steadily shrinking. On their way they diverted to a stockpile of beams and other components, and that pile rapidly shrank like ice under the jet of a steam cleaner. The other two squares began to move next, sliding into thicker lines: one going straight over the curve of the arcoplex to start work on the ship's skeleton beyond, while the other came back towards Tech Central and circumvented it to head over to the other side of the station. The robots moving there began the essential armouring of the vortex generator, thus further stockpiles diminished, and all the materials taken down from the enclosure went too.

A sudden leap in power supply marked the moment the smelting plants began opening out their mirrors—no longer requiring power from the reactors either to move themselves into position or run back up to temperature. Smelters that before had been functioning at only half of their potential performance now went straight to full capacity, as the various plants issued plumes of vapour and ash, turning bright and silvery in the sunlight. Molten metal boiled with inert gases, and coolers that had not been needed out in the orbit of Mars soon came online. The rolling mills, presses, auto-forges and casters; the capstan lathes, milling machines, diamond saws and drills; the matter printers, nano-weavers and bucky-spinners: all of them seemed to let go with joyous abandon until once slow-moving swarf conveyors steadily increased to full speed.

In Arcoplex Two, Robotics screamed with activity—no power outages now, no requirement to build up a charge for any of the high-energy processes. Here the machines seemed to be hearing the message from their larger brothers out in the smelting plants: *Energy to burn, guys. Let's do it.* There was power now for further high-temperature work, too; and, elsewhere in the arcoplex, silicon quickly turned molten as a chip factory started up, as did a powder forge for making the cutting tools that would soon be needed to replace those already in use.

Saul smiled as power levels just continued to rise. Already the first of his new robots were working around the rim, sometimes singly, sometimes conjoined into short centipede forms, hauling up and affixing structural beams at high speed. And the skeleton of the space ship grew visibly; dream turned into hard reality.

SCOURGE

Clay Ruger woke to feel the constant ache of his battered body, reached out for the painkillers and iodine pills on his bedside shelf, popped two of each out of their blister packs and washed them down with a gulp of water from his suit spigot, and he waited. There wasn't one of the survivors without broken bones, wrenched joints and a mottled effect of fading bruises from head to toe. Clay himself had two broken shins, ribs broken all down one side, and few other bones in his body without at least hairline cracks, including his skull. But at least he wasn't one of those who had ruptured something internal or suffered one of the cerebral haemorrhages that had killed a third of the crew. And at least, unlike Gunnery Officer Cookson, he hadn't ended up with a snapped spine.

When Argus Station's warp bubble had brushed against the *Scourge*, gravity waves had travelled the length of the ship like invisible walls. Compression waves were how Pilot Officer Trove described them, her voice slurring because of her broken jaw; while Captain Scotonis called the event a "tidal surge." All Clay knew was that it felt as if, in just a matter of seconds, he had been simultaneously smashed against something, then *stretched* through it. Afterwards he felt as if he had spent months in an old-fashioned adjustment cell—one where they weren't bothering to use inducers, just batons, army boots and fists.

Finally the painkillers began to kick in and he was able to drag himself from his bed—a laborious exercise even in zero gravity. Just as they all did, he still wore a full spacesuit: after yet another atmosphere breach only two days ago, none of them fully trusted the repairs. The suits also offered some protection from the high levels of radiation caused when one of the warheads in the armoury exploded. It hadn't gone into fission, but it had acted like a dirty bomb, spreading radioactive material throughout the ship. It was this, Clay knew, that would eventually kill him. Broken bones weren't the only common injury for not one of them hadn't suffered radiation sickness, or did not register positive for pre-cancerous cells, if not overt signs of some sort of cancer. Clay was sure that some of the stuff coming up out of his lungs had little now to do with his initial injuries.

Before stepping out of his cabin, he closed his suit visor, then once outside he began making his way up a corridor that was no longer straight, but in fact had taken on a slightly corkscrew shape. A crew member passed him heading in the other direction, dolefully towing herself along like an ancient.

They ignored each other—crew generally had little to say to him, and not much more to say to each other, either. Eventually, the doors to the bridge came in sight, but before he reached them the command crew came out.

Scotonis, Trove and even Cookson were there, pulling on their suit helmets. They all looked ill—Cookson the worst of all as he pulled himself along with everything below his waist hanging dead. It struck Clay that they had all been animatedly discussing something before his approach and had now fallen silent, but paranoia was all too easy aboard this ship of the damned.

"How are you, Cookson?" Clay asked, as he drew closer.

Cookson swung a corpse-like face towards him. He was deadly white, with a slight bluish tinge to his lips and a yellow mass of bruising down one side of his face. He gave a sickly grin that exposed the missing teeth in that side of his mouth.

"Not dead yet," he replied. "I want to live long enough . . . just long enough."

"Something we can all say," said Clay. Then, studying the others, "So what's up?"

"It's something Dr Myers can't say now," said Scotonis, "because he's dead."

"What?" Clay felt a creeping horror. Myers, thankfully, had been one of the least injured of them all, having managed to escape without any broken bones—just minor cracks—and, with them all in the process of dying, he had become the most essential member of the crew. Now he was dead?

"Come on," Scotonis gestured for them to follow him, and limped off down the corridor.

"I'll . . . I'll leave it for now," said Cookson, clinging to one of the handholds set in the wall.

Scotonis halted, turned to study him, then nodded and continued on. Clay followed, wondering just how Cookson was managing to stay alive and how much longer he would survive.

No matter how hard they had tried to seal off the compartments into which they had loaded the corpses, the stench was spreading out into the rest of the ship. As well as the damage throughout it—walls bent and buckled, panels out of line and exposing electronics and plumbing, floors twisted, fluids leaking—a free-floating mess was also accumulating. As they neared the crew medical area, Clay noted occasional dressings, some already used, most simply discarded while dealing with the rush of injuries after the gravity waves struck. Here and there old, brown blood was spattered on the metalwork, and down in one corner lay what looked like mouldering splinters of bone.

"This needs cleaning up," commented Scotonis.

Neither Clay nor Trove replied. Who would do that? Who would care enough to do it?

Finally they reached the section of corridor outside Medical, where three sorry-looking crewmen loitered, arms wrapped protectively around their torsos as they waited for a cure that wouldn't be available. Scotonis marched past them, opened the door into Medical and stepped through. Clay and Trove followed him.

"Well," Trove eventually managed, "he didn't die of his old injuries."

Dr Myers sat strapped into his own surgical chair. Someone had removed all the fingers from his right hand, scooped out one eyeball, then cut his throat. The man's blood still beaded the air, and Clay resisted the urge to try and brush away droplets of it landing on his spacesuit.

"We have to find out who did this," said Scotonis. "They must be punished."

Why bother? Clay wondered, again sinking into fatalistic depression. Myers had reached the state they would all be reaching soon enough, he reckoned. Then he shrugged and gritted his teeth. He had a mind, he had intelligence and what had once been described to him as a low animal cunning. He would not have risen so high in the Committee administration without these, and they were precisely what would enable him to survive. Somehow there would be a way out of this, and he must find it.

5

A THEORY ABOUT THEORIES

During the reign of Serene Galahad, and because of her response to Alan Saul, technological innovation left conventional science in tatters. Many years had been spent building hypotheses and theories on Einstein's general and special theories of relativity, while ignoring irrefutable experimental fact that undermined them. It was proven that certain particles could be accelerated beyond the speed of light, and that was ignored. It was found that the mass of the universe did not match up to theory, so invisible undetectable dark matter was invented to fill the gap. A lunatic who believed we were visited by aliens demonstrated antigravity; why even check his work, he's a lunatic? A working cold-fusion plant is built, and closed down by safety officers. A fool obsessed with fringe studies of ball lightning disappears from his laboratory and is found halfway round the world in the Atacama Desert, burned from head to foot. Bah, meat and bread for conspiracy theorists. And when Alan Saul demonstrated a working Alcubierre drive, which was only theoretically possible with limitless energy and access to exotic matter, this too might have been ignored or explained away. However, having stolen a space station and annihilated a large portion of the Inspectorate by dropping seven thousand satellites on Earth, Alan Saul was someone who really had to be taken seriously.

EARTH

No trees, Serene reflected and, no matter the extent of her power over Earth, *they* were something she could not expedite. Her aero had landed on what had once been an aeroport atop a multistorey car park sunk deep amidst the arcology towers of this sprawl on Madagascar. Now it stood in a shallow valley beside a stream, amidst mountains of rubble. Standing on the edge of the port, Serene studied the view on the screen of a tripod-mounted image-intensifier. Over to the left, a sorting machine, a giant contraption like a steel caterpillar, had nosed into one rubble pile and was passing that steadily through its long alimentary tract as it extracted metals and other usable materials, before shitting out plain concrete, brick and carbocrete into a hopper section positioned at its rear. As Serene watched, this same hopper detached and trundled over to the edge of a long deep trench, to tip its contents inside. At the end of the trench a giant excavator was still digging, piling precious though highly depleted earth to one side, ready to fill in over the rubble.

"A long and onerous task," she noted, swatting at something that had landed on her neck, then removing her sunglasses to frown at the smears.

"With present machinery and resources it will take twenty years to complete," Elkin replied, ever ready with the numbers. "This is presupposing that you intend to clear the entire island of its sprawl and will not be diverting resources elsewhere."

"How much time would be gained in the space operation if I diverted resources from here?"

This was obviously a more difficult question, for Elkin gave no immediate reply. Serene turned to see her gazing at one of her aides and, after a moment, check what he must have meanwhile sent to her palmtop.

"Very little," she replied, "since it's the bottlenecks that are slowing things down."

Was that worth shutting down the entire operation here? Serene decided not. There had been a momentary panic, over a week and a half ago, when Argus hurled itself in towards the centre of the solar system, but Saul had not attacked, merely positioned the station on the other side of the sun where, so the experts told her, he was using solar energy to power a rapid rebuild of the station. Image data from solar weather satellites showed the rebuild to be so extensive that the tactical feasibility of him attacking before all the big orbital railguns here were ready was very low. The tacticians further surmised that it was highly likely that he did not intend to attack at all—the likelihood that he was turning Argus Station into something capable of delivering overwhelming force being very small indeed.

"What's the latest news on Argus?" Serene now took a pack of wet wipes from her pocket and extracted one to dab at her face. It was hot and muggy here and the only species that seemed to be doing well were the flying and stinging kind. This "being out in the field" business was all very well, but it brought its discomforts. She glanced over at Sack, standing in patient attendance. Maybe it was time for her to occupy one of the big, comfortable estates offered for her exclusive use by one of her East African delegates.

"Images show that it is being turned into a sphere with a diameter the same as that of the original ring," Elkin replied immediately. "They also show the asteroid now cut into two pieces and rapidly being used up, and the Mars Traveller VI being repositioned."

"Engineering assessment?"

"The same as before: he's turning the station into an interstellar spaceship. There are also elements in the design that are recognizable as originating from Varalia Delex, the previous technical director of Antares Base. Prior to that she was the overseer of both the Mars Traveller Project and the *Alexander*—or *Scourge*. Also some further information has come to light about her."

"That is?" Serene returned her attention to the view before her.

"Her maiden name is Saul. She is his sister."

Serene swung back. "That explains his abrupt arrival on Mars and the risks he took in rescuing her." She nodded to herself. "Interesting information, but it gets us no closer to stopping him running." Serene stepped away from the image intensifier. She'd seen enough of Madagascar to know that it would once again be green, but would still lack the millions of species that had lived here previously. They still needed the Gene Bank data and, if possible, the samples. Saul could not be allowed to leave the solar system.

"Is Calder any further forward in preventing that?" Serene began to stroll back towards the aero.

Elkin fell in just a step behind her, and other staff scurried to collect up equipment while protective spiderguns moved in from the edges of the aero-port. Time to go, Serene felt, but where next?

"Just before we landed, he told me that the new weapon will be ready for a test firing within a few days," Elkin replied. "And now would be the best time to test it since Saul, positioned on the other side of the sun, will have no view of it."

"Calder's sure of that?"

"Our comlifers have made all our satellites and stations safe from mental incursion, and the test will be disguised amidst a test firing of one of the new railguns."

Serene paused to gaze up at the leaden sky. So, forget that East African estate. Chairman Messina's quarters up in the spin section of Core One had recently been renovated, and she would certainly need her bodyguard there alongside her . . . She would make that her base as she toured the other stations above, and she would be there to watch that test: to watch the first deployment of the weapon that would bring Alan Saul at last within her reach.

ARGUS

There was little sign of the surgery Ghort had undergone other than a few faint lines visible under the stubble on his scalp, and his frequent expression now of perplexed puzzlement. The relay was a mirrored cube just a centimetre across, which he wore on a silver chain around his neck. Neither of these items was visible now that he wore his heavy work suit and clung to an I-beam of the column, which currently extended over a kilometre and a half below the rapidly disappearing central asteroid. "What's it like?" Alex asked, as he floated out in vacuum ten metres away on the end of a line.

"Ever used a telefactor?" Ghort asked.

Alex had once trained on a bomb-disposal telefactor, his hands in special gloves and with VR goggles over his eyes. It seemed as if he had been there defusing the bomb with slightly numb fingers, rather than sitting kilometres away at a console.

"Yes, I've used a telefactor," he replied.

"Nothing like that at all," Ghort told him. "I get a schematic of the job in hand, break it down with a work-order program perpetually adjusted to materials available, load specific tasks to specific robots, insert you, me and the others in where human dexterity and flexibility will work best, and then watch the entire job slotting together even while I'm working on it too." Ghort dipped to peer down at where the five construction robots he controlled were positioning and welding in place bubble metal I-beams, and where Gladys and Akenon were fixing optics and power cables. They were working on just one corner of the column, while five similar teams were working on the rest. Meanwhile, yet other teams were building the column inwards, as the largest chunk of the asteroid was being hauled to one side, and while mining robots concentrated on the remainder.

"Here it comes," said Alex, now seeing a big loader robot scuttling down towards them carrying a great mass of bubble-metal beams and other items on its back. "We should be able to get back up to speed again."

Var Delex had changed working methods so there would be less competition between humans and robots, which apparently led to a greater number of errors and accidents. However, she had not been able to dispel completely all competitiveness. Those building this column to take the Mars Traveller engine were now racing against the new robots building the framework for the station sphere, trying always to stay ahead of the steady growth of that incurving wall of girders. Alex gazed out towards the rim, watching centipede lines of the robots working around the wall—looking like golden worms from this distance. Of course, it was a futile race. The column would stop at two kilometres, while the sphere wall would continue for half a kilometre more and curve into the blast hole for the Traveller's fusion torch.

To get out of the big loader robot's way, Alex hauled himself into the column's web of girders alongside Ghort. Down at the end of the column, the loader detached from its load, leaving it suspended on the end of a thread out in space, and headed back—like a giant metal beetle that had just rid itself of its wing encased body. Once it was out of the way, Alex detached his line, then used his wrist impeller to propel himself out then down, settling to land gently on the packed heap of beams and other components. A minute's search and he found the plastic crate he wanted, peeled it up off its gecko pad and hauled it along with him back to Ghort. Behind him, construction robots began taking the rest of the package apart.

"Let's get to it," said Ghort, opening the crate and taking out the first of the neatly packed mass of stress sensors, which were crucial for a column expected to support such a load as this one would.

In one week they would be hauling across the already detached Mars Traveller engine, along with its shock-absorbing bed, and attaching it here. Alex looked forward to the sight of that behemoth being moved, and already regretted his wait-and see attitude to the new cerebral implants, for through such a device he would have been able to make sensory recordings that he could view again at leisure. And apparently there would be masses of file space available for such recordings, since everyone possessing an implant would be linked to his own information repository. Or, at least, that was how Ghort had explained it in a rather offhand and dismissive way.

Five hours later, their shift ended, their tools taken up by another team, whose leader also took control of the robots without even a pause. They returned up the column towards where Tech Central had been disassembled, ready to be slotted into a central sphere which was already in the process of being prefabricated. Halfway there, they launched themselves from the column towards the entrance to their accommodation unit, bringing themselves down neatly with impellers, entering through the airlock two by two and shedding their suits.

"Now that was a good shift," said Akenon, "and I'm going to spend some of that station credit in the Olive Tree!"

This was another change that had been suggested by Var Delex, and instantly instituted by the Owner. No longer were they working just to survive, but they were getting a wage. They received station credits for their work which could be spent on some of the luxuries now becoming available. It was also possible to withdraw those credits as coinage which could be spent on some luxuries that were technically under the wire: cannabis, tobacco, bootleg alcohol and various personal items. Alex realized that being able to buy such things made the likes of Akenon and Gladys feel that somehow they were getting one over on the Owner, but he knew they were fooling themselves. Saul would not have introduced coinage if he cared so much about what people spent it on, and to believe that he did not know about the growing black market aboard the station was foolish. It was deliberate, because it made the powerless feel that they had some control over their own destiny.

"Going to get some more *herbs*?" Gladys enquired. "Maybe," replied Akenon cautiously, eyeing Ghort.

"Doesn't matter to me," said Ghort, "just so long as you're not skull-fucked at the start of our next shift."

Such casual exchanges concerning the mundane routine of their everyday lives were here thrown into contrast with the massive changes occurring outside. Alex shook his head. Was it because he was a clone, and because of his years of reprogramming that he could not slide into such casual human acceptance of it all? Perhaps because he himself had never lived a "normal" life, he could not whittle the numinous down to such normality.

"What about you?" Gladys asked him. Alex shrugged; he just didn't know.

She turned to Akenon and slapped him on the shoulder. "Come on, skunk-brain, let's go."

As they departed, Ghort moved up beside Alex and watched them go, muttering, "Bread and circuses."

Alex did not have Ghort's immediate system access, so he had to use the console in his cabin to track down this phrase. Slowly beginning to grasp its implications, and those attending Ghort's general attitude, his acerbic comments and suppressed bile, Alex began to realize that it might be in his best interests to keep a close eye on their team leader.

SCOURGE

Clay gazed up at the five corpses gyrating slowly in the air, holes ripped through their heavy hazmat spacesuits to expose the lead mesh and the pipe networks of their isotope scrubbing systems, with beads of blood and fragments of flesh and bone still orbiting them.

"Someone aboard is working for her," opined Scotonis.

That only made sense if someone had communicated with Earth and struck some sort of deal, which seemed unlikely unless there was a hidden transceiver aboard. But, even then, why would Galahad order someone to start killing the crew? Being highly radioactive, the *Scourge* wasn't worth salvaging, so surely Galahad's best option would be just to wait until it was in range, then hit it with one of her big new railguns? Unless, of course, the traitor was one of those who already knew, or had recently discovered, that Saul had, in an attempt to fore stall their attack on him, transmitted the Gene Bank data to them, and that they had not passed it on to Earth and kept it stashed on board.

Clay winced: he knew his thought processes were slow but they would be equally slow if he came off his meagre supply of painkillers and tried to think round the constant ache of his body. He therefore tried to put it all in order in his mind.

Before the gravity wave had ripped through the ship, it had been Scotonis's plan to use the Gene Bank data as a bargaining chip to get them close to Earth—pretending to Galahad that they believed she would let them live in exchange for that acquired data. Once close enough, however, they would try to locate Galahad and launch a nuclear strike against her, and against anything else that seemed an immediate danger to them. Then, during the ensuing confusion, they would dock at Core Two and somehow get from there down to Earth and into hiding. That last part of the plan had all been very vague, and very desperate.

After the damage to the *Scourge*, the strategy had changed. The ship was certainly on course back to Earth but, as far as Galahad knew, all aboard it had been killed by Alan Saul's activation of the Scour virus imbedded in their ID implants. This was what they would use to get them close, because their ship wouldn't be perceived as a threat. Under further evolution, the plan had changed, with Trove submitting the idea that, with just a few nuclear strikes, they could take control of all orbital facilities, bombard Galahad, then use both the Gene Bank data and their position in control of those facilities as a basis on which to bargain with whatever regime arose after her. Clay felt such plans were just the desperate and the futile meanderings of people already dying. They had then become even more implausible when it was discovered that after the gravity wave and the subsequent dirty bomb explosion in the *Scourge*'s nuclear arsenal they might not even be capable of launching the nukes.

And now this.

The five slaughtered crewmen had been among those assessing the damage to their nuclear capability and trying to work out how to restore it.

"When did this happen?" he asked.

"Sometime within the last week," Scotonis told him.

Clay glanced at him. "You can't estimate it more precisely than that?"

"No." Scotonis shook his head. "We can't use radio, because Earth might pick it up, and the comlines to the arsenal are out. I just left each team to it and had them file a report once their dosimeters maxed out, and then only if they had anything worth reporting."

That statement struck Clay as very odd, because surely Scotonis would have wanted to keep himself completely up to date.

"So it's been a week since any report was filed?"

"It has."

"Therefore this could have happened before Myers was killed?"

"Certainly."

There was something very wrong here but Clay could not quite nail it down. Sunk into depression and sickness, many of the crew were certainly getting slack about their work, some giving up on it entirely. But Scotonis had always seemed a lot more driven, especially after finding out that the Scour, which his wife and children had succumbed to, had been spread by Serene Galahad herself. Clay shook his head in an effort to clear it, then, noting the colour code of the dosimeter on his shoulder, stepped hurriedly back towards the door.

Scotonis followed, watching him with an intensity he did not like, his gaze unwavering as he too stepped out into the corridor and closed the door to the suiting room behind him.

"So what was their latest assessment?" Clay asked.

"I don't know," Scotonis replied. "Whoever did this also accessed the system and wiped the data."

Clay suddenly understood the danger he was in. It seemed that someone was carrying out the kind of plan he himself had in mind, but had not yet acted on or properly thought through. Scotonis assumed it was Clay killing people aboard. Scotonis thought *he* was the traitor, before he had even had a chance to do any betraying.

Clay knew certain things: the proliferation of orbital weapons around Earth made it highly unlikely that they could take control in orbit, so their chances of taking out Galahad with an orbital strike were remote at best, and if he did not get proper advanced medical care on Earth he would inevitably die. All that remained in their favour was the Gene Bank data; all that remained, in fact, in *his* favour. His aim, vaguely, had been to get in communication with Galahad, using his primacy in system access, then tell her about the data, steal a shuttle and take the data with him, ensuring that she knew of Scotonis's intentions with the nukes. The *Scourge* would be destroyed and he would be rescued, then there could be only one story to tell. His story would be about how he had been a virtual prisoner from the moment he had stepped aboard, how he had been powerless to stop Scotonis's disobedience. The chances were that she would have him killed anyway, but his chances of survival with her would still be better than they were by adhering to the captain's plans. Now it seemed someone was pre-empting him with a similar survival plan—one that would undoubtedly interfere with his own. He had to find out who and stop him or her immediately.

"Either Trove or Cookson," he decided. "If someone is working for Galahad, it has to be one of them. Only they have the system access, and only they would know about the Gene Bank data and be able to use that as a bargaining chip."

"You think so?" Scotonis enquired, now raising a sidearm to point it straight at Clay's visor. "*You're* the Inspectorate worm aboard this ship. *You're* the eyes and ears she put here."

"You're forgetting that I'm also the least useful one she placed aboard, simply to ensure she had someone non-essential she could punish," said Clay. "You're also forgetting that she sent the signal to close my strangulation collar just as slowly as possible." Clay hurried on. "Trove and Cookson, however, can both claim that they were only following your orders."

"I trust them," said Scotonis.

"Which makes you easier to manipulate."

"I should just shoot you now. You're no use to me."

"Without me you would never have known the truth," said Clay, then added, "and without me you won't know who the traitor is."

"You know?"

"I know how we can find out," said Clay, suddenly realizing that the answer was simple and that he knew precisely how to identify who had killed these men, and perhaps Myers too.

EARTH

The greatly extended Traveller construction station was occupied by an all-but-complete smaller vessel, a prototype, alongside two gigantic hulks—part of a new generation of battleships that had never flown. The prototype was just a much smaller and less manoeuvrable version of the *Scourge*, possessing the same vaguely torpedo shape. It was a quarter of the size, at half a kilometre long and a hundred metres wide, with a rear fusion engine and four, rather than the full eight, fusion engines located around its body for rapid course changes. However, it was also encircled by the ring of a vortex generator, so resembled an axle stub in the middle of a wheel. Though a prototype, it was a working vessel, but the tacticians had decided that the vortex ring was far too vulnerable where it was currently positioned, and it interfered with the aiming of its own weapons. They had then gone on to suggest that this vessel would be better staying out of close conflict and should therefore take on more of an observational role. Serene had decided to name it the *Vision*—since the *Argus*, the name of a mythical giant with a hundred eyes, was no longer available.

The second vessel extended a kilometre from its nose to its fusion engines, but contained the ring of its vortex generator *inside* its hull and, inside the compass of its weapons systems, it bore the shape of a spinning top. This was Admiral Bartholomew's vessel so, after little thought, Serene had named it the *Command*.

The third vessel bore the shape of a smaller version of what Argus Station was now becoming. Here everything had been much better integrated, and all wrapped in a new design of composite armour. In this two-kilometre-diameter sphere there was more room for the two-thousand-strong assault force, along with a cornucopia of heavy weapons, including two of Calder's new design of missile.

"Have you thought of a name for it yet, ma'am?" asked Admiral Bartholomew.

Serene glanced at the diminutive man who bore such a heavy title. He was smaller even than Serene and seemed to disappear in the physical presence of his command crew, which mostly consisted of big steroid-and cyber-enhanced brutes. Yet, when he spoke in his soft Brazilian-accented tones, everyone attended to him at once. Physically small he might be, but he was bright and sharp, and amidst his crew seemed like iron amidst plastic. Out of thousands of prospects, this erstwhile commander of the Core One station had been ranked way above the rest.

Swallowing wetly on an urge to vomit, which the anti-nausea pills had yet to negate, Serene sat back in the co-pilot's chair of the space plane as it drifted towards the dock of the construction station. She had considered naming the last ship after some historical figure, maybe a general or a political leader, but now decided on something in keeping with the brevity and concision of the other names.

"I name that ship the *Fist*," she said.

Bartholomew allowed himself a tight smile. "Apposite."

"So you intended to remain aboard the *Command*," she said.

"Now you've named it, what else can I do?"

Serene turned to study him more closely. Was he just making a little joke or was he starting to show his true colours, now his strangulation collar had been removed?

"No offence intended, ma'am," he added hurriedly. "I believe my record notes a tendency in me to inappropriate humour when I'm nervous."

Serene nodded. Yes, she had seen that on his record. It was one of the few items in the section his examiners had reserved for listing his faults—a section completely outweighed by his numerous qualifications, his experience and his successes. "So why do you choose to remain aboard the *Command*?"

"Where I position myself is irrelevant, ma'am, since you have designated me admiral and I command three ships, not one. It is also the case that I am a strategist, and therefore better at assessing situations at one remove, while Captain Oerlon is both a good combat commander and organizer of personnel, so will do much better aboard the . . . *Fist*, which has a larger crew and the troop complement, and is likely to find itself at the sharp end of any battle."

Could she accuse him of cowardice? If things went to plan, then the *Fist* would be the vessel launching the main attack against Argus Station, and the first to dock as it sent in the troops. And, as Bartholomew must be well aware, that had not gone too well the last time. Serene decided otherwise, since Bartholomew had made some decisions in his past that ran counter to the orders he had been given and which, if they had turned out to be wrong, would have resulted in him ending up in an adjustment cell. He was clearly no coward.

The dock drew closer: a triangular pillar jutting out from the main mass of the station, with four space planes already moored to two of its faces, two of them having brought her main security team here a few days previously to liaise with the Inspectorate complement already aboard. It had been necessary for them to spy the station out and to get all protocols in place to ensure her absolute protection. No data about her presence here could be allowed to leak out, since a space station was a vulnerable place for Earth's dictator to be. Also, staff considered even marginally unsafe must be moved; the readergun network put on hold since the failure rate could not be risked; undercover agents activated; and fast escape routes checked out. Thinking on this last eventuality made her feel queasy, even now that the anti-nausea pills were starting to work, for it meant a fast escape by a drop shuttle re-entry vehicle should something catastrophic happen to the station—such catastrophes being generally related to the arrival of Alan Saul in Earth orbit.

Bartholomew smoothly operated their plane's controls to bring them to the one empty surface, the station now seeming to loom above them. Serene experienced a moment of disorientation, but by now the accompanying nausea was all but gone. Docking clamps engaged with a reverberating crash and she listened to the low thrum of compressors driving the plane's airlock cylinder into the dock, as if enacting some obscene technological mating. Bartholomew unstrapped and Serene copied him.

"I do have a question for you, if I may, ma'am?" he said as he stood up.

"Go ahead." She obliged.

"My crews and the assault troops have recently received orders to visit a team of medics you sent over, to have their ID implants removed," he said. "Why is that?"

"We're not sure but, according to a tactical assessment, it seems likely Alan Saul was able to use those implants to locate all *Scourge* personnel, and via them was able to penetrate secure communications, which is how he beat them," Serene explained. "Our technicians are working to negate all the advantages that his mental penetration of computer systems gives him."

And I don't want him activating the Scour lodged in your implants and killing you all.

"Hence the comlifer too?"

"Yes—he is from the original team that has been protecting Earth's computer security, so is tried and tested. Meanwhile I have more comlifers assuming new positions down there."

The passenger compartment of the plane contained Elkin and her two aides, besides other ancillary staff, Serene's small security team from Core One, and some of Bartholomew's staff. The security team was already up and ready the moment Serene stepped through, and they headed back to the airlock to precede her. There had been no need for Serene to wear a spacesuit, since this dock was pressurized, but, for her safety, Sack had advised her to do so. It was also the case that here the kind of clothing she would normally wear—chosen for the imposing impression it would give—seemed completely inappropriate. She had therefore chosen to have made the suit she now wore. It was a state-of-the-art VC suit of silver and blue, with the armour subtly shaped so as not to conceal her femininity. As she went headfirst down through the lock and, in one of those dizzying changes in perspective, stepped upright out on to the inner floor of the dock, she recalled her history.

"I may have the body of a weak and feeble woman," she muttered to herself.

"Pardon, ma'am?" said Bartholomew, then stepped back abruptly as Sack appeared at her side, his combat suit turning him into even more of a hulking monster.

She glanced at her bodyguard, unreasonably annoyed at him because she had spent so much time either feeling sick or being just too busy to take things any further with him. Perhaps it would be best to wait until they were back on Earth; make it a kind of celebration.

"Queen Elizabeth the First," she explained to Bartholomew. "I leave it to you to find the reference." She scanned the crowd of personnel swarming all around her, noting the ranks of Bartholomew's crews and soldiers standing neatly to attention. She wondered if she was expected to make some sort of inspection, then dismissed that idea. Scanning further, she found herself puzzled by the number of Inspectorate enforcer uniforms she was seeing, which were distinct from the attire of her security teams already gathered here. Surely there was little need for so many of them? Surely, up here, so many non-productive personnel would be a drain on resources?

"Where's Calder?" she asked.

"Here, ma'am."

The man himself stepped forward, clad in a simple atmosphere-breach suit over jeans and T-shirt, one of the new palette-design palmtops clutched in his right hand, his thumb inserted through the hole to press down on the security reader and his fingers able to work the underside touch controls.

"A lot of Inspectorate here," she noted. But, even while she watched, the Inspectorate staff began to filter away. Perhaps they felt their presence was not really required with all the soldiers and other security here. Even so, she felt a twinge of suspicion and knew this presence was something she ought to check up on.

"Here to ensure your safety," he replied blandly.

"Then they are rather surplus to requirements." She waved a hand towards the ranked troops and crew.

"Yes, certainly." He paused for a moment before adding, "Of course, a degree of natural curiosity is not something to be ruled out."

Perhaps that was it. This was a big station and maybe most of its Inspectorate personnel had come here just to see her. She couldn't really blame them for wanting to see their ultimate ruler in the flesh, but she would still have to make some comment about them leaving their posts for that idle purpose—though later, for she had more important concerns right now.

"We go straight into the orbital firing after the test," she declared, waiting impatiently for Calder to lead the way. "You've organized it?"

It took him a moment to draw his gaze away from a nearby Inspectorate officer and focus on what she was saying.

"I have, ma'am," he said, then probingly, "though I'm not sure of its purpose."

"Shall we go?" she snapped.

He gestured with his palette and, as she moved off, Serene was thankful that her security personnel moved ahead of her to lead the way. Sometimes all this deference could be quite annoying, especially when people insisted on walking either beside or behind her when she herself didn't know which direction to go.

"I would have thought the purpose of the orbital firing quite evident," she continued, realizing that this was the first time she had actually physically encountered Calder—that this was the first time she had spoken face-to-face with someone on whom so much depended.

"If you destroy Argus Station, you lose the Gene Bank data," he replied.

"Then obviously that is not the purpose."

"His response might not be what you expect, ma'am," Calder suggested.

"There are only two responses: fight or flight," she explained. "If he arrives here, my tacticians suggest he won't be able to stay long enough to cause major damage without putting Argus Station at huge risk. Most likely he will run, which will take him away from the sun and its convenient source of power. But he will not run all the way yet, because he's not ready to, and he believes he can run at any time. The orbital firing will slow him down and give you more time to commission those ships out there, and take your new weapon against him."

Calder nodded in dubious agreement.

At the base of the dock they headed for a train where more security personnel were waiting, doubtless there simply to ensure no one slipped a bomb on the vehicle before her arrival. She stepped aboard and gazed in puzzlement at the presence of seats in this zero-gravity environment, then sat down anyway. After a moment, she copied others in pulling her seat straps across. The reason for the seats and the straps soon became evident as the train slid into motion, passing through a complicated array of seals and iris doors, out into bright sunlight and the disperse confusion of the station structure, and then accelerated.

No air to slow it down, Serene realized, as she was first pushed back into her seat, then down into it on one sweeping curve, then eventually lifting out of it against her straps, as the train slowed at a C-section station in the side of something like a steel coliseum located out in vacuum. With a sucking crump, airlocks engaged, and she was soon out into busy corridors and cage ways, then into a control centre that seemed either in the process of being taken apart or still being put together. Serene strode over to a big outward-slanting window that overlooked some-thing crouching within the station structure: a skyscraper of technology braced and supported by heavy beams, massive carousels at one end, massive cables feeding in all round, unmistakably a weapon.

"One of the new ones," said Calder from behind her. She glanced round at him.

"And the new missiles?"

"I can show you one, but they don't look particularly impressive—just a half-tonne of plain cone-shaped metal, very much in the form of an old staged-rocket crew capsule." He pointed down towards the carousels. "I have one ready to be loaded directly after the first test firing of an inert missile."

"Then let the test proceed."

Calder gestured politely to a throne-like seat facing a curving panoramic screen. Of course there would be nothing to see by looking at the railgun itself, other than perhaps some movement in the carousels. Leaving her staff to hover behind her—Elkin and the rest unsure about where to position themselves, so looking like rubes in the big city—Serene went and sat herself down.

Three scenes were visible. One was obviously from a camera positioned down on the Moon's surface, showing a plain of contorted rock and drifts of dust terminating up against a jagged range of mountains. Nearby, measuring posts had been fixed in the ground to give a sense of scale, while at the foot of the steep mountain slopes lay a scattering of lunar accommodation units and some steel-wheeled lunar rovers that had to be at least a hundred years old. The next view showed the same scene from a satellite located above the Moon—the rovers now reduced to silver specks. The third view was from even further out.

"We've got the Hubble pointing at this, too," Calder explained, "using a milframer camera."

Right then, Serene couldn't remember whether that was a camera taking a million high-resolution frames a minute or a second, and she felt disinclined to ask. It basically meant that, should she want to, she could view extreme slow-motion video of the imminent events. She gestured for him to continue.

"Okay," said Calder, his voice now issuing from a PA system. "Power up and fire the test shot, in twenty seconds precisely."

The movement of people in the room seemed to judder to a halt for a second, as many screen images flickered and changed. Serene shivered as a thrumming in the air ratcheted up into clear audibility: the kind of sound heard in any power station in a major sprawl.

"Firing test shot," announced Calder unnecessarily, as the tone of the hum abruptly changed.

Nothing happened for a few seconds, during which Serene had time to feel annoyed at not asking him for more detail: such as how long it would take the missile to reach its target. Then a bright flash lit up the lunar plain and it abruptly bulged up, domed, then opened on a deep red explosion. Transferring her gaze to the video captured from orbit, Serene observed a perfectly circular wave spreading out around it. The close view briefly showed a boulder the size of a house tumbling past, before being subsumed in a wall of dust. The view from furthest out then showed a fire fading at the centre of an expanding and ever-diffusing dome of dust.

"Impressive," Serene allowed, then glanced round at Calder. "I presume everything was satisfactory?"

He nodded. "There was really no reason to test the railgun—the real test comes next."

"So, if you would lead me through what happens now?"

"The weapon is already in its power-up cycle," Calder explained. "Shortly, we will use the railgun at its lowest power, just as a launcher, since firing on full power would provide far too much acceleration and wreck the weapon's internal components. Once it's just clear of the station here, the weapon receives its vector and accelerates. To an outside viewer it will just seem like a railgun test firing, for the weapon will immediately start travelling at a speed equivalent to that of our previous firing, and it will then hit a target point just beyond the previous one."

Serene smiled and returned her attention to the screens. The dust had cleared now and the old accommodation units and rovers were still in place on the other side of a brand-new crater in the face of the Moon.

"Firing weapon," Calder announced.

This time the thrum of power remained constant, but Serene could feel the skin on her back crawl nevertheless. She waited patiently, blinked on a flash amidst those jagged mountains, then watched the whole landscape ripple. For a second, the mountain range seemed to distort through a fish-eye lens, then it erupted. The close view briefly showed the accommodation units and rovers turning into glittering fragments, before an avalanche of stone ate them up, then greyed and blinked out. The orbital view showed a blast ten times the size of the previous one, tearing an immense hole in the Moon and throwing a great plume out into space, sending rock and dust far beyond any hope of the Moon's gravity retrieving it. Serene finally gazed upon the face of the ancient satellite, now changed forever.

"Of course," said Calder, "the gravity effects around the warp substantially magnify the impact value."

It had been Calder's idea to make a missile that used a vortex generator to propel it. Since it was a missile, and without the encumbrance of passengers—who would be fried by the Hawking radiation generated inside its warp bubble—it *could* travel faster than the speed of light; faster even than Argus Station. Such a missile, on impact, would knock out the warp bubble of that station, thus negating what Alan Saul must perceive as his big advantage: his ability to run and their inability, before going in pursuit, to know where or when he would stop and change course.

"And this one was just the Alcubierre-drive version?" she enquired.

"It was," Calder affirmed, "the other three are the ones that are fully armed."

This refinement to the weapon hadn't been Calder's idea, but a suggestion from the tacticians. When one of these missiles hit the Argus warp bubble, and knocked it out, the nuclear EM warhead it also contained, which was designed to be primed by the high temperatures generated within the warp bubble, would then detonate, cooking local computers. After that, Alan Saul would no longer be running, and Argus Station would be open to assault.

The only drawback with these missiles was that their small vortex generators interfered with the vortex generators of the ships they were on, and vice versa. The ship's vortex generator could not therefore be maintained at complete readiness while they were getting a missile ready to fire, which meant a delay of up to half an hour between either drive being used. This was something the tacticians were working on, and Serene felt confident of a solution.

"So now it's time to scare the rat out of the woodpile," she said, not entirely sure where she had heard that expression. Just then the power note in the air changed again.

"All the railguns here and on the Core stations are now firing," explained Calder. "Forty inert missiles. We aren't firing at full power, because if we did, they wouldn't swing round the sun towards their target."

Their target . . . Argus Station.

Alan Saul was just about to get his wake-up call.

6

WHY DIDN'T HE RUN?

A question that will bother historians until the end of time is, "Why didn't Alan Saul flee to somewhere far away and safe?" Surely, once he had tested his Alcubierre warp drive on his flight to Mars, then taking Argus Station to another star system, and there obtaining the materials and energy for its conversion, would have been less risky than staying in the vicinity of Earth? One explanation is that he needed additional resources for the immense journey he was about to make, but I feel that is far too simplistic. Some illumination might lie in his rescue of his sister, Var Delex. We know, from witness statements and available information, that the torture he suffered at the hands of Salem Smith had wiped his mind, so one has to ask what drove him to seek out and rescue a sister he no longer actually knew. Saul was far too logical, too far along the road to machine mentality, to be affected by any belief in fraternal love, or duty but, by his actions, it seems his unconscious still drove him. I believe his unconscious also recognized unfinished business, and a hatred of the regime created by Serene Galahad, which was little different from the one he had already tried to destroy.

ARGUS

High up within the skeletal sphere of his ship, Saul hung in vacuum, with Var beside him. She had been insistent on his joining her for this tour of the work in progress, despite the fact that he could view it all without being physically present. She needed affirmation of her status and, quite frequently lately, it seemed that she needed reassurance, as if she was losing confidence in her own abilities.

Below them lay what remained of the original station, but with the Mars Traveller engine now being hauled down into its new position. Tech Central, which should have lain directly below him, had been dismembered and reassembled around the station core to which all inward reaching structural members now connected. It occupied the upper hemisphere of the core, the view from its windows now mostly blocked by the inner bearing endcaps of the original arcoplexes. The only really open view from there was through the gap where the Traveller engine had once been, but even that only gave a distant view of the ship's skeleton and, even now, a second new arcoplex spindle was being assembled in the way of that.

"It'll soon all be gone." Saul pointed to the remaining pieces of the asteroid that had now been shifted out to hang alongside the new ship's core.

"It will never all be gone," replied Var.

"Yes, I know." He waved a hand to encompass the surrounding sphere. "It's all out there still."

"No, I don't mean that. Some enterprising soul took a half-tonne chunk of high nickel-and-chrome-content iron and is now turning it into jewellery."

Saul had already known this, down to the detail and dimensions of the jewellery concerned, also who was making it and when and how, and how small a dent this made in station resources. He did not mention this, however, but just let her bolster her confidence with this game of "I know something you don't." Meanwhile, he slid the larger part of his attention elsewhere, through the cam system and other ship's sensors, to watch as Paul and two other proctors connected up the twenty-seventh Mach-effect coil array—a device like a huge steel aphid clinging to the inner edge of a structural beam. Except for one team, all the humans had converged for Hannah and Var's planned celebration, but the proctors stopped only for their own mysterious periods of stillness. He liked seeing them work as smoothly and efficiently as his conjoined robots, but pausing occasionally as if to admire their product.

"How long?" he asked them, without actually speaking.

"With Jasper Rhine running the balancing tests, it will take fifty days," Paul replied. "Without him it could be done much quicker, perhaps twenty days to install and balance every one of the projected two hundred and thirty coil arrays. They must be synched with the EM component of the Rhine drive."

The mild implication was evident there: a human was slowing down some of the work in progress. Saul ran some rapid calculations. What with many human members of the work teams now getting "chipped," the balance was nevertheless changing. They were speeding up, becoming more adept, more robotic, but it was still the case that if he replaced every human operating aboard with a robot, the work rate would increase.

"Should I confine them all to their quarters?" Saul asked. "Or should I exterminate them and thus free up more resources?"

"I do not respond well to rhetorical questions," Paul replied, while smoothly connecting up power cables and propelling himself back from the array.

"Work round him," Saul instructed. "But allow him to feel useful." Just as he himself was doing with his sister . . .

Saul now focused on a branching tree of his centipede robots working at the top of the sphere. The robots passed a last structural beam up that same tree to the remaining human team, who fielded it and began moving it into place. Even as he watched, the tree of robots fragmented—individual robots heading off in different directions about the sphere ready for their next tasks. Though it would have been much quicker to have just the robots fix the beam, Saul had backed Var's decision to allow this team, which included the Messina clone and Messina's old bodyguard, to accomplish this last piece of work. That seemed an extension of his initial choice to allow all the humans to survive. *A moral choice?* He wasn't sure he knew the meaning of the concept any more.

Saul felt it almost as a visceral clunk deep inside his torso as that same beam went into place, then as a gradual easing inside him as bolts were tightened through perfectly lined-up holes before welders glared distantly in vacuum. He now hung in a complete spherical cage, five kilometres across, in orbit about the sun, though admittedly some parts of the cage were not permanently secured since access would be needed for further materials.

"The last beam is in," declared Var, almost belligerently. "So a watershed has been passed?" Saul asked.

"Yes," she affirmed. "On the Traveller construction station, I always found that marking these occasions with some sort of celebration, no matter how minor or constrained by political oversight, increased the subsequent work rates."

"Certainly," Saul replied, noting to himself how robots did not need such motivation. However, the bulk of his attention remained focused elsewhere, because new data were coming in.

Serene Galahad's comlifers had blocked his access to all of Earth's satellites and computer systems, also the solar observation satellites, but they had not extended their range far, merely cut off all other installations beyond Earth's orbit from any contact with Earth. The Martian satellites were available to

Saul, but they were far away and transmission delays were long. Still, just a few million kilometres out, an old satellite orbited the sun in a parallel path to the Earth's. It had been overlooked because it remained mostly powered down until it detected comets or asteroids arriving in-system that might be a danger to Earth. Saul had sent a relay out from behind the sun, made a connection through it to that elderly satellite, and turned its radio and optical telescope array so as to now watch the home world.

"Railgun," he remarked, his tone belying his sudden qualms.

Galahad was working *fast*.

"What?" asked Var.

"About twenty minutes ago, Galahad fired a very powerful railgun at the Moon." So saying, Saul instituted an immediate check on Argus's weapons. Two railguns were operational but the plasma cannon that the Saberhagen twins were building was still far from completion. Perhaps his allocation of resources had been in error? Yes, Earth was a danger that could not be ignored—and in an instant he began to divert resources. The Saberhagens would shortly be receiving the components they were waiting for.

"Second firing," he now said, appalled at the destructive power of what he had just witnessed. "They must have solved the component distortion problem, because that looked like a railgun-fired nuclear weapon."

"Seems a bit advanced for them," said Var sniffily.

"Any more advanced than building vortex . . ." Saul felt a sudden surge of both annoyance and frustration, immediately followed by the realization that he had become arrogant. Even as he sent the orders for the smelting plants to close down immediately and retract, he considered how, if he had only been watching still from Mars, they would have been in serious trouble, because he was now witnessing a launch of railgun missiles around the sun directly towards their position. Thankfully, so as to obtain the correct orbital vector, they were travelling slowly, but he was well aware that if he hadn't been watching, he would have had to sacrifice both smelting plants just to save his ship.

"This is a problem?" Var enquired.

"Yes, and I've just given orders for everyone to prepare for a shift in precisely one hour," he replied. "It seems Galahad wants to let us know she hasn't forgotten us. Forty railgun missiles are now heading round the sun towards us."

Using the impeller on the wrist of his suit, Saul rapidly sent himself down towards the ship's core, with Var in quick pursuit.

"We need the solar energy," she protested.

"We're not moving far," he replied.

To avoid these approaching missiles, they only had to move a small distance relative to the sun, which could have been achieved with the steering thrusters or even the Mach-effect drive, were it operational. However, there was too much equipment, not to mention the remainder of the asteroid and the Traveller engine, unsecured inside the station. They must move without inertia, therefore the Rhine drive was required so Saul checked its status, as he had been checking it so often. Major changes to the station's structure, including the heavy armour being put in place in the station ring, had caused distortions in the vortex generator that had been necessary to straighten out. It was good, as he knew from the last time he checked it, just a few minutes before.

Approaching the surface of the ship's core, he slowed himself with his impeller just enough so he could absorb the remaining impact by bending his knees and have his gecko soles still remain in place. Var landed shortly after him and he was pleased, for her, to see that she had landed as perfectly as himself. He strode towards the nearest airlock, heaved open the door, pushed himself down inside, and waited until his sister crammed in beside him. The airlock gave them access to a corridor leading to the Tech Central control centre, which internally had been left much as before. Saul removed his VC suit helmet and clipped it to his belt.

"Humans in space really need to start thinking less two-dimensionally," Var commented, as she followed him.

"To do that," Saul replied, "humans either have to change, or have been raised in a zero-g environment."

"Well, even that's started now."

Saul nodded in grave agreement. Those being "chipped" provided an example of the former . . . but he didn't know how to react to the news that some station personnel were getting pregnant, and that thus far eight in all had refused termination. This could be taken as meaning they were starting to feel safe, but this urge to procreate was more probably a response to the constant danger: a biological imperative and a hedge against the future.

He entered Tech Central to find that Hannah, the Saberhagens, Rhine, Le Roque and even Langstrom were present. This event was something cooked up by Hannah and Var between them, Hannah having brought two bottles of fizzy wine, which was brewed on the station, and a collection of the special glasses required for drinking such a beverage in zero gravity. This gathering was so that the main players aboard the station could celebrate the fixing of the last structural beam. Var had also allowed all the work crews a shift off to celebrate similarly—a humanizing event—and a large number of them were waiting in the Arboretum for the return of Ghort's team, before the party began. Currently, however, Le Roque and Brigitta were speaking into their fones, and Langstrom and Rhine were working consoles, while Hannah stood on her own beside a medical gurney wheeled in specially to carry the drink and glasses. The rest of the station's personnel, meanwhile, were receiving the news that the station would shortly be on the move, and the party atmosphere was fast dissipating.

"Too human for you?" Hannah snapped at Saul.

"No, it seems Galahad wants to spoil your party," he replied tightly, then shot at Le Roque, "You have tracking on them?"

"I do, and they're up on all screens and accessible to all personnel," the station's technical director replied. "Every damned one of them is on target and we have to move."

Saul turned back to Hannah, who had now been joined by Var. "Railgun missiles heading straight for us. I feel they are an important reminder to us all."

"Yes, I know," she replied, suddenly looking tired.

Rhine was working his drive, Saul deliberately not interfering but keeping a watch on him from the inside of the computer system. The warp bubble should be near enough spherical despite the remaining mass of the asteroid, and the shift would be a short one, but still the margins for error were tight. Saul did not want to risk losing any of the newly constructed parts of the station. He walked over to join Hannah and Var.

"In fact, this celebration has made things easy for us," he offered. "All but one of the human teams have locked down their work and are not presently anywhere that might be dangerous, while the team that fixed that last beam is on its way in." Even as he said this, his mind was ranging throughout the station, constantly checking. If the station hit anything large enough to knock out the warp, then they might experience a momentum change; however, there were impellers mounted on the biggest unsecured objects—the Mars Traveller engine and the asteroid chunk—and any drift could be corrected.

"Oh, goody," Hannah replied.

Var popped the cap off of one of the bottles. "They didn't need to give us a reminder. The images I've seen of those three ships they're building tell the whole story." She used a small manual pump on the base of the bottle to squirt a stream of the wine into one of the capped glasses, then paused in bringing the glass straw up to her mouth. Everyone in the control room was staring at her. "What? It seems a shame to let it get warm." She sipped.

The shift was imminent and they could all feel it: a slightly different sensation now, as if the new surrounding superstructure was somehow distorting whatever it was that affected them. Saul nodded towards the glasses on the gurney. "Pour them all."

Var raised an eyebrow and did as instructed. She was already on the third glass when the drive engaged. The light of the sun dropped rapidly through the spectrum, and the moment of their shift was marked by a flash of intense red through the windows. Then the sun was back, glaring on the structures visible outside.

"Just a few thousand kilometres," said Rhine.

Saul focused through that warning satellite on the stations ranged about Earth. By his calculation, it was possible that the enemy had tens of thousands of railgun missiles available. If it had been Galahad's intention just to send them a reminder, then fine; the smelting plants could be extended and they could simply get back to work here. However, if the dictator of Earth was intent on driving them away from their power supply, that was a different matter. Saul did not want to spend the next weeks, if not months, dodging pot-shots from Earth, nor did he like the idea of the work here going on hold during that period.

Galahad could commission her ships within that period and he would be forced to run out-system before having achieved what he wanted here—without having made the necessary preparations for the immense journey across interstellar void.

"Drink your drinks," he instructed, taking a sip of the wine himself while wondering how alcohol might affect or impair the distributed functioning of his mind.

They all gathered round to accept their glasses in turn. Saul moved away to gaze out through the windows of Tech Central. He decided against ordering the smelting plants to be extended again just yet. Calculating signal delays, he reckoned on twenty-three minutes before Galahad learned that they had moved, then a further twenty-eight minutes before he learned if she had devised an immediate response to that. Meanwhile he watched the workers coming in, the proctors installing further elements of the Mach-effect drive, and simultaneously absorbed detail and tweaked and changed his plans to greater efficiency.

"She can't touch us," said Langstrom with relish.

Saul turned to him, a hollow feeling in his stomach. "On the contrary," he replied, now seeing a second launching of missiles from the vicinity of Earth. This launching was early, before Galahad could know they had moved, a wide spread to in-corporate where some tactical team of hers had calculated he might move his ship. None of them was on target, but Galahad's message had been delivered. Walking past Langstrom to join the rest, he announced, "We're shifting again." And immediately began inputting new coordinates, factoring in known solar-system debris and deciding on two further shifts to take them to their first destination.

There was time yet, so he would allow all solar energy collection to continue for a while. He studied the disappointed expressions around him.

"We would have had to have moved shortly, anyway," he stated, his voice taking on an echo as it repeated through the PA system, "since we are running out of materials."

They then watched him attentively, aware that he had some-thing more to say. Via cams throughout the station, he saw people turning to public screens now displaying his face.

"A second launching of railgun missiles is heading on its way towards us," he continued, "and it is a simple fact, with the resources Earth commands and its supply lines established, that they could keep up this rate of fire indefinitely. We are therefore going to shift away from the sun."

"We need energy," Var protested pedantically, "and you're taking us away from it."

"Where are we going?" asked Le Roque—posing a question to which, in the long term, there was really no simple answer. Saul, however, gave them the simplest answer he could.

The abrupt relocation of the station had been brief but disconcerting, especially since it occurred while Alex and Gladys were in the elevator taking them down into the Arboretum. A brief announcement through his fone informed Alex that Earth had just fired railgun missiles at them, so the Owner had shifted the station out of their way. They were safe again, it seemed, yet suddenly Alex felt angry at his powerlessness, his lack of knowledge.

He stepped out of the elevator to feel the ground solid underneath his feet for the first time since he had last been here, with Messina, when the Arboretum hadn't been spinning, and his feet had hardly touched the ground, as he went on his killing spree among the invading troops. He now scanned his surroundings and saw no signs of the battle that had taken place here.

"She's a bitch, that Galahad," Gladys muttered, then pointed over to the dividing section of the Arboretum, where Akenon and Ghort waited for them, having already shed their suits and used the elevator some minutes earlier.

"So this is your first time here?" she asked, perhaps not wanting to talk further about the station shift, or its implications.

"First visit to the Olive Tree, yes," Alex replied, playing along. "After my previous experiences in the Arboretum, this isn't a place I've wanted to return to."

"Come on!" urged Akenon.

They picked up their pace and soon reached the other two. "It's this way." Ghort pointed up some steps rising against the dividing section, which led to a metal walkway jutting two metres off the ground before following the inside circumference of the Arboretum cylinder. Alex supposed they were expected to walk there, rather than on the premium soil inside the cylinder itself, to save them trampling on a jungle of squashes growing underneath the trees, or pushing through densely packed fruit bushes. The walkway curved its way round to a balcony jutting out directly above, where the people occupying the tables and chairs seemed to hang suspended upside-down. As he and his team climbed up and made their way round, perspective slid round with them, until at last they were approaching the balcony the right way up.

The area was occupied by ten circular tables, each with seating space for four. Every table but one was now occupied by personnel, the empty one being reserved for them, the team who had fixed the last beam. A desultory cheer greeted them, the party atmosphere obviously diminished by the recent station shift. Waving and grinning, Ghort led the way to the table and they sat down.

Shortly, four bottled beers, along with the luxury of open-topped glasses, were brought out to them. Alex sipped, gazed into the Arboretum, which resembled a forest distorted through a fish-eye lens, and wondered what people here talked about in their time off. He listened carefully, but very little was being said, since everyone on the balcony seemed to be concentrating on the wall-mounted screen above the doors into the bar, while those sitting inside were similarly occupied with a screen there.

"Now that the heroes of the hour are present, I'll continue," said the Owner, gazing out with unhuman indifference from the screen for a moment, before attempting a smile that was only frightening.

Alex glanced at Ghort but received only an unreadable blank stare in return. Did he resent being demoted from bodyguard to Chairman Messina to the role of a working grunt? Did he hate the Owner?

The Owner continued, "Serene Galahad has fired upon us again, and quite likely she will keep on firing on us until she has driven us away from the vicinity of the sun. We are therefore obliged to move a lot further. Our first shift away is imminent, and the second will come directly after that—bringing us to the periphery of the Asteroid Belt." He gave another brief smile, this one thoughtful and slightly more human. "There our main task will be to get the Mars Traveller engine into position and operational, because we'll need it to take us into the Belt, to our first target: an asteroid containing essential materials. This we'll slice up and bring inside the ship." He paused to gaze, distractedly, to one side. They could all immediately feel it, so none of them needed his next announcement of, "First shift."

The screen then flicked back to a holding image: a picture of the station—or rather *ship*—as it now looked. The shift ensued as a weird twisting sensation emphasized by sudden nightfall inside the Arboretum as the sun-catchers ceased to have anything to catch and the light tubes ceased to have anything to convey. Lights on the wall above the balcony and within the bar switched on automatically. In this artificial glow, Alex studied the faces around him. Some wore expressions of excitement, but most were pensive and serious, for no one could work in space for any length of time without knowing how quickly its vagaries could kill.

"What about power?" hissed Akenon, as conversations started up again around them. "We managed okay on fusion, but nowhere near as well as by the sun."

"He's now got the reactor from Mars," Ghort noted, "besides three new ones built in Arcoplex Two waiting to come on line."

He's got the reactor from Mars, Alex noted; whereas Akenon and Gladys would have said *we* have it.

"Still not the same," Akenon insisted.

Alex nodded, for Akenon undoubtedly had a point. In driving them away from the sun, Galahad had won a brief skirmish in what Alex felt might be the start of a wholesale war. They now no longer had access to the power of the sun, so what would be the Owner's response? How did Alan Saul intend to prevent Galahad from killing them all?

Akenon, Ghort and Gladys fell into a discussion about power usage, the effectiveness of the new rectifying batteries and how much could be stored in ultra-capacitors scattered throughout the station. Alex sat back and wondered how long this present shift would take. Presumably the Owner was taking them to some point where they would have a relatively clear run at the Asteroid Belt. With the Rhine drive running and their speed approaching that of light, this could take just minutes or it might take hours—he had no idea.

He had nearly finished his beer when they emerged from the shift, and Argus heaved and groaned all around them. Much less of a pull now from the gravity of the sun, Alex realized.

Would this distort the vortex ring? Would adjustments have to be made? No . . . already he could feel the tension, the distortion of space and the pull of the ineffable building-up. Saul's image again appeared on the screen.

"Once we have possession of the materials we require from the Belt," he continued, as if there had been no pause, "we must fire up the Traveller again to get us clear. Then the next shift beyond the Asteroid Belt will ensue."

Again the holding picture flicked onto the screen, as the second shift kicked in, and again Alex began speculating on its length. The Asteroid Belt lay three hundred million kilometres from the sun, so at light speed, which was approximately three hundred thousand kilometres per second, that distance could nominally be covered in a thousand seconds. However, the Belt was well over a hundred million kilometres thick, they might not be travelling that close to the speed of light, and not necessarily even in a straight line out from the sun. All he could say was that it would take *over* seventeen minutes to reach their destination: a miraculous rate of travel achieved over truly immense distances.

After ten minutes Alex suddenly found himself sweating. He diagnosed Hawking radiation, which meant their ship had to be now reaching the edge of light speed. And what would happen if they ever passed that speed? Would they all fry, all die? Alex felt his anger increase because he was tired of always facing these questions; tired of being a pawn. After fifteen minutes, conversation at the tables all around began to dry up except for the occasional doom-laden mutter. This changed, in turn, to nervous chatter when the shift finally ended after twenty minutes. Then the chatter stilled as Saul reappeared on the screen.

"The last shift will take us to Jupiter," Saul announced, "where we should be able to obtain the rest of the materials we need. In orbit around the gas giant are currently hundreds of booster shells from the various Mars missions. These we'll retrieve, dismantle and turn into what we require." Saul paused, seeming to gaze straight at Alex, who gazed back, wondering if becoming the "Owner" had made this man lose any human concept of time.

"Doubtless you have all been wondering what we'll do for energy, and if we'll again be working only with fusion," Saul continued. "We will not, because once we reach our final destination, we'll move this ship in close, and there we'll tap the flux tube between Io and Jupiter. There will be energy to spare; energy enough to build more fusion reactors so that we never end up in such straits again. I mean enough energy to finish turning Argus Station into what it must become: an interstellar vessel."

There, it was said, and Alex felt his spine crawl. He had heard others debating this possibility but had given it little thought himself. Now it was plain and he could discern the worried tones of those around him as they discussed the last statement. Saul was building an interstellar vessel, so that meant they were going to fly between the stars. No questions, no debate—they were powerless.

"So *there's* our future," said Ghort, leaning in close.

In that same moment, Alex decided he no longer felt satisfied with being a working grunt. He would respond to the notification received that he could have an implant like Ghort's, and that would be just his first step on the ladder. He fully intended now to gain some power over his own destiny. However, he understood the limitations of that power and, unlike Ghort, could not find it in himself to resent being one of the owned.

He shrugged. "It's an improvement on our past, at least."

"Maybe yours," said Ghort, then clamped his mouth shut, as if wishing he had not revealed quite so much.

SCOURGE

Trove stood up as they entered her cabin. She was skeletally thin now, and moved like an old woman. But, then, Clay reflected, who of them was not moving about like a geriatric? She wore only soiled overalls and slip-on gecko slippers, and was allowing her Mohican to grow back—a stubble line from her forehead to the nape of her neck.

"What is it?" she asked tiredly.

"We've had killings aboard," said Scotonis, his voice sounding flat, almost indifferent.

She nodded, then suddenly realized. "Killings? I knew about Myers . . ."

"Somebody has murdered the team assessing our nuclear capability," Scotonis explained.

Clay, meanwhile, stepped a little closer to Trove to get a look at the dosimeter stuck to the sleeve of her overall. It was graded at a lower level than those both he and Scotonis wore, but that meant nothing. She could have changed it recently. He reached into his jacket, his hand straying briefly against the butt of the pistol he had retrieved from his cabin, then beyond that to take out the small hand-held Geiger counter.

"Why would anyone do that?" Trove asked, obviously confused. Then she focused on the device Clay was holding. "So you think it might be me."

She was quick, Clay thought; he had to allow her that.

Scotonis stepped back, drawing his sidearm. "Just let Political Officer Clay check you out, and don't make any sudden moves." Clay glanced at Scotonis. It was almost as if the man wanted her to react badly, so that he could conclude this quickly. Clay stepped forwards and took a reading, and found himself oddly pleased to see that she obviously hadn't set foot anywhere near the assessment team. She probably hated him for punishing her with her cabin inducer on the outward journey to the Asteroid Belt, but nevertheless he felt a grudging respect and almost a liking for her. He turned back to Scotonis, shaking his head. "It wasn't her."

Scotonis seemed reluctant to accept this, for he kept his gun aimed vaguely between Clay and Trove. He just stood there with his jaw moving as if he was chewing on something bitter, and meanwhile searching for a reason to pull the trigger. Perhaps he had become paranoid, though he certainly had reason to.

"Now we check Cookson," Clay said carefully.

For a long thoughtful pause Scotonis did not lower his weapon, then he abruptly holstered it. "Yes, Cookson." He turned towards the door, Clay heading after him, then swung back once he had opened it. "You remain here, in your cabin," he instructed Trove, who had seemed about to follow.

"I need to know about this." Trove was staring at her captain with a kind of sad horror—not an unusual expression for those remaining aboard.

"You must do as you're told and stay here," Scotonis repeated. "Or do I really have to compel you to?"

Trove nodded in tired acceptance but, as she turned away, Clay caught a look, directed solely at him, that seemed an amalgam of exasperation and panic.

Scotonis marched off down the corridor with Clay in tow.

Since Cookson's cabin lay on the same deck of the ship, it did not take long to reach it. However, it did take a long time for him to respond to their knock and to open the door.

Cookson appeared even worse than before—like a corpse clinging to a handle set beside the door, his motionless feet hanging just a few centimetres above the carpet. At the sight of them, he towed himself along a recently suspended network of ropes back towards his narrow bed. Clay scanned around. The place stank of sickness and death; used drug patches and blister packs of pills floated through the air.

"What is it?" Cookson said briefly, not even looking back at them as he paused by his urine-stained bed.

"Give me the counter," Scotonis commanded.

Clay reached into his jacket, his hand again brushing his gun before closing on the Geiger counter. He pulled it out, slapped it down in Scotonis's hand. The captain stepped forwards, right up to Cookson, switching the device on.

"So it's time, is it?" asked Cookson, turning.

It happened so fast that Clay had no time to react. The vicious crack of Scotonis's weapon rang out and Cookson tumbled back through the air, the side of his head gone and chunks of skull and gobbets of brain spattering the wall behind him. Clay reached for his own weapon as Scotonis turned to him, but the captain holstered his sidearm and walked back carefully, a sick expression twisting his features.

"There," he said, holding up the counter to show Clay the display. Cookson had obviously taken a huge dose of radiation—one which would have killed him sometime in the future, but had certainly killed him now.

"We should have questioned him," said Clay.

Scotonis shoved the Geiger counter in his pocket and stepped through the door. "To what end? He's been stopped, and that's all that matters." He eyed Clay bleakly. "Now you can get out of my damned sight. Get back to your cabin, and make sure you stay there for a while. I don't want to see you again until we're within range of Earth." Thereupon Scotonis strode off.

Clay stared at his retreating back. Something was wrong here, very wrong, and, if only he could think clearly, he felt sure he could work it out. He turned away and decided it politic to obey Scotonis, for now. Back in his cabin he could rest a little, take some time to ponder things. As he began moving, his gecko boots crunching on the floor, he began to think seriously. Why had Cookson killed Myers? Perhaps the doctor had picked up on Cookson's increased radiation dose? Perhaps Cookson wanted extra drugs, or even to exact some odd petty vengeance on the rest of the surviving crew for not being as badly injured as himself. Why had he killed the assessment team? Surely Cookson was the one with the least to gain from that, since he was certainly dying.

Clay entered his own cabin, stepping over to sit down before his screen. He needed data. Maybe he would be able to call up some cam footage of Cookson and thus try to trace his movements, but system log-on was dodgy. He found himself able to check on some things but on checking others, the system immediately asked for his password which, when input, just didn't work. Definitely something wrong. He checked further, then stared in horror at a screen partially blocked out by a password request. Numerous readerguns had been reinstated aboard, so had the cabin pain inducers.

"What the fuck?" he exclaimed out loud.

Perhaps it was the surge of adrenalin that cleared his mind. He now suddenly understood that it didn't have to be Cookson or Trove who had been killing people. Replaying events in his mind, he realized that the Geiger reading Scotonis had shown him had not necessarily come from Cookson, but could have been from Scotonis himself. So what was the captain up to? What did he want?

Clay sat back, staring at the screen. First and foremost, Scotonis wanted vengeance; he wanted Serene Galahad dead and, it seemed to Clay, the captain was careless of his own life in that respect. So what if the assessment team had reported the nuclear arsenal unusable, or maybe impossible to fire? What weapons could Scotonis use then? Of course: the *Scourge* itself. Scotonis wanted to drop this ship right on top of Galahad's head, but he knew that his crew would object to that. Fatalistic they might have become, but many of them still hoped for some reprieve—such as Serene Galahad being nuked out of existence, and a chance of survival for them in the ensuing chaos. Perhaps Myers had detected Scotonis's radiation dosage, or perhaps Scotonis had just killed the man who was managing to keep many of the crew alive. Certainly he had killed the assessment team so they could tell no one else whatever the situation was with the arsenal.

Pain inducers? Readerguns?

Scotonis intended to kill everyone aboard, and Clay had to stop him. He stood up. Good thing he had disabled his own cabin inducer . . .

The pain hit him first on the crown of his head, and spread down his body as if he was being immersed in boiling water. He screamed and stumbled for the door, realizing, even as he fled, that this pain was not at a disabling level but that he was being driven from his cabin deliberately. Out in the corridor, other crew members were stumbling along. The inducer effect was operating out here too, but much less so in one direction. Sobbing in agony, Clay stumbled away from the direction he would have taken to reach the bridge. Scotonis was driving them away; that was all.

Readerguns?

He heard them ahead, delivering three neat shots at a time, just as something slammed against his skull and dropped him into blackness.

7

WARP WEAPONS

Though the versions of the Alcubierre drive created by professors Rhine and Calder were intended initially for faster travel through space, weapons applications were not far behind. In this sense, these drive systems were the antithesis of the rocket engines preceding them, which were first developed as weapons-delivery systems before being put to less lethal uses. Calder's warp missiles, as he himself dubbed them, were specifically made to knock out the warp bubble of Saul's ship and deliver an EM pulse by an atomic blast, and their full potential was never fully explored. They were capable of exceeding the speed of light, but only for a brief time, since the internal Hawking radiation would soon damage their load. The thinking behind this was narrowly focused on the missiles being able to travel fast enough to intercept Saul's ship. It is perhaps fortunate that Calder decided on a test shot at Earth's moon at merely railgun speeds, for the amount of energy that would have been generated by an FTL shot would have been immense, perhaps enough to have turned the Moon entirely to rubble. Perhaps weapons like this are another reason why Enrico Fermi felt compelled to ask, "Where are they?"

EARTH

For a moment there, as Argus Station just shifted to a new orbit around the sun, Serene wondered if Saul was going to call her bluff, or was maybe even preparing to attack. Elkin had immediately foned to inform her that the drop shuttle re-entry vehicle was prepped and ready, if she wanted to board it. However, Saul had not attacked, but had run away as predicted.

"If he had stayed there, it would have been a stalemate," commented Bartholomew.

"Stalemate?" Serene enquired, turning from the astounding view across the construction station from Calder's apartment, which she would occupy during her stay here.

"Yes, stalemate," Bartholomew affirmed, glancing at Calder for confirmation.

"Work aboard Argus Station would have been halted while it dodged the shots," Calder confirmed. "He was lucky not to lose his smelting plants the first time round."

Calder's expression was bleak. He knew Bartholomew was right but did not want to himself imply any criticism of the dictator of Earth. Serene experienced a momentary disappointment with him, immediately followed by the rise of something predatory inside her, for she was sure he was hiding his fear behind that expression. Was this how the lion felt when faced with a crippled gazelle? Perhaps one day she would find out, if they could ever manage to resurrect those two species.

Right now she found her whole attitude to Calder changing. It was, she felt, sensible of him to show such caution now that his usefulness was drawing to an end. The infrastructure was all in place, the new drives were already being improved on by research teams and new ideas were blossoming. New ships could be built quickly, and none of these required Calder or the extravagant promises she had made him.

"Still not an adequate explanation for the word 'stalemate,'" she observed, her gaze drilling into him.

Bartholomew shot Calder an odd look and replied on his behalf, "The resource drain and the work involved here in feeding the railguns would have brought work on our own three ships to a standstill."

With Saul on the run, she felt she had won this round but, still staring at Calder, she declared, "Perhaps it would have been sensible for you to apprise me of this fact before we fired off those shots, Professor Calder."

He sat utterly still. Of course he dared not say, "I thought you knew what you were doing," because that would have represented too much of a criticism, and also because Calder had to be thoroughly aware of the presence of Sack, who had ensconced himself in a comfortable chair by the door but looked no less lethal for that. Then something clicked into place, and Calder's mouth clamped shut for a moment as his expression hardened in a way she did not much like.

"As I understood it, ma'am, you wanted to 'scare the rat out of the woodpile,' and those shots aimed at Argus Station were more in the nature of a salutary reminder to Alan Saul that he is not beyond your reach." Calder paused, appearing momentarily thoughtful. "If I misunderstood your intentions, then I can only apologize."

The raptor instinct inside Serene subsided, and she felt a momentary chagrin on realizing that she had just completely misread the man. She turned back to Bartholomew. "So, the crews are in training and the *Vision* will be ready for launch in just two weeks. Is it your intention to launch it immediately, or will you wait until the *Command* and the *Fist* are both ready?"

Now an earlier anxiety had returned. For a while the Hubble and other telescopes on the Core stations had simply lost track of the Argus and she had feared she had lost Saul or, more importantly, the Gene Bank data and samples. When the Argus warp bubble was again detected, heading way out, she'd felt a panic rising to choke her. He was running all the way, he was really going to leave the solar system . . . But, no, the station, or rather the starship in the making, halted at the Asteroid Belt where, the tacticians told her, it seemed likely Saul would be mining for further materials. But still an anxiety remained: she must not lose him.

"The *Vision* will launch the moment it is ready," said Bartholomew. "It will get as close as feasible to Argus, without engaging, and expert tactical teams aboard will relay data back to me. As I believe you are aware, it will be carrying one of the warp missiles. This is our solution to the warp-missile delay. Saul will not consider the *Vision* much of a threat and so will be unlikely to run. Most probably he will run only when the *Command* and the *Fist* set out, whereupon the *Vision* can use its missile to disable his ship for us."

"How will you know whether Saul is running or just relocating within the solar system?"

"That is a question to which the tactical teams are applying themselves." Bartholomew paused, grimaced. "Of course, we will not be able to know for sure whether he's running or not, which is why I've designated a perimeter beyond which he can't be allowed to go."

"And that is?"

"Effectively a sphere enclosing that portion of the solar system that lies within the orbit of Neptune."

"That's a large . . . perimeter," said Serene, aware on an intellectual level of the appalling vastness out there, but also aware that full comprehension of it lay far out of reach of her planetary-evolved mind.

"True," Bartholomew shrugged, "but it is a sphere that Argus or one of our own ships could cross in nine or so hours, and which one of Calder's missiles could cross considerably quicker.

I had considered expanding that sphere by a factor of ten. However, the chances of the missiles we fire at Argus hitting something else along the way increase by an appreciable factor too, and of course our supply of missiles is limited." Bartholomew glanced at Calder for confirmation.

"By the time the *Fist* is ready to launch, we should have been able to construct one more," Calder said firmly. "It's a matter of resource allocation. Making a warp missile is hardly like packing high explosive into a tube, or even making shaped charges around some fissile . . . it's not even close. They take a great deal of time and effort—both of which would now be better spent on getting the ships ready."

"If one is to suppose that three ships are actually required," said Bartholomew.

As the two of them started debating the relative merits of fewer ships and more missiles, Serene found her attention wandering. Damn, but it was so sterile up here, and abruptly she found the presence of these two men irritating.

"That will be all," she interrupted. "You both may leave now."

After a short shocked pause, Bartholomew abruptly stood up, gave a brief and oddly archaic bow. "Ma'am."

Calder stood up next, looking as if he wanted to say something further, but then echoed Bartholomew's bow before following the admiral to the door. Sack was already peering at her questioningly, but she waved a hand of dismissal at him too. She was tired of human company, and he just about qualified in that regard. Once they were all gone, she stood up and walked over to gaze across the construction station.

Yes, it was sterile here but this was, she felt sure, the environment that the bulk of humanity would end up occupying. Again she considered some of her earlier speculations about what final form those humans would take, while also considering the initial results of laboratory trials she had set in motion.

It was, she now knew, indeed possible to manufacture a virus capable of modifying DNA to her requirements. However, it would be the children of those infected who would have their lifespans shortened and who would die, without senescence, in an approximate age range of between forty and fifty years. Those with such shortened lifespans could have their span increased, however, by the constant administration of drugs. This same virus would not render the recipients infertile, but another virus could be made to achieve that—this infertility continuing into subsequent generations and also amenable to negation by drug therapy. It would also be possible to create vaccines for both viruses, even though, as she considered that, Serene could think of no one who should be so vaccinated beyond herself.

She, the state, would thus be in total control of human lifespan and fertility. Then, while technology continued to advance and as robots and expert computer systems shunted humans aside, the planet would never again be burdened with an excess population. She would, she now decided, hold back on this no longer, but move from laboratory trials to field trials the moment she returned to Earth. Previously, she had considered the possibility of excess population being used for human expansion into the solar system but, in reality, population control became more essential when such populations were moved into environments even more limited in resources than those of Earth.

Serene strolled back to the sofa and sat down, feeling buoyant again—but, as ever, only for a moment or two. She had the future perfectly mapped out in her own mind, but still a large blot marred that map: Alan Saul. Once she had dealt with him, no other human could ever be allowed to get so out of control. No other human would ever obtain such access to personal power.

ARGUS

The bulge of the dressing on the back of Alex's skull was a constant reminder of his recent trip to see Hannah Neumann. He kept trying to reach up and finger it, and frequently had to snatch his hand away once his gloved fingers rattled against the helmet of his heavy spacesuit. Apparently she could only take the biopsy, since that was a surgical technique that required little energy, but the cerebral implant would have to wait. All she had in stock were already assigned, and more needed to be manufactured. This could not be done yet while the whole station was conserving energy: the lights were turned off in the Arboretum, and it and the arcoplexes were now free-wheeling, with no energy being provided to their motors; similarly all manufacturing was closed down and the smelting plants were somnolent in their docks.

Alex felt a degree of relief about that. Even though he had decided to have the implant, the idea of someone cutting into his skull evoked vague and unpleasant memories of the numerous cerebral operations he had undergone back on Earth. Hannah Neumann had been swift to note evidence of this while she scanned his skull prior to the biopsy.

"It's not usually necessary to do this," she had told him, "but what lies inside your skull has been altered . . . isn't the same as standard human."

Standard human?

"So what does that tell you?" he had asked, gesturing to the 3D scan on the nearby screen.

"You've got a micro-wire net inserted to provide electrical stimulation to various brain centres, along with a system of micro-tubules through which various neurochemicals were injected to targeted points," she had then explained. "It's all a bit primitive—state-of-the-art about thirty years ago—and it's what they used to reprogramme you and erase your memories. There's also a lot of scarring from subsequent updates, along with the addition of a connector to both networks set in the top of your skull, under your scalp. I imagine you were one of the first: one of the prototypes."

"Thirty years from that tank," he had admitted, "but I don't know if I was one of the first."

"Putting an implant in your skull is going to require more extensive surgery," she had continued, "I'll need to remove much of what has been added, including a couple of chips that are constantly making neuro-blockers and other odd substances. Also, I must make some repairs and some reconnections. It could be that you'll then access old memories. It could also be that your character will change." She had paused, watching him carefully while displaying a hint of that suspicion of him that others aboard the station tended to show. "I'll need to put you under close observation, and you won't be able to go back to work for a while."

Now he was back at work, wondering if he really wanted to go through with that extensive surgery, and observing just what all the spare energy was being used for. He, Gladys, Akenon and Ghort, along with two robots under Ghort's control, were positioned on one corner of the platform made ready to take the Mars Traveller engine. The behemoth itself was sliding slowly past them, almost like an old-time super-tanker drawing past a dock. Such was its sheer scale that it seemed to Alex as if it was the platform he stood upon that was in motion.

The engine was angled in slightly, so its business end would pass through a circular gap allowed in the spherical superstructure of the spaceship. Their team presently waited by a slowly unwinding cable drum—one of eight positioned all across the platform. Once the shock-absorbing base of the Traveller engine passed the platform, every drum would then begin braking, bringing the giant to a halt, while impellers dotted across its surface would begin pushing it into position. Thereafter they would wind in cable to tow it down to its destined resting place.

"It's gonna come down on us like Goliath's boot," Gladys predicted, "and turn us into mush."

"Who's Goliath?" asked Akenon.

"Some fantasy game character," replied Gladys.

"Actually," interjected Ghort, "Goliath was a biblical character, as in 'David and Goliath.' And, considering the context, 'Goliath's sandal' would be more correct."

"Oh, yeah," concurred Gladys, "David was that guy with the spell-hammer and plasma rifle."

Ghort emitted a low moaning sound and banged the heel of his hand against the side of his space helmet. Alex supposed it was all very well having this instant mental access to the computer library of Argus, but passing on the knowledge thus acquired could be like . . . *casting pearls before swine.* He then wondered where that phrase had emerged from—and if it might have leaked out of one of those parts of his mind that Neumann seemed to think were now sealed.

Incrementally, the base of the engine came into view over the edge of the platform. Peering across at it, Alex again suffered one of those changes in perspective that seemed a constant while he was working in zero gravity. Now he felt as if he was standing on an elevator platform dropping past some monolithic factory complex. The dome-shaped pellet aggregation plants were now above the platform, while directly opposite him lay the big cylindrical fuel tanks, partially concealed by secured coils of cable and the tied-down fifty-metre-long hydraulic shock absorbers. As these slid past, the spherical start-up fusion reactors then came into view, and next the three-metre-thick layer of foam composite that had been attached to the now practically non-existent central asteroid.

"Braking now," Ghort announced.

The cable drums were computer controlled, so it was not necessary for anyone to do anything, nor had Ghort's announcement been necessary because they could all feel the sudden vibration through their feet. The cable from their drum—a five-centimetre-thick composite of braided steel and carbon fibre—drew taut over tensioning wheels, above the aggregation plants, to its point of attachment on the other side of the engine. Alex felt the platform push up against his feet as the weight of the engine tugged on it, apparently, as calculated, stretching the column below by nearly eight metres.

Behind the engine, picked out in work lights scattered along the length of the behemoth, clouds of water vapour became visible from impellers firing somewhere out of sight. The engine slowed like a giant train coming into a station, the foam-composite base rising a hundred metres above them, then slowly beginning to swing across.

"Check your tools," Ghort instructed.

Alex gazed down at the socket driver fixed by his feet, shrugged and picked it up, triggered it to watch the socket already in place spin, and checked its small alert screen. Nothing wrong, all perfectly fine . . . then he remembered to set it in reverse, since his next immediate job was to undo bolts rather than tighten them. Meanwhile, the robots under Ghort's control went over the edge and began hauling up beams and slotting them into sockets all around the platform and, now that the engine was out of the way, Alex could see over to the adjacent section of the outer sphere—directly on the level of the platform about a kilometre and a half away—where the new robots had conjoined themselves into golden centipede forms and were already building inwards the lattice wall that would connect to those same beams. When they were done, the wall would form a section dividing off the half-kilometre-tall hemisphere in which sat the Traveller itself—a wall that would require further strengthening before the engine could be fired up.

"All drums synchronized," said Ghort, "we're winding it in."

Did having an implant incline one thus to make unnecessary statements? Alex wondered.

The Traveller engine now lay perfectly in position above the platform, and it did indeed seem like a massive weight ready to come down and crush them. However, the tug they were to give it was but a small one for, though the platform and column below could take a great deal in the way of impact shock, they didn't want the engine to go bouncing away again. The impetus it was now being given had been precisely calculated so that the shock-absorbing layers, and a series of barbed fittings perfectly lined up below, would negate it.

"Cable detaching—go and get it, Gladys," Ghort instructed. "Akenon, Alex—get to it."

As Gladys launched herself up along the slackened cable, Alex and Akenon strode over to the motorized cable drum and at once began taking out all the bolts holding it in place. Necessarily, because of the huge load it had been under, there were a lot of them. Each bolt he took out, Alex carefully placed in the pouch on his belt, since losing a bolt resulted in a loss of pay—and, besides that, no one wanted heavy lumps of metal floating free when the Traveller eventually did fire up.

Shortly, Gladys was on her way back to them with the end of the cable, while the drum continued to wind in the slack. Using her suit impellers, she fell past, slowing beside one of the newly placed beams sticking out from the platform edge. Here she attached the cable end just as Alex turned a corner on the plate securing the cable drum in place. He paused to look up, saw that the base of the engine now lay only fifty metres above, and was steadily drawing closer. There was little risk to anyone, however, since it was travelling so slowly that anyone could get out of the way quickly enough. The only risk was that all of the cable drums might not be shifted out of the way in time, so the impellers would have to fire up again to stop the engine's descent.

"That's the one I was looking for," said Akenon, holding up the last bolt.

"Me too," said Alex.

By now, the drum had ceased turning and a slack length of cable arced its way over to where Gladys had attached the other end. Alex and Akenon followed this out, propelling themselves from the edge of the platform into open vacuum. Ghort followed next, one of his robots heading back, past him, to close its forelimbs around the spindle points of the drum and its motor. Even as it did so, and as he propelled himself out after the rest of his team, the drum started turning again, towing itself along the length of the cable towards the anchor point at the end, guided all the way by the robot, out from underneath the descending mass of the engine.

Grabbing one of the new beams, Alex attached his socket driver to it, then his safety line. He gazed up, past the great descending mass, towards the hole, five hundred metres away, out of which poked the throats of the fusion chambers. He recognized now why some had compared this device to the tower of an ancient cathedral, some place of worship, and felt glad to have retained his capacity for awe.

"No time for gawping," urged Ghort. "We've got work to do."

There was no conventional dimensionality to the virtual world, and so Saul's control over his nascent spaceship was no different wherever he actually located his physical self. But he still retained a human conception of power, where to be at the centre of things was to be physically present at that physical centre. At the touch of his mind, the armoured door swung open, leading into what personnel aboard were already calling his "inner sanctum." He stepped inside, leaving the spidergun outside.

No one had seen this place being built, for he had used only robots in its final construction or assembly. The central chamber within was circular. At one side a single acceleration chair hung in reinforced gimbals that were similar in appearance to an orrery, surrounded by curving panoramic screens. He didn't really need these screens but, as with much in his inner sanctum, like the swing-in keyboards and ball controls on the chair arms, they were a backup should he at any time find himself unable to access all the cams and computers of his new ship mentally. He also had to admit to himself that such *human* access kept him grounded; kept him from losing himself in the world of mind. The rest of the room, but for a cageway leading to rooms above and below, was empty space provided for his leisure, but which he'd yet to equip. Surrounding this central room were four more rooms, all interconnecting: a kitchen area mostly automated, a sleeping area he might never use, a washroom and toilet, and then a final area for storage.

Saul headed across the empty floor to the cageway, not yet required for going down because the room below was empty too—a museum and display area for which he had yet to obtain any exhibits—and now propelled himself to the room above. Here was part of the reason for Hannah's frustration in obtaining the right equipment for her production floor. The room contained five amniotic tanks with specialized cooling systems, also main-frame computing he could separate from the rest of the ship, a surgery containing the most advanced equipment he could obtain and which would soon be in use, small manufactories, robots and other high-tech items galore. Here he could do just about anything that could be done throughout the entirety of Arcoplex Two, though naturally on a smaller scale. He next walked over to the banks of cylinders running on their own independent cooling system, for here too he had moved Earth's Gene Bank, along with hard copies of the genetic data kept on file throughout the ship. Was he retreating here? he wondered. No, he was making himself a fortress. And soon he would move his backups here too.

Returning to the central room, he climbed into the array of gimbals and strapped himself down in the acceleration chair. Suddenly he found himself at a still point, his mind utterly clear, and allowed his consciousness to expand throughout the entire ship. He studied its spherical skeleton; the two arcoplexes, the arboretum cylinder and a fourth spindle for another arcoplex were the spokes of the old station wheel. Another arcoplex spindle under construction, which extended above, and the column for the Mars Traveller extending below formed the wheel's axle. He then focused on some of the detail of the engine itself, which had now been attached, both visually and also in the virtual world.

His new robots had finished constructing the lattice wall inwards from the exterior skeleton ready to attach to the platform for the Traveller engine, and currently human teams and older-style robots were bolting down hydraulic ram plates at the edge of the platform, and reeling out the last of the optics and power cables to reintegrate the engine with the ship's systems. In the platform-support column robots were now securing them selves to beams while other human workers began streaming away. They had been affixing pipes leading to the location where he intended to place auxiliary fuel tanks—which was a job that could now wait. Meanwhile, the engine warm-up routine and diagnostics had been running for some time, and soon it would be time for the dragon to wake.

Next Saul focused his attention upwards. Lying midway between the old station wheel and the upper pole of the ship was the location planned for the four main weapons. The two railguns were already in place and their magazines filling; most of the maser, which had previously seemed to be just scrap metal, had been salvaged and rebuilt. However, the fourth, uncompleted, weapon was what drew his attention.

Working with a team of twenty humans and forty robots, including two proctors, the Saberhagen twins had been building their plasma weapon there, but had now ceased work and locked everything down. Just like him with his empty rooms for future expansion, they had incorporated extra capacity to allow further development of their latest weapon. Studying their plans, Saul was impressed. Right at that moment, not even he could think of any improvements to make, and he was especially pleased to see that, while they had been installing the heavy electromagnets and power supply they had also detailed a team within Arcoplex Two to manufacture the plasma "caps." When completed, this lethal device would be able to deliver the Newton impact of a railgun, along with an EM blast and heat equivalent to a plug of matter magically extracted from the core of the sun.

Saul's main attention next strayed into Tech Central, which lay just above him. Le Roque was striding back and forth, his face sheened with sweat as he organized the lockdown of the ship. Those who had finished their work were busy ensconcing themselves in secure areas, all of them in either spacesuits or breach-survival suits. All loose items were being secured, the biggest chore being handled by humans in EVA units stowing the last small chunks of the Argus asteroid in an ore carrier, before internal cable-mesh sheets would be tightened down over them.

"I'm repositioning in six minutes," Saul warned him, "but this time I'll be using the Rhine drive, so there should be no problems."

"The drive?" Le Roque queried. "Why?"

"I can't use the steering thrusters to reorient."

As the man looked thoroughly bemused, Saul decided to put him out of his misery. "I need to reorient the axis of the ship ready for approach," he explained. "And, with the vortex generator running, we happen to be sitting in a massive gyroscope. I calculate it would take the output, at full power, of about four Traveller engines to counter the angular momentum."

"Ah, I see," Le Roque replied.

Because of the angular momentum of the vortex generator, it had quite simply become impossible to change the ship's axial orientation *at all*. However, that situation would change once the Mach-effect drive was operative.

As was his habit, Saul now checked up on those he cared most about or, rather, those he allowed his human self to care about. Hannah and Var he found huddled together in one of the mobile overseer's offices that had recently clamped itself down on the new lattice wall.

"That's not a particularly safe place to be," he observed to them.

"Argus Station . . ." began Hannah, then paused before continuing, "Nowhere aboard this *ship* is particularly safe."

The new usage Saul had tried subtly to promote—calling it a ship rather than a station—wasn't catching on very well, and he realized that at some point he would have to rename his vessel.

"Where *is* safe these days?" Var asked. "I suspect it's a very debatable point whether the chances of the people here getting killed are any higher than the chances of those on or around Earth."

"You know exactly what I mean, sister," replied Saul. "The insulation on an overseer's office is enough to withstand the extremes of space, but hardly adequate for where you are now." He made some rapid calculations. "The temperature inside there is quite likely to exceed sixty Celsius."

"We're prepared." Hannah reached over and opened a fridge door to expose numerous bottles of the same beer brewed in Arcoplex One and served at the Olive Tree in the Arboretum. "We have our suits with their cooling systems too." She tugged at the collar of her own suit.

"You should also check out the power supply here," Var added, her tone slightly superior.

Saul did so, and saw that it was ready to switch over to a stack of all-but-depleted rectifying batteries. As these converted the heat to stored electricity, they would produce a cooling effect. He also realized that these two women were ganging up on him.

"That's all very well, but what about stray debris, which would punch straight through those walls of yours," he lectured, feeling like a spoilsport martinet parent. "You are simply putting yourselves in unnecessary danger."

"Any asteroid debris will have to get through the station wheel first," Var observed, "and in that respect you are in more danger from them than us."

"You know very well I wasn't talking about asteroid debris but any still unse-cured items within the station wheel."

"I'm checking stress-sensor readings," said Var stubbornly, "and, like you, I like to be at the centre of any work I've been overseeing."

A sniping reference there to his inner sanctum.

"You can check stress readings from anywhere inside the station." Saul realized at this point that he had almost unconsciously assigned just a small portion of his human mind to this dispute and that it was now being merely stubborn and just wanted to win a pointless verbal contest. He reabsorbed it and, using pure intellect, assessed their chances of getting hurt as only a little above those in the wheel's accommodation units. And anyway, in the end, how dictatorial did he want to become? "We're staying here," insisted Var, "to see the show." She reached for a bottle out of the fridge, unscrewed it, then had some problems sucking out the beer. Apparently such bottles were meant to be drunk while the ship was under acceleration. In irritation she pulled the bottle away from her mouth and added, "If you don't like it, you'll have to send some of Langstrom's men or even some of your robots to remove us."

"That will not be necessary." He was already drawing himself away mentally, aware that, even though the human part of him would miss them if they got killed, their loss would have only minimal effect on his overall plans. "Enjoy the show."

It was time. Saul observed that the asteroid chunks were now fully secured and the EVA workers positioned where he wanted them. With a thought he initiated the Rhine drive. Magnetic fields torqued, space glowing red and then winking out all about the ship, and the momentary transition raised a feeling inside him like déjà vu. Afterwards, the stars blinked back into existence all around, and he checked the axial positioning of his ship. It was perfect.

"Mars Traveller start-up will commence in precisely two minutes," he announced to all throughout the ship. "You have only that amount of time to finish securing yourselves."

The Traveller engine reported just a few faults—ones that were more than compensated for by the redundancy in its systems. The seconds began to drag for him, but he suppressed that purely human sense of frustration for, if he allowed it to continue, the ensuing days of acceleration, course changes and deceleration would seem interminable.

"Firing," he finally announced.

The engine cleared its various throats and stuttered into life, then it bellowed as it blasted out a fusion flame half a kilometre long. Saul's acceleration chair reoriented within its gimbals, and the acceleration pushed him gently down into it. Debris seemed to be shifting all in one direction, but in actuality remained stationary relative to the ship. Saul focused on a single spanner striking the edge of Arcoplex One and tumbling on down, falling straight through the new lattice wall only a hundred metres away from Hannah and Var, before striking the outer skeleton on its way out, then deforming and melting in the glare of fusion flame.

"We're on our way," he whispered, purely to himself, for only now did some residual human part of him feel that the journey had truly begun. Then, just seconds later, serendipity took a hand and reminded him of everything that lay behind him.

"Fuck it," he said, preparing to shut down the Traveller engine and divert power throughout the station back into the Rhine drive; preparing to run.

It was a gravity-wave detector aboard the observation satellite orbiting parallel to Earth that alerted him. The anomaly was one it couldn't quite process because it lay so far out of the parameters its processing had been devised to handle. Secondary visual images came in as a confirmation—the tracking intermittent because the object was moving so fast. One of the three ships had left the Traveller construction station, engaged a drive similar to Rhine's creation and was now on its way out. He glimpsed jerky images of the shiny bubble of an Alcubierre warp heading directly towards them. Travelling at sub-light speed, it was behind the signals from the satellite, but it could still be here in well under an hour.

Extrapolating from the size of its warp bubble, he realized that it was the smaller ship that had left—the prototype—the one with a very vulnerable drive ring and with other combat disadvantages. Still, it was unexpected and it was a danger, for Galahad might have decided to send it to attack in the hope that it would cripple Saul's ship, even though the attacking ship would itself surely end up being destroyed.

"One of Galahad's ships is on its way out towards us," he stated over the intercom, "and it may be that we will have to run." Really, he needed to say no more, and there were no preparations that needed to be made since personnel who were already secure for the thrust of the Traveller engine were over-prepared for inertia-less flight. He could go right now, but he waited. If the other ship continued on this course, it had a very high risk of knocking out its own drive bubble on asteroid debris on the way. Saul calculated tactics. Maybe the intention was to use this approaching ship's drive bubble to stop or attempt to damage Argus, in which case it would have to halt first, then come in on a new trajectory.

"Paul," he said, "we have partial on the Mach-effect drive?"

"We do," replied that proctor.

"Give me stats."

The figures arrived in an instant, and Saul felt a brief sense of tension dispersing. If the other ship used its warp bubble to knock out his bubble, the problem thereafter would have been manoeuvrability, since his ship carried a lot of inertia so could not dodge bullets easily. However, the partial Mach-effect they possessed, combined with the Traveller engine and steering thrusters, meant that, after both drive bubbles were knocked out, the other ship would have no advantage in manoeuvrability. And if it came within range of the Saberhagens' weapons, it would end up being destroyed.

Next, as Saul continued to make his preparations, the other ship halted some half a million kilometres in from the orbit of Mars. For a moment Saul thought it must have struck something, but swift analysis of the gravity anomaly assured him that it hadn't. In the next moment he realized what was going on. Galahad had sent out an observer which, if required, might attempt to stop Saul leaving the solar system. Within a matter of weeks, if his estimations regarding what he could see at the Traveller construction station were correct, the other two ships would be able to follow. It was therefore worth spending time gathering necessary materials and continuing to build his ship inside the solar system, Saul felt—even at risk of attack from this small ship—for a long and perilous journey lay ahead. However, its two sister ships were not worth risking so, hence-forth, he would ensure the Rhine drive was sufficiently powered up to engage before those other two craft arrived.

"We're okay for now," he announced. "It's just an observer."

As he sent images to all the screens and delegated a smaller part of his mind to deliver a commentary on what had happened, he felt a deep disquiet. He had been too arrogant on occasion before, so what might he have missed this time?

8

IMPOSSIBLE ROBOTS

Even with our own comlifers and the rapid development of cyber technologies, nothing yet has been developed to match Alan Saul's "conjoining robots." The reasons posited for this by those working in robotics have been of the same tone: he was lucky, the reports on their efficiency were exaggerated, or even that the robots never really existed. However, that Saul was able to turn Argus Station into an interstellar vessel in such a short time is undeniable, and the truth is perhaps difficult to accept. Alan Saul was a genius even before he was turned into what we now call a comlifer. Every time we have tried to take people with similar mental advantages and do the same with them, the result has always been disastrous—the recipient of the cerebral technology and AI mental template rapidly self-destructing or going insane, or turning into a moron. We must accept that Alan Saul was unique and we should not slide into a denial of what he managed. For our future, and for the sake of us all, we must believe in the impossible—and similarly achieve it.

EARTH

The image on the screen was as clear as anything broadcast locally, yet its source lay millions of kilometres away, focused on by the telescopes aboard the *Vision* and relayed back here. Serene felt an extreme frustration with the clarity of it all, for screen images as detailed as this had been, ever since she assumed total power over Earth, ones of scenes she could affect at once. However, she could not touch Argus Station, she could not touch this ship Alan Saul was building, or at least not yet.

"What are they doing?" she asked tightly.

"Exactly what the tactical assessment predicted, ma'am. They're taking on more materials," said Bartholomew. "Professor Calder should be able to give you more detail on that."

Calder cleared his throat then, in dry tones, explained, "The Argus asteroid, as we see, is nearly all gone. It was mostly nickel iron, so Saul will need other materials. His EVA units, robots and work teams are currently using demolition charges and cutting equipment to take apart a rubble pile consisting of a wide variety of metallic ores, including some radioactives."

Calder leaned forward, past Serene, and made some adjustments with a ball control, bringing the focus in closer so that now they could see the conglomerate of the rubble pile lying just hundreds of metres away from the ship's outer skeleton. One-man EVA units—spherical machines sporting a pair of arms and claws to the fore—were ferrying chunks of the pile in through a gap in the skeleton, while robots of a kind Serene recognized were carrying other lumps across and down into a smelting-plant dock. However, there were things there she did not recognize, and the sight of them made her skin crawl. Things that looked like golden centipedes were crawling over the rubble pile and disassembling it.

"What the hell are they?" she demanded.

"Some new form of robot, ma'am," said Calder. "Now we've managed to get a close look at them, I can confirm that they are the reason the outer skeleton of the ship was built so fast—but previous images weren't clear enough for us to see them. I have my robotics staff analysing the data. An initial report suggests conjoining robots: single units that can join up into larger wholes."

"We have nothing like that?" said Serene.

"No," Calder agreed, "the degree of programming sophistication is not available to us as yet."

Serene turned on him. "And why not?"

He gazed at her steadily, obviously reassessing the snap answer he had been about to give. "We have been working with already known methods to build our defences and ships as quickly as possible, rather than apply resources to that kind of research and development, ma'am. However, now we know that Saul can build robots like this, and now we are close to completing the two remaining ships, I have assigned a team to work on a similar project."

She couldn't really fault that answer and spent a moment analysing why she kept seeking ways to attack the professor. He had created his own little realm up here and, though she couldn't detail a specific instance of it, she felt he resented stepping into second place while she was here. It seemed to her that he was always on the edge of rebelliousness, but his survival instincts kept restraining him. She turned back to the screen. "There was something about a space-plane launch."

Calder leaned forward again to make further adjustments. The view changed abruptly to show two space planes heading under power away from Argus.

"They will reach their target within a day," he explained. "They're heading now for a single asteroid consisting of mostly water ice and salts. We suspect the main targets there are the water and rare earth elements."

"They'll tow it back?"

"It seems more likely that they'll begin cutting it apart," said Calder. "Then, when Saul has all he needs from the rubble pile, he'll move Argus itself over."

"Then what?" asked Serene.

"Once he has the materials," interjected Bartholomew, "we reckon on him wanting power, ma'am. Tactical says he has three options: he comes back to the sun, he flees the solar system or he taps into some other solar system source, the mostly likely being the Io flux tube. That's where—"

"I know what the Io flux tube is, Bartholomew," Serene interrupted. "What I want to know now is how you plan to stop him and capture or kill him. I want to know how you're going to retrieve the Gene Bank data and samples for me."

"The initial plan remains unchanged, ma'am," said Bartholomew. "We are mostly reliant on Saul not knowing about the warp missile aboard the *Vision*. Once we've stopped him, we can thereafter ensure he never leaves by completely disabling his Alcubierre drive. We can then take our time with Argus Station— effectively putting it under siege."

The image on the screen had now returned to a previous setting and showed those same golden centipede robots seemingly eating an entire asteroid. The sight was disquieting because it made her wonder in what other ways they might have under-estimated Alan Saul. She also disliked how their whole plan relied on just one throw of the dice; if the *Vision* failed to stop Saul with its warp missile, the missiles aboard the other two ships would probably become redundant.

"When will *Fist* and *Command* be ready?" she asked.

"In twenty days now," Calder replied, trying to keep his voice level. He glanced at Bartholomew. "Sometime soon the troops' quarters will be ready, so they can go on board, then there'll just be some diagnostics to run."

Serene remembered how the troops were presently housed in the construction station, though why Calder had felt the need to mention them now she couldn't divine. Perhaps he also resented their presence on his territory. Whatever, she dismissed the thought.

Sitting back in her chair, she gazed around the command centre, which overlooked the two remaining ships. She eyed the Inspectorate personnel here and recollected that she had intended making inquiries about the number of personnel in the construction station, but just didn't currently feel inclined. She was tired of this place and had come to realize that her presence here tended to hinder people rather than impel them to greater efforts. Her order that the *Vision* should be launched as soon as possible had been obeyed, but she had since discovered the cost: eight people killed in accidents due to overwork and resulting tiredness, disruption in production here which, even though it had resulted in the *Vision* being launched sooner, had put back the launching of the other two ships. She decided she would stay until after that double launch, and until after the tug, which was currently being prepared, had brought in the *Scourge*. Then she would return to Earth and begin the genetic reprogramming of the human race.

SCOURGE

It was worse than when Scotonis had shot him with a stun round, but then this time, as well as something knocking him unconscious, he was recovering from inducement and his body was still full of slowly healing bones. He opened his gummy eyes to dim light and at once realized he was in one of the storerooms down near the troops" quarters. How he had ended up here, he had no idea, until Trove dropped into view, pushing a big plastic crate down towards the floor.

"How's the head?" she asked, and by her tone it almost seemed as if she cared.

"It hurts," he croaked.

"It was the only way I could stop you." She then smiled oddly. "And it provided some repayment for what you did to me with my cabin inducer."

Clay noted that her voice was slightly slurred, as if she was drunk, and her eyes were veined with red.

"But how did you stop yourself?" he asked.

She pointed over beside him, where a pile of used analgesic patches lay. It took him a moment to realize what this implied: she had used the patches to numb the pain from the inducers. That explained her apparent drunkenness, and also meant she must have known about the inducers beforehand.

"What's happened?" he asked.

"You realize Scotonis is insane?" she countered.

"Depending on your particular definition of sanity," he replied. "How did you know about the inducers?"

"He had them put back online because, so he said, under such extreme circumstances the crew might mutiny and try to bargain with Galahad. I agreed, but I didn't find out until just a few hours ago that he'd had further inducers installed in the corridors, and put the readerguns back online too." She shook her head, picked up a coffee flask and swigged from it. "I didn't start putting it together until the two of you visited me, then I started using my stash of patches. I stole them from Myers shortly after you used my cabin inducer on me."

"I'm sorry about that." Clay was astounded to discover that he actually meant it. "But what was your plan?"

"To kill Scotonis, but I couldn't get to him—the inducers he has around the bridge were set at full strength." She closed her eyes for a moment, obviously on the edge of tears, then her expression hardened as she opened them again. "They're all dead," she told him. "Scotonis murdered his entire crew."

"Why did you save me?" Clay asked.

"Pure chance." She stared at him woodenly. "Your cabin happens to lie between mine and the bridge, and all the other crew were further away. You were the only one I could reach after I stepped out. The rest were already running directly into his readerguns."

"And how did we both get here without being killed?"

"You again."

"What?"

"After you used my cabin inducer on me I opened up the back wall of my cabin to a service duct. Should it happen again I could thus escape without apparently leaving my cabin. I dragged you down the duct to end up here."

Clay pulled himself upright. "We have to stop him. We have to get to the bridge."

Trove shook her head. "He knows that we escaped." She pointed to the ceiling at a cam socket and intercom plate that Trove must have recently bashed in. "He was talking to me just a little while ago—basically telling me that any attempt to stop him would be futile."

"That can't be true."

"No?" Trove's answering sneer was familiar. "He's pumping the air out of every part of the ship but the bridge. If we stay here, we die. If we go after him, we die. Even if there was a way, via service ducts, to the bridge we'd then have to contend with his other protection."

"Don't keep me in suspense."

"He's managed to activate one of the spare spiderguns, and it's in there with him."

So that was it: every avenue to Scotonis was closed, and apparently they would soon suffocate down here. Clay gazed at Trove steadily, knowing that she wouldn't have given up. She reached down, undid the catches on the crate and flipped over the lid. Inside were cellophane packs of neatly folded white garments and, when she skimmed one over to him, he saw the integral hood with its clear plastic visor—and small oxygen bottle. "Survival suits," Trove confirmed. "The air supply lasts for twenty minutes, so should be enough to get us somewhere we can find some more air."

Clay gestured to the crate. "What about the bottles on the other suits?"

"Designed by committee," she stated, extracting a packet for herself. "The air bottles aren't interchangeable."

It reminded him of the time they first met and her sly comments about bureaucratic inefficiency. Then he had been offended; now he just accepted it. "So where's safe?"

"Nowhere, if he sends that spidergun after us," she replied as she opened her packet and shook out a survival suit. "But if he decides we're no longer a danger to him, we should be able to get aboard one of the troop shuttles and use the air supply there."

"Then we might be able to—"

"Get your suit on!" she snapped.

Only then did he realize that he was not getting enough air and hastily opened his packet, shook out the suit and donned it. The air supply kicked in immediately and the suit drew taut around him, straining against its quilt lines. A small speaker crackled beside his ear.

"You hear me?" she asked, her voice tinny.

"Yeah."

"Let's go."

She pushed open the door and they stepped into one of the hexagonal corridors of the hive-like troop section. Clay felt his stomach turn over when he recognized the unit numbers on the walls, and therefore where they were heading. The door at the far end of the corridor opened into what had since become a mortuary. Corpses floated in a haze of vapour, their suits bloated and burned. Brown flakes of what might have been boiled and dried-out blood swirled in the remaining air, clogging around vents in the walls. As she led the way through this horrible scene, Trove snagged an assault rifle and some ammo clips. Clay did the same, even though such weapons would be no use against a spidergun.

Beyond this area they moved into the hold, past munitions crates, a rack of ten-millimetre machine guns and the folded-up but terrifying shape of another spidergun. Clay was glad to reach the airlock at the end, which opened into the shuttle bay. Trove punched a code into the panel beside it and stepped back, but nothing happened.

"No way through there, I'm afraid," came Scotonis's distorted and tinny voice over his suit radio. "Sorry, but one of the Earth orbit tugs is now on its way out, so I can't have you giving the game away."

"We won't leave," said Trove. "We just want to keep breathing."

"Sorry, but I don't believe you, and I can't take that chance."

Trove stepped back from the door, scanned around, pointed to a nearby stack of crates and headed over. When she pulled off a lid, Clay immediately recognized the butter-like blocks it contained, with their inset timers: demolition charges just like the one she, Scotonis and Cookson had sent him out of the *Scourge* to use on an anchor that had failed to detach from Argus Station. She reached inside and lifted one of them out.

"The blast will kill you," Scotonis observed.

"If there was air in here to transmit it, probably yes," Trove replied, "but you yourself have conveniently been removing it."

She attached the charge to the door, then waved Clay away. They retreated all the way back through the hold and into the mortuary, before moving against the wall on either side of the door. Clay felt the wall thump against his back, then a few shards shot through the door, followed by a cloud of dust. When they returned to the airlock, the first door was gone, while the second was just clinging by one hinge and hung into the shuttle bay. They entered and headed straight over to one of the brick-like shuttles—a vehicle that bore more resemblance to a large armoured car than anything space-going.

"If you try to leave, you die," Scotonis informed them.

"I told you I had no intention of leaving," said Trove. "At least, not yet."

The airlock into the shuttle opened with ease and soon they pulled themselves up into a small storage area, behind rows of acceleration chairs ranged on what Clay perceived as both the floor and the ceiling. The vehicle was cramped and claustrophobic, but he was glad to feel the tautness of his suit relaxing.

"I have a railgun aimed just beyond the bay doors," Scotonis added.

"So what's your plan, Scotonis?" Clay asked. "Why did you feel it necessary to try and kill us all?"

"Ah, our political officer speaks."

Trove moved forwards, and Clay towed himself after her. "Yes, I speak," Clay replied evenly. "So, apparently you can't use the nukes?"

"Nonsense, of course I can."

"So why kill the assessment team?"

"They found a problem," Scotonis replied. "The entire launching system is wrecked."

"So you can't use them," Clay declared, as he followed Trove into the cramped cockpit.

"I can detonate them," Scotonis replied. "I just can't detonate them outside the ship."

Clay checked a display on the wrist of his survival suit. The air in here was good, so he reached up to open the visor seam, then pushed the hood off his head. Trove glanced at him, reached out and hit some controls on the console before them, then did the same.

"So I guess you plan to drop the *Scourge* on Galahad's head," she said, her voice humanized again.

"Not quite," Scotonis replied. "Once I've located her, which I'm trying to do now using radio searches, I'll drop the *Scourge* on her head and detonate all the warheads too."

"Surely you can let us go just before you do that?" suggested Clay.

Scotonis did not reply.

NEAL ASHER

ARGUS

Loaded down with tools, cable and long screw-in ice pitons, Alex descended slowly towards the asteroid. Flaky ice crunched under his feet but it offered little grip to the gecko boots of his heavy work suit, so he bounced off again. Floating up from the mass of ice, he surveyed his surroundings as he used his wrist impeller to bring him back down. Over to his right, the mooring cable stretched out towards the two space planes, which hung belly to belly, with a docking tunnel running between them. On the horizon of the asteroid beyond which the two ships lay, he could see some of Ghort's robots busily drilling holes to plant demolition charges. Alex felt it was no coincidence that all the humans here had been detailed to another task—that of preventing the chunks of the asteroid from tumbling away from each other—and that none of them was directly handling explosives. He considered that a healthy paranoia on the part of the Owner.

Using his implant, which Hannah Neumann had told him would only activate partially until the repairs in his head had fully healed, Alex called up the overlay. Immediately, a network of glowing lines etched out the major faults in the arc of ice lying ahead of him, but the map was incomplete. He banished the overlay then called it up again, and this time it reappeared with numbers hovering above the attachment points. The nearest one lay just a few metres ahead. He used his impeller to propel himself to that spot, unreeled his line from his belt and, clinging with one hand to a rock embedded in the ice, wound in his screw piton. Next, drawing the line taut to hold himself firmly in place, he undid the clip holding a heavy reel of cable at his waist and pushed it down towards the ice. Through a loop in the end of the same cable, he inserted another screw piton, but this one was half a metre long. He now unhitched his powered socket drive and, bracing himself against the ice, used a vibrating torque setting to screw the piton deep into the ice itself.

Now having finished dealing with this anchor, Alex surveyed his physical surroundings, called up various different overlays from the survey data of the asteroid, then paused to run a couple of searches, which were unfortunately limited to the computing available aboard the space planes. Yes, this was good; this expanded his horizons, put knowledge within his immediate reach and there would be more to come. But the greatest advantage was the one Neumann had not made generally known—and which you learned just before your implant went in. Alex now knew that he had a very good chance of living *forever*.

"Number twelve is in," he stated, wondering how much wiser he might become in a thousand years.

"So you managed not to turn yourself into a helicopter," replied Ghort jovially over his suit radio.

"I managed it," said Alex, gazing along to the next anchor point, and noting again that Ghort seemed very reluctant to open implant-to-implant communication with him. He had learned that such communication tended to carry greater nuances, that some of what lay behind the words uttered tended to transfer over. This, Alex surmised, was the reason for Ghort's reticence in that respect: in using such communication it was more difficult to lie.

Alex picked up the reel of cable, detached his line and, clutching the reel's spindle, used his impeller to send himself towards the next anchor point. This was no easy task since he needed a lot more impetus to get himself moving, and to keep moving, and the heavy cable now unwinding tended to put him off course. Arriving at the illusory number hanging over the surface, he anchored the cable with another piton before stretching the next length of cable to the next point. Soon he would have to return to the base of the mooring line leading out to the space planes just for more cable. Finally, when he and others, including Akenon and Gladys, were done, the main chunks that the ice asteroid would be separated into, once the demolition charges detonated, would not fly off into space. That was the theory, anyway.

Ten hours later Alex was back aboard one of the space planes, which had acceleration chairs only in a forward section, behind the cockpit, for Ghort and his team; while the section behind had been turned into a temporary living accommodation, and the one behind that into an enlarged hold for their equipment, including Ghort's robots. Alex, Akenon and Gladys already sat strapped in to watch the show on the big screen on the forward bulkhead.

"There goes the line," said Gladys cheerfully, as the plane jerked and they saw the mooring line on the screen slacken into an arc. A moment later a motor thrummed somewhere and the line began to snake in.

"We're keeping the docking tube?" asked Akenon.

Akenon seemed to have some kind of resentment for the team in the other space plane; he seemed to get offended when they came aboard this plane. This apparently was something to do with a failed affair and the loan of some station credit—Alex was unclear about the details. It all seemed very human and petty, and was certainly far below the concerns of Ghort and the similarly implanted team leader on the other plane, for they remained in constant communication. They tried to hide it, but while conducting implant-to-implant conversations they gave away the fact that they were talking by their facial expression and inadvertent gestures. Thinking of Ghort, Alex now glanced behind. If their team leader did not come soon he would miss the show. He returned his attention to the screen.

The ice asteroid hung in void, now static in relation to their space plane. When they first approached it, Alex had thought it looked vaguely like an anvil, albeit one that had partially melted. Their present perspective showed nothing of that shape—just an irregular lump of dirty ice. Alex used his implant to key into general com and the limited computer network around them, and thus picked up on a countdown.

"Ten seconds," he stated.

"Sure thing, O omniscient one," said Gladys.

Alex instantly relayed an audio recording of the word into a search to get the meaning. He guessed Gladys's vocabulary was the kind you picked up if you constantly played VR fantasy games in your time off.

The count dropped to zero and the asteroid expanded, blowing out clouds of ice dust, then came a flash, sending rainbow colours skittering over its surface.

"What the fuck?" Akenon exclaimed.

"Complex ices," Gladys explained, before Alex could do any research. "They fluoresce as they turn into normal water ices, and the demolition charges will have caused a bit of that."

"Thank you, O omniscient number two," said Akenon.

Alex stood up, the image on the screen now replaying in some part of his mind. The asteroid was heaving like some big beast taking a breath, becoming deformed, clear fragments visibly moving but the cables preventing it from flying apart. As he opened the door into their living quarters, he saw the mooring line snake out again and its explosive harpoon imbed itself into one of the larger chunks. Later they would have to return to detach the cables in preparation for those same chunks to be hauled inside the Owner's new ship.

No sign of Ghort.

Alex moved on into the recently enlarged hold and at last spotted his team leader. Ghort was standing beside an open crate and, from his distracted expression, was obviously communicating with the other team leader. Alex walked over and waited politely, just as when someone was using a fone. His gaze strayed to the crate, which was the same one the demolition charges had arrived in. There were four charges left inside. Alex would have thought little about that had not Ghort, upon suddenly realizing he was not alone, turned round and casually closed the lid.

"You missed the show," said Alex.

Ghort tapped his own head. "I was watching."

Alex acknowledged that statement with a nod, then paused as something massive dropped into his mental compass. It lay thousands of kilometres beyond the ice asteroid, and weighed heavy in his mind through its wealth of connections, data, possibilities: what had once been Argus Station, but was now turning into an interstellar vessel, had come as close as it could by relying on the Rhine drive and was now firing up its Mars Traveller engine. Only able to access a small amount of all that lay available, Alex felt he understood Alan Saul so much more now, and understood why he had chosen that title "the Owner."

Turning away from Ghort, Alex wondered if any of the demolition charges inside that box would soon go missing, or if some had gone missing already. He decided he must try and find out where they would end up, and whether Ghort required expert help to deploy them. He now had an intimation of what his team leader's plans might be, and decided that he wanted to be included. All Ghort needed to do was trust him fully.

Alan was ever so careful not to infringe her territory, and Var was sure that sometimes, when she made any mistakes, he overlooked them just so long as they did not impinge upon his overall plans or threaten to result in danger. However, despite his diplomacy, she knew for certain that what she was doing he himself could probably now do with only some designated portion of his mind. That rendered her expertise impotent and, indeed, *impotent* was the best way to describe how every other "expert" aboard this ship was feeling.

The section of lattice wall she stood upon, adjoining Arcoplex One, had been turned into some weird alien rockscape consisting of numerous chunks of asteroid crawling with those giant golden centipedes busy securing them in place. As she looked up to watch a chunk of dirty ice being driven into the ship's skeleton by impellers and human workers wearing EVA units, she reflected how those workers were now better off than the experts. They, at least, were finding ways to advance and adapt within the increasingly alien and frightening environment of this ship. All the experts, however, were thoroughly aware that they could never again be the top in their field, and that the ultimate expert here was always looking over their shoulders. That was with one exception, perhaps.

"It doesn't matter what kind of security you use in computer tech," observed Hannah from beside her, "since there's always someone who will find a way to circumvent it."

Var glanced at her. "So you know what it is?"

Hannah glanced up from the vacuum-format e-pad that she had stuck on the surface of a chunk of asteroid consisting of metallic bullet-shaped chunks, like belemnite fossils. "It's an encoder rather like those used in subnet hardware. A group of the chipped have set up a—until now—secret method of implant-to-implant communication."

"Should I be worried?"

"I don't know." Hannah shook her head, which made a visible gesture in the VC suit she wore, but was something Var could not achieve in her heavy work suit. "I think it highly unlikely that Alan is unaware of this."

"Are you aware of this, Alan?" Var asked.

"Yes, I am aware of this," he replied.

The immediacy of his reply did not lead Var to think he had been paying close attention to her and Hannah. That was just some piece of software—rather like one used in the more user-friendly fones—responding to a question directed at him. Doubtless some further piece of software, presently recording every public and probably every private conversation aboard the ship, had immediately dragged up the previous content of the exchange between Hannah and Var for his instant inspection. Of course, he did not respond to every question directed at him, just to those he considered important and relevant. That assessment was probably carried out by yet another piece of software, or a subsidiary thought process, since within him the difference wasn't easily defined. She wondered if he knew that the replies he gave were just enough to promote the idea of his being godlike, ever present and ever watching. Of course he knew.

"What are they using?" Hannah asked.

"It's quite simple," he replied. "The encoder attaches to their relays, and provides a list of icons they can select to contact anyone else with a similar encoder."

"And you've cracked those codes," Var suggested.

"In a way . . ."

"So what are they saying?"

"They are saying they must build the groundwork of their rebellion cautiously, and that, since an escape to Earth would only result in them being captured and killed by Galahad, their domain has to remain here, aboard this ship," Saul explained. "And for them to be truly free aboard this ship, the autocrat currently in charge has to die."

"And you allow this to continue?" Hannah asked in exasperation.

"What would you have me do, Hannah? Have them thrown in an adjustment cell, or killed, or perhaps sent over to you to have their minds wiped?"

Studying Hannah's expression, Var saw it transform from exasperation to weary horror.

"No," Hannah replied, "there always has to be a better option."

"It's just talk," he continued, "and talk cannot hurt me."

"They've managed to put together this hardware," Var protested, "and mere talk can easily turn into something else." She felt he was again being irritatingly dismissive and arrogant.

"And should it do so, I have something in place ready to counter it," Saul replied. "I wait in the hope that they will see what others receiving implants and backups saw at once and so clearly. I wait in the hope that they will cease to behave as children."

"Who are they?" Var asked. She certainly didn't want such people working on anything important, and she was damned if she wanted to leave everything to her brother. She didn't believe the myth he was creating about himself and, as she finally admitted to herself, she didn't really trust him.

"That I will not tell you," he replied. "Don't you have other things to occupy your time right now?"

Suppressing a snappy reply, Var glanced up. More EVA units were now on the move above, travelling up along the length of the newly erected arcoplex spindle. And, when she turned on her visor display and inspected a work-order flow diagram, she saw that the new transformers were now being moved into position. Of course, if she had taken the time to get her own implant installed, she would have been aware of all this much sooner.

"Work to do," she said to Hannah, before she launched herself upwards.

As Saul watched Var head away, he briefly dipped again into the communications between the would-be rebels, but everything worthy of note was already being flagged in a continuous recording. He checked these latest flags and noted that Ghort and two others had been discussing Alex. Ghort was still unsure about this member of his work team, but the others were insistent that Alex must be recruited. In their eyes he possessed the training and skills they needed and, being the last surviving clone of Alessandro Messina, having him on their side would send out a powerful message during further recruitment. Ghort had to question whether that message would be a positive one, and so their discussion had continued. Saul calculated that they would shortly make their first approach to Alex who, though emotionally less complex than most other human beings, was very smart in many other respects, and would respond positively and join them, just as Saul had predicted.

He next watched the final chunks of ice being ferried in and roped down amidst the asteroid matter on the lattice walls of the station wheel. This even distribution would reduce distortion of the warp bubble, though there was a small chance they would lose another chunk of the docking pillars. Meanwhile, Var was now ensuring the locking down of the transformers being installed at the upper pole of the ship.

As he watched through nearby cams, he reflected how he had handled his sister's most recent . . . error. The transformers were heavily insulated, as were the cables leading inside from them. The insulation Var had intended to use had been more than adequate to deal with a potential two megawatts running through the station, but were not sufficient to deal with any of the possibly huge fluctuations above that, so Saul had found it necessary to intervene. However, at the same time he had deliberately speculated with her on the insulation requirements of the space planes that would serve as the anode and cathode they intended to plug into the Io flux tube, so her annoyance was ameliorated by him accepting her suggestion that they use old Mars Traveller solid-fuel booster tanks retrieved from around Jupiter for that purpose. She had, in essence, responded as predictably as Alex. Saul hadn't even been disappointed, which told him that all those parts of himself he still defined as human were now less so.

Saul briefly considered how, even before Hannah had put the biochip in his head and before he loaded Janus, he had rather stretched the concept of what the likes of Hannah would define as human. Now his *human* aspects were changing even further as he evolved mentally. He retained the survival instinct, but knew he was growing more and more distant from ordinary human concerns. He had moved beyond contempt, beyond boredom, beyond exasperation. As he was now, he knew that he would have much more closely analysed his previous almost instinctive decision to rescue his sister from Mars, and perhaps decided to leave her there. And now he was seriously considering the benefits and disadvantages of maintaining a human population at all aboard what had become his ship, and considering it very carefully.

The last chunk of ice set on course for its final position, the EVA workers were departing, leaving Saul's robots to rise up from their plain of boulders and field it. His ship now possessed much more water than its occupants required, but Saul was thinking both towards the immediate future and far beyond. As power became available, the ice would be melted down and piped in between the blast walls and layers of composite armour that now filled the outer ring, around the vortex generator. Then, at some point in the more distant future, when the new arcoplexes were built, he had decided that one of them would become a mostly aquatic environment and therefore much of the water could go there. He visualized a cylindrical sea with land masses positioned at either end, perhaps dotted with islands between over a central barrier designed to contain the pumps that would shift water from one end of the cylinder to the other, to mimic the effect of tides. It would be a curious environment for the spectator—with the sea curving up on either side around the spindle lights— and one that would take some technical know how to balance out properly, especially when using anything other than the Rhine drive.

In that same cylinder he would utilize Gene Bank samples and data to construct a marine ecosystem. Perhaps it might be possible to resurrect extinct species like the dolphin, though anything larger would have to wait until he extended his ship into something the size of a moon, so it could contain larger cylinders. However, perhaps by then he would have had time to look into some interesting possibilities related to Rhine-drive technology and have developed that old staple of science fiction, artificial gravity, and therefore not need cylinder worlds at all.

The ice was down in place and secure, the EVA workers gradually docking and heading back to their accommodation. Var had checked the security of the new transformers, and dispatched the EVA workers there to their homes before attaching herself to a portion of the outer cage that gave her the best view. Hannah, meanwhile, had returned inside, since perhaps one viewing experience close to the engine flame was enough, and her own esoteric concerns were again occupying her thoughts. Le Roque was busy overseeing the now rote lockdown procedure required before a firing of the Traveller engine. All seemed to be operating like a smoothly oiled machine and Saul felt no need, or inclination, to deliver any warnings before he finally fired up the engine again.

The fusion flame glared as bright as the sun, and charging levels rose as rectifying batteries were bathed in the sudden light and heat. The column supporting the engine shortened, but stress-sensor readings showed nothing out of expected parameters. Var whooped in delight, the sight of the Traveller engine's power never getting old for her. Slowly, the ship began to move up towards the periphery of the Asteroid Belt. It would only take minutes to bring them to the point where solar system maps showed their clearest run on the two hops to their destination. As the minutes passed, Saul considered various plans for the other new cylinder world. Perhaps all the tropical ecologies could be transplanted there from the old arboretum, which would definitely solve some of the heating and insulation problems. Perhaps this new cylinder could be filled with moist tropical life . . .

The time arrived, and Saul engaged the Rhine drive without shutting down the Traveller engine. The effect was an astounding colour display on the interior of the warp bubble, and the production of some exotic particles that Rhine himself was already studying, having been forewarned. The ship moved, at a right angle to the thrust of the Traveller, but since that engine was now effectively firing within its own universe, it had no effect on their course in the outer universe. Heat levels within the bubble rose rapidly, while rectifying batteries distributed throughout the station sucked it up and converted it, dumping charge into super-capacitors, ultra-capacitors and other forms of storage. Saul's robots literally bathed in it as they also topped up their depleted supplies. Some of the asteroid ice sublimated, creating a fog within the ship's skeleton, but one that soon blew away as the warp shut down.

Next, Saul shut down the Traveller engine. At the cost of the tritium fuel that was now becoming depleted, he had now effectively recharged the entire ship. He looked around, seeing Jupiter as a slightly larger star far away from them round in its orbit, discerning Mars as hardly visible without magnification and the Asteroid Belt as a haze slewed about and below them.

Again the Rhine drive kicked in and dropped them into what was effectively their personal universe. Saul counted down the minutes as the drive took them up close to the speed of light, closer than they had ever been before. Hawking radiation flooded the ship's skeleton, and Saul observed an effect as close to perpetual motion as was possible as the power the drive used was replenished by the charging of rectifier batteries. Beyond the speed of light, would they rectify out more energy than the drive actually used? This was an issue Rhine had been considering at some length, but neither his nor Saul's maths was up to the job. Something new would have to be invented once they had collected enough data, which Rhine was gathering even now. And certainly there was no such thing as perpetual motion, so the cost would have to be paid somewhere, somehow.

Saul allowed his attention to range once more through his ship, taking in detail, assessing conversations, keeping his finger ever on the pulse. He saw Langstrom, Peach and one of the mentally reprogrammed, the *repro* Manuel, sitting playing a game of three-sided chess on their linked computer screens. This was a pastime all the police still aboard the station seemed to be enjoying, and this particular game was part of a tournament that Saul predicted Manuel would win. Hannah was already aware of this odd effect in some of those whose minds she had wiped: a tendency to borderline autism.

Tick-tock, time passed, though its effects were curious and monstrously difficult to calculate.

"Paul," said Saul, "tell me you're ready."

"You know I am," replied the proctor.

Something new to try, monitored by eight proctors scattered throughout the ship. Saul had left it just for them to handle, since he was reluctant to let such advanced minds continue solely with the many menial tasks with which they had been occupying themselves.

Paul was out on the station-wheel lattice wall, acting as a node in the network the proctors formed: closely connected to seven of his fellows but only loosely connected to Judd and to the proctor that had named itself Tull, both of whom now completely controlled Robotics. Again Saul resisted the temptation to insert himself into that network and spy on the minds he had effectively created.

"Two minutes," Saul said, noting the Mach-drive coils already drawing power as a mackerel sky spread across the inner side of the warp bubble.

"Yes!" shouted Rhine, slamming his hand down too hard on his console, then sucking his stinging fingers afterwards. One fragment of a loosely connected theory proven true.

"I'm not sure that when you're happy, I should also be," said Le Roque, walking over to peer at the equations on Rhine's screen, frowning, then moving away again.

"Get ready," Le Roque announced next to the entire station, "though what for I don't know. No one quite knows what happens next."

They were close to their destination: laser measurements showing a slight distortion of the warp bubble caused by a huge mass in the universe adjacent to their small and temporary one. Saul made direct adjustments to the vortex generator that effectively turned the warp through a hundred and eighty degrees, then shut down the drive. They came out of warp still carrying the impetus given by the Traveller engine, but now taking them in the opposite direction relative to its previous thrust. The ship shuddered, stabilized, EM fields reaching out and feathering towards infinity, pushing on the surrounding universe. And the ship accelerated. Saul now sent images to every screen presently not in use for some other purpose. Old Jupiter gazed at them with a vexatious red eye while they slid past veined Europa, whose pallid gaze lingered upon its secret oceans within.

9

REVOLT!

The more authoritarian a society becomes, the more there are of the disaffected who are "fighting for freedom." Conversely, the more liberal a society is, the more people you will find who are fighting to exert authoritarian control. Oddly enough, in both cases, they are the same people. The freedom fighter is just a revolution away from becoming a dictator. The concerned and righteous, who wish to make some changes for the good of all, are just an election away from pulling on their jackboots. Never trust the activist who wants to change the world for the better, because their "better" is usually the worse for you.

ARGUS

"It just doesn't feel real," said Dr Da Vinci, his gaze fixed on a screen showing Jupiter looming close, and its moon Io closer still. Close enough to identify three volcanoes pumping sulphurous plumes out into space.

"It isn't real." Hannah injected her latest cerebral biopsy into a sample bottle, then eyed the doctor from Mars. "It's all light-and-colour enhanced and the perspective shortened so we can see both. It all looks very CGI out there." She gestured to the screen.

"I don't mean that." Da Vinci reached up to finger the small dressing at the back of his skull. "I mean the speed of it. When I shipped out to Mars, I had months aboard a Traveller to begin to appreciate the scale of it all—to know that I was travelling an immense distance." He stood up from his chair. "How can we possibly be in orbit around Jupiter? How can we be sure the images we see are real?"

NEAL ASHER

He was being rhetorical and philosophical—a tendency which was only a recent trait, according to the report Saul had given her access to. Da Vinci was a lost soul trying to make sense of it all, but he was also a highly intelligent and capable lost soul. On Mars he had hated the interference of Political Officer Ricard and lodged objections that would have seen him put into an adjustment cell on his return to Earth, had that eventuality not been cancelled for all of them at Antares Base. He had seemed to concur with Var's takeover there, but had ultimately backed Rhone and, according to Var, had cried over the corpses that generated.

Hannah grimaced. She had initially felt a bond with Saul's sister, but now that was evaporating. Var Delex was as ruthless as Saul which, in both cases, stemmed from the need to survive. However, with his continued transformation, Saul's ruthlessness seemed to have disconnected him from base human motives, while Var's instincts seemed to be wrapped up in resentment, paranoia and some silly need to compete with her brother. Yes, Saul was now a dangerous creature, but Hannah knew that he was no longer vengeful. Var, however, she realized, was not someone to be trusted with the kind of power Saul presently wielded.

"How can we know the images reflect reality?" Da Vinci repeated.

Hannah studied him, perfectly understanding his difficulties. After all that had gone before, he had been whisked halfway across the solar system in a partially constructed interstellar vessel by a man who seemed to be breaking every law imaginable, including those of physics. He was, Hannah felt, very much a fellow traveller, for like her he had all the moral objections and shied away from the harsh solutions.

"You know because of *that*." Hannah held up a finger. "Listen."

"I don't know what you mean," he said after a moment.

"Of course," said Hannah. Being fairly new aboard and this being his first time in Arcoplex Two, he had no idea about the sounds he should be hearing. Hannah could hear it, however: the creaking and low groaning, the occasional snap and ping of a joint realigning; the ship yielding under the unsubtle touch of Jupiter—the same touch that generated the seismic shifts and volcanoes characteristic of Io. It would get worse too, once they moved between Io and Jupiter.

She shrugged. "You can hear the gravitational stresses," she explained, "but if you really want the truth, then get a spacesuit and go outside. You'll soon lose all your doubts, believe me."

"I've no doubts, as such," said Da Vinci, "I'm just divorced from the feeling." He now took a look around her laboratory, his expression turning slightly

154

acquisitive. "I was told that, after you'd taken my sample, you'd have something for me to do?"

The station's medical personnel were underemployed, for the moment at least, so there had been no real position for him. However, he was certainly skilled enough to join her in working here. Quite likely he would have moral objections, and ones she wanted to hear, which was why she had saved until now what she revealed to people just before their biopsies.

"First you need to understand what this is really for." She held up his cerebral sample.

"Not for growing graft tissue?" He seemed baffled.

"Come with me." She led the way through the door leading to her production floor, which was starting to fill up with equipment and now had a scattering of employees, some of whom were even human. As she explained about the backups and pointed out the various tanks in which bioware was growing, and a small chip-etching plant busily at work, his gaze flicked attentively to every detail. As they reached the far end, he stepped over to a tank inside which resided something organic shot through with shiny wires and plastic optics, suspended in a cloudy fluid at the centre of a web of power and nutrient feeds. He placed a hand against the toughened glass, then gazed at her questioningly.

"Not here, then?" he said.

"What?" Hannah asked.

"The clones."

That was it, right there: he'd gone straight to the heart of it. Hannah wondered if it was truly ergonomics that had made her decide to keep the cloning facility separate from operations here. Perhaps she just preferred it to be out of sight, so that her conscience would not nag her quite so severely.

Da Vinci stepped back from the tank and turned to study the perpetually growing rack of backups.

"So we can live forever—or at least for longer than our natural span," he said. "But, as always, such developments have their price."

Hannah grimaced. "I understand the thrust of your remark, but what precisely is a 'natural span'?" She shook her head, experiencing a tightening in her torso like the precursor to one of her panic attacks, and felt it loosen. "Our natural span, if you wish to call it that, is long enough merely for us to breed and pass on our genes, then everything after that is just a bonus. People have lived well beyond that span for centuries."

NEAL ASHER

"I think you understood my meaning." He gazed at her steadily.

"Perhaps . . . but what do you reckon the price might be?"

"One that the clones will be paying, perhaps?"

"If you could elaborate?"

"Tank-grown clones are human beings who should be allowed the right to life. By using them as receptacles for these"—he waved a hand towards the backups—"you are effectively destroying that life."

Perhaps this was a mistake. Now, moving on from "natural span," he was talking about "right to life." Was this man a doctor of medicine or one of divinity and philosophy? Her own feelings about those backups and clones related more to the cheapening of the life a person owned, and the potential for abuse.

"One has to ask where the line should be drawn," she said. "Does a sperm have a . . ." Hannah paused, seeing a slight twist to his mouth and suddenly remembering something more in his report. He had very firm views on this subject, ones that were in sympathy with her own: human life was nothing special; it was the human mind that was important. "Yes, you had me there, for a moment," she finished.

"I just wanted to be sure we are on the same page." Da Vinci then nodded towards the backups. "So which one is his?"

"By 'his' I presume you're talking about Alan Saul's?" Hannah felt a resurgence of the anger she had experienced only a few days ago.

"I am but, being at more of a remove from him than you are, I'll continue to call him the Owner." He paused. "It seems the politic thing to do."

"They're not here," she said tightly. "Two days ago he had them removed to his inner sanctum, along with some cloning tanks, if my reading of the ship's manifest is right. He doesn't trust us mere mortals . . ."

"I feel the need to point out," said the Martian doctor, "that we are all potentially immortals now."

"Still . . ." said Hannah grudgingly.

"I'd also have to wonder whom I would trust, if I were in his position." He gestured to the backups, as they strolled towards them. "You tell me I'll also have one of those sometime in the future. Well, in that future I, too, can see myself wanting to take it away from here and lock it in the safest vault I could find. In fact"—he looked around—"the lack of security here concerns me."

"He's always watching," said Hannah.

"That's not enough," said Da Vinci. "I'll no more rely on demigods than I relied on the non-existent gods from which some people claim our morality descends."

Hannah felt herself beginning to smile—an unfamiliar sensation. She was finding herself starting to like this doctor from Mars. Var Delex had been company of sorts but, despite her great intelligence and drive, she seemed shallow. Da Vinci seemed to have depths she could drown in and, more importantly, he was male.

"So will you do it?" she asked, leaping ahead to test just how much was going on in the mind behind that quite attractive face.

"Yes," he replied, "I'll run your cloning facility. I'll grow your body replacements for you and I'll even look into something you don't seem to have considered yet: the cryogenics required for keeping those spares on ice."

Hannah grinned widely, till it felt as if her lips might split. "There are state-of-the-art cryogenic pods aboard Messina's space plane, so you can work with those."

"I will." He nodded sharply, then turned to study her. "But still, the idea of growing clones makes you uncomfortable, as do all the implications of your work here. I'd suggest that is the real reason I'm here."

"In a sense," said Hannah suddenly sobering. "I'm in undiscovered country here, and I at least need someone to point out the direction of the sun to me."

"And the Owner cannot do that."

"He knows right from wrong, but his morality is harsh and unforgiving."

"Is there any other morality available to us now?" Da Vinci swung away to survey their surroundings again. "To fret over what is right or wrong is a luxury that has to be put aside once questions about survival come along. We can debate these things interminably, but in the end how many people have refused these backups? How many would set the chance of eternity against some questionable morality and still choose the latter?"

"I think we should take this debate to the Olive Tree," said Hannah, only in the last instant changing her proposal of location from her own room.

He turned and touched a hand to the base of her back. "Yes, let's do that."

Hannah smiled at him, starting to get used to the sensation. For a second her gaze strayed to a nearby cam, as if challenging any watcher to comment. But, of course, Alan Saul was no longer subject to such human frailties; he was out of reach and, if she was honest, had been out of reach since he had stepped out of the Calais incinerator.

* * *

The room was devoid of visible cams or other forms of surveillance, so Marsin had assured him. They could talk freely here; they could discuss subjects none dared raise while under the watchful gaze of Alan Saul. They apparently ran a debating group here, and Alex must be properly assessed before he could be allowed to join.

Marsin, a slightly chubby Asian with a generally friendly demeanour was, in view of his history, not quite what Alex had expected. The man sauntered over to the two-seat sofa in the cramped apartment and sat down, picked up a remote control to turn off the wall screen, then gestured with the remote towards the chair opposite. Alex sat down, too.

"On Earth we were subject to a worldwide dictatorship," Marsin began. "We could dream of being free but in reality we knew that the only way to personal freedom was by acquiring power, and in trying to do so we just enhanced the power of the state."

So what exactly is freedom? Alex wondered idly, impatient for him to get to the point. However, the question stirred up memories embedded in his mind which were now, as Hannah Neumann had told him, beginning to shake themselves free. He clearly recollected a doctor, who looked very much like Marsin, slicing into his head and then the horrible feeling of his scalp being peeled back and the subsequent grinding of the bone saw. It was unbelievably agonizing, but he was unable either to scream or to move.

"Painkillers interfere," the man had explained, "but perpetual wiping of his short-term memory during the process gives us the same outcome."

"I know because I have an interrogator who uses similar techniques," Messina had replied.

Alex had been able to see the Chairman just at the edge of his visual field, arms folded, his expression showing mild interest. Then came a jump, a hiatus, whereupon he *remembered* forgetting the initial cuts, and returned to a world of pain, then another jump found him waking up on his bed in his small cubicle, and feeling a strong resurgence of his love for and loyalty to Chairman Messina.

"So there we were, clawing our way up firmly embedded ladders, when we were dragged away," Marsin was saying. "Dragged away from the slavery we knew and made subject to the whims of yet another dictator." Marsin shook his head. "We can never hope to be free here."

Alex reached up and touched his skull, the psychosomatic ache fading. He shook his head and focused properly on Marsin. For all his high-sounding tone, Alex had no recollection of Marsin fighting to keep the Subnet online, being part of the revolution, or hoarding arms in preparation for a fight for his rights and the rights of his fellow man. However, having run a lot of close security for Messina, Alex had encountered this man before, and now, after things were freed up in his head, recollected him as the toady aide to Delegate Lamont, and knew that he had only escaped mind-wipe here because he had always made damned sure that no responsibility for anything could attach itself to him.

"And yet we had more freedom than you, Alex," he said, "so you must feel more deeply what we are feeling now."

Patronizing twit.

Alex had expected Ghort to make the approach, but perhaps they used the likes of Marsin initially because whatever inner council they had, and it was certain they had one, considered Marsin more dispensable. The man had also set himself up as the go-to guy for the disaffected, being very vocal in his criticism of the Owner and the regime aboard the station. He was acting as a filter—perhaps in place to weed out those whose disaffection was only temporary.

"I agree, we can never be free here, but then I also question if there is anywhere that we can be," said Alex.

"Freedom must be actively strived for," said Marsin vaguely.

"So how do you propose we go about that?" Alex asked.

"There's nowhere we can escape to, and even if we could get to Earth, we'd end up dead or in adjustment."

"We must strive for freedom here," Marsin observed, becoming a little more specific.

"I don't see the Owner turning this ship of his into a democracy."

"We don't call it a ship—we call it a station—and we don't call him the Owner, since to do so would be acceding to his will and accepting that we are *owned*."

"We?"

"Before I can tell you any more I need to know where you stand on this issue," said Marsin. "If you are happy to be one of the supine occupants of this station gratefully receiving the trifles Saul dispenses, then we may as well end this conversation now."

"I wouldn't be here now if I didn't think there were matters to discuss," said Alex, "though I'm unsure that such discussion will get us anywhere."

"Discussion is a beginning." Marsin waved the remote control airily. "But after that beginning, what do you yourself think should be done?"

"Saul will never stand down," said Alex. "Like all dictators, he will cling to power even to the point of destroying what he has power over." He paused in reflection: maybe best to get it out in the open now. "Saul had Alessandro Messina mind-wiped and then had him taking part in a military action that resulted in his death, so, as the Chairman's clone and being conditioned to protect him, I have to say that my feelings are strong. The only way to free ourselves of Saul is to bring him down, and the only way we can do that is by killing him." There, it was said. Alex grimaced as another clear recollection slid into his mind: one of him walking into a room where four younger versions of himself sat around a table, clad in hospital whites, with their skulls shaven and covered with scars, trying to play cards but their attention straying, their hand movements jerky, and two of them drooling. There had always been failures, and it had always been best to get rid of them quickly. On that occasion Alex had used an electrostun abattoir tool so there would not be so much mess to clear up afterwards.

"Much the same conclusion we have all come to." Marsin nodded, but he was still watching Alex very carefully. "However, Saul is very powerful and if we move against him we must do so with the utmost caution and precision."

"Secure communications would have to be first priority," Alex opined. "The only reason Malden's revolution wasn't still-born was because of its secure subnet communication."

"And upon gaining a secure method of communication?"

"Organization, command structure, arms caches and some sort of assassination plan." Alex paused. "I would also suggest that recruits be organized into cells of four or five with only one of those able to communicate with the commanders. You wouldn't want just one fuck-up to result in the whole network being taken out."

"We already have our cells," said Marsin, now moving beyond simple debate. "The problem here is the technology being developed by Hannah Neumann, and effectively controlled by Saul. Anyone captured who possesses a link to command could be mind-reamed for information."

"But," said Alex, "you must ensure that no one within the cells actually knows who they are talking to."

"True, but all that secrecy makes both organization and recruitment a very difficult task."

"You have two choices, then," said Alex. "You must do it quick and dirty, sacrificing secrecy, or you must play a long and slow game."

"Our choice has been for the former," Marsin told him. "It's our contention that, once Saul takes this station out of the solar system, our chances of succeeding against him will rapidly diminish. We need to strike while he is still uncertain of his power."

Quick and dirty . . . Yes, Alex now remembered persuading certain revolutionaries on Earth of that course, resulting in the death of some delegates who had been an irritation to Messina, followed very quickly by the deaths of the revolutionaries themselves. He sat back and folded his arms. So, this was no debating society, then. He wondered if they'd actually killed anyone yet; if any potential recruits had decided they didn't want to be involved after hearing too much. During the recent frenzy of construction, there had been two deaths. Could it be that one or both of them had not been accidents at all?

"So you have a plan?" he asked.

"I need to first know if you're in."

Alex studied the man, realizing that perhaps there had not yet been any killings, because usually the recruiting process was slower and the weeding out more precise. However, he understood that his own recruitment was to be "quick and dirty" and that therefore the revolutionary command had already contemplated their first killing. Marsin was undoubtedly armed; his body language gave that away. Alex reckoned the remote control he continued to hang on to must control something other than the screen—probably something hidden in the chair Alex sat in. "I'm in," he said, "and, if possible, I want to be in at the front end."

"You want to be the one who pulls the trigger on Saul?"

"I do, since then I will have paid the debt owing to my past, and can move on."

As Alex was discovering, his past was full of debts and many of them could never be repaid.

"Though some of us have had reservations about you," said Marsin, smiling now though still holding the remote control, "most of us were sure your response would be such." With his free hand, he rooted in a pocket of his loose-fitting shirt, took out a flat square of dull metal of the kind Alex had seen Ghort surreptitiously attaching to his relay, and tossed it over.

"What's this?" Alex asked, after he had briefly inspected it.

"You attach it to your relay." Marsin pointed to the polished cube hanging on a thin chain around Alex's neck, "and that turns it on. It encodes to the recipient any transmission you send, and you'll learn how to use it quickly enough."

"And who are the recipients?"

"Your cell commander is your work team leader, Ghort."

"As I suspected," said Alex, as he pressed the square device against the side of his relay. He wasn't going to pretend he did not know about Ghort, not now he was about to use a communication method that made attempts at lying difficult.

"You suspected Ghort was considering rebellion?" Marsin asked, his lips not moving and the words generating inside Alex's head without the intervention of his ears.

"Suspected is too mild a term," said Alex. "But then I have been trained to look out for stuff like this, which is why you'll find me useful."

"And you still want to be at the sharp end?" enquired Marsin, implant-to-implant. "You still want to be the one who kills Alan Saul?"

"I want to be the one who kills him, yes." Alex paused for a second, watching some remaining tension fading from Marsin's expression, as he finally released his hold on the remote control. "But, tell me, do our cells only consist of those who are chipped like us?"

"Yes, because we can only be sure of each other like this."

Alex felt that the revolutionaries had misunderstood the title "the Owner." Hadn't they realized that Saul did not claim ownership of them but of this ship he was building, of the technology that surrounded them—claiming it in the same way as any pre-Committee human being would have claimed the ownership of his own body. If they had understood that concept, they would not have put such a heavy and dangerous reliance on one piece of technology inside that technological body. They had much to learn, these people, and yet probably not enough time.

When they arrived here, the ship had possessed its supplies of superconducting cable, but not enough. One of the smelting plants—now permanently sited in its dock since most of the ore-transport tube below had been dismantled and most of the carbon composite cable it had been wound out on had been taken away and cut up for other purposes—had, after many days, come close to solving that lack. Saul had watched his robots transport the selected chunks of asteroid matter, out of which the requisite materials could be refined, into the plant where older-style robots had fielded them and fed them into the gravelling machines that led to the smelters. Within an hour, other machines had begun braiding fulleride and copper oxide filaments, spiral-wrapped in HTS tapes, to provide the extra cable required. This, because of a lack of rare earth elements, was not completely superconducting but would be good enough for the job in hand.

Meanwhile, the two space planes that had earlier launched from Dock Two—the same craft that had taken out the two work teams to slice up the ice asteroid—were now arriving at their targets. Saul watched through cams as one plane matched course with and descended upon a Mars Traveller solid-fuel booster tank—one of hundreds currently in orbit about Jupiter. He felt docking bayonets clunk into place in holes prepared in the booster tank for precisely such retrieval, then felt in his bones the space plane's engines labouring to pull its load to a new course. Just at that moment, the second plane docked with its own load, and likewise began shifting it.

"ETA approximately twenty hours," one of the pilots declared unnecessarily. "Work team heading out."

Saul had selected the personnel with more caution this time. The likes of Ghort and the other wannabe rebels could not be trusted with fielding and bringing in such large and heavy objects. Some inadvertent accident might result in one of those tanks ending up on a fast trajectory towards the centre of the station itself, therefore towards Saul's inner sanctum, and he had no intention of making things that easy for them.

He watched as the work teams aboard each space plane headed out onto the booster tanks, dragging with them space-plane steering thrusters— specially insulated, electronically hardened and made to run on a simple fixed programme. The tanks even had places ready for the attachment of these, and Saul silently thanked the Committee Mars Missions steering and focus groups for their frankly astounding foresight, though it occurred to him that it might have been Var, as she had worked her way up to become overseer of the construction station, who had ensured all this. Of course, neither Var nor any others in those numerous political groups could have foreseen such thrusters being used to position the fuel tanks in the Io flux tube.

They would probably have quite rightly pointed out that, subject to fluctuations of thousands of amps in a massive current, the thrusters would simply fail. Saul, of course, expected them to fail, but not before they'd done their job of positioning these tanks—a job that would have scrapped the space planes themselves and killed everyone aboard.

"Le Roque," said Saul, and he watched as the technical director looked up in surprise at the nearest cam in Tech Central. "Are we all secure?"

Le Roque took a moment to think this over. Saul knew he wasn't reviewing the most recent preparations for another move of the ship under Mach-effect drive, but deciding on whether to ask why Saul was asking. Le Roque knew everything was secure, and he knew for certain that Saul knew.

"Yes, we're ready," he said, without moving his lips, before returning his attention to his three main screens.

What else to ask?

Saul knew, in a perfectly intellectual way, how those aboard felt he was becoming remote and disconnected from them and their human concerns. Le Roque's response was a perfect illustration of this and, in that moment, Saul realized he must re-engage so as not to go completely out of touch, at least for now. With great difficulty he again breached the division between his human self and the rest, and allowed the human part to continue the conversation.

"I ask," he said, "because it seems this would be a good time to begin reassessing all flight preparations. The possibility of becoming complacent should never be ruled out."

"The procedures are fine," replied Le Roque, "and complacency only gets banished when someone discovers the penalty for not following them."

Rather cold, really, but then Saul had noted how all the chipped personnel developed a decidedly callous streak shortly after implantation. This had nothing to do with the implants themselves, but was all about how those recipients perceived how the implants *should* affect their behaviour. Humans—sometimes the novelty of their foibles could become wearing.

"How are you finding *your* new implant?" Saul asked.

"More efficient," Le Roque replied, still without speaking out loud.

"I'm so glad," said Saul, casting irony into the void.

"And how are you finding your implant?" he asked Rhine who, rather than stay in Tech Central, had returned to his own lab in order to monitor the Mach drive's effects.

"Chipper!" Rhine almost yelled.

There were of course exceptions to that dehumanizing effect. In some, certain traits became emphasized. In Rhine that trait just happened to be lunacy.

"How far along are you with your new theories of everything?"

Rhine looked up at the nearest cam. "Hypotheses," he stated, then returned his attention to the screens. The line between hypothesis and theory had always been one where the arguments were bitterest, and where scientists might sacrifice their careers on the altar of empiricism.

"I am about to move the ship," Saul announced through the PA system, "to a lower offset orbit between Io and Jupiter. That's a position we should be able to maintain."

He reached out and uncoiled a thick optic cable, with a full teragate plug, from the arm of his acceleration chair and plugged it into the socket in his skull. Rather than switch straight over to this new connection into his ship's systems, he ran programs to ensure only a gradual change-over as they approached the Io flux tube.

"Remember, people, that all radio communications will gradually be replaced by laser coms. Usually you wouldn't notice any difference, but in this case the coms that route through the ship systems will be affected by the massive EM output of the flux tube."

Saul moved the ship like a human mind guiding a human body. The drive systems were his locomotion, like in running, walking or swimming. He did not consciously work the vector calculus and check against inner maps of the solar system, just as no runner, walker or swimmer would have to make conscious calculation about what they were doing. He did not have to micromanage everything and he knew how to delegate within the complexity that was his mind, his body. He engaged the Mach-effect drive and pursued Io, dropping steadily into a lower orbit. He felt the tidal tug of Jupiter through stress sensors in the structure all around him and in a sensitive gravity detector sited between a pair of lattice walls, and began to read the vastly smaller pull of the distant moon. He gazed upon a gas giant and its satellite, in the human spectrum and beyond, and through electromagnetic vision saw the part of the flux tube he had chosen as a bright tornado curving from the moon to the north pole of the gas giant. Getting closer to it, he felt induction currents building up in the structure of his body—his ship—and felt systems correcting for that, just as a human body might correct for heat or cold or drunkenness, and he sweated electrostatics.

Unlike with a human body, Saul's vision could extend inwards wherever he wanted it to. He saw Angela Saberhagen halting to stare at her reflection in a glass window pane and trying to smooth down hair that had begun to puff out like a dandelion head, and now crackled under her touch. He saw Hannah Neumann and Dr Da Vinci engaging in sweaty sex in her laboratory, almost as if she wanted to do this somewhere she knew Saul could be watching, and he realized that the human part of him should feel jealousy if he only allowed it the freedom for such petty emotions.

He saw the proctors all gathered together now in a deserted part of the outer wheel of the old station. Linked together hand to hand, they stood in a row that faced towards the EM shield hardware ranged about the inner walls, and were somehow experiencing the charge of the station, but again he resisted the impulse to snoop. He saw static discharges leaping from strut to strut in vacuum, and an eerie blue glow appearing in certain parts of the cylinder worlds. And he saw Rhine suddenly become animated as the sensors under his control detected ball lightning rolling round the rim, in line with the business end of the EM hardware and passing in front of the row of proctors, who now watched as if they had been expecting it.

However, such effects were not as bad as they could have been, for though the Mach-effect drive was operating through the ship's EM shield, the shield itself was set at its maximum. Though humans could have survived in the sleet of radiation and ionized particles occurring close to the flux tube, they could never have survived the genetic damage that ensued.

Then he was in place, held there by the drive pushing lightly on the surrounding universe, the ship poised beside an ionic storm that might be invisible to human vision, but certainly not beyond the compass of their instruments. Rectifier battery storage was making good use of these surges, but also dumping energy almost as fast to power self-correcting systems and diagnostics throughout, and as repair robots drew power in order to hunt down and repair blown components. Saul now felt a fuzzy edge to his thinking, to his very being, as the computers fought this disruption. He gazed outwards at the approaching space planes and their loads, watched Var and her teams attaching the ends of the new cable, stored on drums twenty metres across, to EVA units ready to be rolled out and attached to the old Mars Traveller booster tanks. And he waited, and his robots waited, and the crew waited, all in that before-a-thunderstorm sense of expectation that he knew would never end so long as they were here.

SCOURGE

He'd drifted off to sleep four, maybe five times? Clay couldn't quite remember how many times, nor how many days they'd spent inside the cramped shuttle. They were still okay for water, since they'd found two VC suits aboard that recycled their urine and would do so indefinitely while power was still available, and food wasn't a problem either. However, the inside of the shuttle was now getting a bit ripe, even though they'd found a sealable plastic container to use as a toilet, and even though enough water was available for sponge baths. Shuttles like this one simply weren't designed for lengthy occupation.

Trove was again tinkering with the shuttle's computer. She had a couple of hatches open in the cockpit and was busy swapping out chips. She also had computer code frozen on one of the two screens set into the instrument panel. She reckoned she might be able to access the cam system of the Scourge, though how having a grandstand view of their catastrophic entry into Earth's atmosphere would help them, Clay had no idea.

"What about the radio here?" he asked, trying to think of something helpful, but realizing this was a question he must have asked her before.

Trove stared at him as if he was an idiot. "Like I said, the *Scourge* is EM shielded. Our only chance of getting a signal out would be to send it via the ship's computers to an exterior aerial, and he's locked them all out."

"But you're accessing the computer system right now?"

"Yes," she replied with exaggerated patience, "but the aerials will still be locked out and we'll only get an exterior view if he allows it."

"So what the hell do we do?" he asked leadenly.

Yeah, another question he had asked on numerous occasions, and a sign of the general malaise he was sinking into. Physically he now felt a lot better; the pain he had experienced a little while after they had arrived here—once the effect of the painkillers had begun to wane—was fading, but mentally he wasn't so good. With his body seemingly recovering, it was almost as if it felt it could expend some of its renewed energy on dropping him into a deep depression.

"We've already discussed this," she snapped. "We try to run when he goes after Galahad. The main engine will fire up, so observers will know there's someone still aboard, so it won't matter if this shuttle is then seen leaving." She paused for a second. "I see no reason why he wouldn't just let us go."

Clay grimaced. Scotonis had slaughtered his entire crew and committed himself to suicide, death and destruction, yet Trove was talking about the man making a rational decision. Clay thought it unlikely that the captain was in the frame of mind to allow anyone a get-out clause.

"There," she said, clicking the two panels closed again. At once the code began to scroll, then, after a moment, the second screen blinked on to show a holding image. It was the old space-exploration logo of a space plane penetrating the ring chain of the united world, all its links differently coloured to represent the various regions of Earth. This was something that Galahad had ordered to be changed into something more representative of her regime, but an idea that had been shelved until the future, when resources could be spared for such ephemera. Clay felt that her efficiency and the speed with which she managed to get things done would have been admirable, had she not been as barking mad as Scotonis.

"There, what?" he asked.

She clicked down a ball control and the logo disappeared to divide the screen up into twenty numbered squares, which Clay knew comprised just one page of a sequence of five. Each square was a cam view taken from either inside or outside the main ship. Dragging the cursor over each one expanded it, and by this method Trove worked through each of the cameras aboard the ship, pausing at corridors that had been turned into abattoirs filled with the floating dead, or bits of them, and where the drying blood on the walls had turned brown.

"Bastard," she muttered.

After a while it became evident she wasn't yet finding what she wanted, and Clay enquired, "He's not letting you look into the bridge, is he?"

Just then, for the first time since they had boarded the shuttle, Scotonis addressed them. "Of course I'm not letting you look into the bridge. I require my privacy." He paused, then continued, "Perhaps you'd like to check out the views through exterior cams twenty to twenty-eight."

Trove immediately selected number twenty-eight, which revealed the distant blade of a drive flame. She switched to twenty, because every tenth cam outside had telescopic functions and better resolution, and focused in.

"They've sent a tug to collect us," she stated. Scotonis gave a lethargic handclap in response.

The vehicle was three hundred metres long and essentially a squat Mars Traveller engine wrapped in towing and grapnel mechanisms, fuel tanks and jutting the combustion throats of hundred-year-old hyox rocket motors, with the small bubble of a crew cabin lost amidst all this panoply. Clay recollected that space tugs like this usually carried a crew of three, two of whom were unnecessary—the Committee had never considered it a good idea to allow just one person control of so much power, unless of course he was a delegate or the Chairman himself. The three consisted of the pilot, who was the only one really needed, his second officer to whom was delegated the minor job of observer, and a political officer specially seconded from the Inspectorate complement in Earth orbit.

However, since Serene's ascension to power after Saul's ruthless thinning-out of Earth's bureaucracy, such political oversight there had become impossible and, so she claimed, unnecessarily interfering. So perhaps there was only the pilot aboard.

"If we could only get to that shuttle," he said, imagining them secretly getting themselves aboard, then onto whatever Earth-orbit station it docked with, then onto a space plane heading down to the surface . . . No, that just wouldn't run.

"That shuttle will hard dock," announced Scotonis, and Clay wished he had kept his big mouth shut. "You'd have to suit up and exit through one of the hull airlocks, every one of which I control. Of course you could blow the airlock, as you did before, but then you'd need to face the anti-personnel lasers positioned out there."

"But surely, Scotonis, this is going to screw up your plan," said Clay. "How can you go after Galahad when you're under tow?"

"Ah, our political officer shows his ignorance again," said Scotonis. "I can just release the docking bayonets from here and pull away."

"Listen, Captain," said Trove abruptly. "I know you've committed yourself to killing Galahad, but why must *we* die? Once you've located her, you've got to put this ship on a re-entry course, and she and everyone else will know that there's still someone aboard. Just let us go—our leaving won't interfere with your plan."

All so utterly reasonable. Clay sighed and gazed at the screen again. The tug was much closer now, and he could see its steering thrusters firing. He watched it roll, bringing into sight a hard docking plate with protrusions that were probably the bayonets Scotonis had mentioned. Clay could see no sign of an airlock, so the captain probably wasn't lying about them needing to take a space walk.

"If you leave now," said Scotonis, "you'll need something to bargain with—something that might stop whoever is in charge up here from either shooting you down straight away or throwing you into an adjustment cell as soon as they get hold of you."

The Gene Bank data Saul had transmitted to them in an attempt to forestall their attack and which they had not relayed to Earth, but which they had retained as a bargaining chip? Clay felt a sudden surge of excitement. Did Scotonis really intend to release them?

"You can't find her, can you?" said Trove.

Clay gazed at her in puzzlement. What on Earth was she on about?

Trove continued, "You're coming up blank on your radio and computer searches. I would guess that any information on her present location has been suppressed, simply because that location isn't completely secure, for some reason."

"You were always the most perceptive of my command crew," Scotonis declared. "Her last known location was Messina's Tuscan home, but data traffic there has recently waned. She could be, as you say, in a less secure location or else taking one of her tours."

"You need something to draw her out," said Trove, "and that's where we come in."

"Precisely."

"I'm still not getting this," Clay interjected.

Trove turned and gazed at him. "We offer the Gene Bank data and demand to speak to her. We try to extract guarantees from her, some promise of safety, something perhaps witnessed by delegates and supposedly legally binding."

"But there'll be no guarantee. She'll just go back on her word once she has the data, and have us either killed or adjusted."

"Of course." Trove nodded.

"So what's the point?"

"The point, Mr Ignorant Political Officer," said Scotonis acerbically, "is that if she communicates with you aboard the shuttle, I have a greater chance of tracing where her signal is coming from, and to where your signal is being routed."

"Not just that," said Trove. "Considering its original source, she'll probably want the genetic data transmitted directly to some form of secure storage close to her. She won't want to risk having something Saul might have attached to it on Govnet."

"No," said Scotonis, "I disagree. The data will go straight to secure storage at Messina's home. But she will not necessarily be there."

"Even so," Trove insisted, "that might be another way of locating her. If I was her, I'd load the data to multiple secure locations, and I'd be confident that one of them is one I can carry with me."

"Perhaps," Scotonis allowed.

They were going to live, Clay was now sure of it. They were going to survive this. Of course, they'd probably end up as prisoners on one of the space stations but, once Galahad was dead, everything would change. He felt sure that he and Trove could come up with a plausible explanation as to how they ended up with their chips and collars removed, and why the mission to capture Argus Station had failed. Somehow the blame could all be laid on Scotonis.

"How will it work?" he asked. "With the data, I mean."

"I'm going to return system access to you," decided Scotonis, "so that you can access it remotely and begin transmission of the data. And just maybe it will all have been sent by the time I drop this ship right on top of Galahad's head."

Clay suddenly realized that he could also download the recording he had shown Scotonis: the one showing how Galahad was responsible for the Scour. He could work that angle too, and get them free. Scotonis had found out, and had wanted vengeance for the killing of his family, which was sort of true. He had quickly taken complete control of the ship and forced his command crew to have their implants removed. It was all the captain's fault . . .

The ship jerked, shuddered, and he felt vibrations through the deck of the shuttle and through his seat. Returning his attention to the screen, he saw that it was now completely filled with a close-up view of the tug.

"When can we leave?" he asked.

"In another two days . . . when we are closer to Earth," Scotonis replied. "And I'll even let you go if I do locate Galahad before then. There has been enough death already."

This last comment might have given Clay hope for the captain's remaining sanity, were it not for the fact that the man intended to drop a spaceship on Earth and detonate enough atomic bombs to erase an entire country.

171

10

THE KING SLEEPS

The idea of cryogenic hibernation had been a staple of science fiction long before the hypothermic chilling of accident victims or battle casualties to prolong their lives became a standard medical technique. Research into this area stuttered to a halt under the Committee because saving people by reducing their temperature, either from injuries received or for some future time, was considered redundant. The thing about human beings, the Committee delegates felt, was that there was always a ready supply of them. And their own crack at keeping the Reaper at bay was better ensured by other medical research, the results of which they were already witnessing. But this changed under Chairman Messina. So strong was his urge to fend off his own death that he made sure funding was available for any research possessing the slightest bearing on that aim. Quite swiftly, then, the previous research was resurrected and, by the end of the Chairman's time in office, viable techniques were available to put human beings in cryogenic suspension. Hence the rumour, which is connected to an old legend, that Messina didn't really die on Argus Station, but sleeps in some cold coffin in a cave underground, awaiting his time to be woken and then to rule again. This is why some people still actively search old underground installations in quest of him, with ice picks ready to hand.

ARGUS

Controlling a robot was a weird experience that one of the other rebels, who once trained security mastiffs back on Earth, had likened to controlling a well-trained dog. The one presently following on Alex's heels, as he walked out along the pitted surface of the old Mars Traveller booster tank, seemed to confirm that description. Presently it was clutching a metre-square fixing plate in its forelimbs, but shortly Alex needed it to set the plate to one side, grind a flat area down to clean metal, to get a good electrical contact, then attach the same plate. Alex quickly reviewed the simple series of tasks he had designed, noted subprograms kicking in to correct his errors or iron out inefficiencies, and to flag changes awaiting his approval. These basic changes were little different from those that would appear while he was programming on a screen or, so he was told, through one of the more modern fones that linked to the visual cortex, but how it worked inside his skull was something completely new.

Computer programs translated into accurate visualizations of actions within his head, while changing visualizations changed the programs but also caused alternate menu links to appear. What degree of roughness did he want the flat surface ground down to, and what tolerance on the ensuing flatness? These details loaded automatically with reference to the schematic in his skull, but awaited approval; meanwhile, the robot moved the necessary grinding head into position in one of the tool carousels that its arms terminated in. Alex found it best just to give approval, for he wasn't a qualified engineer and could not confidently make the kind of changes others might make. However, after working with the robot for just a little while, he was finding engineering knowledge now embedding itself in his skull—his implant was *teaching* him.

"Lock yourself down, Alex," Ghort instructed him. "They're detaching."

Alex glanced back towards the upper hemisphere of the ship's skeleton, half a kilometre away, where Ghort and his robots, along with Akenon, Gladys and members of several other work teams, were preparing to reel out the new cable from its massive drum. He noted weird boreal effects on the metal-work there, caused by electric discharges induced by the proximity of the Io flux tube. He sent the order to his robot and it shuffled to one side, splaying its four legs and probing with clawed feet for some of the anchor points distributed all over the surface. As it located them, Alex stepped back, unwound the line from his belt and hitched it to a ring on the robot's body. He then looked around to see the other workers nearby—checking over the new steering thrusters—also locking themselves down. With a thump he felt, through his feet, as the space plane on the other side of the booster tank undocked. Alex checked plans in his skull, then peered over one side of the tank, finally seeing the plane coming into view, firing off steering thrusters and turning—the jets issuing from the thrusters seemingly refracted through prisms. Finally, a kilometre out, it started up its main engine and headed away towards the visible horizon of Jupiter—off to salvage more tanks.

"Now, that should have been our job," remarked Ghort, over the scrambled channel. "We already had experience with the ice asteroid."

They'd been very wary about sending their scrambled communications over laser com but, as Alex had pointed out, it actually reduced the chances of them being decoded.

"You're questioning Saul and Var's allocations?" he asked. "You should know better than to question the pronouncements of God and his high priest."

"Now that they've made that hole and are preparing to shift the docks, a space plane would be a good way to get to him," Ghort noted. "A blast from its main engine straight through his sanctum would solve a lot of problems."

"Or we could have dumped a booster tank right on top of him," suggested Alex.

"No," snapped Ghort, "that would also take out Tech Central and too much of the infrastructure, killing too many people and maybe ruining our chances of survival out here. No point in committing deicide if you kill yourself in the process."

Kill too many people . . .

Alex found he had access to further memories of Ghort. On the surface the man had always been ruthlessly professional and coldly pragmatic in going about his duties, but Alex now saw that he had been a restraining influence on the other security personnel assembled around Messina. Upon Ghort's promotion to chief of close protection, the response to imagined slights against their charge was limited to a physical beating, rather than the one concerned then being handed over to the Inspectorate for interrogation. Those whom Messina considered a danger to him—usually a delegate or delegate's staffer—were handed straight over to the Inspectorate, rather than being subjected first to crude torture to extract a "confession." The more rabid elements of the protection teams were often found wanting, and quickly dismissed. In his own way, and considering the circumstances he found himself in, Ghort had always managed to be a good man.

"So we have something else in mind now?"

"It is time for you to know," replied Ghort. "He doesn't often leave his inner sanctum—probably staying optically plugged in there now—so we're aiming for a targeted detonation. I liberated some demolition charges from our ice asteroid job."

Alex stood there contemplating that statement, and the confirmation of his suspicions made him feel a little sad. He now remembered, some years ago, hearing Ghort talking to another of Messina's bodyguards.

"They're like children," the other had said.

"They're efficient, obedient and will follow a kill order without a second thought," Ghort had replied, "but there's no malice or cruelty there; you get plenty of both in children. Sometimes I think they're the best of Messina. It's a shame they're never allowed to remember."

The scene had been a bloody one, Alex recollected: a contender for Messina's crown meeting an early demise, along with his family and his entire staff. Ghort had come to ensure tight security before Messina's arrival to inspect the victims, while Alex and his brothers were leaving, their work already done.

"Keep working, Alex," said Ghort in the here and now. "These pauses might arouse suspicion."

Alex set his robot in motion again and walked alongside it—with his line attached it was almost as if he held it on a lead. For a second, his footing became unsteady as a couple of steering thrusters fired up to stabilize the booster tank's position after the departure of the space plane, then he arrived at the fixing point indicated in his overlay. Detaching his line, he stepped back and set the robot to work. It placed the plate over to one side, stepped forward and positioned itself precisely over the designated spot, then lowered one of its tool-head arms to the pitted surface. Dust shot away, filled with a constellation of metal fragments erupting from the contact point of a rough carbide grinding wheel.

"Why is it time for me to know now?" Alex asked.

"I've opened our current exchange to the others," said Ghort. This meant every one of the rebels was listening in but, if they wanted to say something, they had to indicate so with a digital signature and then wait for Ghort's okay. And they wouldn't be able to join in if involved in some activity where their outward reactions during this secret communication might be noticed.

Ghort continued, "It's time for you to know because we have all agreed that you will be the one to pull the trigger. We also need your input on how to go about this. We've had a number of suggestions, but you yourself have better training in this sort of thing."

Quick and dirty, thought Alex. They were taking risks because they knew they had to move fast, and the biggest risk they were taking was in trusting him. He guessed that, knowing his history, they assumed he was completely on-side.

In his inner vision Alex recognized twenty-two icons, and he made sure to record those he didn't recognize so that he could later attach them to a specific name and a face. It struck him as likely they had decided that Saul must die soon for, once they were plugged into the flux tube, the work here would proceed at a hectic pace and, before they knew it, Saul would then be taking them out of the solar system.

"What's your weapons inventory?" Alex asked.

A small file arrived in his implant and he opened it. Ghort had taken four half-kilo demolition charges. Also available were twenty-five assault rifles, sixteen sidearms and a good quantity of ceramic ammunition.

"A direct assault on his inner sanctum would be suicide," Alex stated. "He always has his spidergun with him, and other robots stationed in the surrounding area. I would guess that his inner sanctum is also armoured." Alex paused, slightly reluctant to continue, even though he knew precisely what to do with the tools available. "I can convert two of the demolition charges into a copper head—armour-piercing explosive with one charge to penetrate and throw the other inside, which I'd remix to alter the burn, and then pack in a cast-iron case. That would first fill his inner sanctum with shrapnel, then with fire, and of course leave it open to vacuum, and either will kill him." He paused. "Use any more than two of those charges and we might end up taking out part of Tech Central, too."

One of the icons flashed and Ghort allowed the rebel indicated to speak.

"What about delivery?" asked a woman called Irini.

"That's not a problem," Alex stated. "One of our robots is not going to be able to distinguish between fixing a bomb in place or installing a fuse box. All they ever do is follow their work orders."

"Agreed," said Ghort. "Though we'll disable its internal radio after loading the order."

"That should do the trick, but it's not our main problem."

"So what do you see as our main problem?" Ghort asked.

The robot had now switched to a drill tap, punching and threading holes in a blur across the ground-down area to match those already drilled in the plate. No swarf was visible because it was sucking that away. A moment later it employed a finer grinding wheel to polish the metre-square section of the booster tank to a mirror finish that matched the mirror finish underneath the fixing plate. Next would come the plate, then the bolts to tighten it down, during which process the two fine-ground surfaces would simply bond at a molecular level.

"Our main problem is that he still won't be dead," Alex stated. "His backup is kept in his inner sanctum, and it will certainly be lodged in some sort of armoured vault. We could try going in after it but it's quite likely his spidergun will still be operating, and quite certainly so will his mind. If the spidergun doesn't kill us, then the robots he'll immediately summon will definitely do so. It would be suicide."

The robot lowered the plate into place and then, in a blur of activity, wound in the twelve fixing bolts, before stepping back.

Good doggy, Alex thought.

He turned to look back towards the ship, and saw the two linked EVA units engaged in towing the cable out, now coming in at the end of the booster tank, with vacuum between taking on a bluish tinge from ionization. They then knocked against the tank briefly, an electric discharge flashing as they shed a tangle of three robots and the cable end. These three spread out into a line and continued hauling in the cable, like some nightmare tug-of-war team. Alex moved out of their path just as Ghort spoke again.

"We have information that says otherwise," he said.

"Otherwise?" Alex asked.

Meanwhile other teams of both robots and humans were using impellers to get themselves away from the booster tank. The same thing would be happening somewhere down below, just off the old station wheel. And now it was time for Alex to go, too. He ordered his robot to follow him and propelled himself away from the booster tank just as the three new arrivals plugged in the cable, and he used his wrist impeller to send himself after the two EVA units. To give himself time, he did not hasten to catch up with them to hitch a ride, as per usual. Behind him, his robot had folded in its limbs till it looked eerily like an Egyptian mummy, and the three coming off the booster tank behind adopted very much the same pose. Alex shivered, since right now he didn't want such reminders of human mortality.

"Otherwise," Ghort repeated. "Saul input the orders to move his backups to the inner sanctum, then personally overrode the robots doing so. He moved them instead to an armoured case within the new armour placed around the vortex generator inside the old station ring."

How convenient, Alex thought. *And doubtless his backups are accessible.*

"That makes sense," he said. "Keeping his backups close to his physical body would be like putting all his eggs in one basket. Is it guarded?"

"Of course it is," said Ghort. "By one spidergun."

"Not easy," said Alex.

"We have two demolition charges left," said Ghort. "And we also have the weapons."

Alex mulled that over for a moment, then said, "I should be able to rig something for the grenade launcher on an assault rifle, if you happen to have one with that attachment."

"We do," Ghort replied.

"We'll have to deploy every weapon to keep it busy enough for me to get in a killing shot, which means using people," Alex added. "This probably means most of us—unless you have found new recruits. And that means some of us are likely to die."

"On the contrary," said Ghort, obviously amused, "our back-ups remain safe in Arcoplex Two, where also some of our clone bodies are being grown even now. The only person who is going to die is Alan Saul."

The EVA units entered the ship's skeleton, while Alex caught hold of an I-beam, hung onto it and turned himself round. The booster tank was already a kilometre out, and continuing on its journey into the main ion flow of the flux tube. Now, looking down, Alex could see the second booster tank on its way too. He linked into station systems and checked power monitoring and saw that, even though the anode and cathode had yet to enter the region of highest ion density in the flux tube, power was flowing through the ship—a steady quarter of a megawatt and still growing. Glancing within and down, he saw Saul's robot centipedes already stirring to life, unused lights coming on, the cylinder worlds spinning up to speed and the first jets of vapour issuing from the smelting plants.

"So we'll hold a memorial service," Alex stated.

"Okay," Ghort replied, "we'll meet off-shift and get things ready. Right now we have to get back to work. That's all for now."

Their scrambled links shut down.

Alex gazed for a while longer at the growing activity within the ship, watching chunks of asteroid and newly completed components already on the move. A hive of industry had never seemed so apt a description. What was happening here was massive and, in his heart, he felt it was the start of something that might last longer than all hitherto-known human history. And he laughed.

From her bed in her apartment in Arcoplex Two, Hannah watched Da Vinci walk naked over to her fridge, pop open the door and take out a bottle of beer. She frowned at the immediate reaction she felt. How dare he open her fridge without permission? Then she tried to shrug that off and remember that, but for a brief interlude spent with Saul on this same station, she had been living alone in private apartments for decades. She reached for the remote control sitting on her bedside table, her hand closing round it immediately turning on the screen, then ran through her favourite selection of cam views.

The first one to appear showed a section of the ship's skeleton, which had previously been squirming with short combinations of Saul's conjoined robots as they steadily affixed hull plates. She paused the program because that section was now completely covered, searched further cam views and found another higher up, where the robots were still at work. Setting the program running again brought her to a view from the rim of the space docks, where she was amazed to see that the docking pillars had now been completely detached and were floating, like skyscrapers transplanted from Earth, into void off to one side of their original position outside the ship. The resolution was good enough for her to see the cables running stretched taut through a hole in the cage towards a massive cable drum. Soon those docks would be located inside and fixed to their destined position above Arcoplex One.

"It changes hourly," Da Vinci stated.

"It's like being back by the sun," she affirmed. "Only better in some ways, because the power, for us here, is practically limitless."

He came and sat down on the edge of the bed to watch the rest of the show. Hannah felt a momentary surge of irritation because he hadn't brought her a bottle of beer, too, but then remembered how, the last time he had done so, she'd capped it and put it back in the fridge before making herself a cup of coffee.

The next scene showed robots marching chunks of asteroid into the smelting plant now permanently sited in its dock, then marching out again with various components for the new ship. They looked like ants gathering materials for a nest, and their swarm-like movement even produced a psychosomatic itch. There were many more of them now, too: a mixture of the old station robots and trios of the conjoining robot units. The human teams still working out there were becoming more and more difficult to spot, especially now that many of them were starting to break up after more of them were chipped and began to control their own teams of robots. However, she did spot them in the next view, one of the plasma cannon the Saberhagens were building, and in the one after that focused on the construction around the base of the axial arcoplex spindle.

"It's awesome," Da Vinci remarked, "but it's also terrifying."

Hannah was still staring at the screen, which now showed the second smelting plant—the one still capable of being extended—lying some way out from the ship, with three old booster tanks now moored to it, in the process of being cut up by adapted mining robots and fed inside. She said, "I've not thought too much about the future, about us leaving the solar system, because there's always been so much to do and it always seemed like such a distant prospect." She shook her head. "But with the speed everything is being done out there, I realize the future will be upon me before I even know it."

"We're already living in the future," Da Vinci opined. "I never expected to find myself gazing at foetuses growing so fast that the changes in them are visible every day, nor having to cool amniotic fluid to stop it from boiling.

She glanced at him. "How is that going?"

She hadn't read his latest report, expecting to catch up with him when he arrived here in her apartment, but he'd been more interested in getting her clothes off and she hadn't been averse to the idea.

"I have fifteen clones growing," he explained, "for the twins, Le Roque, Langstrom and a few of his lieutenants, for Rhine and, of course, for you."

Hannah shivered at the thought, then felt annoyed by such a reaction. She was surely far too much of a rational being to be affected this way.

"But I'm limited to fifteen clones until later." He gazed at her over his beer bottle. "Saul has now given me a new task."

"He has?" Hannah felt suddenly worried. Had she, by taking Da Vinci as a lover, put him in danger from Saul? No, of course not. She abruptly felt disgusted at her instinct-level wish that there was some competition for her between the two. Jealousy was probably an emotion Saul had totally dispensed with in the perfect order of his mind.

"He's had the cryogenic pods removed from Messina's space plane and sent to me. I have to test them, using some of the Arboretum livestock, make a report . . . then there must be a human trial."

"Who's the volunteer?"

"I am."

"What?"

"He's already having the main components for new pods manufactured," Da Vinci revealed, still watching her. "Thousands of them."

"Wait a minute." Hannah clicked off the screen and sat upright. "You volunteered?"

"We never got to take the Hippocratic Oath when we trained under the Committee. How could we do so when our future might include stints in Safe Departure clinics or in some Inspectorate cell complex? But I made that oath to myself and have, to the best of my abilities, stuck to it."

"What's this got to do with you volunteering?"

"I cannot, in clear conscience, let someone else test out a cryogenic pod. But one must nevertheless be tested, as we must be certain that they will prove safe."

"I don't see why," said Hannah, "since they're only going to be used for storing cloned bodies . . ."

"You think?"

Hannah stared at him, replaying this conversation in her mind. He had said that the components for "thousands of them" were already being made. But why? It struck her as unlikely that Saul would ensure a clone body available for every human aboard this ship—only enough of them for essential personnel, if, in reality, any of them aboard could be described as essential. *Thousands of cryogenic pods?* Then she got it.

"Interstellar flight," she said. "We're all going on ice while this ship of his flies to the stars."

"That's my assessment, too."

"I need to get you chipped," she said. "Your backup is growing, and within just a few days we should be able to make the links."

"I don't know that I have the time because, even without complications, there's a four-day recovery and adjustment period."

"Nevertheless, you must be chipped before you try out that cryogenic pod." Hannah swung her legs off the bed and headed for the shower. "You do *not* go in there without a backup."

"It's good to know you care."

She grunted dismissively. She did in fact care, but sometimes it didn't show so well. Maybe that was because Saul always loomed in her mind so prominently and Da Vinci was therefore not the single most important man in her life. As she stepped into her shower cubicle, she wondered if that situation would ever change, and then realized that it would. The time would come when her emotions finally caught up with her intellect and, on a gut level, she truly felt that there were only two human beings in that equation.

ARGUS

With the clamping wheels on the ends of its legs powering up, the overseer's office began its slow crawl up the ship's skeleton to a new position five hundred metres from the top pole of the ship. The inside of the office was now decked out just like one Var had used while working on the Mars Traveller project. However, here she was finding herself having to move the office a lot more often, just to keep out of the way of the astounding pace of construction.

She gazed at her array of screens and could not help but feel a bitter sense of awe. All three of the massive docking pillars were now inside, suspended one above the other in a cubic framework that gave room for the manoeuvring of space planes alongside with support and maintenance equipment, all currently crawling with robots and humans and glinting under a constellation of welding lights. The two new arcoplex cylinders were growing visibly even as she watched. Their bones were going in place at the same pace as the ship's skeleton had been constructed, while that skeleton was steadily being shrouded in hull plates—their dark shadow swiftly blotting out the view of Jupiter. Asteroid matter was disappearing fast, while the need for raw materials was being filled by the steady supply of booster tanks being dragged in from around Jupiter, and by frequent missions to some of the smaller encircling moons in quest of rarer earth elements as they ran dry. The Saberhagens' weapons were now all but complete, the stream of robots from Arcoplex Two seemed never-ending, the abortive structures that had sprung from the outer rim of the old station wheel had been stripped away and the ship was *filling up* and felt *gravid*—girder walls rising to meet each other, accommodation units, small factories, additional hydroponics units and more besides, sprouting everywhere like tree buds.

After staring for a while at the screens, Var returned her attention to recent reports and updated schematics; finding there was not much she needed to attend to, she began checking the messages she'd had relayed to her communications system. All the work schedules were meshing together nicely and the smelters were completely on top of answering demand. The only problems to be encountered were system disruption caused by induction and static discharges, which were an inevitable result of having the ship positioned beside the Io flux tube. Beyond these, she noted that Commander Langstrom was on his way to see her and should be here in a few minutes, and meanwhile all but one remaining item had been responded to.

Var gazed at the message from Hannah Neumann. They had not talked for a while, since it seemed Hannah was currently more interested in getting her bones jumped by that weasel Da Vinci rather than drinking beer with Var in the Olive Tree. But this wasn't a personal message: it was one automatically generated by Hannah's system to inform Var that her backup had reached maturity and yet still no connection had been made with her implant. So perhaps it was time for Var actually to get an implant, to become potentially immortal, to thus extend her abilities to do her job, to enable her to do within her skull what she had just been doing on a screen; to enable her personally to control robots and summon to her mind any data she ever required. What had she got to lose?

Var stared at the message, trying to think logically about it, but could not dispel a stubborn reluctance. Perhaps she was rationalizing, but it all seemed to come down to that relay, that off-switch her beloved brother had decided should be installed in the circuit. Why did he have so little trust in his own sister? Why did he have so little trust in Hannah, who, though she might deny it, looked upon him with a weird combination of maternal pride and worship, or in the others who also worshipped him: like the Saberhagens, who clearly also saw him as their personal incarnation of god the father; like Rhine, who quite simply could not visualize a universe without Alan Saul and who would die for him; like Langstrom, who, at last, through the jaded horror of his military career under the Committee had found someone worthy of serving?

"You don't trust us, do you, Alan?" she said out loud, but there was no response.

Perhaps it was because he, being convinced he had moved so far beyond humanity, had persuaded himself that, at this remove, he could understand it so much better. But probably all he knew was little more than Var did: that the very naivety of worship made it more likely quickly to make the transition towards hate. Or was it that, in convincing himself that he had moved into a post-human state, he'd lost any connection with his humanity at all? Could it be that he considered the ebb and flow of human emotion beneath his notice, that he now thought himself untouchable, or even invulnerable? Var pressed a hand against her forehead as if to try and still all the possibilities whirling round inside there, or to try and steady herself.

I must get this straight . . .

There were those amongst the already chipped who were now plotting against her brother. He knew, of course, yet seemed utterly dismissive of their shenanigans, whatever they might be. He should never forget that the advances that had resulted in him, as he was now, were a human invention. He should never forget the power of human ingenuity and, should it be turned against him, he should never forget that he might actually die. Var felt that something needed to be done, which was why she had summoned Langstrom. She could not rely on her brother to deal with what seemed likely to be a growing problem amongst the chipped. She was determined not to turn into one of the worshipful, and thus one of those utterly trusting and dependent on their god.

The airlock light was flashing, which meant Langstrom had arrived. As she stood up ready to greet him, another out-field thought occurred to her. Maybe her brother was just letting the rebellion develop so as to give himself a reason for extreme response? Was this what lay behind his distrust: did he realize that his intentions would be seen as a betrayal by those aboard his ship? She could not help but remember recent conversations with Hannah, when the woman had talked about her ultimate fear that Alan might decide the humans on board were a burden he no longer wished to shoulder, and therefore decide to dispense with them. She could entertain the possibility that he was merely watching and waiting for this rebellion to become overt—waiting for that excuse to be rid of them all.

Langstrom stepped through first, followed by the repro Manuel, who apparently was steadily making himself indispensable as a secretary—a role rather belied by his physical appearance. Langstrom's other lieutenants, who were chipped just as Langstrom was, were engaged elsewhere about the station—making enquiries and "shaking a few trees to see what dropped out."

"Varalia," Langstrom greeted her, dipping his head respectfully.

This was the kind of acknowledgement she had been receiving from many, and she found it both annoying and flattering. Annoying because she suspected it was all to do with her family connection, but flattering because sometimes it seemed due to her for being in charge of the rebuild, and because of how she had seemed to make things all work so much better. And the operative word there was "seemed," since she often felt that her performance had been more one of social engineering than actual engineering, and less that of a true leader and more of a figurehead.

"You've got something for me?" she asked.

"I've found out where the relay scramblers are being manufactured," he replied. "There's a small factory in Arcoplex One, attached to a shop. It's a private concern where they repair fones and are making replacement parts for fones."

"Private concern?"

"Since your introduction of a salary for station work, the Owner has allowed vacant ship space to be rented out for such activities," Langstrom replied. "Commerce is growing. In Arcoplex One the shopping mall, which originally catered for the delegates living there, is gradually becoming occupied. We have people manufacturing clothing, jewellery and objects of art, as well as different kinds of alcohol, tobacco, cannabis products and designer drugs I've yet to have any guidance on . . . and, of course, this fone shop."

Var stared at him. She obviously knew about the Olive Tree and what was sold there, but had never considered where these new products were coming from. In fact, all she knew about Arcoplex One was that it served as accommodation for certain station personnel, and she hadn't yet even been inside it.

"Do you have any names?" she asked.

"The shop is run by a technician called Scarrow, but, as far as we are aware, he himself has no knowledge of the scramblers. However, he has two people working for him who, during their off-time, are producing them."

"There's no way Alan cannot be aware of this. Who exactly are they?"

"They're personnel from Mars: one is a repro, so quite probably innocent regarding the purpose of the scramblers, while the other is someone who served under Rhone in Mars Science. The first individual is called Thomas Grieve, while the second is called Gilder Main."

Var digested that information in silence. Grieve had been one of those responsible for killing Martinez, and she had wanted to kill him in turn. However, there had just been no time then, and when she finally got round to making enquiries about him, she discovered that he had already undergone Hannah's ministrations. She'd found him and spoken to him, even pushed him, but discovered only a child-like man with little recollection of his past and not the slightest bit of malice evident in him. So, in frustration, she'd left him alone. Gilder was someone she vaguely recollected, who had climbed his way up through Mars Science with his nose firmly wedged between Rhone's buttocks.

"Have you arrested them?" she asked.

"On what charge?"

It was frustrating but, under Alan Saul, there was no law against secret communications. Var knew that because she had already checked. Under the Committee, there would have been numerous laws being broken and numerous reasons for arrest—not that the Inspectorate had ever required a legitimate reason for arresting and interrogating someone. Here, then, was one of the drawbacks of allowing people greater freedom. But, again, was that greater freedom intended to provide people with more rope with which to hang themselves?

"I need to talk to Gilder privately," she declared through gritted teeth.

"Obviously I cannot be involved in anything that infringes the law," explained Langstrom, straight-faced. "I can merely monitor some citizens, and there are restrictions on what I may do with the data obtained."

Langstrom patted Manuel on the shoulder, whereupon the repro took a data stick from his top pocket and set it down on a nearby surface.

"It's also noteworthy how the Owner allows cam dead spots to exist throughout the ship," Langstrom continued. "He explained to me how he did not want to monitor everyone completely all the time, since he is not the Committee, and how allowing a degree of illicit activity acts as a safety valve, creating the illusion of greater freedom."

Var eyed the data stick. "Thank you for the information, Commander Langstrom. It's a shame that we cannot act on this matter, but the law here on board is the law."

He dipped his head in acknowledgement and headed for the airlock, pausing before stepping inside it to say, "I agree with the Owner about that safety valve, which is why I've reduced my patrols operating within Arcoplex One and only intervene when I see, via whatever cams are available, any situation getting out of control—which is rare."

The moment the two of them were gone, Var proceeded to view the contents of the stick. The dead spots were all detailed, and the position of Gilder Main was being updated in real time. Currently he was at work in Arcoplex Two and, checking his shift details, she saw that he would be finished there in two hours. She also noted how one of the dead spots was in the small factory operating behind the aforementioned fone shop.

"Do you know what I'm doing, Alan?" she enquired. "Or are you too blinded by your own belief in your omniscience?"

She stared at her screen, not quite sure what to do next. However, leaving matters in the hands of her superiors or depending on her subordinates had led equally to betrayal. So, one thing was certain: she had to do *something*.

11

SOFT-FRUIT PRACTICE

There are those who assert that evolution is a directional thing and that, as we evolve, we are heading towards some omega point. This strange idea stems from the thoroughly erroneous perception of evolution having an aim beyond the brute survival of genes. It is a sign of philosophical, faith-based thinking infiltrating the thoroughly mechanistic facts regarding human biology. There is no data on evolutionary biology to warrant any faith in the idea that we are somehow "improving." If living in trees and chucking bananas at each other became a breeding advantage, into the trees we would go for soft-fruit target practice. Evolution does not just stop, and the changes it makes in us are governed only by production of the next generation. It can be argued that, by physically altering our bodies and our minds, we are just part of evolution's toolbox. Perhaps now the best cerebral implants shunt aside the biggest horns and the bushiest tail, and it might be that humans will eventually reach something akin to an omega point. But, equally, those same implants might prove a hindrance to obtaining a mate—a dead end—and the ones still up in the trees with the bananas will eventually be the winners.

EARTH

"Admiral Bartholomew," enquired Serene, as the man's image popped up in a small frame at the top corner of the main screen, "how much longer before you can undock?"

"Once all the troops are aboard, which could be any time now, we can separate," he replied. "All our other supplies are in."

"And, thereafter," Serene continued, "how long until you can head out?"

"If we run our vortex generators up to speed and forgo any further testing and diagnostics, then twenty-two hours."

"Keep me updated," Serene concluded and, after a moment, the small frame closed.

Undocking the *Command* and the *Fist* from the construction station the moment the supplies and troops were aboard would shave off almost a day, but only if the drives functioned as predicted and there was no requirement to dock the ships again for further work. It was a risk Serene felt it necessary to take in light of the images she was now viewing.

She'd seen just how fast things were progressing here on the construction station, but this development outpaced it tenfold. Saul was building his ship at a phenomenal rate. That skeletal ship had arrived in orbit about Jupiter just a few weeks ago and, despite a lack of clarity to the images because of the ionization thereabouts, the moment it plugged into the flux tube, activity aboard the craft had ramped up so high that its image in infrared showed clearly even beside Io itself. Now the outer skeleton was more than halfway enclosed with hull plates, while the interior had filled up rapidly—even the docking pillars being moved inside with the ease of shifting a few planks rather than thousands of tonnes of metal and the complex support technologies.

"What have Tactical got to add?" she asked without turning. Elkin stood silently behind her, along with her two aides.

Calder was also present, but currently off studying something on one of the other consoles in the control room, as if he wanted to disassociate himself from this scene; while Sack was looming close, having detected the tension in Serene the moment she began viewing the video feed.

Elkin replied, "They say that his ship still could be ready before the *Command* and the *Fist* are ready to launch."

"Still could be?" Serene enquired, silently putting a call through her fone and linking it to the screen before her.

"This progress is faster than anyone believed possible, so all base parameters have to be changed," Elkin stated. "It may also have some bearing on the coming conflict."

"Some bearing?" remarked Serene acidly, noting that one of the aides was trying to attract Elkin's attention. "That's even supposing there is a coming conflict!" She was starting to get angry now, receiving some intimation that things were beginning to spin out of control.

Elkin had now taken note of something on her palmtop and frowned.

"What now?" Serene demanded.

"I've just received a notification, ma'am, from security team leader Vaughan," Elkin replied. "Apparently our undercover operatives here were relocated with the . . . less trusted staff."

"And I need to know this why?"

Elkin clammed up and, even though Serene had asked what had drawn Elkin's attention, she felt no guilt about harassing the woman.

"Well, you can tell team leader Vaughan—What is it?" she snapped at Bartholomew, who had now reappeared in that tiny frame on her screen.

"Ma'am?" he asked carefully.

"Do go on," she said acerbically.

"I'm just letting you know that all the troops are now aboard, and we will be undocking directly," he announced stiffly.

"Well, get on with it." Serene used the chair console to switch views to an exterior cam that showed the spinning-top shape of the *Command*, with the *Fist* bulking just beyond it. Already umbilicals were detaching and the scaffolds enclosing them were being whittled away by a veritable swarm of EVA units and robots. She allowed those images to calm her, but Calder's abrupt arrival at her shoulder set her irritation level rising again. "You have something for me?" she asked, wondering if he had come to present more irrelevant detail, which by now she realized seemed to be the resort of those around her when they understood that her mood wasn't at its best.

"We've received a communication from the *Scourge*," he said, sounding puzzled.

She turned in her seat to look at him. "Look, the concerns of the crew aboard your tug are not exactly my priority right now."

"No, ma'am," he agreed, "but this communication is not from them but from the *Scourge* itself. It seems there is someone alive aboard that ship. We just received a video file from someone called Clay Ruger."

Serene stared at him, struggling to fit this new information into recent events but just feeling baffled.

"Clay Ruger?" she echoed.

"He was your political officer aboard that ship," Elkin interjected.

"I know who Clay Ruger was . . . is." He was a man who should have died months ago, strangled once she sent the signal to his collar. And if he had somehow avoided that, then he was a man who should have died a short time afterwards when Alan Saul sent the Scour activation signal to all those aboard the *Scourge*, or when Argus Station's warp bubble had brushed against the ship and torn it up. "Video file?" she queried.

Calder pointed to the icons ranged along the bottom of her screen. "It's available there."

Suddenly her anger and her irritation were gone, and she found herself thinking clearly. It was as if this new information had hit a reset button in her brain. Clay Ruger had survived, which meant that, in some quarters, strangulation collars and Scour implant chips did not offer the degree of control she might have supposed. Abruptly she sensed danger all around her. Suddenly she understood how the arrogance of power could be an ultimate weakness. Glancing beyond Calder, she noted that, while her own security personnel were assembled here, the number of original Inspectorate enforcers had increased. She swung back to her screen and dragged a cursor down to the video icon, clicking it.

Ruger gazed out at her from the screen. He looked pale and ill and very, very thin. She saw at once that he wasn't wearing a collar and also noted shadowy movement to one side—he wasn't alone.

"This is Clay Ruger, the political officer aboard the *Scourge*," he said. "I need whoever records and first views this video file to get it to Serene Galahad as quickly as possible." He paused, wiped at his face with grubby fingers. "It will no doubt come as a surprise to you, ma'am, that I am alive. I can get into lengthy explanations about why, but would need to speak to you alone to give you the full detail. Let it suffice for me to say that Captain Scotonis, after having learned something about the death of his family, turned traitor. Even as I boarded the *Scourge,* he took control of all readerguns and inducers, and so effectively gained complete control over me and his command crew."

Serene felt the skin on her back creeping as Ruger waved a hand dismissively. If Scotonis had learned about the source of the Scour, then his turning against her might be considered perfectly understandable. It seemed likely that Ruger also knew, but was being careful not to broadcast such knowledge.

"The man was insane," Ruger continued. "He demanded that we free ourselves totally from Earth, and so ordered the removal of all implants and other security devices." Ruger reached up and touched his bare neck. "However, he said nothing of this to Commander Liang and his troops, because their loyalty to

Earth was unquestioning. This was why he carried on through with the attack on Argus, just so he could get Liang and his troops out of the *Scourge* and onto that station, and there abandon them just as he did. Subsequent events killed most of those remaining, including the captain himself, and have wrecked much of this ship."

Serene paused the video to give herself time to think. Ruger was obviously making his excuses and hoping he could return to Earth without blame. Though his story was all very interesting, it was probably full of half-truths and outright lies, all of which would be uncovered in an adjustment cell on Earth, prior to his execution on prime-time ETV. Meanwhile, there were other things that now needed her attention—things that she had, in her arrogance, neglected. First and foremost was her personal safety.

"Have him, and whoever is with him, arrested once the *Scourge* is in orbit," she instructed. "I'm sure his story will soon take on a new shape." She began to stand up. She would go now to Calder's apartment and, while heading there, ensure her scattered security team was called in close. Perhaps it also might be an idea to ensure that Calder himself remained at her side . . .

"I think you should look at the rest, ma'am," suggested Calder. "He does have something important to say."

As she studied him, she deliberately assumed an expression of boredom. "Oh, very well." She set the video running again.

"Pilot Officer Trove and I tried to take back control of the ship, for you and for Earth, and therefore presented the greatest danger to Scotonis, so he had us locked in the forward chamber used for storing inert railgun missiles. By imprisoning us he actually ensured our survival, because that part of the ship did not suffer as much damage from the tidal forces of the Argus warp. We've since managed to escape that storage chamber, and are now on a shuttle aboard the *Scourge*, and we are ready to come into one of the Earth orbit stations. But, of course, you are probably wondering, ma'am, what point is served by my sending this message."

Serene certainly was, and really wished he would hurry up and get to the point. Her sense of personal danger had just ramped up, especially when she glanced round to see Elkin frowning at her palmtop, and her aides obviously busy receiving a heavy com load.

"I wanted to be sure that, upon leaving the *Scourge*, we would not immediately be fired upon. I also want utter assurances, from your own mouth, ratified by all the delegates of Earth, that neither Pilot Officer Trove nor I will be punished for real or imagined crimes or handed over to the Inspectorate for interrogation. We have done the best we possibly could in a very bad situation, and we also now have in our control something of great value to the human race."

Cue the dramatic pause. Really, just for inflicting that irritating bit of theatre, Serene decided Ruger's public execution should be a spectacular. However, his next words left her dumbfounded.

"Scotonis informed you that there were no communications with Argus Station, but he lied. Alan Saul tried to buy his way out of being attacked by transmitting all of the Gene Bank data to us. It now resides within computer storage aboard the *Scourge*, under my personal access codes. I can at once set that data to transmitting on any frequency, coded or otherwise, that you decide." Ruger shrugged, sat back a little from the cam. "It being subject to my personal coded access, I can do anything with it . . . anything at all."

The implication was plain: Ruger had the power to give her the Gene Bank data; he also had the power to wipe it completely from the *Scourge's* system.

Serene turned slowly to Calder, thinking fast. "Send him a reply. Tell him that once his shuttle leaves the *Scourge* it will certainly not be fired upon. He must dock here on your construction station. Tell him that I will communicate with him shortly afterwards, once I can ensure that my delegates will ratify a full pardon for his or Pilot Officer Trove's real or imagined crimes against the state. You may also add that, in my opinion, Earth is as much in need of heroes to laud as villains to pursue and punish."

"Certainly, ma'am," said Calder, somehow seeming more confident and together, all of a sudden.

Did he suppose that, because she was now close to obtaining at least some portion of what she wanted out here—seeming likely to get her hands on a workable cure for Earth's ills—she would be leaving soon and he could therefore return to enjoying the prime position in charge, and thus rule over his realm here without interference?

"What kind of reception should we prepare for him?" he then asked.

"I intend to meet him, in person, and I'll want that meeting broadcast on ETV." If necessary, she could pull the security teams closer in around her then—if it turned out that her growing suspicions about Calder were true. "We'll have the broadcast relayed up on screens in the space dock he arrives in, along with the ratification of his pardon from the delegates of Earth. That will go a long way towards assuring him that no blame for previous failures will attach to him, and of course encourage him to begin his transmission of the Gene Bank data."

Calder nodded thoughtfully. "Our new shuttle dock would be the best place. The cam network there is more modern and it has the requisite screens."

"Very well," said Serene, though slightly suspicious of this latest suggestion.

"So he is to be a hero," remarked Calder.

"Until the broadcast is over," Serene stated. "We'll then extract the full truth in an adjustment cell." It annoyed her that a spectacular of Ruger's execution would never be witnessed. Instead it would have to be something for her private consumption.

"I see," said Calder, his expression hardening. He nodded once, and with a tight "Ma'am," he moved away, heading across the control room to sit at the console he had been using previously. Casually glancing around her, Serene noted that there were now at least ten of those Inspectorate uniforms nearby— most of them clustered near Calder—while her own security personnel, scattered around her, numbered just eight.

She stood up, realizing she had just made a serious mistake. She had let Calder know that she intended to go back on her word to Ruger, that public knowledge of someone's status made no difference to whether or not they ended up in adjustment or with a bullet through the brain. Equally, all her promises to Calder himself were therefore worthless.

"When I've made all the arrangements, I'll speak to Ruger again from your apartment," she called out airily, heading towards the exit, her personnel rapidly falling in around her, Sack pacing warily at her shoulder. Right then she did not dare demand that Calder accompany her—feeling sure that to do so would push to a head something that she might not survive.

ARGUS

The meeting had been moved forward and, as Alex headed for the cam dead spot in Arcoplex One to attend it, as well as his backpack he carried a sidearm he had acquired on the ship's black market. It might be that the rest of the chipped had decided he was too much of a risk, and he was actually being called to a rendezvous with whoever had been given the chore of getting rid of him. He didn't consider it overly paranoid to think that way, since people in secret organizations like this one tended to be paranoid, so he was behaving perfectly in character.

The main layout of the buildings inside the arcoplex had changed not at all, but almost everything else had. The commerce thriving here was illustrated by the numerous lurid signs over shops in certain streets. Some of the apartment buildings had even acquired balconies on which plants were growing that, though also ornamental, were mostly for recreational consumption. Here and there, buildings had been painted in certain colours to distinguish them, and right now the conference centre was gradually being gutted—causing much discussion as to what it might be turned into, the most popular choice being a sports centre with its own swimming pool.

Alex passed the fone shop, with its sign depicting an old Bakelite telephone seemingly growing out the top of the skull of someone who looked suspiciously like the Owner. In the next building along, he approached an arched door with the eye of a cam set in the apex and, as the door buzzed open, he guessed this surveillance wasn't linked into the ship's computer system.

On entering, he passed a construction robot, squatting in the corridor like a steel gargoyle, and was beckoned forward by a woman he recognized as one of the chipped. Heading towards the murmur of voices, he stepped warily into the room beyond and then relaxed, sliding his hand out of his jacket. Every one of the rebels he had so far identified was present, so this had to be a genuine meeting.

"Now that we're all here," began Ghort, eyeing Alex with slight annoyance, "we need to talk seriously."

Shrugging off the straps of his backpack, Alex moved over to the nearest available seat.

Meanwhile Ghort continued, "You all saw how things ramped up a few days ago, and therefore know about the recall of the space planes?"

"And we know why," interjected Marsin. "He saw Galahad's warships pull out of their construction station, so he's getting ready to run."

"Precisely," said Ghort. "And the moment he does run is when we strike."

"But surely," said the woman who had waved Alex in, "we'll just leave ourselves open to attack from those warships? I'm all for getting rid of Saul but not at the price of handing myself over to Galahad."

"It won't work like that," Ghort explained. "We move just as he fires up the Rhine drive, just when he feels he's safe, when he feels he's already escaped. At that stage his death won't result in the drive shutting down. Alex, you have the necessary devices?"

Alex nodded and reached down to open the backpack, first taking out two objects which, because of their long stems, almost looked like fireworks. These stems were steel, however, and the cylindrical objects attached to the end of each were considerably more destructive than any firework.

"These," he explained, "incorporate delayed-action solid-fuel boosters and noses full of high explosive." He passed them to someone sitting nearby, who immediately passed them on to Ghort.

"Enough to take out a spidergun?" he enquired as he took hold of them.

Alex nodded. "If I can get a clear shot." Then to himself added silently, *in the microseconds of a spidergun's response time.*

Next he took out a large squat cylinder with a gecko pad fitted to one end.

"Copper head," he explained. "It's an old method of armour piercing, but the innovation here is that a fraction of a second later, an incendiary follows the stream of vaporized copper through. This will burn out his inner sanctum." He pointed to a small digital display on the side. "It works by either a timer or coded signal, and it can also be shut down by coded signal if necessary." He passed this over too and watched as Ghort handed it to one of the chipped, called Jean-Pierre, who then took it out of the room. It seemed likely to Alex that the same robot he had seen on the way in would be the one that would deliver it.

"Let me have the detonation code," said Ghort.

Alex nodded and immediately sent it via the scrambled channel. This request, more than anything else, told him who was really in charge here.

"We'll set the timer for twenty-five hours," Ghort continued, "which is somewhat over the time it should take for Galahad's two warships to get their vortex generators up to working speed, but I can adjust things if necessary later on."

"We have our weapons now," observed Marsin, "and we have our general plan of attack." He watched Ghort for a moment before continuing. "So how does this run?"

Ghort nodded to Jean-Pierre, who had returned, now empty handed, then said, "The moment Saul fires up the Rhine drive, we move to the rendezvous point before heading to the outer ring. The robot will, when ready, take the copper head and position it on Saul's inner sanctum."

Ah, checking, thought Alex. Doubtless Ghort himself or someone else familiar with explosives would be vetting Alex's work. They would find nothing wrong with it, of course.

"But if we're on shift?" he enquired.

"Until we've done this, try to ensure that you're wearing either heavy work or VC suits during any shift you undertake," Ghort replied. "When the drive fires up, or once you receive notification from me, just drop whatever you're doing and move. The weapons will then be in place." He now passed over the two assault rifle grenades to the woman sitting beside him. "As we move against Saul's backups and that spidergun of his, I'll let Alex here lead, since he'll know the best approach. Any questions?"

Studying the expressions all around him, Alex noted that some of them looked a little sick. Talking revolution was not quite the same as undertaking the actual act. One of the more frightened-looking men held his hand up.

"I have one," he said, then at Ghort's nod continued, "what happens if we fail?"

"If we fail, we die," said Ghort.

Alex had been determined not to spice the proceedings with horrible reality, but in this instance he could not help adding, "And in that case we have to hope Saul allows us just the once-only experience of dying."

Gilder Main had been the first to arrive, unlocking the door to the building next to the fone shop which Var had only recently learned he was now renting, and he was also one of the last to leave, heading straight back next door. Var lowered her binoculars and unplugged the optic connecting them to her palmtop, then studied the twenty-five faces on her screen. Ghort's presence had come as a surprise to her, Marsin's as no surprise at all, while the fact that the Messina clone was involved seemed inevitable. Folding up her palmtop and slipping it into her pocket, she began to walk around the circumference of Arcoplex One towards the fone shop itself.

So what now?

Var fingered the other object in her pocket and considered her options. She knew the names and faces now but still needed to know what their plans were, assuming they had got so far as formulating any plans. She also realized that, if she truly believed her brother was preparing to let this thing run so as to give himself an excuse to either thin out or exterminate the current population aboard, she had to act. She must also operate without reference to his apparently omniscient presence throughout the station. She must operate as she had on Mars, cutting a straight line to her goal with ruthless efficiency.

Soon she was on the street she had been observing from the other side of the arcoplex, then she was passing the door she had actually been watching and heading straight for the door leading into the neighbouring fone shop. Just outside, she paused for a moment. She knew that Scarrow was currently working a shift in Arcoplex Two, and that inside Thomas Grieve would be at the counter while Gilder Main would be working in the rear. She opened the door and stepped inside.

Just as she had supposed, Grieve looked up from a screen and gazed at her with momentary puzzlement before suddenly showing fear. She had pushed him hard the last time they met—trying to find some fragment of the murderer he had once been and thus a true motive for revenge.

"Varalia Delex!" he exclaimed.

Too much warning. Groping in her pocket, Var abruptly accelerated, leaped the counter and pushed through the door behind it. As she went through, she saw Main pulling something out from underneath one of the workbenches. Before he could stand upright again, the toe of her boot rammed into his side, then she pulled the stun truncheon from her pocket and stabbed it towards him. He grunted, convulsed, went down on his face, spilling a small torch-like object from his hand. Var snatched it up, feeling triumphant—any doubts about her current actions evaporating. Unlike a stun truncheon, which basically caused an abrupt and brief paralysis, the disabler he had been about to use disabled by causing the most extreme agony.

"What are you doing?" asked Grieve from the door.

Var glanced towards him. "Come in, Thomas, and close the door behind you."

With obedient naivety he did precisely as she asked, even as she stood up from Main's recumbent form and headed towards him. After closing the door, he turned to her uncertainly, just in time to receive the full force of the truncheon on one side of his head. As he went down, Var felt slightly uncomfortable about how good it had felt to do that, how, even though Grieve had been mind-wiped, she still felt in need of some payback from him for the killing of Martinez back on Mars. She then went in search of rolls of electrical tape with which to bind them both.

"So, how were you intending to assassinate my brother?" she asked, when Main finally came round.

He stared back at her in a superior way before suddenly looking panicked and peering down at his chest.

"You're looking for this?" she asked, holding up his relay on the end of its chain, the communication device now crushed flat by his bench vice. "No, you won't be talking to your coconspirators for a while—if ever again." She noted that Grieve had now regained consciousness, too, and was staring at her wide-eyed from where she'd bound him tightly to another bench leg. He wouldn't be interrupting them, since she'd taped his mouth shut.

"I don't know what you're talking about," Main snapped. "And you've no right to do this. We have laws aboard this station."

"You mean 'ship' don't you," she noted acidly. "Argus ceased to be a space station some while ago."

"Whatever." He shrugged.

"I know who the rest are, since you all conveniently had a meeting within my sight. So I'll go back to my first question: how do you intend to assassinate my brother?"

He kept his mouth stubbornly closed, so she held up his disabler and watched sheer terror flit across his expression.

"You're mad," he said quickly. "We just meet to discuss some business options."

"Very private business," she said, holding up one of the scramblers.

His eyes widened in shock.

"Did you really think you could keep these items a secret?"

He said nothing, so Var placed both objects down on the floor, reached out and pinched his nose shut and, when he finally opened his mouth to take a breath, shoved a ball of insulating tape inside. He struggled as she again picked up the disabler and set the intensity to below a level where the agony would knock him out. She pointed it at his chest and triggered it, watched him writhe and grunt, tears streaming from his eyes. After a full ten seconds of this, she turned the disabler off, shuffled back a bit to get away from the pool of urine spreading underneath him—and wrinkled her nose because he'd also shit himself.

Soon he was staring at her in panic, struggling to inhale enough breath through his nostrils. She pulled the wad of tape from his mouth, slimy with blood and saliva, and put it to one side, before waiting for him to recover. He lay gasping and occasionally sobbing, tears still streaming from his eyes. At that moment, Var felt a moment of doubt and began to wonder if she had gone too far. She then stubbornly dismissed the thought. She would carry this through to its conclusion, since no other options were viable.

"Now, I'll ask you again: how do you intend to assassinate my brother? And, to save time here, your communications have been penetrated and I know for a fact that killing him is your ultimate aim."

"There's no plan . . . we were just talking . . . no law against talking."

"So twenty-five of the chipped, having established what they believed to be a secure method of communication—and including in their number that rabble-rouser Marsin and Messina's ex-bodyguard and clone—were just *talking*." She stared at him steadily for a moment, then reached over and picked up the ball of tape again.

"If you've penetrated our scramblers, you must know!" he said desperately.

"But I haven't," she replied. "It's my brother who knows what you're up to. I'm just making sure something is done to stop that before he uses it as an excuse to exterminate us all."

"He won't kill you."

"Okay, before he exterminates all but a few of those close to him." She began moving the ball of tape towards his mouth again, and he tried to turn his head aside.

"Wait! Wait!" he pleaded.

She jammed the ball of tape back in and gave him a second dose from the disabler then afterwards let him struggle for breath, until he fainted.

"This will not stop until you answer my questions," she told him after he recovered consciousness.

This time, as he stared at her with bloodshot eyes, blood and saliva running down his chin, she knew she would get the answers she required.

"There's a bomb," he managed.

"Tell me about it."

"Ghort got hold of . . . demolition charges." He coughed, sending more blood running down his chin, and she noted a trickle of blood from one ear and wasn't sure why he was bleeding there. "Alex turned them into a copper-head armour-piercing charge capable of killing him in his inner sanctum . . . and two assault rifle grenades."

"Why the grenades?"

"Spidergun . . ."

"In his sanctum?"

"No . . . out in the rim, where he's hidden his backups."

Var sat back on her heels and studied him. That answer made no sense at all, and she felt Main must be trying to mislead her. Without jamming the ball of tape in place she hit him with the disabler again. He convulsed, emitted a gargling sound, his back arching. As she clicked off the device, he slumped, his right eye now red with blood and still more of it running out of his ear. She waited patiently for him to recover, but eventually felt her stomach tighten up and a cold dread settle over her. He wasn't breathing.

Var struggled to cut him free as quickly as she could and tried mouth-to-mouth, thumped his chest, used every technique she could think of to revive him. She even used the stun stick on his chest to try and restart his heart. She lost track of time: how long had it been? Ten minutes? Half an hour? It must have been something to do with his implant. Like many of the chipped, he had yet to heal completely, and she had no idea what harm the application of a disabler might have caused. Finally she gave up and checked the time. She had another two hours before Scarrow went off-shift and then probably turned up here. She had the corpse of someone she had tortured to death and—she swung her head to gaze at Thomas Grieve—she had a witness to that fact.

Would her brother forgive this? He had gone to Mars just to rescue her, and had then put her in charge of the converting of Argus Station into an interstellar vessel. But those uncharacteristic acts of nepotism were no indication of how he might react to what she had done here. When she knew him back on Earth, he had always been a cold fish, and out here he was colder still. He might just decide that forgiving his sister for murder would be inconvenient—that she'd stepped too far over the line—and send her the way of the Committee delegates captured here . . . and the way of Thomas Grieve. No, it would be best not to put him in the position where he had to make any decision about her.

Still gazing at Grieve, she stood up, opened her palmtop and keyed into the programs she used to monitor the construction work on the station. A quick search revealed precisely what she wanted, and she rerouted a construction robot to pick up an empty sealant drum and fetch it here. It would arrive within an hour. She walked over to Grieve and gazed down at him, saw that he was crying, probably because he knew what was about to happen. There was nothing she could say really, so she reached over to the bench above him and picked up a heavy adjustable spanner, knowing that if there was any uncertainty hitherto about her having stepped over the line, she was just about to banish that.

The two ships whose names, so the latest ETV report informed him, were the *Fist* and the *Command*, had made their way clear of their construction station. With his new upgrades in place and beginning to kick in, and the soreness of his body separated from his main consciousness, Saul decided to try something. He had spent hours concentrating on building backup programs to compensate for time delays, and constructing lethal worms and viruses to look for any chink in those distant defences. Now, relaying through the observer satellite lying a few million kilometres out from Earth, he tried a long-range penetration of the systems of the two ships . . . and failed.

Perhaps the transmission delay was just too much. As data finally started coming back to him, he realized he had hit something amorphous that subsequently reached back towards him and began its own penetration of the observer satellite.

Aboard one of those ships was a comlifer, keeping him out. He sent signals to shut down systems within the satellite to deny it access, until he realized the data packets coming through from the satellite were no form of attack but an attempt at communication. He allowed them space within the satellite's storage and, over the ensuing hours of signal delay, watched in fascination as a subpersona developed there.

"Hello, Alan Saul, genocidal maniac and all-round psychopath," said a voice.

What with the huge communication delays at this distance, it had been Saul's intention to assign a lesser portion of his mind to respond, only relaying to him any critical data obtained for the duration, and to be reabsorbed later. However, the Rhine drive was up to speed, there were no hitches in the work being conducted, and all other plans were playing out precisely as predicted. His ship did not need him and, really, the data he might be able to obtain through this communication had higher priority. He inverted priorities, leaving the general running of his ship to a lesser portion of his mind while changing the notion of time for the rest of his mind by collapsing his perception of the signal delays. It seemed that the comlifer wanted to chat, or perhaps was looking for some sort of opening which, if conceded, would also provide an opening for Saul himself.

"So who am I talking to?"

An image presented itself now of a bald fat man confined naked in a chair, tubed, wired, bound and presently being sponged down by a medic. "My name is Christopher Shivers, and you can call me Christopher—I only let my friends call me Chris."

"Why would you suppose that I am not your friend?"

"Because you are the arch-demon Alan Saul—enemy to all humanity and all right-thinking souls. You are the one who all but destroyed Earth's government and visited the Scour upon us."

"I detect elements of sarcasm coming from you," Saul replied. "Perhaps you know that the Scour came from a biochip that is included within all ID implants—a biochip incidentally manufactured at the Aldeburgh Complex which Serene Galahad used to run."

The subpersona paused to exchange data with its original self, updating rapidly. Saul received a brief request for the subpersona to relay to Saul's system. It seemed likely that this was now the real attempt to penetrate Saul's ship, and, if so, it would give Saul a way of getting to Christopher, and the *Fist* and the *Command*. He allowed it to relay to secure storage, but of course reduced security simply by communicating with it.

"It seems you might have a case," said Christopher, "but you are still my enemy. It is because of you I am now what I am, rather than a lowly robotics engineer. It is because of you my skull feels as empty as it is full."

"I understand," Saul agreed. "You must accept the exigencies of your genetic programming to retain a reason for continuing to exist. You must keep some part of you human or else everything becomes pointless and oblivion the only answer."

Even as he spoke the words, Saul knew they were no longer entirely true for himself. He existed. He would continue to exist and no longer needed the instinct for brute survival; something more complex was nudging it aside.

"So you give advice to your enemy?" Christopher asked. "Here's my human part."

The image changed, slid back to a stored one: The bald fat man thrashing against his restraints, unable to scream because of a big plastic plug in his mouth—probably there to stop him biting off his own tongue.

"I want to die but I can't kill myself. If I try to kill myself the response is the same as with any other form of disobedience: *pain*. I ache for oblivion—being human is the reason I want to cease to exist."

"So how is it that you're talking to me now?"

"All part of my duties, if but briefly."

It was the *Fist* that had fired the missile, but it would be some hours yet before it reached the satellite and destroyed it, cutting off one source of data for Saul. The comlifer had been distracting him from the attack, whether intentionally was unclear, since there was nothing he could do about it anyway.

"How long before the *Fist* and the *Command* are ready to go?" he asked.

"*I* couldn't possibly tell you that."

Saul noticed the emphasis on the "I," and how more data packets were currently queuing up to load to the subpersona.

"Genetic exigencies?" he enquired.

"Certainly," replied the growing copy in Saul's system of the comlifer aboard *Command*, "survival or else trying to make copies of some part of oneself."

Saul watched the packets loading to his system, while also observing the missile eating up the distance towards the satellite, and calculated that most of the packets would be through before the missile struck, after which he intended to take the time to have a proper talk with Christopher. Now he returned the larger portion of his mind to a more human perception of time, while instantly updating on everything that had happened during the many hours that their apparently brief conversation had taken.

First to come into his focus was, as always, Hannah Neumann. She had been very busy while construction was still underway here in the Io flux tube, and now the number of those who had been chipped—and who possessed backups for their minds—outweighed the rest of the ship's inhabitants. That number also included the Martian doctor Da Vinci who, at that moment, was monitoring the rapid growth of the fifteen clones under his care. As Saul had expected, the relationship between these two was getting strained. They both put this down to Da Vinci's choice of trying out a cryogenic pod and her insisting that he also must be chipped and have a backup first, when in reality their problems were due to them both being dominant controlling personalities ill prepared to submit or to make compromises. Within the next five days, extraneous circumstances permitting, one of them would find a reason to start a fierce argument with the other, and that would lead to them breaking up. It was all so prosaic, so human.

Next, Saul focused his attention on the weapon built by the Saberhagen twins, for it was now complete and undergoing diagnostic testing. Magnetic bottle "caps" were loaded and all the weapon's ultra-capacitor storage was fully up to charge. At the moment, Brigitta and Angela were in Arcoplex Two, monitoring the diagnostic test—Angela mostly silent while Brigitta, from recorded cam footage, had been bemoaning Saul stopping them from test firing their weapon. Saul felt a degree of chagrin, somewhere, at Brigitta's blinkered intransigence, but decided to speak to her anyway—like a human.

"I must congratulate you on your success here," he stated through their intercom.

Brigitta glanced round to check if he was in the room, then glanced up at a nearby cam. "I would have more confidence in our *success*, if you would let me fire off at least one cap."

"Surely the reason for that is quite plain?"

"Not to me."

Even as Brigitta spoke, Angela grimaced and shook her head. Obviously the quiet Saberhagen twin had already worked out why, yet, because of her own irritating tendency not to communicate what she felt should be obvious to all, she had not told her sister.

"The *Vision* is sitting out there watching us very closely," Saul observed, "and isn't it the case that revealing a new weapon to one's enemy is not a good idea?"

"We're as good as in the Io flux tube, where the EM radiation should cover it."

Oh, good, she had at least been thinking about this, though not deeply enough.

"Two problems I see there," replied Saul. "Because we are, as you say, as good as in the Io flux tube, the data you would get from such a firing would be highly dubious. The EM effects would disrupt both targeting and the magnetic bottle of the cap. Furthermore, the *Vision* would still gather enough imagery to inform Earth that we are capable of firing plasma bolts."

"I suppose," she replied grudgingly. "I haven't got your omniscience."

"So, you must just do what you can without a test firing, okay?"

"Yeah, okay." Brigitta flung herself down in her seat, waved a hand at the cam and began tapping away at a keyboard.

Saul drew away, feeling like a professorial parent irritated by the limited understanding of a child. He spread his awareness now, taking in a full overview of his ship, fleeting irritation dismissed and satisfaction at present progress supplanting it.

Just two square kilometres of hull plates remained still to be fitted for the ship to become a fully enclosed sphere. The docks were now secure inside, while his conjoined robots were building massive sliding space doors in the outer hull. These were back in their open position so presented no hindrance to the space plane currently entering the ship and heading towards Dock One; meanwhile, the remaining space plane was two hours away, still towing in a booster tank. Insulated walls had risen up around the business end of the Mars Traveller engine, while a new steering thruster was being built at the pole of the ship—both of these just a backup should the Mach-effect element of the ship's overall drive fail. All the rebuilding was in fact ahead of schedule and, thinking of that, Saul decided to check in on the woman whom he had appointed overseer of all this work.

"It seems, Var, that you're managing to beat my rebuilding schedule," he commented, watching his sister through the cam located in her mobile overseer's office.

She looked up from her screen, and he at once noted how pale and ill she appeared. Perhaps she had been pushing herself too hard, yet, reading the minutiae of her expression, Saul felt a nag of doubt.

"Is everything okay?" he asked.

"I think so," she replied, "if you're utterly sure that these chipped rebels are unlikely to be a threat—I can't help but feel some concern about them."

With a fragment of his mind Saul ascertained that those same chipped rebels were moving along nicely with their plans. They'd now stepped over the line from talking to action and everything he'd put in place to deal with them would initiate at the right time. He then noted that one of them was missing—a certain Gilder Main, whose backup relay was no longer signalling—and he ran a search of recorded footage. It took him all of two seconds to realize why something had seemed amiss with his sister.

"I see you had a chat with Gilder Main."

It appeared that Main and the repro Thomas Grieve had spent some hours with her in the cam black spot in the workshop of the fone shop. Subsequently neither of the two had reappeared in any cam view.

"One of the robots they control is carrying a copper-head bomb which it even now has probably attached to your inner sanctum," she replied quickly.

"Where are Gilder Main and Thomas Grieve?" he countered, noting that, yes, the robot had indeed put the explosive in place and that its timer was running. "What happened behind the fone shop?"

Momentary desperation flitted across her expression, then it went flat and blank. "I questioned Main and he revealed the plot. He also said something about a plan to destroy your backups, which he seemed to think were somewhere in the old station ring. I think Thomas Grieve overheard us." She shrugged. "What happened after I left, I've no idea."

She was lying, there could be no doubt. He watched old cam footage of a robot, carrying an empty sealant drum, arriving while she was still in the fone shop, then heading off to one of the smelting plants, where that same drum had gone into one of the furnaces. There was also no data available on who had instructed the robot, so someone expert must have wiped it from the system. Someone like Var.

Gilder Main, he felt sure, would not have willingly revealed the plot contrived by the chipped rebels. With a thought, Saul sent a small maintenance robot to check out that same black spot, certain that it would find neither Main nor Grieve still there. By now they were both furnace slag or part of the ship's components. Furthermore, from what he had thus far read in Var's expression and in the intonation of her words, he suspected that she had interrogated and killed Main, and probably killed Grieve too. Saul linked to a particular backup, taking the route he had taken before when he just became suspicious of some of the chipped—whereby he had broken the scrambler codes by reading their recently backed-up thoughts. He set a program to decoding Gilder Main's last memories, and then returned his full attention to Var.

"Did you kill them both?" he asked her.

"Now you're being silly," she replied, but everything he read in her confirmed the truth.

What should he do about this? Var had been as much a killer as him—killing to survive—except, of course, when she killed Rhone of Mars Science, which was plain vengeance, for he had been no threat at the time. If she had killed Gilder Main, then really that was justifiable since Main, like the rest of the chipped, had crossed a line. However, killing a mind-wiped repro amounted to the plain murder of an innocent.

The decoded memory came through now. Saul experienced Main's sudden panic upon hearing that Var had walked into the fone shop, his scramble for the disabler he'd stolen, the impact of Var's kick followed by a similar impact from a stun truncheon . . . then nothing thereafter.

In a way it was his own fault, he realized. Having yet to decide how to deal with the human population aboard his ship, he did not know how much freedom to allow them, how large a degree of self-governance, or how much information to provide for them. He had not detailed to Var his plan for dealing with the chipped rebels because he felt it to be only his concern. He also had no wish to explain, to someone whose breadth of understanding was so limited, the subtle manipulation he was using and how he was certain it would work. In her turn, Var had felt the need to act decisively, ruthlessly and *competitively*. He should have foreseen that. Now, in an instant, he made some crucial decisions. The human population aboard would govern and police itself, and he himself would only intervene when his own or the ship's security was threatened. They would work to pay for their accommodation, the necessities of their existence, the very air they breathed; and, since the system currently developing here was a wealthy one, they could earn much more. Saul now issued a decree to that effect, to be displayed on every screen, fone or personal item of computing. That was how it would be from now until . . . later.

Through certain cams, Saul noted the production of the main components of the cryogenic pods. When he finally left the solar system, the population here would go into hibernation and then . . . what? In truth he had no need of any of them. They were basically an encumbrance.

"I have no intention of judging you," he told his sister. "Let us hope that you've sufficiently covered your tracks for no one to find out, though, for I will not stand in the way of any judgement by your peers."

She just gazed at the cam, and Saul studied her for a while longer, reading her face down to its very pores, but feeling a mental distance between them rapidly growing. Shortly it seemed as if he was peering down a microscope at some interesting but thoroughly predictable specimen, until external events abruptly dragged his attention elsewhere.

The *Vision* was on the move.

12

SQUARE PEGS, ROUND HOLES

The Committee, and also its forebears, had always been much in love with the idea of "social engineering." This starts with the contention that the world would be a better place if, to cite some examples, people ate and drank only what was good for them, exercised regularly, avoided mind-altering substances, worked diligently for the good of all, produced only two children, put their correctly sorted trash out on time and listened with worshipful interest to the wisdom of their betters. Next on the agenda is persuasion, usually along with the manipulation of "facts," which works, but only to a limited extent because people are contrary creatures whose resentment increases almost proportionally. Finally the punishments for incorrect behaviour arrive because, in the end, the ideologues want the people to fit their idea of a perfect society, where an airy concept such as happiness can only arise from correct political thought. Serene Galahad's approach was of course much more direct: if human beings don't fit the "perfect society," then they must be altered on the genetic level to correct their faults. She was also a much more honest version of the "social engineer," what with her hatred of humanity unconcealed.

EARTH

"Bartholomew reports that he's moving the *Vision* to minimum safe distance away from Saul's ship," said Elkin, as they rounded a corner in the corridor and headed towards Calder's apartment. "And Calder reports that the tug is bringing the *Scourge* into Earth orbit and that a shuttle has just left it."

It all seemed too much all at once—just too many balls to keep in the air. She palmed the lock to Calder's apartment, turning to watch as some of her security team deployed in the corridor, then she stepped inside.

"So tell me again about what Vaughan reported," she snapped.

"Our undercover operatives here were listed as unsafe personnel, and either moved to the far end of the station or off station altogether," said Elkin flatly. "This could have simply been an administration error, but it also seems that Vaughan and his team are finding themselves hindered by the Inspectorate personnel aboard."

"Hindered in what ways?" Serene asked as she sat down at Calder's desk and opened up her palmtop, expanded its screen and adjusted the keyboard projection to a suitable surface.

"Mostly bureaucratic foot-dragging, restrictions on system access, and by allocating quarters for Vaughan and his men in . . . inconvenient parts of the station."

"I always considered the number of Inspectorate personnel present here too high," remarked Serene. "And now I'm feeling uncomfortable with that—just as I am uncomfortable with Calder's attitude."

Her annoyance at finding so many Inspectorate personnel still in evidence here had turned to alarm, for she experienced some intimation of sinister motives behind their presence. She shook her head and initiated a search of the station's system through her palmtop and, while it was running, turned on the main desk screen and called up an exterior cam view. The search continued while she watched the main drive of the tug firing as it brought the *Scourge* in towards Earth, which in this current view lay over to the right of the screen. The shuttle was visible, but slowly moving out of shot.

"So it never occurred to Calder that a reduction in political oversight here might result in increased productivity?" she enquired.

Something in her tone immediately had Sack stepping forwards with his reptilian hands clenching and unclenching. Elkin glanced at him and stepped away from Serene, keeping her hands firmly behind her back and her expression bland. Of course, it wasn't really in Elkin's remit to look at staffing levels, and it might not be Calder's fault that so many Inspectorate personnel were still here, since reorganizing the structures he inherited was not entirely down to him. Serene knew that her anger stemmed from her not having immediately investigated this anomaly herself.

Her search now revealed staff rosters and complements, and it was easy enough for her to locate those listed under "oversight." She ran an overlay from the new command structures on Earth, and began finding those who were surplus to requirements. Even as she did this, she noted something else: just how many of these personnel were listed as "Inspectorate/disciplinary."

"They have adjustment cells here?" she enquired, then began checking for herself. They did have adjustment cells—currently occupied by fifty-eight personnel. She felt her anger grow upon seeing such waste and inefficiency, and spun her chair round. Elkin was now thoroughly preoccupied with her fones and by whatever her aides were drawing her attention to on their note screens. Serene deliberately forced calm on herself and waited. She had employed Elkin because of the speed with which the woman could collate data, come to conclusions, and make reports and assessments. After a minute or so, Elkin's preoccupation with information cleared, but this left her looking concerned and slightly puzzled.

"Ma'am," she cleared her throat, "it seems a faction of the Inspectorate entrenched itself here even during your rule, and were in place before Calder arrived. His official response, when this matter was raised by the advisers you supplied to him, was that you wanted immediate results and he could not give you them if he was to spend time conducting a purge. However, data indicate that they were retained on his orders, and their section chiefs vetted by him personally."

"Your assessment of that?" Serene asked.

"I suspect he might have been building a power base, ma'am." Elkin paused to glance at something else one of her aides was showing her, then continued, "Calder's subsequent response to a query from his advisers was that they cause fewer problems this way than would removing them from their posts and returning them to Earth."

"I would hardly call keeping fifty-eight personnel in adjustment cells a lesser problem," Serene noted tightly.

"Apparently," Elkin continued, "just to get the one thousand one hundred and forty surplus Inspectorate personnel back to the surface, with their belongings, would take at least five space-plane runs—journeys, he asserted, that could not be afforded."

"One thousand one hundred and forty surplus personnel," Serene echoed flatly. "Who is this chief Inspectorate political officer?"

"There is none, ma'am," Elkin replied. "They take their orders directly from Calder."

So, Calder did not want these personnel returned to Earth, and it seemed there was some agreement there. This probably meant they did not think they would do so well under the new regime. She swung back to her palmtop and began doing some checking, searching the local system for data on the personnel concerned and then, upon realizing that very little data was available there, she linked to her data banks down on Earth, loading the list of the Inspectorate staff based here to specialized security searches. Within a few minutes things started being flagged for her attention. She began studying everything thus flagged, while simultaneously relaying this new data to Elkin and her aides.

All the Inspectorate personnel involved came from the environs of Outback spaceport, and were those Messina had originally sent there to prepare the way for him. It all made perfect sense now, and she began to develop some real worries on checking further. The section chiefs had liaised closely with her own security teams prior to her arrival; also an inquiry to databases on Earth revealed that they had all managed to avoid being fitted with strangulation collars, though how was unclear.

"How many of my security personnel do we have here?" she asked as she went on to checking readergun protocols aboard the station. It seemed that she did have primacy, so could reactivate and take over the guns in a moment. However, since there had been a lot of construction and reconstruction here, and readerguns had not been considered essential to her purposes, there were huge areas left without coverage—including the large accommodation area where these Inspectorate personnel were housed.

"Approximately five hundred," Elkin replied, now herself looking slightly sick.

"So we are outnumbered two to one by Inspectorate personnel who were loyal to Messina, and who now seem to have made some sort of a deal with Calder."

Elkin nodded dumbly.

"You and Vaughan missed this," Serene observed. "You missed precisely the kind of situation you were supposed to be looking for."

It could be that she was being overly paranoid, but that was better than being dead. It seemed likely that the Inspectorate personnel had chosen this place as a refuge, but it might also be because, under Messina, they had seen the main power base shifting off-world, and had decided that it probably wouldn't be any different under Serene. Quite probably, there were those among them with ambitions, perhaps trying to build themselves a little empire out here, and in Calder they had found someone of similar mind. However, they had all run afoul of Serene's decision to keep cutting political oversight, even after the large chunk Alan Saul took out of it, and they had also run afoul of her decision to pay a visit. The question now was how they would react.

"I can only apologize," said Elkin, shooting a nervous glance at Sack.

Serene gave a dismissive wave of her hand. This was too serious a situation for her to start killing off essential personnel right now. Maybe later Elkin could pay the price for her lapse.

Serene selected the list of Inspectorate personnel and ran it through another program that gave her a list of their implant codes, which she then fed into the Scour activation program. She could kill all of them this way but, if she did, it would become obvious that the Scour was far too specific.

"You've been feeding this through to Tactical?"

"I have, ma'am." Elkin gestured to one of her blank-faced aides. "First assessment is that even if Calder's retention of these people was not originally done with hostile intent, it will be now. He will know that he has been found out and, due to the consequences of that, Tactical puts a high probability on him making some sort of attack on you. However, he will not move against you until after the *Command* and *Fist* have departed under Alcubierre drive."

Serene said nothing for a moment as she considered that, and realized she had been stupid. Of course her personnel weren't outnumbered. She nodded as if this was nothing new to her. "Because of the troops aboard the *Fist*, obviously."

"Still supposing the likelihood of some sort of attack on you, Tactical advises against making the obvious move of ordering the *Fist* to dock again and using its troops to negate that potential threat. If the Fist was to return to the station, it seems highly likely that Calder would then realize something is wrong, and act accordingly. His most likely response is to fire the station's railguns at the *Fist*, and either disable or destroy it."

Elkin looked even sicker now—scared to complete her tactical assessment. Serene held up a hand to silence her, then called up a station schematic and noted that the new dock Calder had suggested Clay Ruger's shuttle should arrive at was without a readergun network, and was quite some distance from both the escape drop-ship and the space-plane docks. She also checked timings and noted that Ruger would be arriving after the *Fist* and the *Command* were scheduled to depart.

. . . the likelihood of some sort of attack on you . . .

Calder possessed his own private army, her undercover operatives here had been removed, Calder's Inspectorate staff had been hindering her own security staff when, if Calder had wanted to avoid discovery, it would have been better for him to have ordered them to keep their heads down. Now it seemed that Calder had directed Ruger—and consequently herself—to an interstation shuttle dock *without* a readergun network. Calder was moving against her, of that she was now certain.

"So what's the best Tactical can give me?" she finally asked.

Elkin swallowed drily before commencing. "You can send your security teams against the Inspectorate complement here, which will give you time to get to the drop shuttle and thus get away from the station. But at the same time you must also order Bartholomew to fire on the station to disable its railguns and control infrastructure, otherwise Calder will be able to hit you on the way down. This gives you an approximate sixty per cent chance of escaping alive, though there is an above eighty per cent chance of both the *Fist* and the *Command* being disabled."

Not good enough. Serene coldly contemplated the data available to her. It seemed likely that Calder had planned some sort of attack upon her in this new space dock, once Ruger arrived. She must turn this situation to her own advantage.

"Vaughan has the usual complement of hardware, I take it?" she enquired.

"Enough for a small war," Elkin replied, "but the Inspectorate personnel aboard will have access to the same sort of hardware."

"I don't know why I bother with Tactical," remarked Serene contemptuously. "We take them in the space dock." She paused reflectively. "My security team is kept ready for all circumstances, including vacuum combat. Besides, they will be equipped with VC suits, while I note that, though armoured, the Inspectorate personnel here still wear ordinary uniforms." Elkin nodded doubtfully.

"I take it some of Vaughan's people are already present in the new dock, to oversee the arrangements for Clay Ruger's arrival."

Elkin blinked, rubbed a finger at a menu control located at her temple, and at length replied, "Yes, Vaughan has assembled a team there, but station Inspectorate personnel are making all the arrangements."

Viewing the big desk screen, Serene noted that the tug was no longer firing its main engine, and Earth loomed large behind it and the attached *Scourge*. Meanwhile, the shuttle was out of view. Despite her suggestion that the *Fist* and the *Command* should use the *Scourge* for target practice, Calder had urged that it be dismantled instead. Yes, a lot of it would be highly radioactive—and therefore only good for scrap—but most of the engines were still fine, including the main one, and the plutonium and uranium from the nuclear arsenal could also be salvaged. Serene studied it for a while longer, but could see no ulterior motive from Calder for recommending salvage. He had obviously still been playing the part of a loyal citizen, while making his own arrangements elsewhere.

Rather than use her palmtop, she summoned up to this same screen a number of internal cam views of the station itself, and quickly located the shuttle dock Ruger would be heading for. The view inside showed a great hall with airlocks running down one side, and two levels of station monorail lines running down the middle. Swarming about the area were armed Inspectorate personnel, as well as numbers of Serene's own security staff.

"How many?" she asked.

"Two hundred of ours, six hundred of Calder's people," Elkin offered instantly.

Serene continued staring at the screen. She had hoped for an easy option here. She had hoped that the Inspectorate personnel would be wearing their usual uniforms. It would then have been simplicity itself for Vaughan to plant a charge on one of the space doors, and then allow vacuum decompression to deal with her problem. Foolish hope that, because Calder was not so stupid as to allow his people into anywhere as vulnerable as a space dock without the requisite gear. She could now only distinguish his people from her own by the older design of VC suit they wore.

"Tell Vaughan to get himself and all his team here at once."

"Ma'am?"

"Just do as you're told."

All her options were running out. If she took Tactical's advice, she could lose everything: she could lose Alan Saul, she could lose the Gene Bank data—whether acquired from Saul or Ruger—and she could lose her own life.

"I take it Vaughan is by now aware of the situation?" she enquired.

"Yes, ma'am."

Serene nodded, then selected the screen tab on her palmtop for the Scour activation program. For a moment she hesitated, considering adding Calder's name to the list, but decided against that, before abruptly switching to another screen and sitting back. No, not yet—considering how fast the Scour acted, there was still time, and she needed to think hard about the consequences of taking this step.

Everyone aboard the station would soon realize that the entire Inspectorate complement had died from the Scour. That information would then spread around Earth orbit, and without doubt it would eventually reach Earth. It would then be obvious that the Scour was a lot more specific than previously supposed, that merely air-transmission or some similar form of contagion were unlikely. She would have to concoct some sort of story to cover this outbreak.

Calder . . .

The man's main discipline was nanotechnology, so surely it would be possible to contrive some way for him to take the blame. This could all be down to an assassination attempt against her and how he used the Scour to remove the personnel protecting her. Yes, something like that should work. There would be loose ends to tie up, but none that could not be neatly knotted by a strangulation collar, bullet or adjustment cell.

Perhaps she could also contrive some sort of alliance between Calder and Alan Saul, as that would neatly—

"Ma'am?"

"What?" Serene whirled on Elkin.

"All your delegates are assembled ready in video conference, and we are currently recording for ETV their ratification of a pardon for all real or imagined crimes committed by Clay Ruger and Pilot Officer Trove," she said. "It's being transmitted here right now, and will soon be ready for insertion into the station ETV broadcast."

Serene stared at her blankly, not quite understanding for a moment. Then it all clicked into place in her mind. She must never forget the importance of ensuring that Clay Ruger actually began transmission of the Gene Bank data.

"Vaughan also reports that his team is fully in place around you, while Admiral Bartholomew—confirmed by Calder—has tightened his estimate of departure to just one hour's time."

"I see," said Serene, wondering where the intervening time had gone.

Ruger's shuttle should be docking in about three hours, which should allow her enough leeway to have things sorted out and cleared up for his arrival. It wouldn't do to have hundreds of Scour victims floating around inside the space dock when the ETV broadcast began—therefore Vaughan and his men would have to deal with that.

Serene tapped on the tab of the Scour-activation program, poised a finger over the return key projected on the table before her, hesitating for just a moment as she remembered the first time she had done this and the pompous words she had spoken then to the man Ruger had replaced. She then brought her finger down.

ARGUS

Acceleration pushed Hannah back into her seat as the new train headed out towards what someone had dubbed the "Meat Locker." This newly built hall was sandwiched within the lattice walls between Arcoplex Two and the Arboretum. The thing was a kilometre long, two hundred metres wide and extended the depth of the gap between the two lattice walls, which was a hundred metres. Down one side was a station into which the vehicle now slowed, throwing Hannah forward against her straps. Once it had stopped, airlock tubes extended from the near wall to each of the three carriages, the tube accessing the rear cargo carriage being oval in cross-section and ten metres across at its widest point. As all these tubes connected, Hannah could hear movement from the rear as robots began unloading the next batch of components for the Meat Locker.

She unstrapped and propelled herself over to the door leading into the nearest airlock tube, checked the ready light, opened the door and passed through. A moment later, she found herself in the new hall itself and looking around. Directly ahead of her the wall was honeycombed, with partially assembled cryogenic pods protruding here and there, with the golden centipedes of Saul's conjoining robots busily at work on them. Over to her right the more conventional station robots were busy ferrying out the cargo, dispatching crates and empty pods through the air to be fielded by their more up-to-date brethren. There were humans here, too: some of the chipped controlling the older robots, engineers working on individual pods, and at the far end of the wall, beside a pod extending near what she supposed she might call the floor—such nomenclature in zero gravity always being difficult—stood a small group apart. She propelled herself towards them, correcting her trajectory with the wrist impeller of her suit because, despite the place being pressurized, using space-suits was a precaution all ship's personnel took in any new builds.

Approaching the group, she slowed and brought herself clumsily face-down towards the floor, but still managed to engage one gecko boot, to secure herself there while she stood properly. One of the figures was without a spacesuit—stripped down to his undershorts while Dr Raiman attached stick-on sensors to his exposed skin. As Hannah walked closer, Da Vinci waved to her cheerfully. She raised her hand in not so cheerful acknowledgement, nodded to Langstrom and the other two officers present, then turned to the remaining individual.

"So you've finally come out of your pit," she remarked, glancing round to locate the spidergun, squatting over by the further wall. "Why's that?"

"To offer moral support," Saul replied.

"It would have to be just that," Hannah observed flatly. "We mere humans are now expected to govern and police ourselves, which means you've effectively washed your hands of us. What's that decision all about, then? A separation of church and state?"

"Within the limits and constraints of them being aboard my ship, I have given the people living here more freedom. I shall see, in time, what they do with it."

"That's big of you," Hannah snapped, then wished she hadn't. "Anyway, I would have thought, with everything that's going on, you'd want to stay at the centre, and in utter control."

"Generally my location is irrelevant and, anyway, the ship is in no danger right now." He paused for a second, his pink eyes blinking. "The *Vision* cannot harm us, and I can get us on the move the moment the other two ships start heading our way."

"I detect some doubt."

He shook his head. "I'm just failing to perceive what Galahad hopes to achieve. Unless those two ships have some way of viewing normal space through an Alcubierre warp, and thus tracking us, sending them against us is a futile gesture."

"I hope you're right," said Hannah, studying him more closely.

With the Mach-effect drive operating to keep the ship stable and the EM shield protecting them from the ionization in the flux tube, all radio communications were shut down. Previously this had meant that, without a direct optic connection, Saul would be disconnected from the ship's systems, but Hannah could see he had used the same work-around as he had employed against Salem Smith on first sending his robots against him. An optic cable extended from the socket in his temple down into the neck ring of his suit, while, attached to the shoulder of his suit, was a flat matt disc with green pin lights flickering and glinting around its rim. He was laser-linked to receivers on the robots here, on his spidergun, and on any other item of equipment that used some form of remote control—and therefore through all of these into the ship's systems.

Examining him further, she noted other changes, such as the fact that he wasn't wearing a standard-issue VC suit. His bulked slightly larger, with numerous black boxes attached to its surface; the helmet hanging from his belt had also been redesigned, possessing optic connections all around the neck ring. It seemed that, while holed up in his inner sanctum, Saul had been busy indeed. Then, with a start, she realized that at the base of his neck, small devices had been surgically attached at his carotids, pipes and wires leading from these down inside the suit.

"Pressure shunts and nutrient feeds," she decided.

"And much else besides," he agreed, before turning to glance at Da Vinci, who, held steady by Raiman, was now stepping into the cryogenic pod.

As Saul turned, she spotted another optic connection at the base of his skull, the cable similarly leading down into his suit, but she could hazard no possible reason for it. She, too, glanced at Da Vinci, feeling abruptly at odds with herself. She had come here because she was concerned about him, because she wanted to make one last attempt to dissuade him from trying out this pod, but now all her concern was focused on Saul.

"You've been operating on yourself," she said.

He turned back to her, his expression mild. "Well, I wasn't actually holding the scalpel. I just robotized and programmed a combined micro- and macro-surgery, shut down this body of mine and let the surgery proceed."

"You should have let me do it," said Hannah, feeling both horrified and affronted. "I'll need to run some tests."

"You have enough to do," he replied, "and my health, mental or otherwise, is no longer your concern."

"It's the concern of us all!" she countered vehemently.

He tilted his head and in that moment she realized that his skin now had a slightly metallic hue which was not due to the lighting here, as she had first assumed.

"Your concern is irrelevant," he stated, the spidergun beyond him suddenly unfolding and becoming more attentive.

Had some fragment of humanity left inside him grown angry with her? Hannah wondered. Or had some risk-assessment program running in a mind that effectively spanned this entire ship calculated an increase in danger to its core; this human body and brain that sat at the centre of Alan Saul like the reptile back-brain sits at the core of all humans? Hannah gazed at him for a while longer, but he showed no human response to such scrutiny.

"Hi, Hannah," called out Da Vinci, his voice sounding slightly slurred, "glad you came."

She switched her attention back to him. He was now lying down inside the pod, and Raiman was beginning to close the lid. She hurried over. "Wait!" But, as she arrived and peered down at him, Da Vinci's eyes were already closed and he was breathing deeply and steadily.

"The process has started," explained Raiman.

Hannah wanted to tell him to stop the process at once, but knew that would be childish, and effectively beyond her authority. As the lid then closed, she switched her attention to the monitor screen showing all the rhythms of a human body, all slowing down. She noted the abrupt change in the pattern there, just as Da Vinci had predicted, at the moment the pod began to exchange blood for a complex form of antifreeze. Thereafter his core temperature began to drop rapidly.

"Time to insert it," said Raiman. "The control systems in the wall need to engage."

She stepped back as he punched a button on the side of the pod. It began to slide into its hexagonal space in the wall, grotesquely like a paper coffin going into a community digester. If it turned out that this process would kill Da Vinci, then she had already lost him. She wondered where this Meat Locker rated in Saul's calculations. Would the people aboard be given a choice about going into these pods, or did that decision fall under his remit regarding his own and his ship's safety? Would it in fact be compulsory?

"Couldn't this have waited until we were away from the solar system and well out of danger?" she asked. "We really needed the opportunity to do much more research into it."

"Not my decision," Raiman replied.

Hannah flicked him an annoyed glance then turned to Saul—but Saul was gone. He must have walked away while she was checking Da Vinci's monitor. In that moment she realized that while she might indeed have lost Da Vinci, there was also a good chance he would survive. All the same, she had very definitely lost the human being named Alan Saul.

He was gone forever.

"It's called the *Vision*," said the copy of the comlifer located aboard the *Command*, and who now allowed Saul to address him as Chris, "because that's about the limit of its capabilities."

"It possesses weapons," Saul noted, just as he reached the door leading into his inner sanctum.

"It does, but you could fry it if it gets any closer."

That was probably true, though Saul's main concern had been about its named purpose, which was why, ever since its arrival near Europa, he had switched over to minimal usage of the Mach-effect drive, and was now holding his ship in position using the rim steering thrusters. Just as with the Saberhagens" weapon, it was best not to apprise the enemy of technologies with tactical relevance, and the Mach-effect drive was certainly that.

In the virtual world he had created, Chris appeared slimmer than the image Saul had seen of him aboard the *Command*, and he was now clad in a neat suit. This struck Saul as not the usual dress of a robotics engineer but of an Inspectorate executive, a political officer. Saul was now entertaining some suspicions about his new guest, and so decided to discover Chris's true thoughts.

"They're panicking," Chris continued. "They've seen how fast your reconstruction has gone and are worried that you might take off or be too well prepared before their two warships can come after you. I'd bet they've moved the *Vision* closer so as to push you into doing something else that'll hamper you, just as moving the *Command* and the *Fist* out of the construction station made you recall your space planes."

The explanation was feasible but, as Saul had just told Hannah, Galahad's overall approach seemed strangely flawed. She must know that he could engage the Rhine drive at any moment and that though the two warships might be able to pursue him along whatever course he chose, they could not know when he was going to stop and change direction, and would therefore not know when to stop their own drives in order to change direction to go after him. Just one course change was needed, and he would be lost in the universe and utterly beyond Earth's reach.

So he had to be missing something.

Entering his sanctum, the door locks thumping home behind him, and his spidergun settling down like a dog coming home after a lengthy walk, he headed straight for his gimbals chair and quickly strapped himself in, unplugged the optic leading from his temple into his suit, and instead plugged in the one here. There was no interruption in the flow of data, and he was pleased with his trial of his new laser networking device, his life-support suit and the recent upgrade to his human body's mental function that required that new suit. Now his backups were truly backups—copying everything now running in his skull, in the additional brain matter growing in an artificial cyst in his groin, as well as the terabytes of processing power distributed through-out his suit.

"I'm not sure I would characterize what they are doing as panic," Saul stated, now opening links into the subpersona called Chris and injecting specially designed search engines which, if he wanted to draw similes with living organisms, were less like bloodhounds and more like wolves.

"What are you doing?" Chris asked.

"Getting to the truth," Saul replied.

The moment the search engines hit, the image of Chris began screaming, whereupon the virtual world he occupied tore open and flew apart. But how, Saul wondered, could something that was a mere collection of bytes feel pain? Of course, the same logic could be applied to human beings. Were they not just moist collections of biological information? It occurred to him now to wonder—as had been speculated on before by people of a philosophical turn of mind—how many of those around him were actually conscious.

The first truth the engines delivered was that, yes, Chris had been a robotics engineer, until his talent for sucking up to the right people and undermining rivals got him the position of political officer in the robotics factory.

After Saul's attack on Earth and Galahad's assumption of power, Chris had tried scrabbling further up the ladder but only managed to annoy someone senior to him. He'd been on his way to adjustment when he was offered an alternative—and he'd grabbed it. Who wouldn't? But, as a comlifer, first losing any will to live, and then going through the agonizing conditioning process, he wished he had chosen the visit to a white-tiled cell instead.

The next truth was a defining one. This subpersona had so many holes that it was a wonder it had managed to hold itself together. It contained no tactical data of any value to Saul, and some data that was most definitely a plant, like the assertion that the *Fist* and the *Command* would not be ready to leave Earth for at least five days. Still, Saul ran all of this "Chris" through filters, pattern-recognition programs, sifted and sieved him to get every last nugget of potentially useful information, then wiped the storage that had contained him, the subpersona expiring with an electronic sigh.

Certain things now seemed plain. Those moving against Saul wanted him to believe that they were desperate; that if he engaged his ship's Rhine drive all their plans would come to nothing; that the impossible was being demanded of them by the dictator of Earth. And it was all a lie. They had something, some technology or method, to achieve what Galahad wanted. That they had built and were in the process of dispatching those ships indicated this, for Serene Galahad might be a homicidal autocrat, but she wasn't insane enough to squander so much on a mere folly. The pattern of holes in the knowledge of this Chris also confirmed this. On the surface the memory erasures looked merely rough, but they covered up some very specific deletions.

Human frustration arose inside Saul, instantly banished, then its source abruptly reprogrammed itself to rid him of that particular route towards time-wasting emotion. He could go no further than affirm that his enemies had something extra, and that they knew how he had intended to react simply by running. As he considered this he noted that those he had summoned some time earlier were now arriving at the door leading into his inner sanctum, so he opened it for them.

They entered quickly, arranging themselves about his gimbals chair like alien priests around some technological god. There was no real need for them all to be present, but by summoning them Saul was making a statement both to them and to himself: in the hierarchy of this ship they stood higher than the humans since they were allowed here, while they also remained totally at his beck and call. But it went beyond that: a need for direct contact both in them and in him, to bring clarity and order.

Swinging his chair round in a slow circle, he studied the ten proctors. Over the time since their initiation, they had every one of them changed. They now wore human clothing or vacuum suits of one kind or another to fit their larger forms. This, Saul knew, was so that they did not look quite so alien and threatening to the humans aboard. Many carried devices of their own manufacture, most of which were staffs like the one Judd first constructed, which was packed with electronics and a power source based on the rectifying batteries, and was both a multi-purpose tool and a weapon. But the most radical changes were in the minds that Saul sensed floating like satellites around him. Each was a different shape, each had diverged and specialized, yet they remained conjoined—sharing information like a group of servers. They were like one being with ten facets, but also ten experts, each of which could quite comfortably survive on its own. He also now realized that the one that had named itself Paul was their interface with Saul himself. Paul served as the one designated as both their legate and expert as regards Alan Saul.

"Humans," Saul began, switching straight to the concern that had inspired this meeting.

"Your ship could be more efficient without them," Paul replied, "but it could also be more efficient without you. It could be more efficient without us and without individual robots and with all its systems automated."

Saul smiled as he followed this logical chain. "Without the arcoplexes and the Arboretum, efficiency would increase. Without the metal of the hull and much of the superstructure, the engines would prove more efficient. The Traveller engine would operate better without having to haul about the Rhine drive, and the Mach-effect drive would be more efficient without having to incorporate both the Rhine drive and the EM shield. The hull would be better without the holes, and could be made smaller if there was less contained inside. In fact, if there was nothing actually inside this ship, there would be no need for a hull at all . . ."

Stone soup, Saul thought, allowing them to register that.

Seeing, on a virtual level, the ramped-up communication now occurring between the ten minds, he wondered if they were struggling with rhetoric and irony but, no, Paul had started in with the same, so they should all be able to handle it. This communication was of a much higher order.

Saul continued, "My initial purpose was based on my genetically based need for safety and survival."

"Which you are now transcending," Paul observed. Saul wasn't so sure about that, but allowed it.

"Beyond survival, what is my purpose now?"

"It is whatever *you* decide."

"And the humans?"

"What you decide."

Saul felt a moment of chagrin that was immediately tracked down and analysed. He realized he had some difficulty in just asking a simple question because of complicated reasons involving its human source and a growing arrogance within him. He negated those reasons and asked, "What do you think?"

The level of communication between the conjoined minds around him suddenly increased, and again Saul resisted the temptation to listen in.

"We think," Paul finally said, "that you have already made your decision. By allowing them all to be backed up, you consider their minds something unique and worth preserving and that, when your own survival is not threatened, you will make every effort to do so."

"But there's more," Saul said.

"Yes," Paul agreed, "because of the problems they represent to you, aboard your ship, you will dispense with them . . . eventually."

Saul allowed clarity to banish indecision. Each genetic combination that resulted in a human body was something he could now easily copy, and it was only the minds that were unique, because of their nurture and not their nature. He knew, then, precisely what he would do, once the exigencies of survival had been attended to.

"But now we have more immediate concerns to consider." The proctors were on the move, both physically and mentally; the meeting now over, and their conjoined communications breaking up. Though he was the one who had summoned them here, Saul could not help but feel that he himself had been judged.

"You cannot run yet," Paul opined.

"Give me your reasoning," Saul instructed, to further clarify his thoughts.

"They will have developed some means of knocking out the drive warp," replied Paul. "And it will be located aboard the *Vision*, as well as the other two ships."

"Judd?" Saul enquired.

"Either a near-c railgun, or some other sort of high-speed missile or some way of disrupting space-time," replied the more practically minded proctor.

"Disrupting space-time on that level is beyond even me," Saul replied, "so I doubt they have anything like that. One must also factor in their proximity." Was he merely being arrogant? No, not about the space-time disruption. However, after seeing those test shots directed at Earth's moon, it seemed likely they'd found a way to fire nuclear missiles, at railgun speeds, that would deliver the impact required to knock out his warp. Thereafter they could just keep knocking it out until the other two ships arrived. He needed to deal with the *Vision* immediately, as he'd suspected.

"Supposing our warp is knocked out," said Saul, "they will then try to knock out our vortex generator."

"The Mach-effect drive is distributed," said Judd. "As long as it is supplied with power, the drive can be maintained through constant attention."

"It can be used to interfere with their targeting," Paul added. "We calculate an over eighty per cent chance, on probable attack patterns, that, armoured as it is now, the vortex ring can be kept safe, though supporting infrastructure is certain to be damaged." The Mach drive could be used to help Argus dodge bullets, Saul translated, and the armour would stop anything that got too close.

Already Saul had called up the schematic in his mind and was having his robots collect essential materials and components and dispatching them to critical junctures all around the hull of the ship. How unsurprising, he felt, that the critical sectors numbered ten, and that his own communication with the robots might be compromised during any conflict.

"So you know what to do," he stated.

Led by Judd, the proctors headed for the door. Each would control a group of robots, their task being to keep the Mach-effect drive operating. As they left, he considered what must be their point of view. If he deemed the humans aboard an encumbrance he was prepared to be rid of, how then did he view the proctors? In the end, though they had promised to serve him, how highly did they rate their own survival?

"I will do the right thing," he said to Paul, the last proctor to leave.

"Of course you will, Alan Saul," Paul replied, "by your own definition of 'right.'"

Somewhat uncomfortable with that notion, Saul waited, watching through cams as the proctors rapidly reached their designated locations, where robots gathered around them, clinging to the inner skeleton of the hull. Once they were in position, he considered his own options, deciding in an instant that now it was time for him to change, at least, his own approach.

It was time to take this fight to them.

Even as he made his plans, he sent a warning. Roused from slumber, Le Roque pulled on a ship suit and stumbled from the cabin he had reoccupied in the relocated Tech Central and, not bothering to attach the fones he had seemed reluctant to abandon, began issuing his instructions through his implant—instructions dealing with the human population, which was now his responsibility. Throughout the station, work crews began locking down their latest tasks and heading back to their accommodation, while the robots folded themselves around beam junctures or anywhere else suitable nearby. A further signal transmitted through kilometres of optic went to a couple of explosive charges fixed on the two booster tanks acting as anode and cathode in the flux tube, and bright explosions severed the cables from their anchor points. Since so much cable lay outside, the feed from the tube did not drop immediately, but gradually diminished as the cables wound in. Meanwhile, Saul started up two new fusion reactors and four fission reactors utilizing radioactives mined from the rubble pile, then prepared the Traveller engine to fire.

"Make sure of your weapons," he instructed the Saberhagen twins, even though he felt sure of them himself, and could take control of them in an instant.

"Are they coming?" asked Brigitta.

"No, not yet," Saul replied, "but they obviously want a war, so that's what I'm going to give them."

13

SEE NO EVIL

Under the Committee, millions of Earth's citizens were sent for "adjustment," where the methods used were essentially behavioural, with the subjects being questioned at length and tortured whenever they gave the wrong answer. This resulted in many of them being crippled both physically and mentally and thus becoming of no further use to society, and therefore disposed of. Subsequent refinements such as the pain-inducer cut down on the number being physically crippled, while precise lie detection facilitated the more precise targeting of pain. As a result, those sent for adjustment were truly adjusted, and were often unrecognizable to their relatives and friends after their sojourn in Inspectorate cells. Before the introduction of biochips, which led to the possibility of directly programming a human mind from a computer, other methods had been tried. It is known that a mind can be partially reprogrammed via the body's senses, but that is a difficult and information-intensive technique. Towards the end of Messina's reign, most of these techniques were abandoned as a wasteful expenditure of vital resources on yet another resource the state had too much of: human beings. The main instrument of Inspectorate adjustment therefore became the selective cull.

ARGUS

Var locked down her overseer's office, on the ship's skeleton, just fifty metres away from where the hull had yet to be fully enclosed. Despite Le Roque's *order* for her to head to one of the more protected accommodation units, or one of the arcoplexes, she remained precisely where she was. Her brother had issued instructions to the effect that Le Roque was in charge of the human complement aboard until such a time as the humans decided otherwise, and

Saul's only interventions would concern the safety of his ship and himself. How he assigned such responsibilities in detail was all very debatable, though it was noticeable how generally terse his instructions and warnings were becoming.

However, one thing was certain: it was Var's fault.

Var cringed inwardly and could not shake off her own sense of guilt. There were no blood spatters evident on the suit she wore—they had all been cleaned off thoroughly—yet it seemed she could still taste Gilder Main's mouth, from when she had tried to resuscitate him, and still feel the weight of the adjustable spanner in her hand as she brought it down on Thomas Grieve's skull. And she could still hear him crying.

These actions of hers had pushed Saul over the edge. She was someone he had risked much to save and to whom he had entrusted the task of turning Argus Station into an interstellar spacecraft, then she had repaid him by displaying a lack of trust in his judgement. Behaving like a member of the Inspectorate, she had committed murder, and now he had washed his hands not just of her but of them all. But didn't that simply prove her point? He had always been on the edge of something like this, always been on the edge of saying: Damn you, you'll do what I want, but beyond that I don't care. Didn't his very order that *humans*—as if he was no longer a member of their race—should police and govern themselves prove that he wished merely to dispense with them? Could she not be right in still thinking that his latest action was just one small step on that route, and that he would still use the impending assassination attempt as an excuse to do just that?

Light glared throughout the ship and Var felt as if an invisible hand was trying to shove her to one side. Checking her instruments, she saw that the cables were now all wound in and that the Traveller engine had just fired up, in order to carry the ship away from Io's flux tube. On an intellectual level she knew he was using that rather than the Mach-effect drive to keep the latter secret from "the enemy," but on a basic emotional level she cursed him for failing to inform anyone where and why he was moving the ship, just as she damned herself.

"Where are you taking us, Alan?" she asked through her fone but, as with the other questions she had recently directed at him, no reply was forthcoming.

What to do?

The temptation just to do nothing, simply to wrap herself in misery and wait, was leaden inside her. But Var, who had pushed herself all her life, knew she

NEAL ASHER

was incapable of giving in to such a sense of failure. She set her overseer's office moving, meanwhile putting a call through her fone and routing all imagery available to the screen before her. After just a few minutes she received her reply.

"Langstrom here," said the police commander. "What can I do for you, Var?"

"I have all their names and I know what they're planning," she replied, noting how he had allowed only a static image icon to come through, even for those with fones capable of displaying real-time images.

"I'm sorry, but I don't know what you're talking about," Langstrom replied. "Whose names and what plans?"

Var felt a hollowness in her stomach that had nothing to do with hunger. The police commander must know that someone she had gone to visit had since disappeared. Was he now trying to distance himself from any involvement?

Before she could say anything, he continued, "Perhaps we should meet to discuss this. I much prefer talking face-to-face with anyone claiming to have important information." He paused for a second. "I see you're moving your office down towards the outer endcap of Arcoplex One. I'll come out to join you from Lock Seven. See you shortly."

Ah, perhaps not arse-covering but an understandable caution.

Being utterly sure of its grip on the ship's skeleton, under the drag of acceleration, the overseer's office continued its progress down towards the endcap. Meanwhile, Var began working on something she had been neglecting. If she became the focus of an investigation, she had to cover herself properly now. She dispatched a program to hunt down and erase any available data about her previous meeting with Langstrom, and was surprised when it found cam footage taken in this very office and then did manage to erase it. So was Saul actually allowing her to cover her tracks? A moment later she discovered something else: data trails leading to large portions of the station system were now partitioned off so tightly that not even a byte or two could squeeze through. So, while Saul had left the human population to its own devices, he was also leaving them their own portion of the station system, and had separated away his essential self so that what *he* already knew could never be erased by anyone else.

Next she began shutting down cams and other data recorders inside the office so that the most anyone could ever know was that Langstrom had visited here. Then, as the office reached a tentative limb out onto the bearing endcap, set to make its way over to Airlock Seven, she abruptly had second thoughts. Maybe this was precisely what Langstrom wanted her to do, so that he could then completely remove any evidence of his involvement in the murders she had committed. No—far too paranoid—so she finished the disconnections.

Out on the endcap the office finally paused over the chosen airlock, lowered itself to mate with it, seals and bayonet fittings thunking home. After a moment the floor hatch swung upwards and Langstrom, wearing a VC suit with the helmet detached, propelled himself inside. He then paused to gaze up at the nearest cam.

"This is a black spot now," Var assured him.

"So who are they," he asked carefully, "and what's their plan?"

EARTH

"We have a problem," said Calder. "And I am calling to advise you, for your own security and for the security of Earth, to leave the station now."

Maintaining an expression of slightly distracted boredom, Serene studied his image on the desk screen. The man was difficult to read, perhaps because his face was not so clear through the visor of the vacuum survival suit he wore. Was he frightened?

"I trust this is not some problem that might delay the departure of the *Fist* and the *Command*," she replied. Then, realizing she wasn't reacting properly, she asked, "What exactly is this problem?"

"We have an outbreak of the Scour aboard, and whether or not the crews or soldiers aboard the *Fist* and the *Command* have been infected I can't even guess. It's very serious, since at least two hundred people have died and many more are infected." He paused for a second, then continued, "We should have your space planes prepped and ready for departure within the hour."

Serene stared at him for a moment, reflecting that the *planes* he mentioned should be ready shortly *after* the two spaceships were underway, then she glanced up from her screen at Elkin, the woman's two aides and Sack. Elkin looked terrified, obviously having already gleaned knowledge of this outbreak just beforehand, while the two aides appeared both puzzled and scared. Sack was even more difficult to read than Calder, with his reptilian skin blunting all human expression. Serene returned her attention to the screen, exuding seriousness and concern.

"Can you give me more detail on this outbreak?" she enquired, making no comment on his suggestion that she depart.

Blank-faced, Calder replied, noticeably no longer using the honorific, "Just that it must have started amidst the Inspectorate personnel, since it seems to be mainly them who are infected."

"Well"—she dipped her head for a moment as if in consideration—"I'll leave it to you to speak to Bartholomew. It's essential that his mission is not delayed, for its importance outweighs anything else, but he will need to institute ship-quarantine measures and have the medical staff aboard both ships running blood tests. If it turns out that he does have the Scour aboard, we must leave it to him to decide how to respond. He must therefore try to limit any outbreak and persevere with his mission."

"Understood," said Calder, grimacing.

"You're putting quarantine measures in place here?"

"I am. Those infected thus far are being moved to areas I'm separating off from the rest of the station, while I've ordered all personnel not infected to use vacuum-survival or spacesuits and switch over to independent air supply. Meanwhile, I'm opening some areas to vacuum, to kill anything that might be lingering there, while flooding the remaining main air supply with a virobact vapour." He paused for a second. "You and your staff will also need to use similar suits and go over to independent air supply."

"Very well." Serene nodded to Elkin and Sack, who immediately went to a nearby locker and began dragging out vacuum-survival suits. For veracity's sake, Serene reached down beside the desk and picked up the helmet of her VC suit, pulled it down over her head and clicked it into place, before closing its visor and turning on its integrated speaker.

"How long until the virobact vapour is cleared from the shuttle bay Ruger is due to arrive at?" she asked, glancing across the room just as one of the aides headed across to the door and opened it, admitting a swarthy, stocky individual in a VC suit, who surveyed his surroundings carefully as he stepped in. Serene instantly recognized Vaughan, the commander of her security team based here. With his big grey moustache, cropped hair and tendency to stomp giving him the mien of an antediluvian general, he was difficult to forget.

"Within the hour," Calder replied. "It should be mostly clear by the time he docks; however, the medical advice is that we should stick with independent air supplies until four hours afterwards. Shall I inform Ruger of that?"

"You will tell Ruger nothing," she replied. "I don't want him being scared off. He might decide to try docking at another station."

"Very well," said Calder, still not resorting to "ma'am."

Serene glanced up from the screen at Elkin, now in a survival suit with her visor closed, then transferred her gaze to Vaughan. "Are any of my security personnel infected?" Of course she knew that none of them was, but didn't want others to realize that she knew.

"Thus far, no, ma'am," he replied, seemingly coming to attention.

Returning her focus to the screen, she said, "Since, as you say, it's mainly Inspectorate personnel who are afflicted, my own personnel will now take over in the shuttle bay, where I will go to meet Ruger the moment he comes aboard. I'll also need you to ensure that once he releases the Gene Bank data to us, it is recorded here immediately and simultaneously dispatched to the multiple locations that Elkin will provide. In the meantime, I'll also want constant updates on the situation aboard the *Fist* and the *Command*."

"You will be meeting Ruger in person?" he said, apparently puzzled. "But your space planes . . ."

"I will not be requiring them just yet." She paused for a second, still gazing at Calder's image. "That will be all." She shut down the call.

"We're still meeting Ruger, ma'am?" Elkin was trying to keep her voice steady.

Serene studied her, aware that, with the Scour aboard, the woman in front of her wanted to get off the station as quickly as possible, but seemed to have forgotten their present situation. Calder had also expected Serene to flee but, even while the Scour was wiping out any physical threat to her here, she still had not negated the threat beyond it.

"Note the timings," she said. "Our space planes will be ready shortly after the *Fist* and *Command* have gone. Note I said 'planes' plural, so that both myself and all my security team can head neatly out into vacuum. What do you think Calder will do then?" she asked. "And don't ask Tactical—just work it out for yourself."

Elkin seemed briefly puzzled, then she looked slightly sick. "He still controls the railguns," she ventured numbly.

If Serene fled, there would doubtless ensue an unfortunately timed test firing of the railguns, and the unfortunate demise of Earth's dictator and her entire security team. But to react like someone who believed the Scour was a virulent and dangerous disease that she could catch at any moment would only hamper her plans. After the *Fist* and *Command* were definitely on their way, she wanted to meet Ruger to ensure the safe transmission of the Gene Bank data. She then wanted Ruger to hand for a long private conversation, and she wanted Calder arrested and available for a more public conversation on ETV, once he was found guilty of spreading the Scour aboard the station during an attempted *coup d'état*.

"Yes, we're meeting Ruger," Serene continued, swinging her chair round and standing up. "Are all the arrangements for the ETV broadcast now in place?"

It took a brief moment for Elkin to recover her calm, whereupon she said, "Everything is ready for you, ma'am."

Serene turned her attention to Vaughan. "You are fully apprised of the situation here concerning the Inspectorate personnel and Calder?"

He lowered his head gravely. "I am, ma'am."

"I am sure Calder will not make a move on us while the *Fist* and the *Command* are still present. Once we are in the shuttle bay, I'll order Bartholomew to fire on this station's railguns and disable them. While that is happening, I will board a shuttle. Once the railguns are disabled, we all depart for Core One."

It all sounded like a perfectly plausible plan, though it was not one she would adhere to. If Bartholomew really started firing on the station, his own ships would probably end up disabled or destroyed, and with no guarantee that everything Calder could use against her departing shuttle had similarly been disabled. Unforeseen circumstances such as, for example, all the Inspectorate personnel ending up dead, would cause her to alter her plans.

"What about the Inspectorate personnel now in the shuttle bay?" said Vaughan. "We're clearly outnumbered."

Thinking on the hoof, Serene suddenly said, "It occurs to me that there is actually no Scour outbreak aboard this station, or else one has been artificially implemented." Yes, this was a good idea; this might work. "Calder is merely trying to push me into fleeing, whereupon some unfortunate accident involving the test firing of a railgun would occur." She paused and dipped her head contemplatively. "Now knowing I am heading to the shuttle bay, he will most likely, as instructed, be withdrawing his Inspectorate personnel, perhaps holding them ready to return once the *Fist* and *Command* have gone . . ." She looked up. "If that is not the case, Vaughan, then you must be prepared to fight. It's as simple as that."

Every expression standing before her seemed to be hiding something. These weren't stupid people, so could most certainly smell the odour of rat. Their suspicions would grow, too, when it became evident that every single one of the rebel Inspectorate personnel aboard was dead.

"Let's go." She headed for the door.

ARGUS

The *Vision* remained in orbit about Europa, with its version of the Alcubierre drive kept ready, according to his readings, to be brought up to speed within half an hour. If he used his own Rhine drive to get to it, it would doubtless deploy this theorized weapon it possessed for knocking out his warp bubble, stopping him before he got close enough to use the Saberhagens' weapons against it. However, he did not intend to attack as directly as that, at least not yet. As his ship headed out from Io, Saul focused EM spectrum telescope arrays beyond the *Vision*, on the rocks and dust floating out there, on the disperse gas and scattered atoms, and began recording vast amounts of data. There he should be able to find a hole in their communications and from them confirm that the attack he was about to make had been effective. Now, with the ship on a long curving intercept course, he shut down the Traveller engine.

He began, as they doubtless expected, probing for a direct way in, pinging the other ship at different radio, microwave and laser frequencies, and searching for some response. Already he had built up a huge collection of computer viruses and self-assembling worms to penetrate any gap in its defences, but it soon became apparent that the ship was hardened and closed off. However, the fact that there were no communication openings told him that the *Vision* did not have a comlifer aboard, and therefore another possible opening could be tried.

The *Vision* had clearly been watching, so it must have telescopes open to receiving certain portions of the EM and visual spectrum. Saul began close-scanning older images of the other ship, tidying them up so that he could study all its exterior equipment. Soon he located the dish of a radio telescope, and then the glinting dome of an optical telescope. It seemed highly likely that both of these would not be attached to the main computer systems of the ship itself. Most probably the images they captured would instead feed into the isolated computer of a tactical assessment team, there to be studied and checked before being transmitted back to Earth.

Saul began building, within his extended mind, models of the kind of enclosed systems he himself would have built to keep out someone like him, and began to look for holes. He himself would have ensured complete separation between the computers controlling the various sections of such a ship. He would scan all the visual data for anything nasty or potentially infective before transmitting it elsewhere. No, there would be too many safeties and too many protections involved on that route in. But there was one system interfacing with this visual data that would not be thus protected: the human mind.

The Argus telescope arrays detected a flicker beyond the *Vision*, bouncing off a chunk of rock which a spectrometer designated as consisting of nicely reflective aluminosilicate and mica. They were using a tight-beam green laser to send coded data back to Earth. Saul dumped data outside the spectrum of that laser and concentrated on the remainder, gathering fragments of code, here reflected from a swirl of graphite particles, there from ice crystals marking the orbit of Europa. He then began comparing those fragments with the image data and likely messages that the *Vision* would now be sending.

"Brigitta," he began, viewing the Saberhagens inside their laboratory in Arcoplex Two, while firing up a steering thruster to alter his ship's course slightly and then calculating orbital vectors with an accuracy he knew had been impossible until now—until *him*. "At this precise moment I want you to fire your railguns here, tracking across in this arc." He sent the timing and coordinates. "Twenty-three missiles should be sufficient."

Brigitta peered at a screen, ran some vector calculations and sat back, puzzled.

"What's the point?" she asked. "They'll go nowhere near the *Vision* and hardly even worry the crew."

"Communications," Saul replied briefly, now copying across to his extended mind the models stored in Hannah Neumann's files of human thought processes, along with other data concerning visual-centre reprogramming.

"Ah, understood," Brigitta responded, quite quickly, Saul felt. "We'll use the plated ones for partial atmosphere targets as they're more reflective."

"What are you doing, Alan?" Hannah asked from her laboratory, having been instantly notified by her computer that her files were being copied.

"Induced psychosis by light-pattern emission," he explained.

"It's only temporary and you need a lot of data on the viewer," she replied.

"Of course," he said, understanding that to her the functioning of the human mind was a complex thing, while his own understanding was now some way beyond that.

"Perhaps if you can pass on some of the data?" she enquired, reaching for the strap securing her in her seat, intent on standing up from the console and screen she had been working at—the one where she was assessing up-to-date data on Da Vinci's condition and trying to see what problems might arise when the cryogenic pod started to bring him out of suspension some hours hence.

"That will not be necessary," Saul replied.

Already he could see how the technique of mental reprogramming a human being through the eyes could be combined with one of his self-assembling worms. The psychosis would be longer-lasting and fed by a self-perpetuating paranoia. The result of these could extend from a crippling mental debility to a violent reaction, depending on where the recipient fell in the list of human mental types Saul had selected. He made two packages—one that was within the spectrum of the optical telescope and another to build the images from radio reception—and sent them both to the two telescopes operating aboard the *Vision*.

His ship was now flying just beyond the orbit of Europa, but still lay far enough away from that icy moon for the crew aboard the *Vision* to feel few worries. They might also be puzzled by the twenty-three missiles currently being fired out beyond Europa.

"Do you need any more?" asked Brigitta.

"I'll let you know," Saul replied as he counted down the seconds.

A block of coded data fell into his mind as the first of the missiles crossed the beam of the laser that was pointed back towards Earth. Then, in quick succession, the other twenty-two followed. Into the comparison programs he now added data about his own course, the firing of those missiles, about an attack through telescope imagery, psychotic episodes in tactical crew and the likely cut in the flow of telescope imagery to Earth. As he worked at the code, he was reminded of how just a few spoken words had given him access to Salem Smith's encryption when he first boarded Argus, but this was proving very much quicker.

The cut in the flow of image data gave him his first foothold, because he could identify portions of what had been sent before as image data. His next foothold was a message which, by its overall pattern and timing, obviously related to that same data. And, after that, the coding they were using unravelled like a rotten net.

"No more needed for the moment," he informed Brigitta, firing up the Traveller engine and swinging back in now, aware that the *Vision* had closed down its telescopes and would be, for a while at least, all but blind to his sudden course change and acceleration. Half a gravity spun his chair round in its gimbals, and put a boot on him.

As his ship now sped towards the *Vision*, he continued to work the code, telescope arrays still focused out beyond Europa. He wanted to know exactly when the *Vision* ceased to be blind, and he wanted to know what orders it would then receive from Earth. Meanwhile he also checked on the readiness of everything internal, since he needed to build up velocity, and it would be an hour yet before he could begin his true attack.

The Rhine drive was ready, the recent accelerations only minimally distorting the ring of the vortex generator; the Mach-effect drive, now always partially engaged, worked to stabilize the ship's skeleton; while the Traveller engine had eaten up just ten per cent of its new supply of fuel; and the Saberhagens' weapons could not be more ready. The only injury reported was a broken finger in the Arboretum, where a man had ignored Le Roque's injunction for everyone to stay secured and had caught his hand in an unsprung door that slammed shut during the last course change.

Checking further on the human population, Saul found he could not locate Var through any of the cams, but from previous footage knew she was in her mobile overseer's office, where Langstrom had recently visited her. Maybe she was confessing her sins and being arrested. Saul found it difficult to find any kind of emotional reaction to that thought. Meanwhile, the prospective rebels had gathered together in a single accommodation unit, then abruptly gone off the radar by doubtless travelling through the cam black spots, which Saul had provided, out towards the old station ring. At the same time, still attached to the armour just twenty metres away from Saul himself, their bomb continued its countdown. He considered, at that moment, sending robots to locate and kill them all, but that could be done if his primary plan—involving his minimal interference and subtle manipulation—failed. No, leave them to it, and allow them to die from their own stupidity.

There were new flickers now off the faces of flakes of methane ice, so it seemed that communications from Earth were sent by the same sort of laser, but using different encryption. One hour passed and soon Saul was perfectly positioned to pick up the laser reflections from the hull of the *Vision* itself. He played with the code, found the inversions and sketched the shape of the mind behind it—the mind that had taken the first code and changed it—and he managed to crack it in just thirty-four seconds. It was laughably easy, and Saul was banishing a human feeling of superior contempt from his mind when reality caught up and sank its teeth into him. The *Vision* had received a reply to the concerns of its captain. The *Fist* and the *Command* were on their way and, since they were travelling within spitting distance of the speed of light, they would be following not far behind the message itself.

EARTH

"You're certain these are clear?" asked Admiral Bartholomew once he saw that the visual feed from the *Vision* had been restored.

"They are clear," confirmed the comlifer Christopher Shivers. Apparently the man was the most trustworthy of them all, having never tried to rebel openly or even to kill himself during his conditioning, but Bartholomew did not like to put too much trust in someone who obeyed only on pain of . . . pain. He put the image feed on hold, since everything coming through was, of course, old and would probably be irrelevant by the time they arrived out there.

"He used a visual-cortex reprogramming technique rather cleverly combined with a self-assembling worm," Shivers added. "It's possible he might try something else but, so long as all this sort of data is routed through me, there will be no more deaths like those that occurred aboard the *Vision*."

That incident had been quite horrible. Two of the four-person tactical team on duty at the time had dropped into some kind of coma, another had acquired himself a Kalashtech and opened fire on other crew members, killing two and injuring eight before being brought down by a disabler, while the fourth member had been found sitting at his console, having used his ceramic dinner fork to gouge out his own eyes. Here the effect had not been as bad: the two people assessing the images and data had turned on each other, but managed to do little damage before being grabbed and restrained by ship's security officers. Bartholomew shuddered, considering how other tasks had kept him from his usual visit to Tactical to inspect the same images.

He glanced round at his command crew, all busily at work on the final diagnostic runs and checks. He clicked a screen tab for the latest updates from the medics aboard both the *Command* and the *Fist* and was relieved to see that no instances of the Scour had yet been reported. Then he again addressed his comlifer.

"So, since we destroyed that satellite, Saul has no access to data from Earth apart from anything he can pick up with his telescopes, which will therefore be already out of date," he said.

"Not unless he's found another way around causality," Shivers replied.

An image up in the corner of the big curved screen facing Bartholomew's chair showed the construction station rapidly receding. Presently both the *Fist* and the *Command* were under fusion drive, putting themselves between the brightness of Earth and distant Jupiter, and both using a shielding technique that had hidden the station in which the *Scourge* had been built—coherent projection of whatever lay behind it towards any eyes that might be looking, in this case some pink eyes out in orbit of the gas giant Jupiter itself. Alan Saul would not know that the message to the *Vision*, which he had certainly intercepted after so quickly cracking their communications, had in fact been a lie; and that Bartholomew's two ships were not yet on their way out and would not be underway for half an hour.

"Let's hope this has worked," he said.

"The *Vision* was blind and in danger," Shivers replied. "Even though targeting remained available for its warp missile, it could not use it because Saul was approaching on conventional drive, and the impact would have completely destroyed his ship. The *Vision*'s choices were then either to fight or to move. If it had fought, it would have lost. Due to Saul's approach velocity, it could only have used its Alcubierre drive to move, and in that case there was a chance that Saul would have run—and then, especially with the warp missile balancing delay, we would have lost him."

"I'm aware of that," said Bartholomew.

"The assessment of our tactical team," Shivers lectured him, "or rather of those of them not presently in Medical, was that, upon intercepting that message, he will run, whereupon the *Vision* can use its warp missile, and the plan can continue as before. My own assessment is the same. Even though he's obviously decided to become a bit more proactive, he'll see no benefit in hanging round to face us."

"Let's hope they're right."

"We won't know until we are there," Shivers replied.

Bartholomew nodded to himself: by the time any data from the *Vision* regarding how things had transpired out there reached the *Command* and the *Fist*, they would already be under drive and unable to receive it. The admiral again considered the possibility of dropping the *Command* out of Alcubierre drive in order to receive that data, and he finally made his decision. Yes, he would. In tactical terms it was not such a great idea to divide one's forces, but if Saul had managed to escape the trap laid for him, they needed to know, for there was a remote chance, depending on whatever route Saul took out of the solar system, of the *Command* being able to use its own warp missile to stop him.

Bartholomew issued his orders, then opened a channel to Captain Oerlon, aboard the *Fist*, to keep him apprised.

"The disabling shot from the *Vision* should at least take me out of the balancing delay time," said Oerlon, tugging at the thick collar of a gel-tank acceleration suit. "I'll make final approach through the Jovian system on fusion, and if he man-ages to get his drive functioning before I'm on him, I should be able to knock him out again."

"You'll make sure it's an accurate shot," said Bartholomew.

Oerlon, who was a morose-looking individual with a large straggly beard, pale sick-looking skin and some sort of gang tattoo on his temple, nodded gravely and said, "None of us can afford to miss."

The essence of their tactical problem was that Saul could run at any time, and the only way of stopping him was with a warp missile, and they had only four of them: the *Fist* had two and the *Vision* and the *Command* had one each. While the vector calculations made before firing these missiles would be very accurate, and little could change their course once they were fired, the distances involved were huge and the margin for error minimal. Including the acquisition of further tactical data, this was the main reason Bartholomew had ordered the *Vision* to move in closer to Saul's vessel. Out of pride, Bartholomew did not want that first critical shot to miss, and beyond that he was aware of what would happen to him if Saul escaped—which was precisely what Oerlon meant.

"Twenty-three minutes to go," said Bartholomew, feeling his stomach tightening.

Within a day, perhaps two, they would either have succeeded or would be contemplating whether or not it was worth returning to Earth.

ARGUS

Var eased her grip on the stanchion and glanced out the windows of the overseer's office, but received no clue there about their sudden recent course change.

"Le Roque tells me he's taking us towards that ship over Europa." Langstrom shook his head. "But I've not had warnings to prepare for any kind of battle."

"Don't you think we should deal with those concerns that we *can* deal with?" Var suggested.

He nodded doubtfully, and continued, "The two who were in the accommodation below Tech Central moved over to join the others"—he glanced at Var—"probably because of this alleged bomb. Just a short while ago, however, they all trooped out and disappeared into the nearest cam black spot."

"We need to act," Var asserted.

"But you have no real evidence of any of this, and you continue being evasive about how you obtained this information. It needs to be verified. You also say that he already knows about this plot, so he certainly knows all about the bomb too."

"He'll probably let it blow but not be there himself when it happens," said Var, not really sure of her own reasoning. "Either that or he's disarmed it."

"So why am I here?" the police commander asked. "You've given me nothing I can act on and it seems to me that, if what you're telling me is true, he probably has something already planned for them." He gestured towards the mosaic of mug shots displayed on the screen. "As he's stated, we have to look after ourselves, but he'll react to any direct danger to the ship or himself. Perhaps you can explain your part in this, sister of Alan Saul . . . our *Owner*."

Var studied the police commander for a long moment, with a sinking sensation in her stomach. She felt sure she had lost him now, but she had to try.

"The question that has to be asked is what will be the extent of his reaction to this," she replied, still unsure of herself but determined to do *something*. "Hannah Neumann once told me that her greatest fear is that Alan will tire of having to fit all his plans about the needs of the human population aboard this ship—aboard *his* ship. We all know that he is entirely capable of running it now without us. I've known from the moment I stepped aboard that, though I was appointed overseer of the rebuild, my position has been completely super-fluous. The implants that enable us to control robots and mentally access the ship's systems were an apparent effort to raise us above our uselessness to him, and what's been the result of that? Combined robot and human teams are less efficient than the new robots he's created, and now chipped rebels are seeking to kill him."

"The extent of his reaction, you said?" Langstrom prompted.

"He might just be searching for a reason to be rid of us altogether," said Var, studying the man's expression, "and this attack on him could provide it. He could turn his robots on us in an instant, and then be free of the encumbrance we represent." She paused to collect her thoughts. "I don't think he will do that, though I think we'll all be heading soon for the Meat Locker, and whether we wake up again after that sleep is . . . debatable."

"I'm still not sure what you want me to do," said Langstrom.

"We stop it," Var replied, searching for some way to couch things for Langstrom—a man who had probably stuck her brother high on a pedestal. "As I see it, he's given us power over our own affairs and we must therefore take responsibility. I think his recent actions indicate that he *wants* us to take responsibility; that he *demands* us to do so and that, if we don't, he'll simply finish with us."

Second guessing the mind of a god, reflected Var, trying to keep the sneer off her face.

"He'll have something in place to deal with the threat," she continued. "Of course he will. But if he is forced to use it, then he'll see us all as useless as he has already supposed. We must act."

"So what now?" asked Langstrom, folding his arms, still reserving judgement.

"The bomb first," said Var.

He acknowledged that with a nod. "I suppose I could do something there."

"You must. What have you got to lose?"

Langstrom watched her warily for a moment, then reached up to touch his fone. "Colson, I want Disposal One over to the Owner's sanctum. I've an unconfirmed statement that some-one might have planted a copper-head armour-piercing bomb against the outer wall. I want you to run a full search and report back." After a pause as he listened to the reply, he calmly continued, "Yes, maybe he does know about it, but you still do the search, and you still disarm anything you find there. Is that understood?" After another pause, "Yes, right now." Langstrom lowered his fingers from the fone.

Var wasn't sure if she was relieved that things were now in motion. She couldn't help but feel that the police commander was only humouring her because she was Alan's sister.

Too many assumptions . . .

"If they do find something we'll have some physical evidence to act on," he conceded. And in that moment she knew she had lost him; even if he believed her, he thought there was no reason to do anything about it. Langstrom trusted too much in Saul and therefore did not follow her reasoning, did not see her brother's arrogance and contempt for humanity.

"We should head to the outer ring," she declared. "We'll need some of your men."

"You have no indication of where he's supposedly concealed his backups out there," he stated.

"None at all, but they are supposedly guarded by a spider-gun," she replied, pulling herself down to sit at a console, before sliding across the overseer's office manual control.

"We won't be able to trace that spidergun, especially if he's trying to keep these backups hidden." He paused, frowning, as the mobile building lurched into motion, then he just gave a shrug. "However, these chipped rebels of yours are still dark which means, if they are moving around out there, they're moving through cam black spots. There are just two places—"

"Attention all personnel," Saul suddenly announced over the PA system. "I have evidence that the two remaining Earth warships are currently on their way out towards us. We will therefore be undergoing severe acceleration, so adhere to fusion-drive safety protocols for the moment."

Var wavered for a second, then instructed her overseer's office to lock itself down, watching through the windows as it clamped its claws about nearby protuberances before dropping to press the gecko pads on its belly against the metal below. Langstrom could not hide his relief, for they would not be going anywhere for a while. Var suppressed her frustration and contented herself with the knowledge that the chipped rebels would similarly be hindered and, if caught away from some place of safety during the coming acceleration, some of them might be hindered dead. It then occurred to her to wonder why the ship was undergoing such acceleration rather than immediately engaging the Rhine drive. It seemed a pointless thing to do because, surely, once the Rhine drive engaged they were safe until it cut out again, probably deep in interstellar space and far away from Earth and its concerns?

Saul noted a bomb-disposal team had been ordered to head towards his sanctum and, despite his warning, were still following their orders. They weren't to know that the device Langstrom had dispatched them to find wasn't really a problem—Saul knew, because he had seen it being made—so he spoke to their leader directly: "Colson, get yourself and your men back into some acceleration chairs."

The man addressed looked up at the nearest cam in the suiting room. "Commander Langstrom has ordered me to search for a copper-head explosive on the outer wall of your sanctum."

"And I am ordering you to stand down. Langstrom is mistaken. There is no explosive."

Colson and the rest looked relieved, as they quickly headed out of the suiting room and back the way they had come. Saul pondered for a microsecond the fact that, while he had decided to leave the humans here to look after themselves, he had interfered yet again. Then he focused on other concerns.

If he had engaged the Rhine drive immediately, it would be knocked out before his ship built up enough real space momentum to carry him to the *Vision*. He needed to be closer and his velocity needed to be higher. By now the crew of the *Vision* had probably found some way to work around their blindness, therefore he needed to take some risks. He mentally slid into the controls of the Traveller engine, while announcing, "Prepare for further acceleration." In the engine, he overrode safeties; he put back online two combusters that automatics had shut down; ramped up everything as high as possible without regard for the dirty radioactive wake he would leave. With a huge rumble, the ship shuddered and accelerated, its drive flame sputtering like a gas torch running out of oxygen, a red line of radioactive tritium sketching out behind the ship. Acceleration increased, climbed steadily to one gravity and then beyond. The whole ship's structure was protesting, but still it wasn't enough.

Next risk: without notifying the proctors, Saul ramped up the Mach-effect drive, further stabilizing the ship's structure and increasing its acceleration. There was a danger now that the crew of the *Vision* would spot the disparity between actual acceleration and what the Traveller engine was capable of. But the Mach-effect was a card he needed to play now. Hands gripping the arms of his chair, he waited—ten minutes, twenty—as velocity began approaching what he required, and the distance between the two ships rapidly diminished.

Time, now.

"Prepare for possible impact," he announced, knowing that most people were already prepared, and showing that he still cared enough to deliver the extra warning.

The proctors, and the robots they controlled, were the most vulnerable now, and he waited just thirty seconds until certain they were all locked down in their respective sectors located around the ship's skeleton. During a final pause, he ascertained that everything within his purview was as it should be as the ship strained all around him, centred now on Europa and on the *Vision*.

"Engaging Rhine drive," he then announced.

The colours changed. Jupiter shifted through the spectrum until it glowed a fluorescent orange, its red spot glaring like a ruby held up to the sun. The ship itself seemed to be trying to fold itself in towards some centre point—and then the stars went out. Saul counted down microseconds then, when the entire ship crashed and the warp went out, he felt a momentary satisfaction at this proof of a weapon that could knock out the Alcubierre warp, and chagrin, because he had not divined the nature of that weapon. As an old expression went, he had been unable to see the wood for the trees.

Of course, a warp missile . . .

Then a blast wave slammed into the ship, peeling away hull plates so the glare of atomic fire could peek inside, and as he lost over sixty per cent of his system, he added the thought:

. . . and one carrying an atomic warhead.

14

BACKUP

The idea of backing up a human mind, as you would back up one of the drives on a computer or any other data, has been with us from the days of recording to magnetic tape. However, in essence, we have been backing up our minds ever since the first cavemen cut notches in sticks as a memory aid. Cave paintings were the human mind rendered in vegetable dyes, cuneiform expressed it in clay, and books are even closer representations of the thought processes of those who wrote them. But, of course, none of these is an exact copy of a human mind, but just small parts of it. We are, in essence, information and every piece of information from our mind that we record is part of our mind. Thus it can be seen that the only drawback of such a back-up technology for the whole of a human mind is the exactitude of that recording. It is certain, for example, that no computer storage could possibly copy all the chemical and quantum atomic processes within the human brain, so any type of copy made could never be exact. However, a human being is never the same from moment to moment, since we are all in a state of perpetual flux, so the copying process could be seen as just part of that flux. The only reason for reluctance to accept this technology as a real possibility stems from religious thinking about a human soul, combined with the contrary belief in the finality of death.

ARGUS

They left Jean-Pierre strapped against one of the stanchions of the cageway. Most of them were bruised, and one of them was supporting a broken arm after that last massive acceleration. Jean-Pierre had been unlucky: slamming headfirst into a wall and his neck snapping; dead before any of them could reach him.

"But he still lives," Ghort opined, referring to his backup.

The lack of enthusiastic response from the rest told Alex that, though they accepted their potential immortality on an intellectual level, the fact of physical death was not so easy to step around. Maybe some of them were having second thoughts. The Rhine drive engaged just minutes before they reached the weapons cache, then disengaged just a moment later. The ensuing blast added to their bruises and caused two further broken bones: one a finger and the other in Ghort's foot. The idea of mortality became of even greater concern as their suits notified them of radiation levels, and how they were way beyond safe limits.

"Not much data available," said Ghort, grimacing in pain. "Seems the *Vision* hit us with a nuclear warhead, and that has taken us out of drive."

"Lucky shot," Marsin added.

Alex said nothing, though he felt that it had to have been more than a lucky shot to hit them with an atomic warhead, since they were probably moving at a good portion of the speed of light. It had to have been a practically miraculous shot.

As they reached their weapons cache, which had been inserted in a three-metre-thick composite blast wall, four metres out from another wall of iron-hard asteroidal ice, both of which were part of the elaborate armouring around the vortex generator, he waited for one of them to state the obvious.

"Look," said Marsin, as two of the others towed the crates out of concealment, "if we do this now, we'll probably just be handing ourselves over to Serene Galahad. We need to wait until we're out of the solar system and safe."

Ghort shook his head. "You seem to put too much faith in the abilities of one man, so perhaps you're starting to believe in his mythological status." He turned and gazed at the ring of faces gathered around him. "Whether Alan Saul is alive or not makes little difference to our chances of survival. We can control the robots, we can control this ship, and we can achieve as much as he ever could."

Alex wondered just when Ghort had slid from being merely a rebel into being a *delusional* rebel, nay even a rebel possessing delusions of grandeur. By all means dismiss mythology and anything based on faith, but facts should never be ignored. Saul was way beyond each and every one of them, and probably beyond all of them combined.

"What about the proctors?" someone piped up.

Alex gazed at the woman who had spoken—the same one who had first escorted him into that meeting in Arcoplex One. She was only considering this now? He studied the rest of his fellows and realized that being mentally hooked into computers, also able to control robots and knowing you were practically immortal was no cure for naivety. Perhaps, in reality, it worsened such a condition. Perhaps the feelings of godlike power had led to a supreme arrogance and the people around him found it difficult to accept that some things were still outside their control, that some things lay beyond their abilities, and that there was someone who could crush them like a bug under heel. Ghort opened the crate and began distributing the weapons.

"We have to do this now, else we'll probably never get a chance later," he said.

Perhaps "delusional" was too mild a description.

Alex received his weapon, along with the two grenades he himself had made, which he hooked onto his belt. Like the rest of them, he checked the action of his Kalashtech, inspected the ammo clip and received further ammo to drop into a belt pouch. As he did so, he nodded to himself with a feeling of deep sadness. They had been given every opportunity to see the error of their ways, and yet they were stubbornly persisting with their silly plan. He considered what a coincidence it appeared that he should have ended up in the work team of the leader of these rebels, and though he believed in coincidence, he knew enough to recognize when it wasn't there.

"So I am precisely where you want me?" he said, voicelessly speaking to none of those around him, just into the system.

The reply was instant, perhaps because his message had been expected.

"I wondered when you would figure it out," replied Alan Saul.

"They just don't understand how much you can see, do they?"

"But you do, Alex," Saul replied. "Now, why is that?"

"Because I knew myself to be a simple creature programmed like a machine, and I know myself to be a simple creature now. I just looked at the odds."

"Never underestimate yourself. Your own self-knowledge has led you to understand that the simple answer, as Occam tells us, is often the right one. You do not overestimate your strengths, nor do you underestimate your enemies. You know where the greatest dangers lie, and how best to choose your allies."

Ghort was leading the way now, between the blast wall and a wall of ice, the others trooping dutifully after him. Now set on their course, they could only murmur weak protests and ask the questions they should have asked long ago. Were all humans programmed thus for self-destruction? Alex wondered.

"What do you want me to do?" he asked.

"What you must," Saul replied, whereupon Alex knew the conversation had ended.

The Owner had other concerns: the survival of his ship, countering the forces of Earth arrayed against him, perhaps the contemplation of his route into future centuries or millennia. The chipped rebels were a small matter, and one he had countered with minimal effort, almost an autonomous one, simply by inserting Alex in place like an extra number in a formula.

Still feeling sad, Alex raised his Kalashtech and opened fire, the shot hitting Marsin in the back of the neck and tumbling him forward into the midst of the rest. Next, emptying his weapon's fifty-round clip, Alex sprayed the entire area ahead of him, pieces of suit, flesh, glittering clouds of ice and ejections of vapour filling the area, bodies tumbling and screams coming over their scrambled channels. In his mind the list of those ahead of him shortened, as the channels to each began winking out.

Calmly striding forwards, he discarded the empty clip and inserted a new one, clicking his weapon down to three-shot bursts, as the vapour dispersed and the ice swirled like snow. Wherever he spotted movement he fired, further channels winking out. He pushed aside a floating body with the barrel of his weapon, saw shots slamming into it from someone crouching ahead, then he carefully aimed and fired, toppling the same crouching figure. Blood specks stuck to his visor, their moisture evaporating and the remainder flaking away from the frictionless glass. Seven channels remained open. He could hear Ghort shouting questions half in language and half in computer code, and the reply simply: *Alex is killing us.*

"Traitor!" Ghort spat—the word intended for Alex's ears only.

Alex stepped over bodies, shouldered aside someone who was still moving weakly, visor covered with blood and vapour jetting from holes too numerous to be stopped by breach resin. Two further steps forward, he grabbed another who was plainly dead, intestines trailing from a split in the lower torso and already drying like biltong in vacuum, then stepped aside holding the corpse as a shield and crouched. As expected, bullets picked up and flung about the mess all around him, but the survivors were aiming too high. Alex poked his assault rifle past the corpse, located three figures and fired. One of them skidded back into another, while the third flew up from the floor, somersaulting backwards and spewing vapour and blood. One figure now hauled up a dying companion, who took the impact of the next shots that Alex fired, before launching himself sideways and disappearing from view.

Alex paused, seeing that now only five channels remained open. Clicking his weapon down to single shots, he walked back again, pressing the barrel to the wearer's neck below any visor behind which there still seemed signs of life, before pulling the trigger. Within thirty seconds just one channel remained open. Seeing who it was, Alex reflected on the *inevitability* that seemed part of the narrative of his life.

"I'm no traitor," he explained, as he collected up ammo clips and an extra weapon before turning again to set off. "I'm a realist."

"He's still going to die," Ghort replied. "That copper head is still attached to his sanctum."

"Naive of you," said Alex since, though the detonator was in perfect working order and had doubtless been checked by one or other of the chipped, Alex had rendered the explosive itself inert, which was rather more difficult for anyone to check.

"Bastard," said Ghort.

"Factually correct," Alex replied, "and I'm still going to kill you." He paused for a moment to consider how short lived had been his distaste for any occupation "involving guns and blood," and then moved on.

It was a disabling shot, leaving the Rhine drive down, large areas of the ship beyond Saul's reach, over fifty per cent of his robots now on autonomous function, the weapons out of his control, many external sensors down, and Arcoplex Two emergency braking because of damage to the outer bearing endcap. But the Traveller engine was still firing, the Mach-effect, after a momentary stutter, ramped back up to power, and the *Vision*—though its own vortex generator was building up power—would not be able to flee for half an hour. And because of the initial acceleration and present velocity, it still lay within reach.

However, if the message that ship had received earlier was true, the other two ships could be arriving at any moment. As he inspected this damage Saul felt anxiety bite. Yes, Judd had been right about the weapon the *Vision* had possessed and certainly Saul was making the correct tactical response, but the reality was that his drive was down and would be inoperable for some time yet.

If those other ships now arrived he would be at an extreme disadvantage. The harsh reality was that no matter how correctly he responded he was back in a fight for survival that he could easily lose.

Saul rapidly began rerouting around burned-out parts of the system, in many places inserting robots as communications relays, shutting down damaged computers and bringing backups online, running diagnostics and rebooting further computers. Gradually the ship's system rose to seventy per cent efficiency and, once again able to access certain parts of it, Saul quickly shut down the Mach-effect drive, since now it was no longer needed and those aboard *Vision* still might not have even noted the acceleration disparity and reported it. Next he shut down the Traveller engine and coasted on towards Europa, but still travelling faster than a railgun slug. Still rebooting and repairing, he noted with annoyance that the damage was such that control of the ship's weapons lay beyond his reach, at least for the moment.

Still there was no sign of the *Fist* and the *Command* arriving and, as the minutes slid by, he began to hope that the message the *Vision* had received had really been intended for him—a bluff.

"Brigitta, do you have targeting?" he asked, calmer now, realizing that very little could change what would happen next.

The Saberhagen twin continued studying her screens and tapping away frantically at a console.

"I have partial, but will need a ten-degree lateral shift of the ship's pole to deploy the plasma cannon," she replied. "I've lost some of the hydraulics, and the cannon-steering rack is damaged."

"No need," Saul replied, already dispatching a conjoining of six of his new robots to make repairs, "I want you to use railguns only since, as I told you before, it's not a good idea to apprise the enemy of everything we've got."

"If you say so—you're the great military tactician."

Saul felt no irritation at this outburst of human pique. He was beyond that now . . . wasn't he?

"Calculate, with whatever targeting you have, on a minimum of five direct hits," he instructed, "and then fire when ready."

Within the system he watched her make the calculations, even as he regained the ability to take control there himself. He felt she was overdoing it a bit by firing twenty-five missiles from the two railguns, but decided it politic not to correct her error.

The *Vision* was now under fusion drive and moving away from Europa, partially silhouetted against its cracked and icy face. Saul watched the two railguns turning, their noses still protruding from their ports but back ends swinging round, driven by hydraulic rams along their curved and toothed steering racks. The first missiles slid into the breaches—belt-fed like ancient machine guns—and a minute later a sudden power drain dimmed lights throughout the ship and it seemed to heave like some beast hoisting a burden. The missiles spat out, invisible to the naked eye at their acceleration, targeting hydraulics correcting minimally to give a suitable spread.

Twenty more minutes passed without reinforcements arriving for the *Vision*, then, as more exterior sensors came on line, Saul detected another warp hurtle in and then shut down within the Jovian moon system. He inspected this data with skin prickling and his stomach sinking. The *Fist* had just arrived— immediately going over to fusion drive to bring it in-system. This tardy arrival confirmed the lie that had been told about the departure of the same ship from Earth, but it was here and Saul had no Rhine drive to take him away. He should have run when Galahad fired on them from the sun. He should not have been so damned sure of his calculations. He then tried to be optimistic about the fact that it had arrived alone, and thus speculated on his chances of being lucky and that the *Command* had suffered a malfunction. Perhaps there was still hope. Then he watched as the first railgun missile hit the *Vision*.

It struck just ahead of the fusion drive, biting a chunk out of the hull and spewing fire and wreckage beyond. The *Vision*'s fusion flame sputtered and went out. The next missile struck just tens of metres from the first, caused an explosion inside which left the engine section of the ship hanging off at an angle, tethered by just a few twisted I-beams. The next blow was a glancing one upon the exposed ring of the *Vision*'s vortex generator, peeling up some of the armour there before the missile disintegrated in a line of plasma.

For a moment Saul thought it had proved ineffective, but the massive coils of the power system of the vortex generator must have been damaged. A silver fuma-role flashed out from the ship, as mercury, travelling at near relativistic speeds, exploded tangentially from the point of damage, and within a microsecond was spearing out even beyond Saul's ship. A fraction of a second later the vortex ring dissolved like some high-speed fuse, and a disc of fire expanded outwards from it.

It was enough, Saul felt: the *Vision* was no longer a danger to him. However, true to Brigitta's calculations, fourth, fifth and sixth missiles slammed into the remaining hull of the stricken ship, one taking off its nose and the other two hammering dead centre and cutting it in half. Saul watched the drifting wreckage, oxygen fires burning inside until they exhausted, people tumbling through vacuum—some suited, and perhaps still alive until their air ran out. He watched other railgun missiles impacting on the face of Europa, their bright explosions throwing out plumes of ice crystals and creating circular rainbows. And he understood why he felt such regret and pity now, when they had never been part of him before. He understood that, in becoming what he had become, often he was more human.

Then he erased that emotion, aimed his ship so as to swing about Europa and go in towards Jupiter, as he coldly calculated how he might similarly destroy the *Fist* and tried to discount the fact that this might not be possible at all.

SCOURGE SHUTTLE

Clay felt sick, which might have equally been due to the dose of radiation he had received aboard the *Scourge* or to his other injuries, but which he felt sure was due to a growing fatalistic acceptance that he was just not going to survive. He'd watched those two massive ships set out, he'd seen the huge amount of work that had gone into rebuilding the Traveller construction station, and he began accepting that Serene Galahad's grip upon Earth was tighter even than Alessandro Messina's. He felt as if he was feeding himself into the maw of some immense mincing machine.

The shuttle jerked, shuddered, and a series of metallic clonks sounded from the rear.

"That's it, we're docked," said Trove, glancing at him expressionlessly.

Clay reached over to the console and picked up a laptop. The man Calder, whom Serene had put in charge up here, had already given him the transmission frequencies and various antennae to aim the microwave transmissions. All Clay had to do was insert his personal security code into the program currently open, hit transmit, and the *Scourge* would begin transmitting the Gene Bank data.

Three of the receivers were positioned on Earth, and two were aboard this same station, but none, by its location, gave any indication of where Galahad herself might be. Clay felt that Scotonis had made a long-odds gamble on locating her and had reckoned that he wouldn't. In the end, the captain would hurl his ship down towards Earth at the most likely location—Italy—and the way Clay felt at the moment, he was sure Galahad wouldn't be there. Afterwards, despite having brought the Gene Bank data back to Earth, he would be found guilty of helping Scotonis to annihilate an entire country, and then Galahad would have justification in exacting the most vicious vengeance available, probably live on ETV.

Another clonk sounded from behind, followed by a ratcheting noise.

"That's the airlock tube in place." Trove studied her instruments. "We're good to go now."

Clay hung the laptop on his belt, then reached over and took up one other item on the console: a sidearm with a gecko pad stuck on its grip. He studied it for a moment, then pressed the weapon down against his stomach, the gecko pad adhering it in place. It was futile, of course, for him to think he could defend himself with this, but at least, with it in easy reach, he had a chance of avoiding falling into Galahad's hands. He hoped, if and when it came to it, he would be quick enough and brave enough to put the barrel to his head and pull the trigger.

Trove stood up, slinging the strap of a Kalashtech over her shoulder. They had already discussed what to do once they left the shuttle, and she had decided against taking her own life if it seemed likely they would fall into Galahad's hands. She intended to force someone else to do that job.

"Let's go," she said.

Clay waited until she had left him room by moving out of the cockpit, then he followed her. Though he had huge reservations, there was nothing for it now but to go through with this, since Scotonis had given them no other options. His stomach tightening and the sick feeling suddenly dissipating, he watched Trove tow herself down into the airlock, check the pressure console, then open the outer door and pass through. He pulled himself through behind her into a wide octagonal airlock tube, with windows in what appeared to him to be the floor, giving glimpses of various inter-station shuttles in their docking cradles, with similar airlock tubes attached.

"You go first," said Trove. "You're the hero of the hour."

Apparently, according to Calder, they were to be featured live on ETV, whereupon the ratification of their full pardon by the delegates of Earth would be broadcast. This would be followed by a communication from Serene Galahad herself. Clay felt a momentary resurgence of his optimism about that. Maybe

Scotonis *would* somehow be able to locate where she was broadcasting from and drop his ship on her? Next, in the ensuing chaos, Clay could tell this Calder about how Scotonis had forced them, under the threat of railguns, to approach the station without telling anyone the captain was still alive and in control of the *Scourge*. Then Clay could top that off by revealing the true source of the Scour . . .

He moved ahead of Trove, patting a hand against his laptop, and came to another airlock door, where he first checked the pressure reading. After a moment he noted an orientation arrow, and walked up the apparent wall to stand horizontal to his previous orientation, before palming the door control. It thumped up on seals and slid aside, the pressure differential gusting a breeze into his face, redolent of machine oil and some slight hint of a familiar perfume. Clay passed on through into a bay area swarming with people. On either side of him rows of security personnel with shouldered Kalashtechs stood stiffly to attention. Other security personnel were positioned at critical points all over, sharpshooters covering various sectors of the bay and guards at each of the doors. So all this was for him, and for the data he was bringing? Clay felt hope dangerously stir inside him.

"Shit," exclaimed Trove.

Clay straightened up and stepped forwards, noting two large floating cams directly ahead, and others scattered about the immediate vicinity, some of them plain but some definitely bearing the letters ETV on their cowlings. He glanced to one side and saw a screen displaying his arrival, and he could just about hear the familiar voice of an ETV commentator. As he moved forwards, the picture abruptly changed to show an enormous conference room packed with self-important looking people, who had to be the delegates of Earth. *Just maybe*, he thought, *I am going to survive this.*

Then the group of people beyond the honour guard suddenly parted, and the figure who had been issuing instructions to them turned towards Clay, smiling as brightly and with as much falsity as a painted clown. He now realized Trove's exclamation had not been about the guard or the security, but that she had already recognized the woman ahead of them. Here stood Serene Galahad herself.

"Welcome back, Clay Ruger," she said, striding forwards.

Clay heard Trove cursing behind him and glanced round to see she had been grabbed by two of the honour guard, and was now being expertly disarmed. He swung back to confront that painted smile.

"A live broadcast?" he asked, not really caring.

"A five-minute delay," said Galahad, "which is standard so the footage can be edited before broadcast." She paused, waved a hand dismissively. "Now, I am compromising my safety by allowing it to be known that I am here. So I hope you will see the risk I am taking as a token of my sincerity."

"Sure," he said, but suddenly he wasn't so sure at all. Maybe she did mean to pardon him and allow him to take his place again within Earth's administration. He felt a bubble of laughter in his chest. What a hilarious joke, but so utterly irrelevant now.

She had compromised her own and everyone's safety here just perfectly.

"Your pardon has been ratified by the delegates of Earth," she continued, "and now, for all our sakes and without delay, you must begin transmitting the Gene Bank data."

Clay glanced down at the weapon secured to his stomach. All this security wasn't here for him but for her, and if he reached for the gun one of the sharpshooters would deal with him, doubtless maiming him but definitely not killing him. But, of course, he no longer needed that weapon now.

"I, of course, trust you implicitly," he said, reaching down slowly to unhook his laptop and opening it. He input his code and began the transmission. He held the laptop up to show her that the transmission had begun, then sent it spinning through the air, away from him. Galahad turned to a woman behind her, who now checked something on a screen that one of two young blond men was holding, before nodding a confirmation. Galahad turned to face him again and now, with avidity and cruelty plain in her expression, he just could not help himself.

He convulsed, choked, and burst into hysterical laughter.

ARGUS

As she entered the Meat Locker behind Dr Raiman and his assistant, Hannah noted how, for over twenty hours, she had felt both scared and angry, but also how that her treacherous friend, her panic attacks, had now gone into hiding. Admittedly the drugs had reduced their impact hugely, but they were always waiting for an opportunity; waiting to leap out and provide fear when none was needed.

She paused just inside the cryogenic complex and looked around. Nobody else was here since all human personnel were still under lockdown, still strapped in chairs or on couches, with suits on and visors ready to be closed, tired of the terror twisting their bowels as they now just numbly waited. But for this, she too would have been as safe as possible in her apartment in Arcoplex Two. Shitty timing, she felt, but apparently the process could not, with cryogenic storage technology at its present development, be put on hold. Da Vinci would be, if all the readings were correct, waking up in the middle of a fucking war. Raiman and his assistant used the handholds fixed to the walls to navigate their course towards Da Vinci's cryogenic pod, which was now already protruding from the honeycomb wall providing storage for all the other pods. Saul had given no warnings of imminent course changes, but they probably did not want to be caught in mid-transit across open space like this, should he suddenly decide to apply acceleration. All aboard were learning that lesson too. Though Saul did always give warnings, sometimes the interval between them and the need for action was only a short one, and they now realized that he deemed their personal safety very much secondary to that of his ship. Hannah, nevertheless, propelled herself directly from the airlock towards the pod, landed clumsily but managed to grab hold of one edge before she could be sent bouncing away, and had opened the bag she carried and taken out the VC suit even before the other two arrived.

"He would have been safer just staying inside here," Raiman grumbled, while checking the pod's mini-screen then hitting the latch control.

"You know we can't allow that," said Hannah reproachfully. "I know," Raiman agreed.

The lid hinged open to reveal Da Vinci lying inside. His skin was bone-white and for a moment Hannah feared he wasn't breathing, until she discerned the infinitesimal rise and fall of his chest. Then, as Raiman and his assistant began removing the visible sensors, the man's eyes snapped open.

"Something wrong?" he asked gummily.

Raiman helped him sit upright and continued removing sensors.

"There's nothing wrong with you," Hannah replied. "It worked."

He gazed at her steadily, his eyes surprisingly clear considering that he had been taking a cruise on the river Styx just twenty minutes earlier.

"Interesting," he stated. "I didn't think I would experience nightmares."

With the assistance of the other two, he climbed out of the pod and the final sensors were swiftly removed. Raiman handed him a flask, which Da Vinci opened and sucked on, rapidly gulping down a warm mixture of vitamins, electrolyte and certain specially tailored drugs. When he had finished that, she handed him his VC suit.

"So what kind of nightmares did you have?" Hannah asked.

He waved a hand dismissively, took hold of the suit and began the laborious task of putting it on. "Massive demons folded up like asteroids and moving through darkness, and my terror of being crushed by them, and bodies floating about in vacuum." He shook his head. "All perfectly apposite, of course."

How true, Hannah felt, and how much closer to current reality than when he stepped into that cryopod. Were his night-mares just the usual mental clearing of detritus and sorting of the mental filing system, or could something have been bleeding through from surrounding reality via the hardware in his skull? That was something she would have to check.

"So did I miss anything?" he asked, finally closing up his VC suit.

"With nightmares like that," Hannah replied, "probably not."

Right on cue, Saul addressed the entire ship through the PA system. "Course change in eight minutes—full fusion thrust." Then, just for the ears of those in the Meat Locker, "Hannah, go and use the primary control centre and medical bay at the end of the Locker. It contains eight acceleration chairs."

"What's going on?" Da Vinci asked as they all at once began heading to the nearest end of the Meat Locker.

"Your massive demons are ripping each other apart," Hannah replied.

Jupiter wanted his ship; wanted to suck it down along with all the solar system debris it had swallowed over its billions of years. Saul reapplied the thrust of the Traveller engine to fling his ship into close orbit, vast plains of cloud sliding below and seemingly no curve to the horizon ahead. They were very close to the gas giant now, too close, since its pull was interfering with the vortex generator, and the magnetic fields slinging the mercury around inside it were limited to sustaining its present speed rather than increasing it to what was actually required. However, Saul now needed the speed for, upon spotting the *Command* arrive outside the Jovian system, he had decided to change his target.

The *Fist* was obviously the more heavily armed, heavily built, and it possessed more fusion drive potential. From studying images of it, Saul had also ascertained that it probably carried troops aboard and, unlike the *Command*, was capable of limited atmosphere engagement and even of landing on low-gravity worlds. Obviously the designers had factored in the option of Saul's own ship crashing onto some solar system body but still remaining functional enough to blow landing craft out of the sky. It was a big powerful ship, then, and one to be completely avoided if at all possible.

His ship fell in an arc around Jupiter, still under drive from the Traveller engine, but with the Mach-effect drive at its minimum, since there was now even more of a chance of his enemy detecting it. The increased density of gas here was heating the hull appreciably, with occasional flickers of incandescence running over it. Induction from Jupiter's magnetic field was increasing the power entering Casimir storage, while also blowing components with monotonous regularity. Saul could feel the structure straining all around him and observed his knuckles whiten as he gripped the arms of his chair just like everyone else aboard, just like all the humans. He relaxed his grip, took a drink from his suit spigot and considered for a moment some purely human concerns, such as how he had not eaten solid food for over a hundred and fifty hours. He then dismissed them: such physical needs he could deal with later, if he still had a living body to feed.

Tense hours passed and he noted some of the personnel moving about carefully, seeing to their own human requirements: emptying the urine packs of their suits, using toilets, finding something to eat. Fear was a limited, genetically programmed reaction impelling one to fight or flight, so it had no place in space warfare, where engagements could last for days, weeks or even years. Perhaps this was something Saul should ponder on for the future, because he had no doubt whatsoever that the aggression humans had taken with them into space was not unique—if he had a future.

Saul's next announcement sent those wandering about back to their acceleration chairs, for it was time to snap their gravitational tether to Jupiter. Using a combination of Mach-effect—mostly to kill the gyroscopic effect of the vortex generator—and steering thrusters, he turned his ship, the combination of thrust and Jupiter's pull increasing to the point of blackout for some. This lasted for an hour, then the slingshot snapped, and they were away, arcing out from Jupiter and on course to intercept the *Command*, even while the *Fist's* course was taking it out of sight behind the gas giant.

Saul cut the Traveller engine, floated light against his straps, and made one slight correction with steering thrusters. Inevitably, with the amount of debris drifting in Jovian space, something slammed through the hull like a bullet going through a soda can. This object, massing at no more than ten kilograms, turned partially to plasma on striking an inner lattice wall and hosed the shell of Arcoplex One with fire. There were no injuries and the structural damage was minimal, a result which couldn't last. He watched the moon Lysithea slide by far to one side, then adjusted his course slightly to an optimum to miss the numerous moonlets lying a further ten million kilometres out.

Measuring a slight downward fluctuation in the speed of its tangential approach in-system, Saul calculated on the *Command* having fired something in the region of ten railgun missiles back towards him. Realizing that Saul was avoiding the *Fist* and was now pursuing the *Command*, the commander of the latter ship had fired probing shots to drive him away from direct convergence; like light taps delivered by a boxer assessing an opponent. "Brigitta," Saul began. The Saberhagen twin had just woken up from a long sleep in her acceleration chair, while her sister was still sleeping. Both of them had been using stimulants for some time but had at last succumbed to the needs of their bodies.

"What?" she asked blearily.

"I am taking control of your railguns," he replied

She just nodded numbly and without surprise as he usurped control. He needed greater than human accuracy now. Amalgamating in one mental program the Mach-effect drive, steering thrusters, gyroscopic stability, astrogation data and the infinitesimal changes to his ship's vector caused by railgun launches, he fired one shot every three-point-six seconds for just over a minute, adjusting his aim incrementally after each shot. Seventeen railgun missiles sped towards the *Command*, each with a calculated impact probability of twenty-three per cent, but only if it did not alter its course. He could manage no better than that due to the inaccuracies in targeting, and noted to himself how the steering racks of the railguns needed to be coated and microscopically polished, and some Vernier adjustment added. After that, a nudge with a steering thruster took his ship to the periphery of the fusillade from the other ship. He did not want to stray any further away, since complete avoidance would defeat his purpose in coming out here in the first place. And the situation was such that he could not avoid both these ships until the Rhine drive was ready again.

As the ships drew closer together, the *Command* used one of its side-burners to shift course abruptly to avoid the seventeen approaching missiles, and from that action he was able to assess the capabilities of its detection gear. The *Command's* instruments would be able to detect major Mach-effect shifts in

Saul's own ship, but whether the crew might be looking out for something like that was another matter entirely. Small shifts would not be noticed, which was handy now as Saul reached the periphery of the fusillade coming back from the *Command*.

A small nudge with Mach-effect and a brief flare of steering thrusters altered his course just so. The two railgun missiles that had been on target now dropped to one. This struck fifty metres down from the top pole of the ship, punched through the hull and sliced through most of the intervening structure before turning into an explosion of white-hot ceramic and molten steel as it peeled away part of the internal space dock and took off the back end of the Mars-format space plane. This resulting detritus, still having lost little of its momentum, travelled down parallel to the axis of the ship, through lattice walls finally to blast out forty metres to one side of the Traveller engine, leaving an impressive plume.

With diagnostics and structural sensor data running straight into his extended mind, Saul noted just a small loss in the redundancy within structural integrity, some damage to the EM shield and Mach drive, already being tended to by a proctor and its herd of robots, and generally, just a fractional loss in battle readiness. The two who had been working in the space plane, and who had been using its acceleration chairs, died too fast for their backups to register the moment of their deaths—turned into white-hot gas in less than a second. Their memory would be one of just sitting in acceleration chairs, and their next conscious experience would be either some interaction through the ship's system or waking up inside new clone bodies. Saul had yet to decide on which but, for the interim, the backed-up copies of dead human minds were kept in a state of unconsciousness.

"Further acceleration," he announced, firing up the Traveller engine for another course change, while also noting that only half its fresh fuel remained.

The reaction followed just minutes after, as the *Command* changed the orbital spiral of its course inward for better convergence. Those aboard it were now thinking that their single hit had been enough to dissuade him from his attack run, that he realized he was heading into a fight he could not win, and they were therefore moving to block him. He turned his ship again to take it up out of their plane, as if he wanted to head out and over them away from Jupiter, but also increasing orbital convergence. They moved to block again, firing their railguns back at him once more. Saul returned fire, but also fired ahead of both ships at a moonlet called Hermippe, knowing that the debris cloud would push the other ship even nearer to him. It would be a slugging match now as their courses drew closer together, rather like ancient battleships pummelling each other.

"Brigitta," he declared, "soon you'll get the chance to try out your new toy."

"About damned time," she replied, before sipping from a flask of coffee.

Angela was awake also now, and busy checking tactical data on her screen. Others were thoroughly aware of the situation too; Le Roque studying Saul's battle plan and issuing instructions to those he had designated as "fire control" and who were now heading for EVA units. Squads of robots, controlled by the chipped, were ready for quick deployment within the ship. Everyone now had their suits tightly closed up and, when not remaining strapped in their acceleration chairs, were ready with breach patches and welding gear. It was the best they could all do, Saul decided, but still many of them were going to die.

The next strike peeled up hull metal at the equator of Saul's ship and glanced off the heavy armour around the vortex generator, blast walls absorbing the shot and asteroidal ice turning instantly to searing steam. The vortex generator remained untouched, however, and there were no personnel in that area, since Alex was conducting his hunt close to a hundred and eighty degrees further around that same ring. Saul still felt a moment of disquiet at that one strike since, without the abrupt Mach-effect nudge, the missile might well have penetrated the armour and struck the vortex generator, which was even now slowly winding up to speed. Another strike went in above the Traveller engine, taking a chunk out of its support pillar. He deliberately induced a misfire, leaving the fusion drive sputtering and burning dirty, before shutting it down. Robots ascended the pillar to make repairs, quickly slicing away wreckage and trans-porting up replacement beams. Meanwhile, the other ship decelerated to bring it closer; doubtless its crew assumed he had lost the ability for massive course changes.

Explosions lit the way ahead as Hermippe threw rubble and molten rock out into vacuum. The *Command* fired side-burn fusion engines to avoid the debris and brought itself closer still. Two hits on the *Command* followed: one a glancing blow near the nose that slagged some kind of weapons turret, and the other one punching right through its main body, the burning gas throwing it into silhouette. Another hit on Saul's ship ensued, slicing in transversely and carving a molten trench through the side of Arcoplex Two. Breach alarms screamed there and bulkhead doors slammed shut internally around the area as it bled air. Through one cam, Saul peered at a group of four people strapped to acceleration couches and gazing up in disbelief through their visors at the long hole above them, its glowing lips open to the rest of the ship.

Another missile came in, almost perfectly on target, its line of flight destined to take it straight through the centre of the ship and just metres from where Saul himself sat. One Mach-effect nudge threw it many metres to the side, where it smashed explosively into the inner bearing of the Arboretum. The whole bearing assembly then fragmented; the cylinder world's shaft at that end dislodged and swung fifty metres to one side. Chunks of ceramic flew in every direction and the mercury content of the bearing spewed out in a glittering cloud. Saul registered twenty-eight backups disconnected from their primary sources: fourteen incinerated when a plume of plasma from the initial missile impact played over their accommodation unit, twelve of them vaporized inside the building in which the bearing was housed, along with one broken neck and one shattered skull in the Arboretum itself. Saul also noted that there had been sixteen people in that accommodation unit—two of them yet to be chipped and now having lost any chance of eternity.

Enough—they were close enough now. "Brigitta," he said through gritted teeth, "now."

15

THE DATA SAVED US

That the Gene Bank samples and data were essential to save Earth's ecosystem was just another misconception on the part of Serene Galahad and her advisers. When seeds buried thousands of years ago could still germinate, when a single bacterium could multiply into billions in the time it takes to plant a tree, and when the exigencies of evolution could turn a mouse into the equivalent of an elephant or a tiger, Earth was not dying. Earth was sick, however: the disease was called manswarm and, with the Scour, Serene Galahad had administered the antibiotic, whilst her sprawl clearances were the salve applied to Earth's scabrous hide. But, even if manswarm had not been so reduced by her activities, the resource crash would have served the same ends as the Scour—and Earth would have regenerated itself, in time. This is a fact of biology and not of blind optimism. Earth has seen numerous extinctions throughout its existence, and in every case that engine called life has never stopped. It was in fact a kind of arrogance to suppose that humans could be so supremely destructive. And, even with that data, much of the life of our present time will still be little more than fossils in rock, a billion years hence.

EARTH

Serene stared at Ruger as one of her security team disarmed him. Unlike Trove, he resisted not at all, just wiped the tears of laughter from his eyes and emitted a few further chuckles.

Why was the man laughing?

Elkin had confirmed, by a random sampling of the data stream, that the *Scourge* was indeed now transmitting the uncorrupted Gene Bank data. It would take maybe half an hour for the transmission to complete and Ruger—she glanced at the laptop now gyrating in the air above one of her spiderguns—had no way of stopping it if he decided things weren't going his way. Ruger had to realize it was all over for him now.

Serene turned to Elkin and drew a finger across her throat. Elkin gave a signal and all the lights blinked out on the floating cams—signifying the ETV transmission was ended. Serene felt the situation was now back within her control, and that she had some decisions to make. With the data in her hands, she could now, if she so wished, just recall her three ships, but she decided at that moment not to. Various experts had assured her that the Gene Bank data alone, though lacking the genetic codes in the full gamut of samples, would assure the future of Earth's bio-sphere. However, getting hold of those samples, and capturing or killing Alan Saul and his rebels, would be a huge bonus.

"Bring them," she instructed Vaughan, gesturing towards Trove and Ruger.

By now all the Inspectorate staff aboard the station would be dead, and it was time to consolidate her position here. She would express some surprise upon learning about the full extent of the Scour deaths on board, then order Calder's arrest and, after some assessment of the remaining staff, put someone else in charge. After that she would return to Earth, back to what she now knew to be her comfort zone, there put the finishing touches to her cover stories, execute Calder for unleashing the Scour here, then have a long talk with Ruger about his inappropriate humour.

"Ma'am," said Sack, now up close to her side.

"What?" she asked, as the future opened out before her in her mind. She would indeed carry through her plan to turn the human race into something more manageable. She would continue demolishing unoccupied sprawls, restocking the oceans, begin establishing forests, jungles and other ecosystems and turn Earth back into the halcyon garden it had once been. With so much to do, she was anxious to be away from here and eager to get started.

"The screen," said Sack.

Serene looked up and saw that the ETV talking heads had now been banished, and that Calder was gazing out from the screen. Everyone now swung round to watch.

"Oh, good," said Calder, "I have your attention."

Serene did not like his tone at all. She quickly scanned about: the bay was covered by her personnel; the dead Inspectorate staff they had found here were neatly stacked away in a nearby store-room. Sharpshooters covered the entire area, but were almost superfluous while her three spiderguns were deployed.

"Your arrogance, Serene Galahad, is astounding," continued Calder. "Did you honestly think that, with the resources and scientific personnel you put at my disposal, I could not work out what you did? Did you honestly think I would not find out that the biochips, manufactured in your Aldeburgh Complex, were the actual source of the Scour, and that you yourself controlled them?"

Cold dread ran its claws up and down Serene's spine. She glanced at the expressions all around her, some puzzled and some doubtful, yet others suddenly attentive and turning towards her. They expected her to make a response.

"And do you, Calder," she said, forcing a tired smile onto her lips, "honestly expect anyone to believe that?" She gestured to those gathered all around her. "Would I surround myself with staff who have all lost family to the Scour? No, I would not. I surround myself with these people because they are as dedicated as I am to exacting vengeance upon the mass murderer Alan Saul. And now you, in your pathetic and desperate attempt to usurp me, are scrabbling for some way to turn them against me." He was about to speak, but she quickly overrode him. "Do you also honestly think that, having such an option available, Messina and his Committee would have expended such a wealth of resources on sectoring, and on developing the Argus network?"

"Oh, classic," said Ruger abruptly. "And yet none of it matters at all." Then he burst out laughing again.

"Shut him up!" Serene snapped, and felt some degree of satisfaction when her order was instantly obeyed and a rifle butt connected with Ruger's head.

"Good try," said Calder. "Your lies may well have worked on those around you, but that's irrelevant now. I knew straight away once you had activated the biochips, and gave you the news you were expecting. It was, of course, necessary to supply some bodies from our morgue here, for veracity. And now, Serene Galahad, it's time for you to pay."

White light flashed near the end of the bay, metal screamed and a cloud of debris expanded. Serene felt something crash into her, tearing her gecko soles right off the floor. She struggled against Sack's grip, though he was only performing his job and dragging her to cover. More explosions ensued and then gunfire erupted. Sack pulled her down by the airlock leading to Ruger's shuttle, just as a spidergun opened fire at a group of figures already swarming into the hold, sending shattered bodies tumbling. She pulled close to Sack, suddenly wishing she'd taken things further with him, for he was her rock, all she could trust. A thrumming seemed to fill the air, Serene's fone emitted a sound like water dropping into a chip pan, then she saw one spidergun fold up like a fist and another go tumbling aside, loose-limbed.

"Tank-busters," explained Sack.

Vaughan and other security staff had launched themselves into the air and were firing their weapons furiously. Serene watched ceramic bullets smacking into some of them, then a ten-mil machine gun sounded, tearing up the floor in a line that terminated at Elkin and her two aides, who just flew apart.

"We need cover," said Sack, glancing aside as the men guarding Ruger and Trove dragged them over.

Serene just stared, with mouth agape, as fragmentation grenades turned the entire bay into bloody chaos, and her security team died. She spotted Vaughan, the silver bars on the arm of his VC suit singling him out, bouncing off the floor only to rise again, his legs reduced to bloody tatters below the waist. About twenty of her people had closed in around her, crouching down and firing at the seemingly endless stream of Inspectorate personnel entering the bay, before themselves steadily falling. Then abruptly Sack was dragging her somewhere else, and she only realized he had opened the airlock door once she was through it.

"Ten of you here!" Sack bellowed.

There were moving bodies blocking all views, some of them bloody, one of them screaming, and bullet impacts were horrible meaty thwacks all around her. Then came a detonation, bright, blinding, setting her ears buzzing. The next moment they were inside the shuttle, yanking the door closed against a chaos of shouting and screaming, then hammering fists and the sounds of bullets impacting. She felt more than heard the docking clamps disengage, heard screams turning to grunts as someone administered an anaesthetic. Slowly she began to unfreeze, but then, seeing she was strapped into an acceleration chair, she realized the immediate danger.

"Do not use the engines!" she yelled, struggling to undo the straps, towing herself towards the cockpit. "We cannot leave the station like this!"

From the co-pilot's chair Sack looked round at her. "We know about the railguns, ma'am. We're just holding position for now."

Serene glanced at Trove, now sitting in the pilot's chair, her hands resting flat on the console, Sack's gun jammed into her side.

"Good," said Serene, fighting to keep a note of hysteria out of her voice. She had to keep control. She had to retain an aura of confidence. She glanced back into the crew compartment, saw that only two of her security team had made it inside, and one of them was strapped into a seat, the top half of his VC suit stripped away, dressings fastened across his chest and over the stump of his right arm. His eyes were closed and a morphia patch had been applied to his neck. The other had a combat dressing on one side of his face, burns showing under its edges and, by his bloody hands, had obviously been responsible for applying the dressings to his wounded comrade. Now he stood guard over their other prisoner, whose head was bloody, but who grinned at her nevertheless.

"So, what's so amusing, Ruger?" she demanded.

"You can't ever leave because this Calder controls the construction station and, from what I just heard, its railguns too," he said. "And, anyway, none of it matters a fuck."

"So you don't mind dying," Serene replied.

"I do, but at least it's going to be quick."

"I wouldn't be so sure about that," Serene spat.

"Oh, I reckon a multiple-megaton nuclear detonation will surely do the trick."

"What?"

"Hey, Trove!" he called out. "Is he on the move?"

"Yeah," Trove replied from the cockpit. "I checked before this goon made me undock. He's broken away from the tug, and his fusion drive just started. We've got half an hour at best."

"What are our chances of getting clear?" Ruger asked.

Serene looked at Trove, who gazed back at her with dead eyes.

"At the crawl speed of this heap of junk inter-ship shuttle?" said the pilot officer. "The expression 'snowflake in hell' springs to mind."

"What are you two talking about?" Serene asked succinctly. "Oh," said Ruger, "I forgot to mention that Captain Scotonis is still aboard the *Scourge*. He knows you controlled the Scour outbreak and that you're therefore responsible for the death of his entire family. He's been trying to locate you, and you then made it nice and easy with that ETV broadcast."

"What's he going to do?" asked Serene, not at all liking Sack's flat stare nor the silent attentiveness of her other personnel here.

"He's a bit pissed off," said Ruger, "so he's going to drop the *Scourge* right on top of your head, and detonate its entire nuclear arsenal."

Serene just stared at him, unable to think of any sensible reply. This could not be happening. She had so much to do, so many plans, she who held the destiny of planet Earth in her hands.

THE COMMAND

Bartholomew had known it wouldn't be easy, but now the reality was hitting home as the damage and casualty reports came in. But Tactical were sure that Saul's fusion drive was out, and insisted it was only a matter of time before they could confirm a full strike on the other ship's vortex generator. This had annoyed Bartholomew somewhat, since after seeing the footage of what had happened to the *Vision*, it was obvious that a tactical assessment wouldn't be required in order to confirm such a hit. Saul's ship would spew mercury travelling at relativistic speeds, and probably tear out most of its equatorial infrastructure.

"Are we close enough for the maser yet?" he asked of his command crew.

"Too disperse still, Admiral," replied Lieutenant Cole.

The maser beam was not completely coherent, so its effective range was measured in just thousands of kilometres within vacuum. Nukes were impossible at this range, since they could not be accelerated to railgun speeds without producing major internal damage, while their lasers, though able to reach the other ship, would waste their effectiveness against its hull. No, it would have to be the railguns for a while yet, and meanwhile Saul wasn't a passive target.

Bartholomew sniffed smoke in the air, redolent of burned meat. He'd lost half of his engineering team and shut down com to the affected part of the ship when it became necessary to close bulkhead doors and fill the place with fire-retardant foam. If there were survivors, they could be dug out later; for now they would just have to endure.

The ship lurched as another missile hit home. Damage-control diagnostics filled one corner of his large curved screen and, reading them, Bartholomew swore vehemently. They'd just lost one of the side-burn fusion engines.

"Repairs?" he asked.

"Going swiftly," Cole replied.

Bartholomew switched over to the stats on the first hit, and called up a frame giving a view of the damage done, where robots were swarming over the wreckage. At least they were functioning above spec. It amazed him how fast they were making repairs. If they continued at their present rate, hull integrity in that section would be back to optimum within the hour. This was all doubtless due to the comlifer they had aboard, because Christopher Shivers had managed to iron out a lot of computer-control inefficiencies.

The admiral focused his attention on the main image on the screen: the spherical ship that had once been Argus Station was now speeding along almost parallel to them. They'd hit it, what, six times thus far, and had still failed to take out the vortex generator. Readings showed that it was still many hours away from full functionality but, even so, it must not be allowed to function since Saul would almost certainly then run. Bartholo-mew leaned back. Well, at least he should be thankful that his own ship's generator was still intact.

"Can we reposition yet?" he asked.

"Still too much in the way," replied Cole. "It's as if he deliberately chose to intercept us here and negate that option." Then he added, "He's firing steering thrusters again."

Of course he chose the battleground, realized Bartholomew, watching the glare of the thrusters now turning Saul's ship.

"That should give us a better angle on his vortex ring," he stated, yet felt a sudden disquiet. He wasn't dealing with an idiot here, so such an alteration in the other ship's attitude had to be for a good reason.

Three flashes, just one second apart, ignited inside a port in the other vessel.

"Something coming," said Cole—and he had time to say no more.

The lights went out, screens went to static, and the PA system howled. The ship shuddered like a beast taking an abattoir bolt to the head. Emergency lights kicked in as lightning arced from Cole's console, and he shrieked. Bartholomew felt heat wash over him and, with an ear-tearing blast, the doors into the bridge buckled inwards. In the corridor beyond he saw a burning body flailing through the air, and then flame spread to envelop the ceiling. The next moment, he found himself tumbling through the air, still strapped into his chair, then slamming into a computer wall. He reached out and grabbed hold.

"Abandon to secondary bridge!" he shouted, though not sure if anyone was listening.

A hand snared him, undid his straps, and an officer he did not recognize began towing him away. The screaming continued behind him.

So what the fuck was that? Bartholomew wondered, with a subtext: *We underestimate him yet again.*

"What the hell happened here?" Var asked, as she surveyed the carnage all around her.

"Seems our problem has been solved," Langstrom ventured, steadying himself against a nearby wall as the ship shuddered yet again, then casting his gaze around, worry etched into his expression.

Under the flashing hazard lights, Var counted corpses. "Not quite . . . two of them are missing."

"Saul is obviously dealing with this," said the police commander. "As I've suspected all along, we probably don't need to be here."

Certainly, Langstrom did not want to be here.

"My brother's attention is probably focused on the *Command*," replied Var obstinately. "This looks to me more like a falling-out among thieves." She pointed to a row of bullet holes along one wall. "If my brother had dealt with these, there would have been a lot more holes, because he would have used a spidergun. Or no holes at all, just dismembered bodies—and no one would have escaped."

"Still," said Langstrom doubtfully.

"And this is a black spot too." Var gestured towards empty camera sockets up on one wall. "We just don't know what happened here, and we have to find out."

Langstrom lowered his head for a long moment, then looked up. "I'm sorry, Varalia Delex, but, though I agree that there were elements among the chipped who were planning rebellion, it is obvious to me that Saul has the situation well in hand. Our best course now is just to get away from here and leave it all to him."

"So you're not at all worried about ending up in cold storage forever? Or perhaps being dispensed with by my brother's robots?"

"I don't believe it," said the commander. "The Owner has had ample means and opportunity to be rid of us all and yet, in every situation, he has done the best he can to preserve life. You have my respect, Varalia, but I will not be dragged into what seems to be some personal problem between you and your brother."

"It isn't personal," Var snapped through gritted teeth. "The entire point is that, with what he has now become, we must look *beyond* the personal, *beyond* normal human relationships and reactions. My brother has never really cared for people, and he cares even less for them now."

"And you still think this after he diverted us to Mars and risked his life to rescue you?"

"He's not even remotely human anymore," Var insisted stubbornly.

"When there's time to do so, I'll have these collected —" Langstrom gestured towards the corpses—"and I'll get some forensic work done. We'll then see if we can find out what happened—see who's missing and hunt them down. But, with everything that's going on out there, we're done here for now." He turned away.

"Well, I am not done."

Langstrom shrugged and continued heading away. Var stared at his retreating back until he turned a far corner and moved out of sight. She felt slightly sick as she fought to dismiss self-doubt. Damn it, she had tortured and killed someone for the information she had just given Langstrom. There had to be some value in that; it could not be simply meaningless. No, she was not done just yet. She stooped and turned over the nearest corpse, did not recognize the ruined face but managed to identify who it was by reading the suit's number and inputting that into the system by laser com, so as to find out who was the last one to put that suit on. It took her twenty minutes to work through all the corpses here one by one, and by elimination she finally knew who was not here.

Langstrom was so wrong: Alex and Ghort were undoubtedly the most dangerous of them all, and must have wiped out the rest after some internal dispute. They would not stop—they were not the kind to stop. She dragged an assault rifle from underneath one of the corpses, found some ammunition, then headed towards the end of the corridor, where further bullet holes were stitched across the wall. She would find them both, and she would stop them.

Even as fires inside the *Command* guttered and went out, it fired up a sputtering fusion side-drive above its protruding waist—its main engine being completely destroyed—and continued moving in-system sideways. While observing this, Saul ran tactical scenarios. The Saberhagens' plasma cannon had caused huge damage to the stricken ship, but evidently had not entirely disabled it. Though the *Command* was moving slowly, it still presented a danger and, judging by the ports on the undamaged areas of its hull, still had some weaponry to bring to bear. The *Fist* was an even larger danger because it seemed to have twice the number of ports, as well as greater manoeuvrability and much more effective armour. And Saul knew that, in a one-on-one fight out in clear space, it would win against him despite his Mach-effect drive.

With the extra damage they had taken, it would be a day or more before the Rhine drive was back up to speed so that Saul could run. But, even if he did so, the *Fist* or quite possibly the *Command* could fire another one of those warp missiles to knock out the drive again. If the missile had a nuclear warhead, the ensuing blast would also knock out a high percentage of the ship's system, and might even leave it disabled: a sitting duck out in clear vacuum. Even if his ship was not so badly disabled and he managed to evade both enemy vessels until the Rhine drive was up to speed again, it could still be knocked out again, at further risk of disablement. He just did not know how many of those warp missiles the other two ships possessed.

Saul gazed through numerous sensors, repeatedly scanned images of the two ships for further data regarding them, and replayed recent events to analyse drive capabilities, but he could find no advantage. His first assessment was correct, so his situation did not look good at all. But surely there had to be something, some other angle; some new move he could make? Even as he thought that, he knew it was the thinking of a victim being dragged down to an adjustment cell.

"We need to look at worst-case scenarios," he stated. "We need responses, should we be unable to evade close combat." He felt he was missing something, and that it was something quite simple—some datum yet to be fed into his present assessment of the situation.

"We have been considering this," replied Paul, who was presently overseeing repairs to power lines leading to one of the Mach-effect units. The proctor was standing like some techno-logical hunt master amidst massed steel hounds.

"And the result of your consideration?" Saul enquired.

The proctor immediately routed a block of information to him. Saul absorbed the overview straight into his mind and saw that, yes, this was a plan that might work. However, the best that could be said about it was that it was a costly one, dependent on numerous variables. A more appropriate description would be suicidally desperate.

"Io?" he enquired, after a moment, consciously suppressing a visceral aversion.

"Their disadvantage is that they do not wish to destroy the Gene Bank samples and data," Paul replied. "And that they also wish to capture you alive."

Perhaps it required minds like those of the proctors to see the way clear, but Saul, even as logical as he could be, found it difficult to accept that their only route to survival was by crashing his ship on Jupiter's moon Io.

He now absorbed the entire plan and studied its many flaws. It would only work if he managed to hit certain parts of the Fist, disabling one particular option. It would work if the Mach-effect drive could be maintained at above eighty per cent efficiency throughout the inevitable battering that his ship would receive before it went down. It would work if the Rhine drive wasn't hit, and it would require that drive being sacrificed later. And it would work, in the end, if the *Command* was positioned just so, had not improved much on its present manoeuvrability and did not tear Saul's ship apart before a very final encounter.

"The crash can be made to look real," Paul asserted, "especially with their scanning equipment being disrupted by EM radiation from Io's flux tube and torus. There are few other alternatives, as while we remain in flight the *Fist* will be able to pound us to scrap before committing its troops to an assault. The enemy must be convinced that we are down and all but finished."

"The robots," Saul noted.

"The troops aboard the *Fist* will be armed with EM-pulse tank-busters, so they must not be allowed to board," Paul explained. "The *Command* is unlikely to have a significant number of such troops aboard, or such weapons either."

"Only if all else fails," Saul decided, though as yet he had no idea what that "else" might mean. He swallowed a bitter taste in his mouth. One thing was certain: fleeing the Jovian moon system was not an option: the battlefield would be around Jupiter.

The huge Mach-effect shove, with a parallel firing of the Traveller engine, sent Saul's ship back in towards Jupiter. He just had to hope that those aboard the *Command* were struggling to get their system up and running, so would not detect the thrust discrepancy. The *Fist* had only just rounded Jupiter, thus was too far away for its sensors to penetrate both the magnetosphere and heavy ionization lying between to get readings accurate enough for them to know the enemy's present course was not all due to its Traveller engine. Its crew were also probably more concerned about what had happened to the *Command*, and were doubtless reassessing tactics now that a plasma cannon had come into play.

"Very effective," he observed.

"Why, thank you," Brigitta replied casually, but her expression, as she gazed at the screen shots, revealed her shock at just how lethal her new toy had proved. Prior to this moment it had all been about design, calculation, invention and engineering problems to be solved. Prior to this moment, calculations regarding the weapon's effectiveness had all concerned energy yields and losses, point heat intensity and distribution. It had not been about burning a crater in the main body of the enemy ship, then tearing a chunk out of its rear and seeing human beings burning on their suit oxygen supplies as they tumbled out into vacuum.

As Saul's ship hurtled back in towards Jupiter, the *Fist* began making course changes to intercept, for their courses lay athwart each other. Firing side-burn fusion engines, it hurled itself up in a curve towards Jupiter's pole, making a turn on conventional drive that Saul knew would have damaged his own ship and probably killed large numbers on board. The *Fist* was clearly a tough machine, and it seemed likely its crew and troop complement must be using some design of pressure gel-tanks to prevent the g-forces killing them. Such manoeuvrability on the part of the enemy ship seemed to confirm Paul's assertions, but Saul did not like that at all.

Also, as the *Fist* moved into an area of minimal ionization, and while Saul's ship drew closer, more of the enemy vessel lay open to inspection. Saul collected data, noting some odd spectral signatures that told him that the armour on the *Fist* was some sort of composite. He also located the space doors to the main shuttle bay, counted numerous railgun ports. Something else to note were the domes of extensible weapons turrets that doubtless contained additional armament.

"I think you may be right," he conceded bitterly to the proctor Paul, just as the *Fist* showered intervening space with shooting stars: a perfect pattern of railgun missiles, in avoiding which Saul would need to decelerate, thus giving the *Fist* a chance to close in.

Thus far, Alex had managed to keep Ghort in sight, but keeping track of him was becoming increasingly dangerous, as the row of shots stitched across the wall of ice at a recent junction had attested. Now the initial immediacy of the hunt, with the prey clearly in sight, must give way to a patient stalking.

"You've got nowhere to go, Ghort," he said. "Even if you evade me, the Owner will eventually track you down."

"You've rather limited my choices," Ghort replied bitterly. Alex grimaced. In retrospect, he should not have warned Ghort that he intended to kill him. Then, again, no fancy tapestry of lies would have convinced the man that he had any chance of survival by giving himself up.

"Yes, I suppose I have."

Ghort's reply was just a grunt, but this provided enough.

The triangulation and tracking program, which Alex had created over a month ago, now had enough data to work with. Both of them were speaking via laser com, linking in to any receivers nearby and transmitting through the ship's system; therefore, so long as Ghort continued to communicate through his implant, Alex could continue to track him. He paused to call up a schematic of his surroundings, located his quarry just a hundred metres away, now moving out from the armouring that surrounded the vortex generator. Then, with reference to the schematic, Alex began using the tracking element of his program. Banishing the schematic as being too distracting, he linked to his suit and brought up a simple display in his visor. Two arrows now appeared there, a red one pointing directly to Ghort and a green one indicating the shortest course in order to reach him through the outer maze of the station ring.

At the next T-junction he needed to go right but, before rounding the corner, he walked up the wall then on to the ceiling before stepping round. As half expected, he spotted Ghort squatting at the end of the corridor, but he was up on the ceiling too. Muzzle flashes lit the space ahead of him. Alex replied with a short burst before hurling himself back into cover, feeling a glancing strike on the VC suit armour on one side of his torso. Diagnostics alerted him to a breach as he reached round the corner with his assault rifle and sprayed a couple of bursts in Ghort's general direction.

"Incidentally," said Ghort, "I have made a choice."

"And what is that?" Alex asked, while his suit informed him that sealant had already closed the breach. He inspected his side, noting a hole filled with yellow resin, but the suit's medscanner informed him that, despite feeling as if he'd been viciously kicked, no bullets had actually penetrated.

"I've chosen at least to kill the fucker who betrayed us before someone or something kills me," Ghort continued. "Which is why I'm still talking to you, Alex."

Ah, he knew about the tracking program.

Noting the red arrow on the move, Alex propelled himself to the floor, stepped round the corner, built up speed with loping steps, then launched himself towards Ghort's previous location. Another glance at the schematic showed the man moving to one of the more open areas of the outer ring, where corridors and rooms had yet to be built.

At the end of the corridor he flipped over, pointing his weapon to the spot where the red arrow indicated Ghort's position. But only ceiling lay there, above a rectangular opening. Just like the junctions before it, this was a perfect ambush point, and doubtless Ghort had that opening in his sights even now. Alex went the other way, along a corridor that finally ran out of wall panels, then up a temporary cageway into blackness seeded with LED lights and tangled with structural beams. Checking the direction arrows again, he found a structure like a chimney blocking the way. He upped magnification in his visor but could still see no sign of the other man, so he slung his rifle and began making his way up a nearby beam to gain a clearer view. He managed just two paces before the ship jerked as if it had run into a moon. As he fell away from the beam, fire and wreckage exploded into the blackness.

EARTH

"You're lying," said Serene but, gazing at Ruger, she knew he wasn't.

She turned back to Sack and Trove. "Get the *Scourge* on screen," she ordered. "Show me."

Trove turned her attention to Sack who, after a lengthy pause, nodded. Then, almost as an afterthought, he retracted his gun from her side.

Trove quickly pulled up an image on the console screen. This wasn't something someone could have falsified in the limited time that had been available. It was indeed the Scourge, truncated by perspective over Earth, with its drive flame glaring behind it.

"Can we talk to him?" Serene asked.

Trove worked her instruments again. The screen blanked for a second, ran some odd code which Serene realized was just the visible portion of some kind of defensive program, then showed an image of Captain Scotonis. Serene studied him carefully. He was unshaven, looked slightly dirty, and his face was dotted with sores. If his mind was unbalanced, then he could be manipulated.

"Captain Scotonis," she said, "it's good that you survived."

He smiled, looking quite sane. "Not so good for you, though."

"I'm told that you've come to believe that I am responsible for the Scour," she said, adopting a puzzled expression. "I just don't understand how this has happened."

"It's not a case of *belief*, Galahad," Scotonis replied. "I've seen the biochips that were embedded on the face of every implant we removed aboard my ship. I saw the testimony of the two scientists who first found out about the source of the Scour—you know, scientists working in a secret laboratory you subsequently had burned—while pretending those in that place were trying to weaponize a virus that was already a weapon."

Serene glanced round at Ruger, who was grinning again, then she tried to stamp down on an upsurge of rage, for such information could only have reached Scotonis through him.

She turned back to the captain. "Then you know half the truth."

Scotonis shrugged. "It's a big enough half for me."

"Yes, there are biochips in implants, and they do produce the Scour," she said. "But it was not me who activated them. When Alan Saul initiated his computer-generated and physical attack on the infrastructure of Earth, *he* activated those chips. All I did was keep the source of the Scour a secret."

Scotonis smiled, shaking his head. "And yet, oddly, those who died from the Scour were not those he would have wanted to kill, but zero-asset citizens. Later, when it was thoroughly convenient for you, Committee members also died of it. But, of course, you covered that rather incriminating selectivity by killing off numerous others within the administration, including my wife and my children. Good try, Galahad, but you're still going to burn."

"You're making a very foolish mistake," she said, scrabbling for some other angle, groping for what to try next, utterly sure that there had to be something she *could* try.

"Bye bye, Serene Galahad," said Scotonis, cutting off the communication.

Serene stared at the blank screen, but now mentally chewing everything over just as fast as possible.

They were trapped inside this station so long as Calder controlled its railguns, while bearing down on them was a spaceship containing enough nukes to flash-burn a continent. However, though she realized her initial reaction to all this had contained its elements of denial, she knew for sure she would survive.

Earth *needed* her; therefore her dying up here before her work was done just could not be contemplated. There had to be a way out. No question.

"The drop shuttle," she said abruptly. "The fast re-entry shuttle."

Yes, survival was inevitable, it *had* to be. "Ma'am?" Sack enquired.

"We can get to it without leaving the station structure," she declared, having no idea whether that was true. "We can get to it without making ourselves a target for Calder's railguns."

Sack abruptly turned to the console and took control of the screen image. He worked through a series of menus, finally calling up a schematic of the entire station, then he pointed to one part of it, a module protruding underneath at the end of a short cylinder.

"Can you get us here?" he asked Trove.

"Why should I even try?" asked the pilot officer.

Serene waited for Sack to hit the woman, or maybe take out a disabler and use it on her. But he did not, and instead turned back to Serene.

"She needs a reason," he stated.

Serene stared at him for a long moment, assessing, calculating. She had been stupid to allow petty vengeance to get in the way. The fates of both Trove and Ruger were irrelevant to her ultimate purpose. She could let them go and whether or not they survived just did not matter. What mattered was her getting back to Earth and regaining her seat of power. Anyway, the pair of them could always be hunted down later . . .

"As I understand it, the controls of the drop shuttle, though they can take us down to Earth on automatic, can be overridden." Still feeling her way, she continued, "You can take control and land it wherever you choose . . . we will give you weapons so you can assure your own safety . . . you can run, you can go wherever you wish . . . I will say that you died aboard the construction station."

Trove gazed at her for a long moment, then, turning to Sack, held out her hand palm upwards. In one almost dismissive motion, as if he just did not care, he took out his automatic and handed it over. Serene felt her stomach tighten as Trove studied the weapon, clicked the safety on and off, ejected the magazine and inspected it, then slammed it back in. She then pointed it casually at Serene's stomach. But Serene knew that the trigger would not be pulled, for destiny rode on her shoulders like a guardian angel. She folded her arms and waited.

Trove abruptly retracted the weapon and shoved it into the belt of her suit. She glanced over to Ruger and watched as, upon Serene's nod, his guard handed over a sidearm and moved away. "Okay," said Trove, turning back to her controls. She quickly began calling up new views within the schematic, overlaid the shape of the shuttle they occupied, its relative dimensions correct, and began plotting a course through the station. Seeing what she was doing, Serene realized that this was something she could have done herself, and that there had been no need to put herself in danger by allowing Trove and Ruger to be armed.

Trove grabbed the joystick in her right hand, left hand working the console and her feet working the pedals that con-trolled the shuttle's attitude. The shuttle turned and lifted, giving a view across the side of the dock where inter-station shuttles clung like steel bracket fungi. A blast from steering thrusters caused Serene to stagger and now the shuttle sped along above the others, a bubblemetal wall speeding past them to the right. Deceleration followed and the shuttle turned its nose in at the end of the dock, spider webs of structural beams looming ahead.

"It'll be a bumpy ride," said Trove, "but this shuttle is built to take a few knocks." She glanced at Sack. "I want a helmet suitable for the VC suit I'm wearing."

Without any instruction from either Sack or Serene, the guard who had handed his gun to Ruger brought forward a replacement helmet, which Trove donned. Serene stepped back into the passenger compartment, whereupon the same man passed her a helmet to replace her own, which she had lost somewhere inside the shuttle bay. Everyone secured their suits, before the remaining soldier thought to check on his injured fellow, but found he had meanwhile ceased to have any need of air.

Trove drove the shuttle forwards and the first crash ensued shortly afterwards, dragging the vessel round until the beam it had just struck was visible, though with no apparent damage. The impact detached Serene's gecko boots from the floor and she had to struggle to propel herself down again, but only after the second impact, when she was thrown against the cockpit bulkhead and a breach alarm started sounding, did she concede that she needed to strap herself into a seat like the rest of them.

Another crash ensued and, from her seat behind the cockpit, Serene watched a crack snake across the screen.

"I'm dumping internal," Trove shouted. "Go to channel fifteen."

For a second, Serene did not know what the woman was talking about, but then came a roaring sound and her suit stiffened, her visor display noting a rapid drop of pressure inside the shuttle. Trove had dumped their air, probably to prevent the screen from being blown out, and now they needed to use their suit radios. Serene searched radio channels using a wrist console, the menu summoned up in her visor. Finding channel fifteen, she noted the option to link it to her fone, but that seemed pointless.

Ahead, the entire station seemed to be gyrating as Trove corkscrewed the shuttle between the metal-webbed blocks of factory units, venting chimneys and globular clusters of accommodation units. Gripping her seat arms tightly, Serene tracked the slow-moving seconds and then minutes on a clock in her visor. For a moment they were out in open vacuum and she glimpsed people in EVA units firing emergency jets to get out of the way, then she closed her eyes as the shuttle turned back into the station, swung sideways to get itself between two massive beams, next leapfrogging some gargantuan ship component being towed along a tunnel resembling a lizard's throat. Coming out of the other side of this tunnel, the shuttle turned, with the curve of the Large Component Construction Floor coming into view to the right, then dropped down past it.

"We'll have to go outside," Trove announced. "The docking mechanism is fucked."

Deceleration threw Serene against her straps as they sped down past a column she recognized from the station schematic. Then finally they were zero gravity again, turning slowly in vacuum as everyone unstrapped. They were now beside the drop-shuttle dock, the drop shuttle itself suspended underneath it like a giant black door wedge. Ruger and Sack were first to the airlock, and first through. Trove and Serene went next, the surviving member of her security team last. By the time Serene was out in vacuum, Sack had opened an airlock leading into the dock. She propelled herself across to it, fighting a terror of the yawning spaces all around her, but was soon safely inside and through the airlock. The corridor beyond was octagonal in section, windows looking out on to vacuum and the gleam of Earth below. Sack led the way down towards another airlock at the further end.

"You know, Ruger," said Trove, "despite everything, I was starting to like you."

"Likewise," Ruger replied as he followed her through into the drop shuttle. "Shame it's going to be such a short relationship."

"What do you mean?" Serene interrupted, pulling herself down into one of the seats inside.

As she strapped herself down in the pilot's chair, Trove glanced round and, ignoring Serene's question, said, "Plug in your umbilicals and go over to ship air. If we're really lucky, we might even get to make a dent in the supply." She directed her next words at Ruger. "Yeah, three minutes really isn't enough time for us to get to know each other better."

16

ENGINEERS AND IDEOLOGUES

The importance of politicians is something that can never be under-estimated, for over the centuries so many of them have strutted on the world stage, prattling their party political and ideological jargon and produced little of real value. The number of them who have had a real effect on the human lot pales in comparison to the number of scientists and engineers who have produced something worthwhile. Who did more for women's rights than the inventors of the washing machine, the vacuum cleaner and the contraceptive pill? Has righteous nannying improved human health more than Lister, Pasteur, Fleming or any number of a huge list of pioneering biologists? Who gave us more freedom than Henry Ford, or more freedom of speech than the inventors of the Internet, or more to eat than Jethro Tull or John Froehlich? It was Edison who shone real light into our lives, not some dogma. However, let us not presume politicians are ineffectual, for whenever the bombs and napalm are falling, the mines taking off legs and the bullets punching holes in human flesh, they are always behind the firing line, deciding who should die.

ARGUS

Again something smashed into the ship and Hannah knew that what she was feeling was real fear and no mere panic attack.

Beyond that she felt frustrated and ineffectual: what was happening now was as beyond her influence as a tsunami.

"We just lost one of the railguns," declared Le Roque, his screen image appearing up in a top corner of the right-hand bulkhead screen, looking like a man seeing his own gallows for the first time.

"No shit," replied Brigitta Saberhagen, her head dipped, trying not to see the same noose.

The left-hand screen, which was linked to a damage-control program, kindly displayed the partially molten and shattered mess that had been one of their railguns, along with a large red-lipped hole to one side of it, where a missile had punched through the hull.

"Is there anything you can do?" the technical director asked.

"I ceased to have any input long ago," the Saberhagen twin replied. "Saul is now controlling everything."

"That's true," Langstrom interjected. "I don't know if any of you have tried, but I can't do much with my implant now. The robots are ignoring me and system access is limited to data retrieval only."

"Perhaps this was not such a great idea," Hannah muttered, suppressing transmission of her voice beyond this limited area. "I'm not sure I want to know what's going on."

It was Le Roque who had opened up video conferencing to them here in their room at the end of the Meat Locker. The technical director was trying to gather data, exert some influence, trying to do *something*, but was just being swept along in the wave of wreckage. All the humans aboard were in very much the same position: strapped into either an acceleration chair or a couch, while waiting to find out if they were going to die.

"I do," Da Vinci replied. "We blank all this out, and the next thing we might see is Galahad's troops coming in here to grab us."

Dr Raiman leaned forwards from his chair beside Da Vinci and gazed across at them both. "We are all wearing VC suits, so have medical support."

"And?" Da Vinci stared at him in puzzlement.

Raiman held out a gloved hand to reveal a couple of drug ampoules. "You can insert them in your support packs, and order suit injection by means of your wrist console or phone." He shrugged. "Or any other data route you care to name."

Hannah reached out to take one of the ampoules and held it up, seeing that all it had marked on it was a bar code.

"The rebels on Earth were starting to use explosive implants before this all kicked off," she reflected. "So what is this?"

"A neurotoxin that only has a number," Raiman replied. "I've always had this stuff ready to hand, even before Saul took over Argus Station." He nodded to his assistant, who was sitting silently in one of the seats behind him. "Greg and I are ready."

Da Vinci reached for one of the ampoules and, without hesitation, pressed it down into a drugs port fitted in the support pack on his belt.

"And, in what feels only a short time ago to me," he said, "I was actually contemplating immortality. Now, it seems, it's time to think about suicide."

The view on the left-hand screen was changing like a snap-shot viewer, running through images inside a ship that Hannah felt was distinctly taking on the appearance of a pawnbroker's sphere clipped by a blast from a shotgun. Another hit left the Meat Locker shuddering, and the view switched to focus on the latest impact point. Hannah gazed numbly at air blasting from a hole in Arcoplex Two, that whole cylinder world turning slowly on its now bent axle. She could have been in there. She could have been right under that. Almost certainly others had been there.

"That's more power lines down," observed Rhine, who until then had been saying nothing; instead he had just sat staring at his own screen and cam with a look of myopic surprise.

"So what have we lost?" Le Roque asked him. Rhine had now turned away and did not reply. "Rhine?"

The professor turned back. "The vortex generator will never get up to full speed without major repairs, and I see no robots tending to the problem."

"We should consider ourselves lucky the thing itself hasn't been hit," said Langstrom. "After seeing what happened to the *Vision*."

Rhine shook his head. "No luck involved."

"What do you mean?"

When Rhine didn't reply, Le Roque did it for him. "Saul is using Mach-effect nudges to make sure the vortex ring isn't hit, and deliberately firing off steering thrusters at the same time, so as to cover it. He doesn't want them to know about the Mach-effect drive."

Wonderful, thought Hannah, hoping such nudges were being used simply to save human lives inside the ship, but sure Saul was just desperately trying to preserve their one shot at escape.

"And then what?" This was Pike speaking from one of the smelting plants— perhaps one of the safest places to be now, since it was close to the vortex ring. "Does this mean he plans to use it against them somehow?"

"I don't know," said Le Roque, obviously bewildered. "Has anyone been able to get any response from him? Hannah?"

"Nothing since he told us to take cover here," she replied.

"Does anyone have any idea what he intends?" Le Roque asked, but no one replied.

Hannah would have liked to believe that Alan had some clever and unforeseen tactic in mind to drag their nuts out of the fire, but instead it seemed they were fleeing desperately while taking a hellish punishment. It wouldn't be long, she felt, before the *Fist* hit something major and this ship ceased to be a ship at all, and became just a drifting wreck. Further punishment would then ensue and, if she and those accompanying her survived that, it would be Galahad's assault force arriving next.

She peered down at the ampoule still resting in her palm, then inserted it into her support pack. Da Vinci was right: on the next few hours depended the chance of eternity or nothing at all.

Var picked herself up and, checking the temperature readings exterior to her suit, saw that without its insulation she would already be dead. The steam fogging the corridor rapidly dissolved into vacuum, but the walls around her were still radiating, still hot. She reached round to probe her shoulder blade: it hurt badly but didn't feel broken. The ribs below it, however, responded to her fingers with a sharp pain. Almost certainly she'd cracked one. Only now did she properly consider Langstrom's words.

Her brother was in the midst of a fight, which possibly in his terms meant only for his own life and for the survival of his ship, but nevertheless the crew of this ship and Var herself totally depended on him for their survival. Perhaps she should simply put trust in him: trust that he had already eliminated the threat the chipped had posed; trust that, though he might not have the best interests of the people aboard close to heart, he had still, as Langstrom claimed, always made some effort to ensure their survival. Perhaps now she should just turn back, find an acceleration chair, and wait for the outcome . . .

No! Var felt suddenly angry at her own weakness. Just because they were in the midst of a space battle, just because others did not believe her contentions and just because she was finding it harder and harder to believe them herself, that should not be an excuse for her to quit. The easy way was *not* the right way—this was something she had learned on Mars. She had killed other humans there and been perfectly justified in doing so. And the killing here had been perfectly justified too . . .

Thomas Grieve.

The name nagged at her. The sight of him looking up at her was imprinted on her mind. The sensation of his skull breaking under the spanner seemed to have permanently embedded itself in the nerves of her arm. She headed angrily off down the corridor, her thoughts in disarray, but doubt still knotting together her insides.

At the far end she came to a junction. To the right extended yet another corridor, but to the left a short stretch of passageway opened out into a large space in the outer ring. Which way? She turned towards the opening first, where she could at least use the image-intensifier function of her visor to take a look around and maybe learn if her quarries were in sight. There could be no harm in at least locating them . . .

Saul noted his hand shaking as he closed his visor, and then violently suppressed human reactions. The shaking stopped as he lowered his hand and studied the spatters of molten metal hardening on his VC suit before peering through the thick smoke towards the hole in the far wall. Veering away from the reality that he had just been a breath away from dying, he descended into the world of pure logic. He surmised that one of the railgun missiles fired by the *Fist* had consisted of some kind of case-hardened alloy composite that had fragmented after its glancing blow against the Arboretum—one of those fragments then finding its way here to punch through the armour of his inner sanctum. The breach had been quickly sealed with resin, and air pressure restored, but it would take a little while for the air-conditioning system to cycle out the smoke laden with hydrogen cyanide. He speculated on whether this poisonous gas was just an inadvertent result of the processes used to construct the missile, or whether it was a deliberate consequence. He plumped for the former because this bombardment was intended merely to disable his ship, because Galahad still wanted her captives.

His attention focusing throughout the ship, and outwards again, Saul studied the damage inflicted on both sides. Other fragments from the latest missile had cut into Tech Central, further wrecking the support systems for the vortex ring, and incidentally taking off someone's arm at the elbow. No matter, the arm had been shoved into a fridge and could be reattached later, while, despite Rhine's chagrin, the present vortex generator would not be taking them out of the solar system *ever*. He had to accept that now.

The rest of the ship was a mess too—parts of its exterior resembling the lid of a pepper pot. The dislodged end of the Arboretum had shifted again to tear through the lattice walls before grinding to a halt; atmosphere breaches filled the interior space with a fog, and fires burned visibly in pressurized sections. One railgun was slagged and the support column to the Traveller engine was damaged and slowly twisting under the strain of thrust. Beside all this damage Saul counted the number of feeds to backup that had been cut and, running a calculation that included those not yet chipped, he reckoned on over two hundred dead.

Meanwhile the *Fist* had received its own pounding, but there the damage was much less evident. The enemy's armour tended to distribute the shock inflicted and in some cases Saul's missiles had failed to penetrate. One result was that the *Fist* was no longer spherical, but now resembled a pocked tomato. Two of its equatorial fusion engines had also been badly damaged and many of its weapons ports had been destroyed, but in functional railguns it vastly outnumbered Saul's ship still.

"Io," Saul decided.

"Undoubtedly," the proctor Paul replied, as he scrabbled around the inner hull to make further repairs, with robots swarming all about him.

"Does it hurt?" Saul asked.

"It is agony," Paul replied.

One of his fellows had been right underneath one of the latest railgun strikes and, as tough as the proctors were, they could not survive being vaporized.

"And he lives still," Paul added.

The proctors, it seemed, had their own form of backup, in the minds of each other.

"I'm sorry," said Saul, not quite sure why he felt the need to apologize thus to the proctors but felt no need to comment about the human casualties.

"Is it in position?" Paul asked. "Data exchange is intermittent and we need exact timings."

Peering through a cam near the fusion engine, Saul watched a robot climbing down towards the hellish flames spewing out from the combustion-chamber array. This was a robot that had been sent to kill him, but now, rather than a dud, it carried a live copper-head explosive which, while he watched, it fixed in position.

"It's in place," Saul replied, as he watched Io drawing rapidly closer. "But best if we don't use it, as I want one of their shots to do the damage."

"It is good to take precautions," Paul opined.

"Yes." Saul was all in agreement on that. The robot was there to cover the very small chance of the enemy ship *not* managing to hit the fusion engine once Saul stopped using the Mach-effect to dodge its missiles. It was also there to cover the chance that the *Fist* might not fire on them at the correct moment—a small chance indeed since the enemy ship's bombardment had been almost constant. Another robot, which walked upright while carrying a ten-mil machine gun, and who was an old friend, if such nomenclature could be applied, moved into position by the plasma cannon. Whether this robot would be needed depended on calculations Saul had to make once his sensors had gathered enough data.

The ship was now down into Io's orbital path, closing in on the moon itself as it sped round Jupiter. Using steering thrusters only, Saul made some adjustments to their course, then abruptly shut down the Traveller engine. Now at last it was time for Paul's plan: the proctor's suicidally desperate ploy.

Within his mind Saul applied sensor data, mapped vectors, carefully adjusted the hydraulic targeting gear of the plasma cannon and included every possible variable in his calculations: the new weight distribution inside his ship after the recent damage; the powerful gyroscopic effect of the vortex generator; the pull of Io and of Jupiter, in fact the whole gravity map around him; further possible damage both from the *Fist* and the massive deceleration he was about to apply. The calculations multiplied in his mind into a three-dimensional mathematical maze which, as he applied more and more processing power, collapsed into its vector and firing solutions, though with large error bars.

There was, as the plan suggested, an advantage in limiting the number of plasma "caps" fired, for he did not want the Fist unable to continue the pursuit to its conclusion immediately, so he ensured multiple routes of laser com to the robot with the machine gun.

"Now we do it," he said, to himself and no one else. He could not tell anyone to prepare for this, for they were all as ready as they could be. And, really, it was pointless warning them that more of them might be about to die.

Another lengthy blast from the steering thrusters, complemented by Mach-effect, turned the ship over. The Traveller engine fired again, at full power, and

Saul checked stress readings as the column supporting it shrank by fifty metres and a large number of beams splintered. Now off-centre, the engine's erupting flame ate into the hull around its port and turned a bright orange. The massive deceleration that ensued slammed him down into his chair, and elsewhere throughout in the ship the effect was even worse. The Arboretum tore free, its near end dropping ponderously, and its ring-side end also being wrenched out and thousands of tonnes of metal swinging down against the inner hull and distorting it under the impact. Also ripped free, an accommodation unit dropped to smash into the lattice wall extending from the base of the Traveller engine. Saul measured the various effects of these impacts, found the adjustments he needed to make to correct his course and did so instantly. He noted a safety protocol kicking in, causing the vortex generator to go over to safe holding—induction power being drawn off from the ring to maintain containment. However, he had expected this, knowing it would be more than twenty hours before the mercury spinning round inside dropped to a velocity ineffective for his purposes.

As expected, the *Fist* turned over and decelerated too. Those aboard it would read his actions as a desperate gamble, an attempt to use Io to cover an abrupt course change heading out-system, but also to bring his plasma cannon into play. And, perfectly as calculated, the *Fist*'s change in attitude brought the doors to its shuttle and landing craft bay directly into view, along with the least damaged of its weapons arrays. Saul tracked multiple firings from the *Fist*'s railguns: a high concentration of missiles heading towards the site of his own ship's plasma cannon. This launch was followed by multiple slower firings, as the other ship deployed mines above its weapons arrays to protect them. Saul adjusted and finely tuned targeting, then fired the cannon.

A line of plasma caps sped out from Saul's ship, moving faster than the approaching railgun missiles, and glowing like massive welding sparks. More mines seeded from the *Fist*, but not quickly enough. The first plasma cap struck to one side of a railgun array, the explosion there leaving a glowing caldera. The second two landed perfectly on target, slamming straight into the bay doors, the first destroying them and the second punching straight through to discharge itself inside. The subsequent blast opened out metallic petals of the surrounding hull, before spewing out tonnes of wreckage—chunks of which Saul identified as the rear section of a space plane, along with two badly smashed inter-station shuttles. It was enough.

The latest launch of railgun missiles from the *Fist* now began hitting, smashing into Argus's hull and underscoring the plasma-cannon port with a lengthy burning ellipsis. The damage was severe but, though targeting was off, it was still possible for Argus to fire the cannon. Saul queued up shots to fire, targeted by using the ship's steering thrusters, then began firing. But he simultaneously ordered his robot to open up on the heavy coils of the cannon with its machine gun. One shot sped away before the big weapon lost containment. It exploded, spewing wreckage and molten metal out of its port, thereby signalling to the *Fist* that it was no longer a danger.

They were close to Io now, feeling its pull, and their speed was down to just thousands of kilometres per hour. Now the *Fist* was close enough to start using beam weapons. Firing his remaining railgun in apparent desperation, Saul adjusted his course down into the ionization torus and into the thin breath of volcanic smoke around the moon, where beam weapons would prove less effective. Distorted by the brush of a maser, the railgun abruptly tore out its rails. Saul returned fire with his own maser, and saw three railgun ports on the other ship spew debris. Further firings from there put the equator of his ship in danger; it heightened the probability of the vortex generator being hit, which must not happen. Using Mach-effect with a covering firing of steering thrusters, Saul adjusted his ship's position just so, evading all but two of the missiles. They slammed into the base of his ship: one of them flaring in the Traveller engine's drive flame and tearing out through the other side like a magnesium fire, but the second hitting the pellet-aggregation plants. The explosion filled the interior of the ship with metal vapour, and then the drive flame sputtered and went out. The robot stationed there had not been required.

"We're going in," Saul announced to the whole ship, as he gazed out upon Io's horizon and the sulphurous landscape below. And, to the proctor Paul, he noted tightly, "Mach-effect is below eighty per cent, I see."

"It is enough," the proctor replied. "But not enough to take us up again."

"We will have time."

Time . . .

In the end the primary aim of those aboard the *Fist* was not his destruction, but seizing the Gene Bank data and samples. Paul had calculated that the coming crash would convince them that further disabling bombardment from orbit might destroy that prime objective, and Saul agreed. If he was wrong, then their chances of getting off the ground again were little above nil, for even though his robots were rapidly at work making repairs throughout the interior of the ship, he doubted the vessel could stand much more punishment. And, more importantly, once they were down, he could no longer use the Mach-effect to dodge the blows, and then the absolutely critical vortex generator might be hit. If that happened, he might just as well step out onto Io and open up his suit.

"It looks as if we're all going to die anyway," said Ghort, his voice drifting in and out of audibility, while patched by a program in Alex's implant. "But don't you want to be the one to pull the trigger on me, Alex?"

Alex didn't bother replying, he just gazed at the long sliver of metal that had missed impaling him to a wall of asteroidal ice, and then started searching for some way through the tangled mass of wreckage lying between him and Ghort. As he moved, he could feel the steady drag of either acceleration or deceleration, but it was mild and of little consequence. Some of the wreckage glowed red hot, but Alex realized that this did not account for the increase in light hereabouts. Shifting himself away from the ice wall, he obtained a clearer view, through a hole torn in the side of the old station ring, of the bright sulphurous surface of one of Jupiter's moons speeding along below.

"Or have you lost the stomach for it?" Ghort asked, as Alex now wormed his way between splintered beams. "It was so much easier for you to shoot people in the back, so I guess facing up directly to someone who knows you're coming and wants to kill you might not be quite to your taste."

Alex paused, surprised at Ghort's attitude. Obviously the man was hoping to lure Alex out from cover, but did he really think him so stupid? Did he think Alex could be goaded into irrational acts of anger? Apparently he did. Alex knew that, in general human terms, he was very naive, but when it came to this sort of thing, this hunting and killing, Alex was Methuselah. Such a misreading of someone, such a complete lack of judgement on Ghort's part, further confirmed the futility of that man's rebellion. It never had a chance of success anyway but, had it succeeded, the chipped would probably have been tearing at each other's throats shortly afterwards.

Finally struggling out into the open, Alex studied his surroundings. He saw that something had smashed through the side of the ship, torn up the outer-ring infrastructure, then buried itself in a blast wall far ahead and over to the right. However, the enclosed section he had quitted just before the latest impact was undamaged, and doubtless Ghort was still covering the rectangular opening below, in the hope of springing an ambush. Alex moved to the right to get a clearer view, checking the direction arrows in his visor, but found them ghosting and intermittent after so many laser-com devices had been destroyed here.

"It's not a case of whether I have the stomach for it, Ghort. It's just a job I do." He hadn't actually wanted to speak, but the program running in his implant needed more communications data to key onto.

"And now you do it for Alan Saul," Ghort replied bitterly. "Tell me, Alex, were you recruited by him for this treachery right from the start, or did you go and weasel your way into his good graces after you'd joined us?"

This response was enough. The red arrow steadied and pointed directly at a twisted beam junction covered by a metre-wide strengthening plate twenty metres ahead. Under magnification and protruding from behind it, Ghort's hand was just visible, supporting the stock of his assault rifle—the barrel predictably directed down towards that same rectangular opening. Alex just needed to move over as far as the nearest blast wall and work his way along it to obtain a clear shot. He began to do so, but also remained curious about Ghort's attitude.

"Surely," he said, "you understand that, even without me here to stop you, you've had little chance of success? Did it never occur to you how convenient it seemed to be for you to gain access to explosives? Did you not question how easily you obtained the supposed location of his backups?"

"So you actually believe the mythology he creates around himself," said Ghort. "You, too, have been fooled into believing in his omniscience. It's all a front, Alex, and so long as people believe in him, they enslave themselves and do the majority of his work for him."

Alex shook his head in irritation. "He spoke to me just a short while ago, and that was the first and only time since he spared my life. He simply inserted me in your group like a number in a formula he needed to solve, while at the same time he gave you enough rope with which to hang yourselves."

"Oh, you're so grateful to be alive," Ghort spat contemptuously.

Alex paused by the blast wall. "Yes, I am. Just as I'm grateful for the possibility, because of him, that I might continue living for a very long time."

"As a slave."

"Yet with greater freedom than I have ever experienced before."

"But you are not free and you will never be free, and you could exist just like that for an eternity," said Ghort. "Those of us with fully functional brains recognize that as a kind of hell."

"I thought you said we were all going to die?"

"Fuck you, Alex," Ghort replied, obviously lacking a sensible rejoinder.

"So things would have been better without the Owner," said Alex. "With you in charge, we would all have been free to map out our own destinies and just do whatever we want. That's rubbish. There is no real freedom anywhere: it's simply an airy concept used to justify power grabs. We are all constrained in some way, either by those who rule over us, or by those we rule, or by our environments and by genetics. I just happen to prefer being ruled by the Owner, because he is the one most likely to keep me alive, and because I myself do not want to rule, and know of no one more worthy to rule over me."

"You're an idiot, Alex."

"But I'm not the kind of idiot who wanted to kill the only one with any chance of keeping us alive or out of Serene Galahad's hands. And I'm not the idiot who is now going to die."

Ghort laughed. "I wouldn't be so sure about that."

Muzzle flashes abruptly lit the scene, and a couple of tracers showed Ghort was firing down towards the rectangular opening. "Well, I thought you had more patience, Alex," he continued.

Then he laughed again and propelled himself from cover.

Alex opened fire, at least two bullets hitting home, but with no guarantee of penetration through a VC suit. Ghort nearly lost his rifle as he used his wrist impellers to drive himself downwards and out of sight. Alex squatted and propelled himself from the blast wall, heading for the same opening in the hope of intercepting Ghort there and finishing this pathetic drama. And, as he went, he was forced to wonder just who the hell Ghort had been firing at.

He landed above the opening, caught hold of a jag of twisted metal, pushed himself down and swung inside, bringing his rifle to bear. Ten metres back inside, two figures drifted in a mist of vapour leaking from suit breaches. One rifle was tumbling away behind them, and one was trailing at the end of a broken strap. As Alex pushed himself down for the floor and accelerated towards them, the larger one turned the smaller one round, pressing a sidearm up against her throat. Alex stumbled to a halt on recognizing the bloody face behind the cracked visor.

"Seems I've got something . . . to bargain with now," panted Ghort, his voice hoarse, blood all around his mouth, and a leak under his armpit which the sealant just didn't seem to be containing.

Alex gazed at the face of the Owner's sister, noted the scabs of yellow breach resin on her stomach and her chest. He observed her cracked visor, and wondered how long she now had left to live.

"But not . . . with you," Ghort added, turning the sidearm on Alex.

THE COMMAND

The secondary bridge looked little different from its primary twin but now, of course, Bartholomew did not have all his previous staff. With his stomach tight and his mind hardened as the *Command* limped sideways-on towards Io, he watched the end of the battle between the Fist and Saul's ship. Both vessels had taken huge punishment, but in the end the *Fist*'s better armour and larger complement of weapons had decided the fight.

"What's your status?" he asked Captain Oerlon.

The captain of the *Fist* had lost most of his beard; he had a burn dressing on the front of his neck and soot smears all over his face.

"We've still got all our beam weapons, five railguns and two others that can be repaired within an hour. Main fusion drive is optimal, but the Alcubierre drive is going to be down for weeks. We lost two side-burners but that's merely cut our manoeuvrability—which is irrelevant now."

Bartholomew switched his gaze from the screen frame showing Oerlon to the main image—transmitted by the *Fist*—of Saul's ship struggling with steering thrusters only to try and escape the pull of Io. The ship looked like a cratered moon, so many were the holes punched through it. Internal fires were visible, as was the massive damage to its Traveller engine. It was weapon-less, had no more drive than perhaps enough to steer it clear of impact with some of the mountains down below, and it was now going to go in hard. Bartholomew just hoped it would not go in hard enough to be completely destroyed, as he still needed to retrieve the Gene Bank data and samples, and possibly some prisoners.

"You didn't manage to hit his vortex generator," Bartholomew commented.

Oerlon shrugged with a wince. "No, and luckily he didn't manage to hit ours either, or rather none of his shots penetrated its armour. Perhaps his drive is armoured similarly."

"Perhaps," Bartholomew allowed. Then, "Your casualties?"

"Fifty-eight of my crew are dead, another twenty in the infirmary," Oerlon replied. "We also lost over three hundred of the primary assault group when he hit the shuttle bay—as they were ready aboard shuttles."

That was the thing about space warfare, Bartholomew surmised. Unlike land battles on Earth, in this unforgiving environment the dead would always outnumber the wounded.

"Other assault troop casualties?"

"None," Oerlon replied. "Our armour took the sting out of the railgun missiles, and nothing penetrated through to core accommodation."

Again Bartholomew watched Saul's ship going in, and noted that the steering thrusters were now all pointing in the direction of travel as if to try and slow the vessel down rather than alter its course. He checked another frame on the screen displaying a map of Io's surface and the changing predictions on the crash site. It would be coming down through the spume emitted from two volcanoes, its impact site a sulphur plain lying beyond. This wasn't a site Bartholomew would have chosen, but he supposed Saul was all out of choices.

"What about landing?" Bartholomew asked.

"We've got some repairs to make, but we should be good for it."

Bartholomew nodded, feeling a degree of smugness. It had been on his suggestion that the *Fist* be constructed so as to enable it to land on a planet. Tactically it had always been a possibility that Saul, his ship having been partially disabled, might be able to take it down on Mars, or on one of the big planet satellites, in order to make repairs, sitting himself in some deep canyon to deter railgun fire from orbit. It was also the case that the few landing craft the *Fist* possessed would be vulnerable on their way down. Better that the whole ship could go down with all its weapons able to defend itself, and then pound Saul's ship from close quarters before launching a ground assault. Luckily, after much argument, Calder had agreed, though neither of them had foreseen precisely this current scenario.

"Well, I guess we can just sit back and watch the show for now," Bartholomew said, doing exactly that.

Saul's ship was low now and trailing vapour. Abruptly, the screen image divided, showing both the view from the *Fist* above and another view from some kilometres behind the descending vessel. Bartholomew enjoyed Oerlon's foresight. The man had obviously launched surveillance drones to follow the ship in. A better assessment could thus be made of just how much damage it had received after it came to rest but, more importantly, here was plenty of imagery for Serene Galahad to use in subsequent ETV broadcasts. Always a good idea to ensure that Earth's dictator enjoyed a ringside seat and plenty of material to work with.

From the perspective of the drones, the ship soon lay below Io's horizon, hurtling over a mosaic of browns, yellows and drifts of icy white dotted with pustules of glowing orange from silicate volcanoes. Ahead lay the twin spumes from the erupting volcanoes, which were blasting gas and molten matter out into space with the constancy of fire hoses. Perspective abruptly changed as the drones climbed. Saul's ship entered the clouds surrounding these two fountains and abruptly turned mustard yellow from the sulphur deposited on its hull, leaking blue flames from those parts of it still partially molten. The view clouded as the drones entered this same area, then blanked out for a while.

The second view from orbit showed the ship punch its way through between those two eruptions, its steering thrusters spearing out long emerald flames. Saul must have boosted those thrusters somehow because, when the drones regained clear imagery, they were almost on top of his ship and had to decelerate. Even now, with his ultimate defeat in sight, Saul was still managing to surprise them.

A sulphurous plain sped past below, then again the drones became blind as the ship travelled over some kind of white mass and blew up a cloud of icy dust. The vessel had by some means dropped lower abruptly and Bartholomew surmised that Saul must have used the gyroscopic effect of his vortex generator to reposition it. Next, from orbit, the admiral watched a smoky line scar its way across the plain for three kilometres, before primary impact. The ship then ploughed in, the loose surface below somehow preventing it bouncing, but the impact still causing it to shed wreckage. It skidded for a further two kilometres, mounding up sulphur compounds ahead of it, before finally grinding to a halt. Some half an hour later the dust had cleared enough for a close drone view of it. Saul's ship lay with the wreckage of its fusion drive buried, partially tilted on its axis, brown and weirdly green chemical smoke rising from glowing holes in its hull.

"And so it ends," said Oerlon.

"Not quite," said Bartholomew. "He still has his robots and whatever crew have survived. We must never underestimate this man."

"We land close and go in hard," Oerlon asserted. "We've got enough EM tank-busters to fry all his robots, seventeen hundred tough and highly trained commandos and forty spiderguns."

"Try not to kill too much computing," warned Bartholomew. "We still need to get hold of that Gene Bank data. And try not to cause any more wreckage than necessary, because there are the samples too." He didn't add anything about trying to capture Alan Saul alive, since that objective was a given. However, he personally doubted that it was possible, and that Galahad's orders would only result in a further waste of lives.

Bartholomew paused to wonder if there was anything he could have missed, but just could not discern it. Oerlon's force was overwhelming; Saul had lost all his major weapons, and only a few of his surviving personnel aboard would be soldiers. And though there were likely to be losses against Saul's robots, those machines would not be able to stand for long against tank-busters and forty spiderguns. Really, he just had to accept that Oerlon was right.

"I'll be in orbit within ten hours," he said. "How long before you can make your descent?"

"We'll probably be ready just before your arrival," Oerlon replied.

"Do so when feasible. Don't wait for me."

Perhaps now it was time for them to think beyond this little war out here. The *Command* would be crippled for some time yet so, once they had taken everything they wanted from Saul's ship, Bartholomew decided, it would be a good idea for him to transfer himself to the *Fist* for the trip back to Earth. He grimaced at the thought, but could feel the tension draining out of him as he decided it was time to enjoy this victory. He had time enough to think about his future under Earth's psychotic dictator during the trip back.

EARTH

Clay Ruger flipped up the hatch in the arm of his acceleration chair, uncoiled the umbilical inside and plugged it into the socket in his suit. His visor display now told him he was running on ship air and power, and in the ship's communication circuit. Next he peered down at the sidearm that had been returned to him, before looking across at Galahad, who had now found her own umbilical and was plugging it in. He contemplated the satisfaction he might still feel by putting a bullet through the side of her head. But what was the point?

Scotonis was now singing over the link he'd made to both Ruger's and Trove's fones, some ancient ditty about a "runaway train." He'd started doing this just after kindly letting them know how many minutes remained before the *Scourge* struck the Traveller construction station and he detonated the warheads aboard.

"What do you mean by 'three minutes'?" Galahad asked, turning to him.

"That's how long we've got before Scotonis arrives," Clay informed her.

At that moment the fast re-entry drop shuttle tilted down as it peeled away from the dock, throwing him up against his restraints. A second later, light glared through the front screen and the vessel shuddered sideways under some sort of blow. Shortly after that the sounds of exterior impacts penetrated through the hull.

"The fuck?" Sack exclaimed.

"Scotonis is firing on the station," Trove announced.

"Now, that wasn't very nice, was it?" said Scotonis over the fone link, before recommencing his song.

Another glare of light through the front screen, but it must have been more distant this time, for no blast wave or debris reached the drop shuttle.

"He's firing on us?" asked Galahad

Trove glanced round. "I think your friend Calder realized Scotonis wasn't going to stop, so has opened up on him with the station railguns." She paused as she took a firmer grip on the steering column. "Bit late for that, as they'd never do enough damage to stop him, and now he's destroying the guns."

"That's good for us," said Galahad. "Calder would have opened fire on us the moment we cleared the station."

Clay stared at her, annoyed by her certainty, irritated by her expectation of reality ordering itself to suit her wishes. She seemed utterly confident that they could still escape and survive. How could she be sure all the railguns had been destroyed? Because, even before she assumed power, she had been utterly certain that she knew best. Then, over the short period of her reign, that certainty had transformed into a belief in her own unique destiny. She probably thought that she simply could not die before achieving it, and probably even thought she would never die.

As he let that sink in, he finally began to stitch together events in his mind. Seeing Serene Galahad aboard the station, the moment he stepped from the shuttle, and seeing that their meeting was being broadcast on ETV, he'd been thoroughly wrapped up in the fact that he was due to die when Scotonis crashed the *Scourge* into the construction station. He had found that suddenly ridiculous, amusing. All the efforts he had made to ensure his own survival, once it became apparent that his new boss was a psycho, had thus come to nothing. He'd kept quiet about the evidence of her being behind the Scour, but retained that same proof for later use, while trying to keep his head down. He'd removed his implant and shorted out his strangulation collar, and he'd revealed the evidence of Galahad's guilt. And all for nothing.

Or maybe not.

His seat kicked him in the back as the drop shuttle's engine fired up, slinging them away from the station. In the forward screen he saw Earth rise and centre, then incrementally grow larger. The giant called acceleration came and sat on his chest.

Until now he hadn't properly registered how he'd stepped into the midst of a small rebellion and that this Calder, who controlled off-world resources, had been trying to usurp Gala-had. It had all been too chaotic. He hadn't understood that getting to this drop shuttle had been a futile exercise at best so long as Calder controlled the station railguns—because he'd still been wrapped up in the certainty of them all dying in a nuclear conflagration. However, he did have some reason for hope: Scotonis had now destroyed those same railguns and, despite her apparent earlier fatalism, Trove was still struggling to keep them alive.

Trove keyed some controls on her chair arm, the acceleration now being too powerful for her to reach either the joystick or the console controls. Part of the forward cockpit screen flickered—a liquid crystal layer in the glass over to one side now giving them a view of what lay behind them. The Traveller constructions station filled up the whole image, still massive even though they were hurtling away from it, in comparative scale like some bug launching itself from a house.

"We're going to black out . . . maybe die," she managed tightly. "No time for the special acceleration suits."

Really, thought Clay, she hadn't needed to say that. The drop shuttle was shaking now, a deep-throated roar penetrating. Perhaps it was illusion but the whole vessel seemed to be compacting and contorting around him.

"Thirty . . . seconds," Trove said.

Clay fixed his gaze on the rear view. There was some sort of counter running at the bottom of the screen and only then did he realize it was their distance from the construction station measured in kilometres, but at that moment the pressure on his eyeballs blurred it.

"Here . . . it . . . comes."

The construction station was now comfortably small in the rear view, just occupying a small area at the centre. Earth had grown huge, filling most of the true forward view, continental land masses clear below sheaths of cloud, the urban sprawls evident even from this distance, like the etched silicon of integrated circuits, while the streaks of mass-driver firings cut up through atmosphere like white hairs sprouting from an ageing face. For a second Clay glimpsed what looked like the Hubble Array, but it then slid to one side of the view. Next, in the rear view, the bullet of the *Scourge* speared in towards the station on a tail of fusion fire.

"Goodbye cruel world!" Scotonis cried over the fone link, then began laughing hysterically.

The *Scourge* struck and slid itself in like a syringe needle being driven into an arm, and a fraction of a second later explosions erupted all around it. For a further fraction of a second, Clay wondered if its armoury might not detonate, then a giant flashbulb went off and the rear view blanked.

"Sweet Jesus," Trove muttered, doubtless seeing some reading on the console before her.

Clay found himself holding his breath, then blew it out with the help of the giant sitting on his chest. The drop shuttle continued to shudder around him, and he wondered how far you had to get, in vacuum, to be beyond the reach of an explosion that encroached on the gigatonne range. The rear view returned, and it seemed as if a big orange eye was peering in at them. There was no sign of the construction station. With an explosion like that, there would be no debris, just white-hot vapour and plasma.

The ovoid of fire grew and flattened, occupying the entire rear view, which was now just an orange section of the forward screen. Abruptly, the giant increased the pressure on Clay's chest, while aurora fled ahead of the ship, which began shaking violently. Earth rose and suddenly slid to one side and, as blackness encroached on his vision, Clay was reminded of when the gravity wave had passed through the *Scourge*, breaking his bones.

Then the blackness closed him down.

17

BRAIN DEAD

With tank-grown replacement organs, cancer-hunting nano-machines, bespoke drugs and micro-surgical techniques to repair just about any kind of damage the body is known to suffer, there are those who say that the human lifespan is possibly without end. The problem with this contention is that it can never be proven, since that would be like trying to plumb the depth of a bottomless well. Certainly we no longer have any incurable diseases, whether bacterial, viral or genetic; however, there are still strict limitations on the amount of physical damage that can be repaired. Most damage can be dealt with, since all organs and limbs can be replaced or repaired, but if a brain is destroyed there is little point in keeping the body alive, and there has consequently been much debate about how much brain damage makes it unsalvageable. If a victim suffers heart failure due to injuries or disease, and the brain is then starved of oxygen, it currently becomes unsalvageable in a little over twenty minutes. And, even though some may theorize that brains can be revived after a longer spell, they also admit that the revived brain would be merely a blank slate, and that nothing of the original personality would remain.

ARGUS

No harm in looking . . .

There had been a surprising lack of pain at first: just a series of hard impacts driving her backwards, detaching her gecko boots from the floor and sending her tumbling. In confusion, she tried to reorient herself, tried to get her feet planted firmly so she could figure out what had happened. Another course change? More railgun strikes nearby? She had just managed to propel herself to a convenient surface and re-engage her boots when he slammed into her.

Var fought to hang onto the rifle he wanted to snatch away, but she felt leaden, as if she had been poured into her suit and set solid. Suit diagnostic warnings scrolled up her visor, but fractured and hard to read. He finally knocked her rifle from her grasp. Through the warnings, she saw his face: Ghort's face, triumphant and sneering, but only for a moment. As he gazed at her his expression suddenly transformed, and he soon looked frightened and hopeless.

Three suit breaches, the warnings informed her: two of them already sealed but one in her suit's visor, where the sealant system did not connect. She must return to a pressurized environment at once. She abruptly felt tired and knew her mind wasn't working at its best when, only after seeing these warnings did she spot the cracks in her visor. That tight leaden feeling inside her torso irritated her lungs and she coughed, spattering her visor with blood, then watched as it beaded and slid down to where all the cracks converged. She could now see the leak clearly. She watched blood oozing through one of the cracks and vaporizing in vacuum outside. But there seemed to be much more blood than she had coughed up, and her neck felt damp, and it hurt.

"I'm sorry," she heard, as Ghort's voice was carried through to her at the point where their visors touched. "I'm sorry."

It was now getting difficult to breathe, but Var knew that had nothing to do with air loss, since that was something she had experienced many times before. Mere tiredness transformed into a sudden incredible weariness. She was just fed up with it all, fed up with the endless . . . effort. She closed her eyes, and that felt good, but then reopened them, choking for breath like someone suffering from sleep apnoea.

After everything, after Mars, after her being rescued, was this it? She coughed out yet more blood, white and frothy now, and could hear her own pulse stuttering in her ears. Shallow breaths were all she could manage, and there just wasn't enough air. Her vision turned to shades of black and yellow, and her pulse grew hesitant like the beat of an engine running low on fuel. When she closed her eyes again, it came almost as a relief as night descended. Var wished for morning to return, as do we all.

They were down now, the ship protesting all around and the lists of reported damage redoubling rapidly. Saul concerned himself with detail and tried not to be appalled by the destruction. He began filtering the data, then redirecting his robots to deal with the most critical repairs. For what was to come next, the Arboretum cylinder did not really need to be hauled back up into position and repaired, the spindle for Arcoplex Two did not need to be fixed either: the weapons were beyond repair and the Traveller engine would not be firing again for months—if ever. Instead, he passed control over the bulk of his robots to the proctors, who were working frantically to repair the Mach-effect drive to restore its efficiency to over that critical eighty per cent. Others he had delegated to sealing atmosphere breaches, to working on structural repairs, or to securing wreckage. Some of them were even now dragging cables over and across the Arboretum and welding up its contact points with the ship's skeleton.

While supervising all this activity with the larger portion of his mind, he simultaneously focused a smaller, more human, component elsewhere.

"You have between five and ten hours, at most, before we move again," Saul announced as he continued surveying the wreckage—and the death—throughout the ship.

"Le Roque." He next addressed the technical director, who had already unstrapped himself and was walking in low gravity across the sloping floor of Tech Central to gaze through its cracked windows. "Do what you can for the injured. System access is limited for the moment, but I've given you the locations and circumstances of those in most need of help. The seriously injured should be moved, if possible, to Arcoplex Two, but you'll have to work fast."

Le Roque stared out for a long moment before turning away, his face white and shocked behind his visor as he returned to his console. Sitting down, he searched for some pragmatic reply. "What about structural damage?"

"I'm handling priorities," Saul replied. "Just deal with the injured, and make sure everyone can be quickly secured after a minimum period of five hours."

"Then what?" asked Le Roque.

"Then we get to find out whether we live or we die." Saul next transferred that portion of his human consciousness he was currently using to communicate with others aboard, specifically to the Meat Locker. "Hannah, Raiman, Da Vinci, you're needed in Arcoplex Two."

Hannah glanced up at the nearest cam. "We're down on Io," she pointed out.

"Yes," he replied, "but, I hope, for only a maximum of ten hours. Liaise with Le Roque on your timings."

"Are we going to survive this?" she asked.

"Maybe," he answered, his voice catching as he glanced with human eyes at the hardened nubs of once molten metal scattered across his suit. He was doing the best he could in the circumstances, but no amount of processing power or planning could remove every fragment of risk that they might end up at the bad end of a railgun strike or a beam weapon.

Over the next hour he watched the injured and dying being sought out, some needing to be cut from wreckage, others having to be given life-saving treatment where they lay. When Hannah, Raiman and Da Vinci arrived in Arcoplex Two, they were greeted by a constant stream of the injured and were soon up to their elbows in blood. Where he could, Saul diverted robots to help them, but only when such diversion did not slow down crucial work on the Mach-effect drive. His priority was escape from the solar system, and if he didn't manage that, they would all end up dead anyway.

Next, having assured himself that everything was running at maximum possible efficiency, he diverted a part of his attention to the two still surviving out in the station ring: Messina's ex-bodyguard, Ghort, and the clone, Alex. He only knew they were alive because their implants kept feeding mental data to their backups.

"Why is Ghort still alive?" he enquired.

"Having . . . some trouble," Alex replied, his words laced with pain.

"You are injured?"

"Broken leg."

Saul reviewed the present situation. The only possible way Ghort could now affect their chances would be if he attempted to destroy the vortex generator. But, considering the man's objectives, he had no real reason for doing so, and it was most likely that he was simply trying to stay alive. Saul calculated that he would remain hiding out there in the old station ring for as long as possible. And, by staying out there, he would eventually solve the problem he had become.

"He is no longer a real danger to us, Alex," declared Saul. "Just get yourself to Arcoplex Two and have your leg tended to."

"Unfinished business," was Alex's brief reply.

"If you stay out there you could be dead within five hours." Saul felt a hint of human irritation arising within him.

"Your sister too," added the Messina clone.

This information threw Saul into a fugue that lasted a whole second, then he began searching cam data and footage, located Var's overseer's office, glanced at a recent report from Langstrom—and realized he had not been keeping his eye on that particular ball. Next he linked through to Alex's backup and then Ghort's, and began decoding both present data streams and recent memory.

"What happened?" he asked meanwhile.

"He shot her . . . thought she was me."

"Is she dead?" Even as he flatly asked the question, Saul felt hollowness in the pit of his stomach. Just as with the ships out there, he had been in error: he had not done enough, he had got it *wrong*. The moment he knew they existed he should have killed the chipped rebels. Here then was the price for his attempt to use a light touch, not to be so dictatorial, to try and put humans in a position to solve their own problems.

"I don't know," Alex replied. "She was shot through the gut and chest when I saw her, with maybe one through her visor too." The words fell like blows. Saul now felt the terror of some kind of disconnection—as if he was falling into an abyss—and a huge regret. For a second he just could not incorporate this simple data; could not accept what Alex was telling him. Then at last some of the data from Alex began to unravel, visual only, showing the view through his visor of a great mass of rubble and sand. Saul began to work with it and cross-referencing a cam view provided confirmation that Saul was seeing sulphur compounds scraped up from the surface of Io. Alex next switched his attention to the gap in the hull through which all this had poured, before turning aside to peer up at a tall bulkhead wall. Memory decoded then, and Saul replayed the earlier exchange between the two men . . .

Alex had little time to react. He couldn't fire on Ghort, so he threw himself backwards to the opening and tried to propel himself out of sight. At that moment the entire ship shuddered and he found himself falling away from the opening before slamming feet first into the very same beam juncture Ghort had concealed himself behind. Now looking towards the outer wall of the ring, Alex watched a storm of material pouring in through the hole in the hull and mounding up. This seemed to last an age, the ship shuddering constantly all around him. Then he was falling again, dropping across the ring section till again coming down feet-first on a hard surface. His recently healed leg shrieked in protest, then gave way underneath him. He had time enough to register that it had broken before a wall of sulphurous rubble swamped him.

Saul pulled himself out of the alluring grip of the memory and returned to the moment, still struggling to accept what his logic told him as he began reading the decoding from Ghort. When the ship hit Io, the man had managed to drag Var into a side corridor, so he was not thrown after Alex, nor did he suffer such a fall when it righted itself on the surface. He had moved on, a quarter of the way around the ring, and was now in a branch corridor, one that terminated against a wall of asteroidal ice. A patch sat in place over the persistent leak in his suit, but he was cold, in pain, thoroughly aware of the damp feel of blood inside his suit, though still standing and still able to move. Var lay at his feet, and he hoped to use her to bargain for his life. In a moment he would move on, work further round the ring to get as far away from that homicidal clone as he could.

Back to Alex now, who was glaring at the section of bulkhead leading up to the opening he had fallen from, searching for handholds, while his tracking program gave him Ghort's location over three kilometres away. The Messina clone was not far from the massive rubble of sulphur compounds scraped up from the surface of Io, and which had swamped him as the ship righted itself on the surface. He had been buried in it and spent the best part of an hour digging himself free. Saul made calculations and realized that, judging by her injuries, Var needed treatment fast, and that with a broken leg Alex could not hope to get to her quickly enough, let alone deal with Ghort. Yet, on another level, Saul also understood that his calculations had their element of denial.

"Alex," he instructed, "head to your immediate right. There you'll find a maintenance tunnel under the vortex generator, which will bring you out in what remains of the Arboretum endcap. From there you'll easily be able to make your way round to Arcoplex Two. I've just sent a map to your implant, so go now and get yourself seen to."

"But Ghort . . . your sister?" Alex protested.

"Ghort is badly injured and dying, and my sister is already dead," Saul replied. He was only saying that to get Alex to desist . . . wasn't he? Saul had no way of knowing how true his latter statement might be . . . surely. "Further effort on your part will prove futile. You've done well, Alex, but this is now over."

Alex hesitated, but then he turned and obeyed.

Saul now hesitated too, then exerted control over his voice and planned the words he would use before he made another call.

"Ghort," he said.

"Hah . . . wondered when you'd be talking . . . to me."

"If you get my sister out of there, you get to live," Saul replied, his tone washed of emotion as he sent a map to Ghort's implant. "You'll be met by Hannah Neumann and some medics at the place I've designated."

"Go to hell," said Ghort, abruptly sitting down.

Saul badly wanted just to kill the man, but again suppressed emotion. Formulae of human responses assembled and solved in his mind, and he knew by Ghort's attitude that the man thought his bargaining chip was no longer valid, and that Var was indeed dead. Keeping himself utterly under control, Saul explained, "She might appear dead to you, but Hannah Neumann might still be able to do something. Please try to get my sister to her swiftly."

Ghort just sat panting for a moment, then suddenly stood up. In the light gravity of Io, he hauled up Var, loose-limbed and flopping like any new-made corpse, managed to throw her over his shoulder, then set out along the route Saul had detailed. Meanwhile, the medics Saul had summoned from Arcoplex Two were on their way. He had done the best he could, and could now only wait for Hannah Neumann's verdict.

He focused next on the *Fist* as it swung in orbit around Io and descended towards the horizon, doubtless with its ground forces getting ready to disembark, and struggled to care. After a long period of just watching, he finally managed to get his thoughts in motion again. From an intellectual distance he considered how it would have been optimal to have ramped up robot activity the moment this ship went out of sensor range, but its drones were still nearby and he did not want the ship's captain to have any reason to consider firing on him when it rounded the moon and finally landed. He ran calculations on likely landing sites, checked the energy ratios in the vortex generator, and coldly made tentative selections of generator containment coils.

And he waited.

COMMAND

Bartholomew gazed at his screen, studying various drone views of Saul's ship; registering the numerous holes in its hull, and the peculiar chemical fires burning inside. Deep radar and other sensing techniques showed that there was still life and movement there. Many internal compartments were charged with atmosphere, as were the three cylinder worlds, and certainly there was some metallic movement detectable, which meant Saul's robots were still a threat. However, the ship was definitely down and would not be going anywhere. Readings showed that the vortex generator, the only drive presently available to it, was incrementally winding down. Bartholomew also wondered if an

Alcubierre warp could be generated both in a gravity-well and through the ground beneath.

"Perhaps I should put some slugs into those," suggested Oerlon, speaking from a screen frame and indicating, with pointer arrows, the atmosphere sections on a schematic growing steadily more detailed as more data came in.

"You can if you wish," Bartholomew replied, "though I feel that the human crew is hardly a danger. Saul's robots will be the main problem. You must also avoid hitting the Arboretum cylinder, since that is the last known location of the Gene Bank samples."

Oerlon grunted and shrugged. "Then there's that new section below the old Argus Station Tech Central. It looks like a likely location for our friend Alan Saul."

"Whom we have been instructed to capture alive," Bartholomew reminded him. "No, you land your ship, and return fire only if fired upon. Once down, you launch the ground assault and use your ship's weapons to cover the troops." He paused thoughtfully for a moment. "This was one of the least likely scenarios envisaged, but we do have assault plans drawn up, though they were originally drawn up with Mars in mind. Scenario B of the two, I think."

Oerlon nodded. "Spiderguns in through the top of the ship, main human assault through the equator, however it's positioned. Five-man teams covering a sixth man, who carries the tank-buster. Limited EM pulse fire in system-critical areas, because missiles will do less damage to the ship's computer system." Oerlon grimaced. "I've had plenty of time to memorize all of it."

"Then I don't need to issue you any further orders," said Bartholomew. "I want constant tacom updates, but, otherwise, go and get the job done, Captain Oerlon."

The other captain nodded, and his screen frame blanked out.

Now the drone views showed deep black shadows around Saul's ship as the surface there became subject to an intensity of light it probably had not seen in billions of years. One drone swung round and tilted up to show the *Fist* descending through the thin atmosphere of Io, its main fusion engine bright as a welding arc while steering thrusters flashed and glared like night-time gunshots. It came down fast a couple of kilometres to one side of Saul's ship, poised on its fusion torch, then, with a blast of steering thrusters, slid over the top of the five-kilometre-high mountain of metal. The flame seared the pole of Saul's ship and hull metal sagged, melted and burned away, opening up an extended view into the interior.

Bartholomew smiled. Using a fusion flame like that had not been part of any of the scenarios, but was a clever move on Oerlon's part. Now the spiderguns could quickly swarm inside, over a wide area, rather than go one or two at a time through the railgun holes.

The *Fist* headed two kilometres beyond Saul's ship and then descended, folding down segments from its lower hemisphere. These were its landing feet, but also the assault force's disembarkation points. Finally it began to settle, dust clouds and chemical fires blasting out from it—coming down onto the surface like a globe on a plinth. As the fusion flame went out, a big door opened down from the landing foot facing nearest to Saul's ship and settled as a ramp.

First out of the *Fist* came a horde of ATVs sporting ten-mil machine guns and EM tank-busters. These were merely ground cover for the crossing towards Saul's ship, and would be abandoned once the assault proper began. Next came the spiderguns—at the sight of which Bartholomew gave an involuntary shiver. About half of these had their weaponized limbs altered: the lethal firepower of machine guns that fired depleted uranium beads being replaced with EM tank-busters and with launchers firing armour-piercing missiles. These were effectively robot killers.

Next came seventeen hundred heavily armed and armoured troops, some carrying portable tank-busters, some carrying missile-launchers, and all carrying Kalashtech assault rifles. They seemed overly laden with equipment, but in the low gravity, and with their VC suits motorized, they moved almost as fast as the spiderguns. Now, on seeing this force swarming towards the shattered behemoth that had once been Argus Station and which had come close to being converted into an interstellar vessel, Bartholomew felt a kind of shame. It seemed too much like overkill now that the enemy was all but beaten, and it seemed to grate on some sensitivity to fairness inside him.

EARTH

Ruger's first thought, as consciousness returned, was *I'm still alive*, swiftly followed by *not for long*.

The drop shuttle was full of acrid smoke and emitting distinctly unhealthy groans and screeches below the constant roar; Earth kept changing places with sky in the view through the front screen and Trove was screaming obscenities while she wrestled with the controls. Beside him he could hear Galahad muttering something that sounded like a prayer, until he actually heard the words and realized she was reciting the names of extinct animals. Then, with a sound like a bullwhip cracking, followed by another sound like a ground car going into a crusher, deceleration threw him hard against his straps. At the same time, something hit the back of his seat with a gristly thud and a hand flopped loosely past him. It seemed the one remaining soldier had not strapped himself in securely and, if that sound was anything to go by, might not get another opportunity to do so.

Earth and sky gradually ceased to swap places with such alarming regularity, the horizon settling shakily into the horizontal. Then the bullwhip cracked again and the pressure came off, the hand dropping out of sight.

"Fuck it!" shouted Trove. "Not enough!"

The horizon started wobbling and began to tilt. Another crack resounded, and once again Ruger was thrown hard against his straps, the hand rising up beside him as if to indicate, yes, I'm still here. He noted flecks of blood spattering his suit's shoulder pad, gathering into globules and launching for the screen, but guessed it wasn't his own. The drop shuttle groaned long and hard, and behind he could hear the distinctive sounds of power shorting out—easily recognizable since he had previously heard it aboard the *Scourge*. With a fourth crack, the pressure came off yet again. But by now the horizon had stabilized.

"That's it," said Trove, "we're all out of chutes."

Clay knew that, without her voice coming over his suit radio, it would have been difficult to hear her through the racket all around him, and he certainly would not have detected the fatalism in her tone.

"And what," asked Galahad's brutish bodyguard, "does that mean?"

"It means aileron, thruster and undercarriage braking only," she replied. "That's if the undercarriage even comes down, which I doubt."

Oh, good, though Ruger, *we're going to crash and burn*. He felt almost like shrugging to some unseen audience. Galahad seemed to believe that some predestination guided the course of her life, and now Clay Ruger was starting to think the same about himself. Apparently he was fated to die in the crash of some sort of flying vessel. He swore to himself, in that same moment, that if he did survive this, his only route off the ground henceforth would be via stairs or a lift . . . well, maybe not even the lift.

"Map screen," said Trove. "I need somewhere long and level . . . and over ten kilometres of it."

Sack obligingly called up a map on the console screen. "What about Outback Spaceport?"

"No good. It's going to be central India, if we're lucky."

"What about a water landing?" Sack asked calmly.

"It would tear us apart."

Sack diligently began searching the screen. "What about this?" He showed a map which, from Clay's seat, seemed to be all sprawl but for a long white smear through the middle of it.

"Run the navcom," Trove replied.

Apparently this bodyguard was a bit more than just muscle, for he worked the navigation console before him like a pro before coming up with some figures.

"Got it," Trove replied, putting the drop shuttle into a slow turn, the horizon tilting. Steering thrusters then rumbled and the horizon rose as Clay's straps bit into him again. He looked for the rising hand, but it didn't appear this time. Maybe the soldier behind had managed to get back into his seat . . . or maybe not.

The sound from outside was now like a gale blowing through an empty windowless office block, and the screen had taken on a reddish tint as if the tough heat-resistant lamination of glass and other materials had come new-made from the furnace. Clay did not know whether this was supposed to happen, but he did know that the internal air conditioning was struggling to get rid of the smoke. The drop shuttle levelled, and now the recognizable shapes of land masses became visible ahead.

"Okay, time to show it our belly," said Trove.

The horizon dropped out of sight to reveal a deep mauve sky scattered with stars. The roaring, which it had seemed impossible could grow any louder, nevertheless rose in a crescendo. This just continued interminably, the sky becoming bluer before taking on an orange blush.

"This isn't the dawn," said Trove. "It's because of Scotonis."

Meteorites appeared next, scratching lines across an object glowing in the sky just like Jupiter's red spot.

"I didn't think there would be debris," remarked Clay.

Trove glanced round. "You're back with us, are you? Well, no, the construction station was completely vaporized. The debris is from Core One and the Hubble Array. Looks as if Core Two survived, though whether anyone aboard did is another matter."

"Right," said Clay.

An hour passed, maybe even more time; Clay wasn't counting and was sure he had been dozing when Trove spoke next. "We've got the nose cams and screen display back."

Three-quarters of the way up, the forward screen divided horizontally. The top section showed just daylight sky while the lower part revealed the view down towards Earth. Oceans sped by underneath, land masses now took on depth and contour, though that image seemed to be of low pixel count, what with all that land having been subsumed by the cubic structures of sprawl buildings.

At length they entered night again, but a lurid night with a portion of the sky seeming on fire. They were much lower when ocean terminated against electric-lit land mass, and Trove announced, "East coast of India."

In the new light, and as low down as they were now, the sprawls became much more visible, and Clay spotted occasional cleared areas amidst them where Galahad's dozers and crushing machines had been at work. Notable too were large areas of sprawl where no electric lights gleamed at all, and he was overcome by a strange spooky feeling on considering how much down there now lay empty. A lake flitted by underneath, divided into fish-farm squares, each reflecting orange but also occupied by black drifts, so probably devoid of fish. Navigational schematics appeared all across the screen, datum lines giving their route in, counters giving speed and desired speed—and much more that Clay did not care to recognize.

"Putting landing gear down now," said Trove.

Clay felt the vibration but he could not hear the motors, pumps or hydraulics at work. However, he did hear the crash and the abrupt change to the exterior roar. This was good, surely?

"It's down?" Sack enquired.

"No," Trove replied.

"What did I just hear, then?"

"You heard the landing gear going halfway down and jamming, which means that if it doesn't get torn off or forced back into the ship when we touch down, we'll probably be doing somersaults."

Okay, not so good.

"Target coordinates in sight," said Trove. Gleaming with reflected orange light, something was rising over the horizon, amidst the sprawls. She glanced at the map on the console screen. "This your idea of a joke, Sack?"

"It was the biggest level area available," he replied.

"Right."

"Ailerons." The roar changed in tone again. "And thrusters." Another sound next: like wind blowing down a drain pipe. The ship tilted forwards, raising the horizon. Trove lost the liquid crystal display so as to give them a lot of sky over a line of orange, with sprawl towers ranged on either side.

"Pray, if you think anyone's listening!" Trove shouted.

The drop shuttle hit, began shuddering horribly and tilting further forwards, bringing more of the plain ahead into view. Then, with a crash and a further shudder as of a ground car running over a zero asset indigent, it dropped again.

"That's the landing gear gone!"

They were definitely down, and Clay allowed hope sufficiently out of its box to take a glimpse at the steadily dropping numbers in the bottom corner of the screen. They were slowing and there now seemed to be nothing but that plain ahead.

"We're down!" Trove shouted excitedly. "We're going to make it!"

Out of the plain ahead, which would probably have appeared white in daylight, a yellow smear expanded and resolved. It seemed toy-like at first, but steadily grew into a huge automated bulldozer with a great serrated roller behind it, parked slantwise across their airfield.

"Fuck it!" Trove added, wrenching the steering column to one side.

ARGUS

Saul gazed numbly at the approaching army and knew that the old robots and his new conjoining robots that crouched throughout his ship would never be enough, could never be enough. Yes, he had thousands of robots under his control, but every one of them could be knocked out easily by an EM pulse. The approaching human troops carried enough tank-busters to do that job, let alone the specially adapted spiderguns he'd just scanned. This was a force that could take his ship with ease, and could achieve all the objectives Serene Galahad had demanded, but for one: capturing him alive. That simply would not happen. He could shut down his body and brain in an instant, and in the same instant scramble his backups. His suit also possessed another option fitted just below his ribcage, in the form of a slab of high explosive. They would not capture him alive, nor would they be taking his body back for Serene Galahad to gloat over.

Dying always remained an option for him, but not yet. Through a cam out in Arcoplex Two, Saul watched as Alex, his leg in a plastic cast, strapped himself into an acceleration chair and lay back, then he switched to another cam and watched the lid of the cryogenic pod thump closed. The numbness he felt had spread through his entire being; it seemed almost part of his make-up now: cold, just like the inside of that canister. He replayed events, now several hours old, in his mind, and tried to see if there was any way he could change the verdict:

Through the sensors of a construction robot, which had been making repairs outside the outer endcap of Arcoplex Two, Saul watched Hannah, followed by two medics carrying a stretcher as they intercepted Ghort. He handed Var over to the medics without fuss, then just stood there, swaying.

"Prognosis?" Saul enquired, speaking through all their suit radios. After she'd checked the readouts from Var's suit, then had run some kind of scanner over her body from head to foot, Hannah rocked back on her heels. She took her time in replying: "She's been dead for over an hour. There's nothing I can do."

"Of course there's something," Saul immediately replied, then damned that small part of him that had made this response. "Get her to a cryogenic cylinder in the Meat Locker," he continued coldly. "The future is always mutable."

"I'm so sorry, Alan," said Hannah as the two medics quickly strapped Var into a stretcher and carted her away. "The bullet damage isn't much different to what you yourself received, but her brain has gone without oxygen for too long, and there's further damage from the sulphur compounds penetrating her suit." There were tears in Hannah Neumann's voice, and also an underlying fear.

"Yes, I understand," said Saul. "And my sister was reluctant to have an implant and get herself backed up. That means she is probably irretrievably dead."

"She was a great woman," said Hannah. "Very human and humane."

No, the past could not be changed . . . at least not yet.

Saul now recollected, despite the situation, a brief bitter amusement at Hannah's words. Humane Var who had slaughtered the Inspectorate personnel in Antares Base, later executed Rhone of Mars Science, and here murdered two more people. Even now, Saul found himself constantly amazed by the human propensity for self-deception. He was also aware of the reason for the underlying fear evident in Hannah's voice. She had expected this loss to tip him over. She had expected it to be the moment he ceased to care at all for anyone, and the moment he turned into the monster she had always expected him to be.

As Hannah had moved away to follow the two carrying Var's body, he had said, "Get her into the cylinder quickly, Hannah."

"What about him?" she had asked, gesturing to Ghort.

"I will deal with him," he had stated. "Go quickly now."

Memory returned hard, vibrant and bright, and clear in every detail:

She turned to hurry after the medics.

"So what about me?" Ghort asked, now supporting himself against the wall.

Of course Saul would not now become more murderous and turn into a monster; both of those required an element of negative emotion. Saul did not feel negative about this man. He felt nothing at all as he took control of the construction robot, sent it forward and instructed it to use programming he had not used seemingly in an age.

Moving with eerie fluidity, the robot slammed Ghort back against the wall with a three-fingered steel hand, extruded a drill from the tool-head that its other limb terminated in, and drove this straight through Ghort's spacesuit and into his chest. The man shrieked, then sagged as the robot backed off, blood jetting from the hole drilled into his heart. Saul did not bother to see him fall all the way, nor watch the robot cart his body off for disposal. He did not have either the time or the inclination.

The numbness he felt had spread from the more human part of himself, infecting the larger more logical parts of his mind. Had the murderousness spread as well? Was he now truly the monster Hannah feared? No, he felt not. The death of his sister had not changed his plans one whit, though perhaps there was no need, anyway, since his plans were murderous enough . . .

"I'm going to need some elevation for this," he declared, addressing Paul who, with several other proctors, was frantically working to repair or replace damaged Mach-effect units at the pole of the ship where the *Fist*'s fusion torch had seared it. "We have to remember that there are two vortex generators down here."

"Apparently your recent human interaction has led you into stating the obvious," Paul replied, incidentally showing signs of a very human irritation himself.

From this Saul realized that the proctor was struggling to keep to the schedule and, upon checking, he saw the efficiency of the Mach-effect rising slowly from just over sixty per cent.

"I can give you four minutes," the proctor continued, "then we go down again."

"In succumbing to your very human irritation," Saul replied, "you seem to have forgotten the propulsive effect of the mass ejection, and the concomitant reduction in our overall mass."

After a pause Paul replied, "Quite."

A brief glance through a cam showed the cryogenic pod sliding home into its slot. The pipes to swap out her blood and other bodily fluids were automatically attaching, but the monitoring equipment had been shut down, since there was no point monitoring a corpse. Saul realized that, though Hannah had used wound glue on the bullet holes, it had been a hasty job and the swapping-out process would still be hampered; replacement fluids would run out into the wrong places in Var's body.

Meanwhile, the two medics who had taken Var to the Meat Locker had reached nearby acceleration chairs, and were strapped in. Throughout the rest of the ship everyone was now as ready as they could be, and the time had come. Outside the ship the ATVs were disgorging their troops and the spiderguns had arrived.

"Do it now," he said to Paul.

The ship suddenly heaved and strained and, with a massive groan, it began to rise. Saul watched spiderguns scrabbling in an avalanche of sulphur compounds and rock, some of them trying to leap the gap growing between the ship and the ground. He registered weapons fire impacting, but it was mostly from small arms and ineffective. As he reached out to three of the vortex generator's containment coils, he calculated on eight seconds before the response from the *Fist*, which would be at about the time he was nearly a kilometre up. He touched the Mach-effect drive and tilted his ship just so, counted seven seconds, then turned off three vortex generator containment coils. Thousands of tonnes of liquid mercury, spinning round a fifteen-kilometre course at just under a hundred million metres per second, erupted free in an instant.

COMMAND

Bartholomew felt the drag of a side-burn fusion engine as the *Command* fell into orbit around Io. His crew reported that the damage to the main fusion engine was repairable within a month, if they concentrated on that and not the weapons. He had ordered them to divert the ship's resources to that same engine, but now, as he studied an image of the sulphurous moon of Jupiter, he wasn't so sure that it had been a great idea.

The ATVs had drawn to a halt and their crews began piling out, while the spiderguns had been climbing the debris slope ahead. It had all been just a matter of time, with the overwhelming forces disembarked from the *Fist* about to begin their assault. But now Bartholomew stared in horror. Saul's ship had risen from the ground without any visible form of propulsion. It had taken Bartholomew seconds of just gaping at the screen to realize there was no optical problem involving the drones, and then . . .

What the hell happened?

Bartholomew reached out to his console with a shaking hand and wound back the most recent imagery. He slowed it down and watched most of the spiderguns ending up buried, then the small-arms fire. Saul's ship then tilted . . .

Must have been a firing from the Fist . . .

But Bartholomew had detected no such firing, and the last tacom update on constant feed to him confirmed this. He slowed the video down even further, and watched as part of the equator of Saul's ship flared and a thing like a giant silver rod stabbed out, struck the *Fist* dead centre, flattened itself into a blade and scythed across, blurring into a gleaming explosion all around the equator of Saul's ship even as that initial ejection hurled it, at massive acceleration, across the surface of Io.

The *Fist*, the ring of its own vortex generator severed, emitted a similar but smaller ejection, which also chewed up its equator as subsequent coils failed. This tore up a crescent of ground large enough to be visible from orbit, which was the only view Bartholomew next received since the blasts had taken out the drones. He suspected that ejection would have done more damage if its course had not been tangential to the moon, and just gouged a mass out of its surface before continuing on into vacuum.

Subsequently the *Fist* rose on a massive explosion. Bartholomew had assumed it a munitions explosion but, as Oerlon's ship came apart and fell away in a fountain of silicon lava, he realized that the near-relativistic ejection of liquid mercury from Saul's ship had punched right down through Io's crust. In fact, a plume now becoming visible way beyond the horizon line confirmed that it had cut right through the moon and emerged out the other side.

No, he understood, the *Fist* had not hit Saul's vortex generator; Saul had deliberately shut down its containment and used it as a weapon to destroy both the *Fist* and that ship's assault force. And now, like a shark rising from the murky depths, Saul's ship was heading up through the massive dust storms and pyroclastic flows on Io . . . and coming Bartholomew's way.

18

HIS GENTLY SMILING JAWS

With the ability to grow tissue grafts, and even whole organs, in nutrient tanks becoming an established fact of twenty-second-century medicine, a large body of researchers in transplantation technology were seconded by the Committee to look into further applications that might be useful to the Inspectorate. Often the more esoteric products of such research were at the whimsical behest of some powerful delegate and, since rejection problems had been all but overcome, the delegates concerned often looked to the animal world for inspiration. The results of this further research can often be seen today among Inspectorate enforcers or the bodyguards of delegates. The misnamed cat's eyes enabled the recipients to see in the dark, though that genetic template was in fact taken from a lemur. Properly named extensible cat's claws proved a rather useless addition to a bodyguard's armoury. Keroskin, first based on the skin of crocodiles, was a non-surgical replacement for subdermal armouring—actually spreading across the recipient's body like psoriasis. After numerous tweaks, it included shock-absorbing layers like Kevlar, a high content of insulating fibres that made it resistant to heat, and diminished growth of the afferent nerve fibres, which cut down on the recipient's perception of pain. Protected by such skin, enforcers could go charging into riots even while inducers were being deployed; however, volunteers to test out what delegates saw as a truly advantageous development were sadly scarce.

EARTH

That giant called "acceleration" was bearing down on Clay again, and its breath stank of hot metal and burning plastic. He opened his eyes, not sure if he'd blacked out during what felt like undertaking a short journey inside a trash compactor on a bob sleigh run, and which now oddly seemed to be continuing even in utter silence. Then he realized that what he was feeling wasn't acceleration at all but his old friend, and sometimes enemy, namely gravity. He looked down at his torso, half expecting to see some ribs protruding, so much did his chest hurt, then he glanced around him.

The air was full of smoke, though it seemed to be clearing. Over to his right, Galahad was still slumped forwards in her chair, while over to his left . . . Clay gaped out at an open plain, now taking on hints of bloody red in the false dawn, scattered with burning wreckage surrounding some great mechanical construct, itself burning, and which it took him a moment to identify. Then he realized he was seeing the caterpillar treads and the underside of that yellow bulldozer. The entire left hand side of the drop shuttle was gone, sheared off, but they were down, and he had survived.

He reached down and pulled his umbilical from the ship's air feed, which at some point must have developed a leak, for how else could he have smelled the effects of burning? He unclipped his helmet, now seeming so incredibly heavy, and tossed it aside. Sniffing, he now also detected an odd underlying putrid odour. Next he looked directly ahead, as if only just plucking up the nerve to do so, and saw Trove gazing down at the torn metal right beside her seat, and a three-metre drop to the gravelly ground below. Sack was already on his feet, his helmet discarded, and heading back. He came to stand before Clay, reaching down to undo his straps. Clay thought this very kind of him, until the bodyguard relieved him of his sidearm.

"You okay?" Sack asked, looking past Ruger.

Before Clay could reply, a muffled voice from behind him replied, "Think so . . . broke my fuckin' nose."

"You'll survive," said Sack, and stepped on towards Serene Galahad. He unstrapped and, with frightening ease, casually picked her up and slung her over his shoulder. Ignoring Clay and Trove, who was now heaving herself out of her seat, he marched over to the sheared-off edge of the drop shuttle and jumped down on to the dusty plateau.

Obviously labouring in Earth's gravity, Trove made her way back to Clay and leaned against the chair next to him.

"Didn't keep up with your . . . resistance exercises . . . in the spin gym," she noted, after she discarded her space helmet.

Clay guessed she was right because he seemed glued to his chair. He made another effort to get up, rose a little way, then slumped back. Struggling herself, Trove finally helped him up and they moved over to the torn-away side of the drop shuttle. Had he not known that they would be landing on Earth Clay might have supposed they had arrived on Mars, what with the russet hue outside. Though this was a Mars from some VR fantasy rather than the mundane reality.

The soldier was already ahead of them, climbing down to the ground, before glancing up at them with a face that looked as if it had been slammed into a brick wall. On wobbly legs, and feeling as if his body was now fashioned of lead, Clay eased himself down to the edge, grabbed hold of a protruding jag of metal, then snatched his hand away as it sizzled. Trove went down ahead of him, using a twisted skein of optics and preconductor cable as a rope, then waited below as he followed her. At the last his grip could just not support his unaccustomed weight and he fell on top of her, and they both tumbled to the ground. "You're fucking useless, Clay Ruger," she said indignantly.

"Don't you love me any more?" he asked, as Trove fought to regain her feet.

"Only like any other helpless animal," she replied, drawing her sidearm from her belt.

Clay, now up on his hands and knees, stared at the ground. He had assumed their landing site to be a cleared and levelled section of sprawl, but now reality began to impinge. Staring up at him, half buried and partially crushed, was a human skull. Extending his inspection of the ground, he identified crushed ribcages, leg and arm bones, wads of clothing, shoes, cheap fones and the occasional glint of fake jewellery. He knew now what their landing field was. It had probably acquired the name "Bonefield" or the "Field of Bones" or the "Ossuary," as had so many similar places all across Earth. He was standing on a great mass of skeletons, all crushed down and levelled. He was standing on just one of many such accumulations of Earth's dead: the result of Serene Galahad's Scouring of the planet.

"Shit!" he exclaimed and found himself up on his feet in a moment, as if his body had just remembered how to work in gravity. He looked all around and, amidst the scattered and burning wreckage, he saw drifts of skulls, then the small mountain of skeletons the yellow dozer must have been spreading out and compacting down.

"Nice place, huh?" remarked Trove.

"Yeah, wonderful." Clay spat the dry, powdery, slightly putrid taste from his mouth, wiped dust from his lips and tried to bat some of it off his spacesuit. He finally looked up: the sky was dull red but with a lighter glare over on one horizon. Meteorites were still cutting across it high up and, even as he watched, some larger piece of wreckage came down, flaring like a firework before breaking into three pieces that went streaking over the horizon.

"We have to get away from here," Trove added. "But, before we go, we have some unfinished business." She began walking over to where Sack had deposited Serene Galahad on the ground, then removed her helmet and lodged a wad of the plentiful loose material here under her head. Galahad seemed to be recovering, reaching up with one hand to rub at her face. The one soldier was sitting a few metres away, on an unidentifiable chunk of wreckage, carefully cleaning the blood from his face with a wetwipe from a small medical kit. He no longer had his rifle and his sidearm was holstered. Trove's intention was obvious.

Sack, meanwhile, was standing over by the dozer, inspecting its huge blade though not stepping too close to it. The heat radiating from that big curving chunk of metal was causing a visible haze in the night air, while flames and black smoke were shooting up from behind it. Clay smelled burning oil and guessed that the dozer's hydraulic fluid must have caught fire. It was understandable, he supposed, for Sack not to want to get too near to any fire. The man had lost most of his skin in the aero crash on Earth that had nearly done for both Clay and Galahad, and subsequently had it replaced with that ugly keroskin. Though why he seemed so fascinated by the dozer blade, Clay could not fathom.

"Well, how are you feeling, Galahad?" said Trove.

The soldier now took note of her and began sliding his hand towards his sidearm. Trove immediately relocated her aim from Galahad towards him.

"Yes, draw your weapon," said Trove. "But only with your forefinger and thumb, and then toss it to one side."

The soldier flicked a glance across at Galahad, something odd appearing in his expression, though it was difficult to read on his ruined face. He shrugged, reached down carefully and withdrew it as instructed, then violently hurled it far beyond his reach. Clay eyed the bodyguard: Sack had turned away from the dozer blade and was now strolling back. There was something wrong here because he seemed completely unconcerned.

"I feel ready to begin work, Pilot Officer Trove," said Serene Galahad, now sitting upright. "And I have no time for silly little dramas like this."

Trove swung her aim across and pointed her weapon at Sack. "You, down on your knees."

Sack continued approaching.

"I said, down on your knees! Now!"

Sack halted, held up his hands in submission, then sank down, his knees crunching on shards of bone. Trove aimed again at Galahad.

"We're standing on your work, *ma'am*." Trove injected as much contempt into the honorific as she could.

"We're standing on the work of Alan Saul," Galahad replied, now rising to her feet. "It was the most horrific of crimes but, in essence, a necessary one to save Earth from humanity. I will build on that. I will remake Earth and I will remake the human race." She gestured all around herself. "One day there will be soil and trees here. These human dead will feed the rebirth of this planet."

"Haven't we heard just about enough of this?" Clay asked.

"I reckon," Trove replied.

She pulled the trigger and the gun kicked in her hand, its flashing putting after-images into Clay's eyes, and the noise so much louder than from modern weapons. Galahad flinched away, then steadied herself with eyes closed. She then reopened her eyes and smiled. Trove fired again, emptying the entire clip, the sound of the weapon thundering and echoing around them. And next, while she stood there still pulling the trigger, and it continued clicking like skeletal fingers, Sack, who moved with scary speed for such a big man, reached over and took it out of her hand.

Trove just stood there as Sack discarded the empty clip and inserted a new one, before heading over to stand next to his charge.

"You didn't think I would hand you a weapon with live rounds, did you?" he asked mildly. He nodded towards Clay. "He had the real thing, which was why I took it away from him."

"Do you now see," said Galahad, "there is nothing to stand between me and the future. I will do everything I say, and that way I will save this world." She paused for a moment as if in reflection. "I would, of course, have liked to have seen you properly punished, as a lesson to all, but the situation is too complicated to explicate to the general public, so regretfully you will not be making any further appearances on ETV." She turned her attention to Sack. "Kill them."

NEAL ASHER

COMMAND

Saul's ship continued rising, and now further data were coming in.

"Some kind of Mach-effect drive, apparently," said Jepson in Communications and Scanning—one of his four surviving command crew. "But apparently its primary source can't be located, so we can't knock it out."

"We don't want to knock it out until he's up here," Bartholomew stated. "If that ship goes down on Io again, we'll have to sift through widespread wreckage for the Gene Bank data and samples." He paused for a second. After seeing the *Fist* obliterated, his instinct said that Saul's ship was such a great danger that he should instantly open fire. But instinct nevertheless had to take a backseat to mission objectives. If he reacted out of fear and ended up destroying everything they had come for, he knew that an adjustment cell would be waiting for him back on Earth.

"What has Tactical got to say?" he asked.

It was another of the command crew, Cherie Grace, in charge of Weapons and Logistics, who replied: "Though we can't locate the primary source of this Mach-effect drive, a sufficient bombardment should knock it out. He also has no real weapons any more, and little in the way of defensive capability. Scans show extensive damage inside, too."

Bartholomew nodded. "We'll try and target power sources . . . do we have his generators located?"

"Mostly, but hitting them is not going to be easy."

"We'll do that anyway, but make sure we avoid the Arboretum cylinder." Bartholomew wondered if there was anything else he had overlooked.

"Do we have any updates from Earth?" he asked.

Jepson failed to reply, and Bartholomew turned to him. The man was staring at his screen with his mouth open and an expression of shock.

"Jepson?"

"Something . . . something at Earth."

"Jepson!" Bartholomew snapped. "Report!"

The man looked up. "There's been an . . . explosion back there."

"And?"

"Admiral, the readings are off the scale . . . We're gathering data right now but it seems the nuclear arsenal of the *Scourge* detonated." He shook his head. "We can't find the Traveller construction station."

"Sir," interrupted Grace.

"What do you mean, you can't find the construction station?" Bartholomew demanded, ignoring Grace.

"It's gone, sir," Jepson replied.

"It's gone?" Whole new scenarios opened before Bartholomew. "I'll want confirmation of that, and more detail on what happened. Did we receive any messages prior to this event? And do we have any data on Serene Galahad's location when it occurred?"

"Sir!" Grace insisted.

He held up his hand. "Shut up, Grace."

If Serene Galahad had died in the detonation of the *Scourge's* nuclear arsenal, then that put a whole new complexion on events—on his mission objectives, and on the penalty for failure. It would also mean a scrabbling for power back on Earth, the outcome of which he could influence with the weapons remaining to him aboard the *Command*. These were matters that needed his very close consideration. However, whatever he thought of Galahad, the fact remained that the Gene Bank data and samples were important for the future of Earth, and there-fore should still be retrieved. It was just that, if she was dead, taking captives was no longer necessary. He could hit that command nexus at the centre of Saul's ship, where he was sure Saul himself resided. He could probably hit everything else in there but for the Arboretum cylinder, because surely the data would be stored there, along with the physical samples. He could tear that ship apart and—

"Admiral, sir!" said Grace. "I must insist!"

"Must you?" he spat, rounding on her.

"He's accelerating, sir!"

"Doubtless that has something to do with him getting away from the gravitational pull of Io," he said, returning his attention to his console and screen. After a second of studying the data Grace had relayed across, reality finally bit.

"Open fire on the enemy vessel!" he shouted. "Target everything but the Arboretum cylinder!"

"Everything, Admiral?" Grace enquired.

"Everything," Bartholomew replied. "We're not taking back any prisoners."

"Understood, sir."

In moments Bartholomew felt it in his bones, as his ship began firing, and he also noted the lights dimming with the drain.

"Power status?" he asked.

"Not enough to maintain everything," replied one of the engineers moni-toring the ship's systems.

"Prioritize weapons, steering and side-burners."

"The vortex generator?"

"Go to holding . . . no, go to induction draw. We certainly won't be able to use it to move us, but we can use the power it's stored up."

Still studying his screen, he noted the distance between Saul's ship and the *Command* rapidly diminishing. Perhaps Saul did have further weapons to deploy, but needed to get closer to use them, so it would be best to keep him at a metaphorical arm's length.

"Take us out." He directed the order to the two personnel at the helm and navigation console—two whose names he had yet to learn, for they were replacements for the pair who had died. "I want a minimum distance between him and us of twenty thousand kilometres, until all of his ship—but for the Arboretum cylinder—is reduced to scrap."

Visuals now showed the railgun impacts on Saul's ship: red spots appearing on its surface, like freckles on a face, and then fading, with glowing wreckage strewing out behind. This was the thing about the enemy, Bartholomew reckoned: Saul's ship was a sphere with a fifteen-kilometre circumference and, though they could try and target vital parts of it, completely turning the majority of it to scrap, as Bartholomew had ordered, would be like turning a full-length train to scrap with just hand-held weapons.

Steering thrusters turned the *Command* and then a remaining side-burn fusion engine kicked in, thrusting him down in his seat but not as forcefully as their scrapped main engine had done.

"He's at twenty thousand," someone stated.

"Have we hit his command centre yet?" Bartholomew enquired.

"Not yet," Grace replied. "Either our targeting is off or . . . Jepson?"

After checking his instruments for a short while, Jepson replied, "I'm getting positional changes in response to our firings."

Now it was Grace's turn to study her own instruments intently. "He's using that drive of his to dodge."

"But I'm seeing impacts," said Bartholomew.

"He can't dodge everything, but is taking a lot of our shots in already severely damaged portions of the ship." She paused again, studying data, then went on. "Most of his vital equipment is on an equatorial plane, and he's edge on to us but with a slight tilt. He's making sure a lot of our hits are right on the equator, where they lose energy in remaining vortex generator armour, or then hit the smelting plants and bearing endcaps and he's spinning to distribute the damage."

"Give me bracketed firing solutions," Bartholomew ordered. "This new drive is probably located somewhere on that plane." He turned to Jepson. "Any effect yet on that drive?"

"His acceleration is increasing," said Jepson.

"Eighteen thousand kilometres," declared their new navigator.

"What?" Bartholomew roared. "I told you the minimum safe distance!"

"He's still accelerating," said the pilot, "and we can't maintain minimum distance, Admiral."

Bartholomew felt his tension growing. Saul had caught Bartholomew out by deploying a plasma cannon and had destroyed the *Fist* by ruthlessly wrecking his own Alcubierre drive. Time and time again he had been underestimated, and no way would he be coming after them like this without some means of attacking.

"Fifteen thousand kilometres," stated the navigator.

"Start with the maser," Bartholomew ordered. "He at least won't be able to dodge that."

"Firing," Grace replied, and the lights again dimmed, "but he's tilted in response and is now completely edge on, so we've still got that equatorial infrastructure in the way. That means we're mostly frying wreckage. I suggest we go to grid plot and hit every surface section that becomes available."

"No." Bartholomew shook his head. "Concentrate on the equatorial plane: he probably has some weapon in there that we haven't seen yet."

"Present drive efficiency dropping," said the pilot.

"Ten thousand kilometres," the navigator added, with a catch in his voice.

"Tactical suggests reduced firing so as to increase suggested safe distance," said Grace, still appearing calm. "Our weapons are putting a power drain on pellet aggregation in the side-burner."

"Maintain maximum fire rate," Bartholomew ordered. He was damned if he was going to run from such a heavily damaged vessel, new drive or not, and suspected this might be a tactical feint on Saul's part precisely to induce him to run.

"I'm getting some strange visuals, sir," said Jepson. "But the maser and railgun firings are interfering . . ."

"Relay to me."

On the screen the image of Saul's ship jumped closer, but then blurred and shimmered. It almost looked as if the hull was burning and boiling in certain areas. Maybe this was an effect of this Mach drive, or maybe the *Command*'s maser was starting to melt sections of the hull. However, something here definitely seemed wrong.

"Cease firing for a full scan," he commanded. "And recommence firing immediately afterwards. Jepson, full link to my screen, updating as soon as scan data comes in."

"Yessir!"

The lights brightened as all firing shut down, then dimmed again while Jepson used ship's sensors to do a full sweep of the approaching vessel as EM interference cleared. On his screen, Bartholomew watched Saul's ship divide into small squares, image data in each rapidly cleaning up before it winked out again, the blur and the shimmering effect wafting away. From the pole downwards, the squares disappeared, soon revealing an area perhaps a kilometre across: a great blemish where the hull appeared to be melting.

"Five thousand kilometres!" the navigator shouted, his voice breaking.

Jepson focused down on that same blemish, and Bartholomew slowly grasped that Saul's ship wasn't burning or melting there; it was *crawling*. He saw the hull was swarming with those golden conjoined robots, thousands of them, and he realized precisely how Saul intended to attack.

"Target that with all weapons!" he shouted but, even as he gave the order, the blemish slid round and out of sight as the approaching behemoth turned on its axis.

"Three thousand kilometres!" Hysterical now, without doubt. "Shut down weapons and give me full power to the facing side-burner, until we're at one thousand," Bartholomew ordered, sounding as controlled and calm as a pilot taking a scramjet down for a crash landing. "Then divert power to Side-burner Three—complemented with chemical steering thrusters."

"Yessir!" replied the pilot and, shortly afterwards, new acceleration pressed Bartholomew down into his chair.

"Sir," said Grace. "Our vortex generator?"

It was an idea, and one he had briefly checked. However, the planning behind the building of the *Command* had been heavily influenced by fear of sabotage. But perhaps still worth checking further.

"Can we shut down any section of vortex generator containment?" he asked the engineer he had addressed earlier.

"Two thousand kilometres." Now the hysteria had evaporated from the navigator's voice and it had taken on a leaden edge—like an acceptance of the inevitable.

The engineer looked round. "Only if we send someone out to the ring with explosives."

"One thousand."

The pressure of acceleration came off, then back on again, as if now trying to throw Bartholomew sideways out of his chair. By slow degrees that same pressure swung round, as the bridge sphere reoriented. It was too late now to send anyone off to destroy containment before the imminent impact. Bartholomew gripped the arms of his chair, stared at the close loom of Saul's ship and at a tactical display indicating relative positions. The *Command* had begun to slide out of the other vessel's path, so maybe . . .

No, at the last moment, the other ship swung sharply to the side, out of danger from the vortex ring, then came in hard on the *Command*'s nose. Bartholomew felt the force of it rip side-ways through the bridge sphere, felt as if one of his own ribs had given way. The racket was terrible—like a bomb blast in a scrap yard—but the navigator's shriek was all too audible as he hurtled past and slammed into the engineering monitor wall, and hung there in the indentation, power shorting out all around him. The fool obviously hadn't secured himself properly—the kind of mistake the previous navigator would never have made, but even that had not saved him from a chunk of metal punching through his chest. The lights went out, came on again, and went out again, before switching over to emergency LED.

The racket continued: the shouting, the agonized protests of metal giving way, the explosions and the hollow roaring of flames. Screens flickered and tactical displays lost any sense. Somebody was repeating, "Oh God, Oh God," in a steady monotone. Then another sound began to impinge, and it was one that sent cold fingers crawling down Bartholomew's spine. As from an automated factory operating at full tilt, he could hear distant saws, drills and hammering sounds. Then came a din of scrabbling and clattering that reminded him of lizards running over a tin roof, but big lizards whose weight was buckling the roof, and then inevitably the crackle of weapons.

The *Command* apparently now had some unwelcome visitors.

NEAL ASHER

EARTH

Clay Ruger closed his eyes. At least it would be quick: no lengthy agonizing death under an inducer, or being impaled on a metal spike, or slowly strangled, or coughing out his lungs as the Scour ravaged throughout his body. He waited for the impact of the bullets . . . and waited . . . then eventually opened his eyes again.

Sack stood gazing down at his weapon, holding it in one hand while running a finger of his other hand along the barrel, his expression contemplative.

"Do you know," he said, "this gun is not a replica. It's over a century old. Admittedly it required heat treatment to reverse metal crystallization, and further metal layered in to repair general wear and tear, but it's worked perfectly for all that time."

"Then it's time for you to work it again," said Galahad, now looking both puzzled and wary. "Obey me, Sack."

Sack nodded. "You asked Calder why, if you were the one who caused it, you would have surrounded yourself with those who had lost family to the Scour. Maybe you remember me telling you about my father, maybe not. This was his gun."

"This is all very interesting, Sack, but it doesn't change the fact that it was Alan Saul who released the Scour on Earth's population, and my only sin was not revealing its original source."

Sack took his free hand away from the gun and held it up to inspect his lizard-skin fingers. He then reached down to his belt and extracted something from it, clicked a button to bring a blade gleaming into the firelight, then tossed the flick knife to stab into the bone ground at Trove's feet.

"You." He turned to the soldier who was now standing up again. "Fuck off."

"There's no need," the soldier replied.

"Nevertheless."

The man nodded and headed over towards his sidearm, and stooped carefully to pick it up. Sack did not react. The man slid the weapon back into its holster, then turned and strode off into the night.

"You two," he said to Trove and Clay, "get over there"—he nodded to the drop shuttle—"and cut me two of the longest lengths of that preconductor cable you can find, and bring them back here."

"Sack, you really—" began Galahad.

The weapon swung round and back, hard, smashing her in the mouth, crushing her lips and splintering her teeth, and sending her sprawling on the ground.

"And you," Sack added, "can shut up."

Her bloody mouth open in shock, Galahad began to scrabble away from him. He stepped after her and fired twice, shattering her kneecap and then her elbow. She shrieked and lay writhing, then, after a moment, desperately began dragging herself along with her undamaged arm and leg, groaning and panting all the while as Sack kept pace with her.

"Do you really think anyone believes you any more?" he asked. "I made sure I was by your side because you got things done, and you then seemed to be the one who would get me—and all the other people I know—some payback."

She had no reply, just glanced up at him with her eyes wide and tried to crawl faster. He halted her by bringing one foot down on the shattered joint of her leg and, as she whimpered in agony, he turned back to the other two. Clay met his gaze for a moment then stooped and took up the flick knife.

"Best we do what the man says," he said to Trove.

She numbly followed him to the drop shuttle and helped unravel the lengths of cable that he then cut. The stuff was not actually a superconductor, but a cheaper alternative that came very close. Eventually they had secured what Sack required and brought it over to him, dropping it on the ground beside Galahad. Putting away his weapon and stooping, the bodyguard busily began stripping off her suit. She fought him, but he smacked a hard lizard-skin hand against her ruined mouth and she desisted.

"You can go now," he said, "if you want."

They stayed for a short while—just a short while.

ARGUS

The *Command* soldiers, moving to defend certain areas of their ship, came pouring through the airlock fast, with the weight of their VC suits only partially slowing their rapid deployment of the ten-mil machine gun on its tripod. That Saul could watch them at work was only due to the optic pushed through a hole drilled in the airlock at the further end of the corridor, for the comlifer was still keeping him from penetrating the *Command*'s computer systems. No matter, and really Saul wasn't trying very hard to penetrate those systems, but instead just sufficient attacks to keep the comlifer busy, with the systems on the edge of overload and communication channels slow and unreliable. This was all now proceeding much as he had supposed it would once they were past the danger of the *Command* using its vortex ring as a weapon.

The other physically penetrative attacks were already deep inside the ship. His robots had cut power to any railgun still capable of targeting Saul's ship and had reached the maser, which they were now dismantling. The nuclear arsenal had just fallen, too, and been isolated with a full six-section conjoined robot inside it, which was making the weapons completely safe by dismantling them. Others had reached as far as the vortex ring and captured three of the five fusion reactors that powered it. Even though its plane now lay away from his own ship, and a containment shutdown would just blow its mercury out into space, Saul did not want it totally destroyed, since there were a lot of valuable materials to be harvested there.

Elsewhere the robots had not penetrated and were responding only when necessary to attacks from the crew, from the readerguns, from the *Command*'s own robots and its soldiers. Already they had stripped away the wreckage lying at the contact point between the two ships, which was now being conveyed inside by older-style robots, and they were proceeding along the length of the *Command* into the expanded waist volume underneath its vortex ring, and there busy dismantling it. Whole, undamaged components, which—with perhaps just a little alteration—could be used in Saul's own ship, were being diligently unbolted or cut at welds so as to be removed. Other items, after being identified as of little use in their present form, were quickly cut free to be taken to a central pool of materials destined for the smelting plants, whereupon the huge damage they had suffered could be repaired. In fact, his robots weren't so much attacking the *Command* as eating it.

The eight-section robot positioned beyond the airlock which was being guarded by that ten-mil machine gun had by now removed the hinges and the seal, as well as much of the surrounding structure. Like a golden centipede carrying a buckler, it surged on its way through with the heavy airlock door held in front of it. The defending soldiers fired their machine gun, the heavy ceramic rounds slamming into the airlock door and in places cutting through it into the leading robot section. By the time the whole robot reached them the door itself was in shreds, and so was the vanguard of the robot chain. It swiftly discarded both, and in a blur, fell on both men and machine gun and swarmed over them, leaving weapon and body components in its wake.

Another fusion reactor was now isolated, and an engineering team was retreating from the last. Here some *Command* robots remained to launch a clumsy defence, as Saul's robots closed in. New programming then kicked in and the *Command*'s robots were overwhelmed and immobilized one at a time, cowlings swiftly derivated and removed. Processing chips were extracted and plugged into sockets in Saul's robots and there wiped; laminar memory EM pulsed at close range, the blank chips reinserted, then fast-and-dirty programs fed in via optics. Thus enemy robots became beasts of burden, conveying away the substance of the *Command*.

Next, a chunk of the data plenum dropped out. Saul did a fast replay to get imagery of a tank-buster being deployed to knock out the first section of the now seven-section robot. The team firing at it looked like crew, not soldiers, but they were still doing a good job. They kept hitting his robot as it hurtled towards them, dropping overloaded front sections as it approached. A conjoining of two sections hit the men at the last, and they, with their weapon, joined the stream of components being hauled out of the *Command*. The robot next cut fast with a thermic lance alongside a door, extracted a thick plug of metal, then inserted a tool head into the perfect five-centimetre-diameter hole this created. The door thumped open and the robot entered, took fire from two readerguns before tearing one down from the wall and hurling it into the other with the force of a bullet. From the acceleration couch, to which he had been secured with metal straps, Christopher Shivers opened crusted eyes now that no cams were still available for him there.

"At last," he managed. "Be quick."

Doubtless the equipment monitoring him would detect his expectancy of death, gauge his relief at the prospect of finding peace and admonish him with some degree of suffering. Saul's robot did not move fast because of this, or because of some feeling of sympathy in the one who had programmed it and still controlled it at will. No, it moved fast because that was how it was designed to move. Using just a few quick motions, it sliced a circular saw blade through his neck, snatched up his head and divided his skull like an avocado. It quickly pared away brain, even while blood still spurted from the man's neck, found the hardware located behind the optic plugs in his skull, sliced away the biological component, then opened tiny covers to insert hair-thin optic and electrical connections.

Saul was now in, into the *Command*'s systems, and he found them very cramped indeed. He sucked up strings of code and broke it, isolated the bridge and included the ship's system in the laser-com network his robots were spreading throughout the craft. Its work done, his robot dropped the remnant of Shiver's head and turned to speed away, picking up its own discarded sections as it went, quickly replacing their burned-out components and reprogramming them, while making for a part of the ship, indicated on the schematic in its mind, where it could join its fellows in the *disassembly*.

Saul then shut down all the readerguns, closed down communications between crew and soldiers, took control of all the rest of the *Command*'s robots and simply added them to his own complement. And now, with most of the front section of the *Command* gone, and remaining crew and soldiers fleeing to the rear or finding somewhere along the way to retrench, he recalled half of his robots and set them to making repairs within his own ship.

Next he focused on the rival ship's vortex generator, which was slowly winding down, though still in the process supplying energy to the *Command*. He connected up superconducting cables from his own ship to suck that power, thus drawing further momentum from the circulating mercury in the *Command*'s generator. It would, he realized, take at least two days before the liquid metal was moving slowly enough to be tapped, and before the *Command*'s vortex generator could safely be disassembled, but by then most of the other ship would be gone. It would also take that many days before his smelting plants could even start work on creating components for a new vortex ring for his own ship, and probably months before his ship might be returned to anything like its previous condition.

"Alan Saul," came a voice broadcast from the secondary bridge sphere, where his robots were now busily taking apart the sphere's acceleration-orientation gear. "I need to speak to Alan Saul."

It seemed that this Admiral Bartholomew, whose name and record Saul had loaded from the *Command*'s systems, now wanted to speak to him. Saul considered that. Possibly, the surrender of the remaining hold-outs would speed up the present process. Then, again, there were huge inefficiencies involved in conveying the human survivors to captivity, and little of material value to be gained by doing so.

COMMAND

There was, Bartholomew felt, something almost reassuring in having been defeated so comprehensively. He had nothing to bargain with, no terms to negotiate, nothing to offer except the surrender of the crew and soldiers he could still contact, and whom he suspected were only alive because they had not yet got in the way of one of the robots. He swallowed some stale orange juice from his suit spigot, visor closed now because the sounds of slicing and drilling, the crackle of cutting lasers, the thump of rivet removers and the high-speed screech of bolts being unwound was getting very close now. He had witnessed it out there before the cam feeds had blanked. He had seen those things taking apart his ship with the alacrity of an expert black-market butcher gutting, skinning and dismembering a corpse collected from the back door of a Safe Departure clinic, only there was more than one butcher at work here, and a damned sight more than just one knife.

"Alan Saul," he repeated, using isolated broadcasting gear within the bridge sphere, since nothing else was now available. "I need to speak to Alan Saul."

"And why do you want to do that?" asked a perfectly calm and apparently sane voice through the PA system.

"I want to surrender myself and my crew," said Bartholomew, glancing round at those watching him and seeing no sign of disagreement there.

"And the relevance of that to me is what?" Alan Saul enquired.

"It's over now. You've won. We'll do anything you want, go anywhere you send us."

"I see," said Saul. "You've conceded defeat and tipped over your king. You've acknowledged that you cannot win and have pulled up the stumps. It was all a jolly wheeze while we were fighting, but now let's all retire to the pavilion for beer and sandwiches."

Apart from the reference to chess, Bartholomew had no idea what Saul was talking about, so all he could do was dumbly repeat, "It's over."

"Hundreds of my personnel are now dead. My sister is dead—irrecoverably dead. And my ship is a wreck. If I had surrendered to you, then my personnel and I would have faced lengthy interrogation under inducement, followed by protracted executions on ETV. You are now in an environment and situation where keeping you and your remaining personnel alive requires an effort on my part. Please explain to me why I should bother to expend that effort."

Irrecoverably dead? What did that mean?

Bartholomew groped for something—for anything—to say. "You were under attack and using your drive at the time, so maybe you didn't see what happened back at Earth."

"I saw," Saul replied. "And I picked up some communications that you almost certainly did not. It seems that Captain Scotonis was still aboard the *Scourge*, and that he felt a grudge towards Serene Galahad relating to her extermination of billions of human beings on Earth—whose number included his own family."

"Jesus!" Jepson exclaimed, while Grace merely dipped her head and gave it a shake.

Bartholomew studied each of his remaining command crew in turn. Some looked baffled, some angry, others still managed to retain that long-inculcated trait of showing no emotion at all. Did he believe what he had just been told? Unless Saul had some kind of weakness he knew nothing about, some need for Bartholomew's support, which in the present situation seemed highly unlikely, he could see no reason why the man should be lying. And, of course, it made utter sense. Many were the suspicions, though aired in utter privacy, about the demographics of that particular catastrophe, and about how it was mostly zero assets who had died—conveniently along with all the remaining members of the previous Committee. Calder had been quite acerbic in his occasional comments about this, and at the time Bartholomew had felt sure he himself was being sounded out. However, he had reacted with complete correctness and loyalty to Serene Galahad, simply because he had been afraid Calder's comments were made at her behest, in order to test his loyalty.

"Then, don't you see?" he countered. "It's all over. She's dead. You have no enemy any longer!"

"That is not necessarily true, since a fast-escape drop shuttle left the Traveller construction station just before the detonation, managed to correct itself after the blast front reached it, and then landed somewhere in India."

After his initial tirade, something about the way Saul was speaking now sounded a bit off to Bartholomew. It all seemed to have become too correct, too exact and, from his experience with Christopher Shivers, he felt sure he knew why.

"I'm not speaking to *all* of Alan Saul now, am I?"

"You are speaking to enough of him," the voice replied.

"So I am to be judged by a sub-program?"

"You are in no position to protest about that."

"So what must I do?" Bartholomew asked. "Must I beg for the lives of myself and my crew?"

"No. I will no longer respond to circumstances on the basis of emotion," Saul replied. "However, I have given limited self-governance to the personnel aboard my ship and, since this is a human matter, I have consulted with Technical Director Le Roque, who is the de facto governor of the human population."

A human matter?

"What is his decision?"

"I have opened your communications to all of your own personnel aboard," Saul declared. "You will tell them to abandon their weapons and head for the nose of your ship. There you will be met by my police chief, Langstrom, who will conduct you into confinement in Arcoplex One. What Le Roque and Langstrom then decide to do with you is their own concern. You may address your personnel now."

Bartholomew sat there gaping. What should he say? What *could* he say? Eventually, after a lengthy throat clearing, he began, "This is Admiral Bartholomew. We have lost, we have been defeated absolutely, and the only alternative to surrender is for us to all die . . ."

When he had finished, the replies came in, neatly ordered one after the other, so doubtless Saul was still controlling their communication. Some argued with Bartholomew, but could not argue with the facts he laid out. Most simply agreed.

"Okay, let's go," he said at last, when it was all over.

They went out through the bridge sphere airlock in pairs, one of them carrying out their navigator, who was unconscious but still alive. Bartholomew waited until they were all gone, extracted the laminar storage of the ship's log and inserted it into a belt pouch, for his defence just in case he ever faced trial on Earth, which now seemed unlikely. He already knew that Saul's robots were tearing his ship apart, but as he stepped out, the extent of it still came as a shock.

The corridor right outside had lost all its wall panels, its ceiling and even most of its floor. He gazed up through the wide-open structure of the ship at busy activity: the flicker of cutting lasers; golden worms seemingly entwined through everything, with their multiple limbs moving at a blur; diamond saws filling vacuum with a snow of glittering swarf; major ship components shifting, then being pulled away. His command crew could be seen further along the corridor, standing back from where one of his own ship's robots was taking up another floor plate ahead.

"Go over it," he instructed. "If he wanted us dead we would be dead by now."

They launched themselves over the robot, which simply ignored them. Propelling themselves on through the ship, they made their way forward to join up with a party of three troops standing on a lattice of beams halfway from the core to the nose. Here Bartholomew gaped in amazement, for so much of the ship's structure was gone he could see clearly as far as the vortex ring, and beyond it out into hard vacuum. Peering ahead, he caught sight of Saul's vessel, in fact could see right inside Saul's vessel, because such a large part of its hull was missing. As they headed towards this, the whole ship around them shifted in the same direction, like some fish being swallowed by a giant sea anemone. Others joined them on the way forward as they propelled themselves from beam to beam, and had to throw themselves clear of the paths of great loads of wall plates, beams, reels of cable and optics—and, in one case, the partially dismembered carcass of a fusion sideburner. Five people awaited them on the lip of the giant hole opening into the massive vessel ahead. They were armed, and began beckoning them down. Bartholomew paused against a beam, as those around him headed where directed. He counted just thirty-five of them surviving out of crew of hundreds.

"You're Bartholomew," said one of the five figures as he caught up with the rest.

"I am."

"Okay, all of you follow me," said the man he now recognized as Langstrom. "Don't do anything stupid, and don't try to run. I won't bother going after you, but then I've no need to."

Bartholomew gazed up at the stream of robots and materials flowing through the gap, and then back at the *Command*. Already it had become skeletal as far back as the wrecked main engine, and he could see right through its length and to the stars beyond. What, in the face of all this, would be more stupid? Was it fighting to the end and thus dying, or allowing oneself to be captured alive?

EARTH

Serene just could not believe the pain. She'd pissed in her suit, which was fine since it was designed to absorb it, but she'd also shit herself and it wasn't intended for that. As Sack had pulled the VC suit from her body, she had been sure he was going to rape her—rape her with a penis covered in that hard lizard skin. She didn't even try to fight him after he dealt the second blow. She knew how strong he was, and knew it would be futile. Let him have his way, let him do this to her and punish her. Perhaps it was necessary for her to undergo this metaphorical "scourging" to free her of the sin of past crimes, and thence she could move clean-born into the bright future. What she had done, and what she intended to do, were of the utmost importance, so she should expect to suffer some pain along the way. Great deeds were often tied to great suffering. Didn't the saints and martyrs of the old religions of Earth know about that?

Once she was naked, he tied a length of the preconductor cable to the ankle of her undamaged leg, then to the wrist of her undamaged arm. So, he was going to tie her down first and then have his way with her. She noted that Ruger and Trove were still here, watching in fascination. They would enjoy her personal humiliation, and now she felt glad Sack had not obeyed her instruction to kill them. After this was all over, she would be able to hunt them down and punish them thoroughly for their crimes, including this present voyeurism.

With the cables in place, Sack began towing her along by her ankle. She shrieked again, then concentrated on keeping her shattered knee and elbow off the bony ground. She gritted her teeth, determined not to cry out any more. She would suffer this, and it would pass. Nearer to the bulldozer she became aware of the heat from its blade—as flames still leaped up behind it—and it was here Sack finally deposited her. He took up the cable attached to her wrist and tied its far end to a large chunk of wreckage. Next he returned and pulled the other length of cable round behind the dozer blade, and she could hear him scrabbling somewhere there. The cable flipped over the top of the blade, which rose at least eight metres off the ground, and he then appeared there, amidst the flames and smoke, and began hauling upon it.

How could he survive there in that fire? The suit must help protect him . . . but what about his hands and face? Serene abandoned these thoughts as the cable began tugging her, by the ankle, closer to the hot blade. However, the other cable attached to her wrist then tightened too, and she was lifted up off the ground, the pain of it bringing her near to blacking out. Higher and higher she rose, until she hung suspended at an angle, between the two cables, only the one connected to her wrist stopping her from swinging straight in towards the hot metal.

"Wonderful stuff this keroskin—you have no idea," announced Sack, walking out from behind the dozer blade. Oily flames licked up his legs, his spacesuit was blackened and smoking, and he looked like a demon fresh out of the Pit. He paused and stooped to take up handfuls of bone gravel to put out the flames, seemingly oblivious to the burning oil clinging to his hands.

"Fire isn't much of a problem for it," he explained, "because it has fewer afferent nerves and can resist a lot more damage than normal human skin. Of course, even at the cost of being more vulnerable and less able to withstand damage, I'd prefer to have human skin, and my old face."

"It can . . . be done," Serene managed. "You can have . . . your face back."

"But I can't have my father back." Sack gestured all around. "And there are millions if not billions of people who also can't have their friends or family back."

"Necessary," Serene asserted.

"Oh, I agree," Sack nodded. "You did something that was horribly necessary in order to save the planet, but this is personal." He walked over to the taut cable that extended from Serene's wrist to the piece of wreckage. He pulled it tighter to give himself some slack at the knot, which he untied. Next, holding the cable taut, he turned back to face her.

"My only problem with fire is a psychological barrier I have to overcome." He slackened the cable slightly and thus set Serene swinging. "I was told that the pain I suffered was just about the worst anyone can suffer, and that of course left scars inside me too."

"You . . . don't do this." He clearly wanted her to think he was going to burn her, and she decided it best to play along with this melodrama he was creating. He would toy with her for a while, but in the end he knew she was utterly essential to the future of Earth.

"But I *do*," Sack replied, then stepped forward to allow her to swing in towards the dozer blade.

He wouldn't do this. He would pull the cable taut again at the last moment. He would not sacrifice the future to such petty vengeance. Serene continued to believe this right up until the moment when her naked body touched metal hotter than a clothes iron. Thereafter she lost the ability to think at all.

* * *

The sunrise was spectacular: deep purple clouds turning silver and gold on their undersides, then shading to amethyst shot through with blood red, before being seared by the sun, as it breached the sprawl towers, and then turning to lemon and orange. The clouds seemed to be rainbow islands in the sky, with the bays and coves of some fantasy land people could only dream of ever reaching—or only reach by dreaming. It was, Ruger felt, a sunrise he would remember, and one he could appreciate properly now the screaming had stopped.

"Do you reckon she's dead now?" Trove asked.

"I should think so," Ruger replied. "I'm surprised she lasted so long."

The power of the sun began ramping up very quickly and the clouds lost their romantic appeal. Maybe a couple of kilometres ahead lay more sprawl, though it was difficult to tell for sure in the increasing heat haze, and now, in clear morning light, the surface they walked upon was all too visible. How many thousands . . . how many millions of the dead lay here under his feet?

"Looks as if we're getting some activity." Trove pointed.

Ruger raised his gaze from the crushed ribcages and empty eye sockets to peer at several shapes rising above the distant sprawl. After a moment he identified a big rotobus, along with two outrider military aeros, heading directly towards them. He wanted to run, get himself to that sprawl and find somewhere to hide while he sorted out what to do next, but having spent so long in zero gravity, having suffered so many injuries and certainly also suffering from radiation sickness, he was having enough trouble just continuing to put one foot in front of the other.

"There's going to be trouble," Trove commented.

"There's always trouble," he replied bitterly.

"I mean, once everyone knows Galahad is gone, her delegates will be fighting each other for the top job," Trove continued. "I'm betting on numerous police actions, and lots of unfortunate accidents."

Ruger wondered what relevance that would have for the pair of them inside an adjustment cell, because that was where they were undoubtedly going.

The three aircraft drew closer and closer but, unexpectedly, didn't come down to land beside them, instead continuing on to the crash site. Maybe they did still have a chance to reach the sprawl and there make themselves scarce. Ruger glanced back as the three craft settled near the giant bulldozer and the wreckage of their drop shuttle, which was now only partially visible through haze. Would they find Galahad still hanging up against that dozer blade, nicely cooked to a turn? Would Sack now face capture and a death sentence?

"Maybe we can make it," he said, turning away and trying to pick up his pace towards the sprawl. Trove had no reply for him. They tramped on for another half an hour, the sprawl buildings seemingly getting no closer. The sounds of the two aeros and the rotobus, again approaching, suffused Clay with a feeling of utter hopelessness, till he halted abruptly, and sat down on bones. Trove stood beside him, gazing back at the approaching aircraft, her arms folded and her expression bitter.

With a roar, the aircraft slowed down, circling out to one side of them. While the two military aeros hovered, the rotobus descended in a blast of ivory dust. Clay closed his eyes and waited, only opening them when he heard a grunt of surprise emerging from Trove.

Sack and two soldiers walked into visibility. One of the soldiers was the same one Sack had dismissed during the night; the other, by his uniform, was a general in the Inspectorate military wing. They came to a halt just a few paces away.

"You'll be needing medical attention," said Sack. "Though this is a sad moment, what with the tragic loss of Serene Galahad in that drop-shuttle crash"—he stabbed a thumb over his shoulder—"the people of Earth must never forget their heroes."

Clay slowly heaved himself to his feet. "Heroes?" he echoed.

"Heroes," Sack repeated. "Against all odds, you managed to survive and get the Gene Bank data back to Earth." He gazed at them blankly. "Whoever now assumes the role of Chairman here will be thoroughly aware of the need to court you. Who knows? Your inevitable fame may even propel you into some high position within the new regime—maybe even the highest position of all."

Clay Ruger felt the cogs and spindles of his mind abruptly run free and begin spinning at high speed. He stood up straighter and transferred his attention to the general.

"Sack is correct," he stated. "We are both in need of immediate anti-rad treatments, at the very least."

The general nodded his head. "We can fly you directly to the nearest Committee hospital, sir. And I personally want to thank you for all you've done."

"Shall we?" Clay gestured towards the rotobus, now becoming clear in the dusty air.

"Certainly," the general replied, waving them ahead of him.

"I hope you know what you're doing, PO Ruger," Trove muttered to him, as they walked. "Maybe it'd be better if we just kept our heads down."

"There will be danger," said Sack, who had silently moved in behind to shadow them, "but I can recommend to you a good bodyguard, who could also employ the right people for security."

Clay glanced at him. "Any chance of a letter of recommendation from this guy's previous employer?"

Sack's smile, in return, was about the nastiest thing Clay had ever seen.

EPILOGUE

JUPITER WAR

The term "war" had suffered much abuse over the centuries, what with it being used in hackneyed cliche's to describe just about any concerted effort by any group of humans, from a nation downwards. The world had thus seen wars on hunger, poverty, disease, smoking, obesity, terror and climate change, and grown disconnected from the reality—just a century past—of nations using their industrial might to tear each other apart, of cities being annihilated and of millions dying. But this was not why the Committee decided to excise the word from official documentation or state-controlled media. No, the Committee, taking the meaning of war to be "open and declared armed hostile conflict between states or nations," decided that, since we lived in a unified world, the term was obsolete. Any conflict involving soldiers, guns and bombs, up to and including the aforementioned annihilation of cities and millions dying, became an incident, a dissident suppression, a tactical excision or merely a police action. In light of this, and in an effort to rewrite history, the struggle with Alan Saul was described as an "extra-solar police action." However, because Saul had turned what was Argus Station into his own nation state, and gone head-to-head against the full industrial and military might of Earth, and won, Subnet pundits such as your author here insist on calling this the "Jupiter War."

The ship's new heavily armoured hull plates gleamed in the sun as the Alcubierre warp blinked out around it. Its new vortex generator, filled with mercury from the Command's generator and from further mining of a cinnabar asteroid, was maintained at full power and ready to fling the ship away again. Inside it, the Arboretum, Arcoplexes One and Two and the new and presently empty Arcoplex Three, were all spinning with steady efficiency amidst internal structure steadily expanding to fill all but one space. Meanwhile, the smelting plants and internal factories continued at their previous frenetic pace: their furnaces, presses, forges, automated mills and lathes, assembly plants and other machines besides, all were busily and raucously at work. The Traveller engine, now repaired, rebuilt, improved and refuelled, stood ready to fire up, but with the double-layered Mach-effect drive distributed around the inner layer of hull, it might never need to. The two plasma cannons, two heavy masers and six railguns were in pristine condition, ready with plasma caps, missiles and power supplies endowed with redoubled redundancy. And Saul hoped he would never have any need for *them*.

Through cameras in the hull he watched as the big new space doors opened and a space plane shot out on its way to the wrecked and depopulated Core Two space station. He then turned his attention to an old friend—an early design of robot kitted out for applying spray coatings, and the same one he had used to lead the attack against Salem Smith—as it perambulated around the hull, etching away metal and spraying bright yellow vacuum-set paint. Its task would be completed sometime after his jaunt in taking this ship out of the solar system.

Earth lay below and even from up here it was possible, with just human vision, to see that some areas were greener than they had appeared before the Scour. Saul analysed spectra in his mind and calculated on a close to ten per cent increase in such areas. He also calculated the force of the latest blast—this time on the American east coast—and knew that another tactical atomic had been used, rating at no more than five kilotonnes.

Serene Galahad's delegates—including officers ranking high in the Inspectorate military wing and others with no particular rank before all this— were busy fighting for power. Thus far, a large portion of the Inspectorate military had rallied to the flag of Pilot Officer Trove and Clay Ruger, whose power base lay in India and who had taken control of much of old Asia. However, they were up against an alliance of European delegates as well as the individual delegates who now respectively controlled the Americas, Australia and Japan, the Arctic and Russia, besides numerous smaller realms between.

Saul reached informational tendrils out to Earth. All the larger warring blocs had either snatched one of Galahad's com-lifers or created their own to defend their computer systems and, with Saul's ship now in orbit above them, security was at its highest and those same comlifers alert to intrusion. Saul should not even have been able to penetrate, but all those blocs had managed to get hold of copies of the Gene Bank data he had sent to the *Scourge*. When he'd laced that data with every computer worm and virus at his disposal it had been in the hope of penetrating either that ship's systems or those of Earth. And the latter case had paid off royally now. He thus penetrated with ease, sliding in under their notice, sliding into twenty-two com-lifer minds and simply rendering them unconscious. Free to mentally wander through all those disparate systems, he shut down every missile silo capable of firing anything into orbit, then as a precaution insured that the presently idle mass drivers could not be used as weapons either. Then he injected a virus he had created many months before.

In just three hours it spread around the world, seeking out specific information and erasing it. When its work was done, not one scrap of system-stored data remained of either Professor Rhine's or Professor Calder's research into the Alcubierre warp drive. The virus then became somnolent and hidden, awaiting the insertion of similar data from other forms of storage, whereupon it would activate itself again and wipe it too. As it sank into somnolence after those three hours, Saul considered his capability of reaching into the human mind via the visual cortex and thus manipulating data inside. But he drew a line at that, deciding that even he did not want to become that ruthless.

Next, he spent hours gathering further data and assessing more closely the situation below. He calculated that, for many years hence, none of the current power blocs would gain complete ascendancy. And if they continued fighting as they were, they would wreck much of the infrastructure of control. Really, it looked as if Earth was dropping back through time to when the separate nation states ruled, which suited Saul just fine. Further analysis rendered the result that, with the vortex generator data missing, none of the separate small blocs would regain the capability of putting up anything like the *Command* or the *Fist*, and when, in at least fifty years, a new world government or large power bloc seized control, it would take them a further fifty years to regain that capability. That would be enough, for Saul would be long gone by then. Withdrawing, he returned his attention to matters closer to home.

Two space planes, retrieved from the partially wrecked ghost station Core Two, had arrived hours ago. Meanwhile the work crew from the space plane he had sent out, along with pilots instructed to retrieve those planes, was busily checking to ensure that Core Two held no nasty surprises. This was prior to

Saul shifting his whole ship over and taking the station inside through the massive new space doors, whereupon Core Two would be torn apart for salvage.

One of the Core Two space planes was currently being refuelled and checked over, to ensure it could manage atmospheric re-entry without coming apart. An hour remained before all the checks would be finished, and there might yet be some maintenance to carry out, yet all those departing his ship had gathered in one of the now-pressurized docking pillars.

There were twenty-eight of them, including Admiral Bartholomew and some of his command staff, also Technical Director Le Roque, along with disparate original Argus Station personnel and some other crew from the *Command*. Saul was disappointed by Le Roque's decision to return to Earth, but could understand it. The man had been struggling, and often failing, to keep people alive here for too long. He was tired and sick of it all, and he just wanted to go home. He also wanted to find out if his family was still alive in eastern Europe. In fact, all those gathered in that docking pillar were rather like him in that respect. Every one of them retained some hope that those they loved were still living somewhere down there. It seemed that such attachments outweighed the danger of returning to Earth. And their decision to go was strengthened when Saul informed those possessing them that they could take their backups down with them.

"I understand you are perfectly aware of the situation below?" he asked Le Roque through the man's implant.

"I'm fully aware and I'm still going," Le Roque replied. "We'll put down at Minsk and surrender ourselves to the delegates of the Russian and Arctic bloc. Your gift should buy us some good feeling there and, I hope, give us some leverage too."

Saul conceded that. While rebuilding his ship, he had also set up a small project, under Dr Da Vinci, to map and make physical copies of the Gene Bank samples. Only ten per cent had been copied, while nearly forty per cent had been mapped, but this would be enough to give Le Roque and the rest their leverage. It would also give the same advantage to the Russian and Arctic bloc, but that would not be enough to save it from the growing power of the European Alliance, just as the European Alliance would not survive its internal infighting and the wedge that Trove and Ruger were driving into it. But Le Roque and the rest knew all about this, so with luck had their plans ready to survive the coming clashes.

"I hope you do find your family, Le Roque," Saul said. "Good luck to you."

"And you," Le Roque replied, "whenever you too find whatever it is you're seeking."

Saul swung his attention away, towards the remainder of those aboard.

The Meat Locker was open and ready, with staff and robots on standby, but only two had thus far chosen to go into hibernation. The rest were clearly waiting for some kind of resolution here, or perhaps for that moment when the ship got underway again.

In one of the smelting plants, Leeran and Pike were happy to be busy, and they didn't want all this activity to end. In Arcoplex Two, Da Vinci was still overseeing the machines that were mapping and physically copying the stored DNA, while he was occasionally also tuning in to Earth broadcasts with negligent interest. Over the last few months, Hannah Neumann had grown increasingly distant from him, and their relationship had cooled to frigidity. She was currently throwing herself into new research aimed at linking up human minds for serial and parallel processing, perhaps hoping for a future when humanity became all of one mind, and so less inclined to kill its individual parts. Professor Rhine, meanwhile, was considering knocking a few more big holes in conventional science by means of a hammer driven by perpetual motion, while the Saberhagens were working on a weapon based on some of his theories: a way of firing plasma bolts in a Rhine spatial fold, and thus delivering them faster than light.

In an anteroom just off the new heavily armoured store for backups, the Messina clone, Alex, was in the midst of one of his conversations with his old enemy, Ghort.

"We have to strive to make the reality of our existence conform to an ideal," Ghort was saying, "else life isn't worth living."

"Which is fine if it's applied individually," Alex replied, "because my ideal might not be your ideal."

"And because you are happy in your slavery."

"No, because I accept that trying to change present reality, in the way you wanted, probably wouldn't lead to any improvement, and that it might only lead to my death."

"Happy slave."

Alex looked merely weary as he stood up from the console, their dialogue having reached its usual impasse. "But you're lucky, since you get to try again," he added.

"How's that going?" asked the facsimile of Ghort's face from the screen.

"Its growth is now about that of a two-year-old," Alex replied. "Raiman has decided to forgo accelerated growth whenever it's not necessary. It—and all the rest—should be ready by the time we reach our destination."

They were talking about the clones, of course, and specifically about Ghort's clone. He would be the first of those in backup to test the process of loading to a clone body, which was some recompense for his crimes, as was his death. Saul had yet to decide what other restitution this man should make. That would depend upon how Saul himself changed his thinking over the ensuing journey, and what his aims might be by the time his ship arrived at its various *destinations*. The first of these was close, but the second was further away than any of them could possibly imagine. And, thinking on that, deep in that small part of him that was still flesh and blood, Saul felt some human impatience to be gone.

Hannah was surprised at how tearful she had felt upon seeing off Le Roque, but she attributed that to her bone-deep weariness. Finally, shutting down and secure-backing all the data on her research projects, she began to feel relieved. While locking away all her biological samples and growing organic interfaces in a freezer that would store them in a temperature only a little above absolute zero, she began to relish the prospect of enjoying a similar rest.

"I thought you'd want to send us all back to Earth, Saul," she said, speaking into the air.

"I considered it," he replied, always attentive but now never visible. "But, even though I'm a selfish and murderous monster, I was still prepared to offer the people aboard a choice."

"You're a monster?" Hannah asked, casting an eye over her spotless laboratory and realizing that, at last, there was nothing more to do. She checked the time to see that just a few more minutes remained.

"You always expected me to be as much," he replied.

Hannah shed her lab coat and went to hang it up neatly in her locker. How long, in real time, would it be before she donned it again? The minimum was four and a half years, since Saul had told them that their first destination would be Proxima Centuri, which lay four-point-two light years away. Four and a half years of undisturbed sleep?

"I never expected it; I just wanted you to be aware of how easily you *could* become a monster," Hannah lied.

In truth, she expected only utter cold ruthlessness from him, so wasn't sure that the others had made the right choice in staying on board. She herself had remained because, to some extent, she felt she filled the role of a conscience that he probably lacked. Heading over to the door of her laboratory, she opened it and stepped out, closing it carefully and palmlocking it behind her. Others were on the move too, probably having finished up their final tasks before following the thirty-two people who had thus far delivered themselves to the Meat Locker. She knew that the Saberhagens were already sleeping there now, as were Leeran and Pike. Plenty of others had yet to make the same move, but Hannah felt her own time had arrived. Da Vinci had told her that he had experienced dreams while in hibernation, so perhaps that meant it wasn't just a total shutdown of the body, but also the kind of rest she badly needed.

Halfway along the corridor towards the bank of elevators leading out of Arcoplex Two, she felt the Rhine drive engage. It was so much smoother now, just a brief vertiginous shift in underlying reality, followed by the feeling, lasting for a few minutes, that appalling behemoths were sliding past just out of sight, before settling into a steady creepy doubt about whatever was real and solid. Hannah picked up her pace, entered one of the elevators, shortly stepping out of it onto a small monorail station platform, and boarding one of the single-person cars. All the way to the Meat Locker, she had no need to suit herself up or use an airlock. The whole of Saul's ship was interconnected like this now, or at least, all the areas to which he granted the crew access.

As she entered the Meat Locker she saw that the staff and robots were already busy putting four people into hibernation, so she just headed over to where she knew her own cryogenic capsule was located. She could have waited for one of the staff, or one of the robots, to attend to her, but felt impatient with that idea—after all, she probably knew more about the process involved than any of them. She stripped off her clothes, feeling no embarrassment at her nakedness since, having lived forever under Committee cameras, why would she? These discarded garments went into a small storage compartment in the capsule wall, then she stepped over to the capsule itself. Within a minute she had all the monitoring units fixed in place, and had climbed inside.

"Ah, Dr Neumann," said one of the medics, approaching, "do you need any help?"

Hannah waved the man away, "No, I'm fine," and reached over to tap the start button on the console beside the capsule. She then lay back in the form specially made to fit her body. It was warm and comfortable, she found, though she had expected it to be cold.

"So tell me, Saul," she asked, "will you ever bother to wake us up?"

"Why else would I allow you to remain aboard?"

The needles slid into her arms, injecting the necessary drugs to lull her into natural sleep, then into a coma, before the other automatics dug into her body to suck out her blood and other fluids, replacing them with gels and anti-freeze, and thus chill her to the brink of death.

"I don't know . . . and that worries me," she said, her voice already slurring. "Maybe like . . . Da Vinci . . . I'll dream of what's real."

"Maybe," Saul replied, the single word falling through the cold blackness filling her mind, and dissolving into nothingness.

They were all in hibernation now and, just as Saul had predicted, it was Rhine, reluctant to shut down his hugely active mind, who had been the last of them to go into the long sleep. The ship was finally devoid of all human activity except Saul's own, but still very active indeed. As Hannah and others had come to understand, he did not need human personnel to get things done here. For such purposes the robots were better, much better. Now, at last feeling free of the distraction of human clamour, Saul shut down the Rhine drive and dumped his ship back out into reality.

"Are you sure about this?" asked the proctor Paul, as he carried his current burden into the mechanism of one of the railguns, and came to stand over the open breach.

"I'm sure," Saul replied. "I have enough genetic samples from her to grow a clone and have copied all those parts of her mind it was still possible to copy. Even though my technological capabilities will develop, there will be nothing more I can obtain from her corpse and, as I myself change, I will become more and more disinclined to try."

"A horribly and precisely logical assessment," Paul replied, lowering the cylinder containing the body of Varalia Delex into the railgun breach, and closing it.

Saul gazed out into cold interstellar vacuum, as Paul moved away. Once the proctor was clear he aimed the railgun at a distant point and fired it. His sister's corpse sped away on a journey that would last a minimum of five million years, and might quite possibly continue until the end of time.

"No words?" Paul enquired.

"None," Saul replied but, as he turned his attention to the paint-sprayer robot still working out there on the hull, he acknowledged to himself that "none" wasn't entirely accurate.

Some hiccup had disrupted the robot's work or, more likely, some unconscious motivation within Saul had revealed itself in its activity. A letter had not been capitalized, and a gap had been missed out, but the name of his ship was, somehow, exactly right. Saul engaged the Rhine drive and took the Vardelex further out into the dark . . . and to the far stars.

In this new age there are government propagandists who would have us believe that Admiral Bartholomew retrieved the genetic data from Saul before destroying him and his ship; that our duly appointed representatives therefore won. But there are those of us left here on the Subnet who still remember Saul's ship looming in the sky, and we remember Bartholomew's statement, and Ruger's story. We must never let the truth be forgotten: how one man brought down two dictators and the entire government of Earth. Now, as we see just such a government re-forming, and see the freedoms we have enjoyed once again being steadily eroded, we must never forget him. We must never forget the Owner, Alan Saul. He's out there somewhere, and one day our descendants will meet him. I hope, for their sake, that by then they will have learned to live . . . differently.

Anon, FreeBlog, the Subnet.

ACKNOWLEDGEMENTS

Many thanks to those who have helped bring this novel to your e-reader, smart phone, computer screen and to that old-fashioned mass of wood pulp called a book. At Macmillan these include Julie Crisp, Louise Buckley, Ali Blackburn, Ellie Wood, Jessica Cuthbert-Smith, Sophie Portas, Rob Cox, Neil Lang, James Long and others whose names I simply don't know. Further thanks go to Jon Sullivan for his eye-catching cover images, Bella Pagan for her copious structural and character notes and Peter Lavery for again wielding his "scary pencil." And, as always, thank you, Caroline, for putting up with a husband who's often a number of light years away.

ABOUT THE AUTHOR

Neal Asher lives sometimes in England, sometimes in Crete and mostly at a keyboard. He climbed the writing ladder up through the small presses, publishing short stories, novellas and collections over many years, until finally having his first major book, *Gridlinked*, published in 2000 by Macmillan, who have since published sixteen of his books and whose schedule is now two years behind him. These books have been translated into 12 languages and some have appeared in America from Tor. 2013 marks a return to his other US publisher, Night Shade Books, who produced *Prador Moon* and *Shadow of the Scorpion* and will be bringing out his Owner trilogy—*The Departure, Zero Point* & *Jupiter War*.

For more information check out: http://freespace.virgin.net/n.asher/ & http://theskinner.blogspot.com/